THE PARASITE & THE WATTER'S MOU'

Also Available in Valancourt Classics

THE ROSE AND THE KEY
J. Sheridan Le Fanu
Edited by Frances A. Chiu

UNDER TWO FLAGS
Ouida
Edited by Natalie Schroeder

NADA THE LILY
H. Rider Haggard
Edited by Gerald Monsman

THE MYSTERY OF THE SEA
Bram Stoker
Edited by Carol A. Senf

THOU ART THE MAN
Mary Elizabeth Braddon
Edited by Laurence Talairach-Vielmas

THE SORROWS OF SATAN
Marie Corelli
Edited by Julia Kuehn

ROUND THE RED LAMP AND OTHER WRITINGS
A. Conan Doyle
Edited by Robert Darby

STORIES TOTO TOLD ME
Baron Corvo
Edited by Edmund Miller

For a complete list of all Valancourt titles, please visit our website at http://www.valancourtbooks.com

VALANCOURT CLASSICS

THE PARASITE

ARTHUR CONAN DOYLE

THE WATTER'S MOU'

BRAM STOKER

Edited with an introduction and notes by
Catherine Wynne

𝔎𝔞𝔫𝔰𝔞𝔰 𝔆𝔦𝔱𝔶:
VALANCOURT BOOKS
2009

The Parasite by Arthur Conan Doyle
Originally published London: Constable, 1894

The Watter's Mou' by Bram Stoker
Originally published London: Constable, 1895

Introduction and notes © 2009 by Catherine Wynne
This edition © 2009 by Valancourt Books

All rights reserved. The use of any part of this publication reproduced, transmitted in any form or by any means, electronic, mechanical, photocopying, recording, or otherwise, or stored in a retrieval system, without prior written consent of the publisher, constitutes an infringement of the copyright law.

Library of Congress Cataloging-in-Publication Data

Doyle, Arthur Conan, Sir, 1859-1930.
The parasite / Arthur Conan Doyle. The Watter's Mou' / Bram Stoker ; edited with an introduction and notes by Catherine Wynne.
p. cm. – (Valancourt classics)
The Parasite originally published: London: Constable, 1894. The Watter's Mou' originally published: London: Constable, 1895.
ISBN 1-934555-56-8 (alk. paper)
I. Wynne, Catherine, 1971- II. Stoker, Bram, 1847-1912. Watter's Mou'. III. Title.
PR4622.P36 2009
823'.8–dc22
2009019221

Design and typography by James D. Jenkins
Published by Valancourt Books
Kansas City, Missouri
http://www.valancourtbooks.com

CONTENTS

Introduction	vii
The Parasite by Arthur Conan Doyle	1
The Watter's Mou' by Bram Stoker	49
Appendix:	
Arthur Conan Doyle, "John Barrington Cowles"	110
Bram Stoker, "The Coming of Abel Behenna"	135
Bram Stoker, "Sir Arthur Conan Doyle Tells of his Career and Work, his Sentiments towards America, and his Approaching Marriage"	153

INTRODUCTION

ARTHUR CONAN DOYLE, in a letter to Bram Stoker sent after receiving an inscribed copy of Stoker's 1902 novel, *The Mystery of the Sea*, compliments Stoker's "Celtic imagination".[1] The novel's setting, although north of Doyle's Edinburgh birthplace, is Scotland, a country and landscape that provides the backdrop for many of Stoker's fictions including *The Watter's Mou'* (1894).[2] As a Dublin-born writer, Stoker had, in Doyle's estimation, a claim to a Celtic inheritance. Aside from their Scottish interests, the two writers' literary, working, and social lives converged on a number of occasions: Stoker, in his capacity as business manager at London's Royal Lyceum Theatre, encouraged the actor Henry Irving to buy the rights to Doyle's story, "A Straggler of '15", in 1892; in the same year, the two were among twenty-four collaborators in a literary experiment, where well-known writers added a chapter to *The Fate of Fenella*; in 1894-95, the texts which are of immediate concern here, Doyle's *The Parasite* and Stoker's *The Watter's Mou'*, were published as volumes one and two in the Acme Library series by the London publisher, Archibald Constable. The editions, which terminated with Dorothea Gerard's *Angela's Lover* in 1896, were sold from one shilling each.[3]

Of course the most famous and enduring literary association

---

[1] Arthur Conan Doyle, Letter to Bram Stoker, private collection. See also *The Conan Doyle Collection* (London: Christie's, 2004), p. 141.

[2] A small number of copies of *The Watter's Mou'* were issued by T. L. De Vinne of New York in 1894 in order to secure American copyright; the first British edition, which is reprinted in this volume, appeared in 1895.

[3] Other works in the series include: F. C. Philips, *A Question of Colour* (1895); L. B. Walford, *A Bubble* (1895); Marquis of Lorne, *From Shadow to Sunlight* (1895); Francis Gribble, *The Red Spell* (1895); Helmuth Schwartze, *An Impressionist Diary* (1895); George St. George, *A Feminine Conviction* (1896); Robert Peel, *An Engagement* (1896); F. Frankfort Moore, *Dr. Koomadhi of Ashantee* (1896). The series was unsuccessful. See Richard Lancelyn Green and John Michael Gibson, *A Bibliography of A. Conan Doyle*, new and revised edition (1983; Boston and London: Hudson House, 2000), p. 84.

that Doyle and Stoker share is in their respective creation of the most celebrated characters of *fin-de-siècle* fiction: Sherlock Holmes, consulting detective, and Count Dracula, Transylvanian vampire. Despite the growing interest in the work of both writers, these fictional products of Doyle and Stoker exist in the public mind in inverse proportion to the public's consciousness of their roles as authors; Dracula is, after all, the most filmed character in history after Sherlock Holmes. The fictional detective has a museum dedicated to him on Baker Street in London, albeit not located at the celebrated 221 B, and is the subject of a recent spoof biography by Nick Rennison.[1]

After "A Scandal in Bohemia", Sherlock Holmes's third documented case, appeared in *The Strand Magazine* in July 1891, the detective became phenomenally popular. Holmes tapped into the period's zeitgeist.[2] He could, after all, promise a degree of stability and reassurance in an uncertain world. The growth of empire in the late nineteenth century and coincident developments in travel and communication enabled the criminal to come from anywhere; and, at home, economic decline, transformations in gender roles, and religious uncertainty provoked a degree of anxiety that is registered in the period's fiction. However, it is well established that Doyle had an ambivalent attitude to his fictional hero. In "The Final Problem" (1893), Holmes is pursued to the Reichenbach Falls in Switzerland by his arch-nemesis Professor Moriarty, and, as they are locked in combat, both fall over the edge; Moriarty never returns. But in the years following Holmes's supposed demise, Doyle was never quite free of his legacy. After a celebrated outing in *The Hound of the Baskervilles* (1902) which was presented as an early case, Holmes was officially recalled to life—he had managed to save himself from the waterfall after all—in "The Adventure of the Empty House" of 1903.

While Doyle's detective enabled Victorian Londoners to sleep more easily in their beds, Stoker's vampires threatened their rest.

---

[1] Nick Rennison, *Sherlock Holmes: The Unauthorised Biography* (London: Atlantic, 2005).

[2] The first Holmes story, "A Study in Scarlet", was published in *Beeton's Christmas Annual* in 1887 and "The Sign of Four" was commissioned by *Lippincott's Magazine*.

Anthony Hope, author of the bestselling *The Prisoner of Zenda* (1894), wrote to Stoker: "Your vampires robbed me of sleep for nights."[1] In a sense, the vampire has consumed its creator. Paul Murray, Stoker's most recent biographer, aptly titles his study, *From the Shadow of* Dracula: *A Life of Bram Stoker* (2004). Like London's Sherlock Holmes memorial in Baker Street, Dublin boasts the Bram Stoker Dracula Experience, near Stoker's birthplace in Clontarf. Whitby, North Yorkshire—the setting of part of the novel—has its corollary undead experience and guided vampire tours. Unlike Doyle's detective stories, though, *Dracula* did not immediately seize the general fancy on its publication in 1897. It fell to Stoker's mother, Charlotte, to be its most ardent advocate: "No book since Mary Shelley's 'Frankenstein' or indeed any other at all has come near yours in originality, or terror—Poe is nowhere ... In its terrible excitement it should make a widespread reputation and much money for you."[2] The maternal prophecy did not, however, come to pass. Although it enjoyed highly respectable sales, Stoker died in 1912 before it became a huge commercial success. In 1922, with the release of F. W. Murnau's *Nosferatu*, Dracula, the screen legend, came to life, just as Stoker was entering into a period of critical oblivion that lasted until the 1980s.[3] The early critical reception of the novel was, however, positive. The journalist H. D. Traill admitted that he read the scene of Lucy's decapitation

---

[1] Anthony Hope Hawkins, Letter to Bram Stoker, 27 January 1898, Correspondence and Literary Manuscripts of Bram Stoker, Brotherton Collection, Leeds University Library. With thanks to A. P. Watt Ltd. on behalf of John Hope-Hawkins for permission to quote from this letter and to the Brotherton Collection, Leeds University Library.

[2] Quoted in Clive Leatherdale, *Dracula, The Novel & the Legend: A Study of Bram Stoker's Masterpiece* (Wellingborough: Wellington Press, 1985), p. 69.

[3] In recent years, *Dracula*-based criticism has been supplanted by more comprehensive examinations of Stoker's writing. See, for example, David Glover, *Vampires, Liberals and Mummies: Bram Stoker and the Politics of Popular Fiction* (Durham: Duke University Press, 1996); William Hughes, *Beyond Dracula: Bram Stoker's Fiction and its Cultural Context* (Basingstoke: Palgrave, 2000); Carol A. Senf, *Science and Social Science in Bram Stoker's Fiction* (Westport, Conn.: Greenwood Press, 2002); Lisa Hopkins, *Bram Stoker: A Literary Life* (Basingstoke: Palgrave, 2007).

to his wife in bed at night.¹ Doyle commended "the very best story of diablerie which I have read for many years".² This introduction briefly examines the biographies of Doyle and Stoker and then charts their literary connections, which are pertinent to both *The Parasite* and *The Watter's Mou'*.

Parallel Lives

Born at the height of the Irish potato famine in 1847 into a Protestant middle-class family, Stoker was, until he reached the age of seven, bed-ridden. This physical impediment exacerbated an active imagination. Transfixed by his mother's folkloric anecdotes and by how she claimed to have seen the looming shadow of the cholera plague in her native Sligo in 1832, his imagination was colored, from the outset, by a Gothic predilection. A science graduate from Trinity College, Stoker was, for eight years, a civil servant of the Crown in Dublin Castle, the seat of British colonial rule in nineteenth-century Ireland. In 1878, at the age of thirty-one, he abandoned his steady progress as a civil servant to become Henry Irving's business manager at the Lyceum in London. This career change would seem to be a rather abrupt one, but Stoker was intent on pursuing a literary career and had already published short stories with Gothic themes in the Irish journal *The Shamrock*. For a number of years he had also acted as the unpaid theatre critic for the Dublin *Evening Mail*.

When he positively reviewed Irving's performance of Hamlet, the actor asked to meet him, and in the autumn of 1878, Irving assumed the management of the Lyceum and Stoker left Dublin to join the new regime. The Lyceum, a microcosm of Victorian culture, enabled Stoker to meet many of the key political and literary figures of the day: the British Premier, William Ewart Gladstone, with whom he discussed Irish politics and his first novel, *The Snake's Pass* (1890); the Poet Laureate Alfred, Lord Tennyson,

---

[1] H. D. Traill, Letter to Bram Stoker, 11 June 1897, Correspondence and Literary Manuscripts of Bram Stoker, Brotherton Collection, Leeds University Library. With thanks to the British Academy for funding my archival research.

[2] Quoted in Paul Murray, *From the Shadow of* Dracula: *A Life of Bram Stoker* (London: Jonathan Cape, 2004), p. 204.

and the bestselling author, Hall Caine, the dedicatee of *Dracula*. Moreover the Stokers were invited to tea on Sunday afternoons with the sensation novelist Mary Elizabeth Braddon. As business manager, public relations figure, host who greeted guests in the foyer, and general factotum, Stoker had access to writers, reviewers, and journalists to help promote his fiction, but existing correspondence also reveals that he had to fulfill such mundane tasks as dealing with queries for seats and the whereabouts of Tennyson's misplaced spectacles.[1]

Arthur Conan Doyle was born in 1859 to immigrant Irish Catholic maternal parentage and paternal grandparentage, and trained as a medical doctor at Edinburgh University. When he crossed paths with Stoker in 1892 after his story, "A Straggler of '15", was bought on Stoker's recommendation by Irving, Doyle was in an enviable position as far as literary success was concerned. Renaming it *Waterloo*, Irving staged the rather maudlin play in 1894, achieving remarkable success in his performance as an old soldier remembering his heroic battle feats.[2] Meanwhile Stoker had produced a dull administrative tome, *The Duties of Clerks in Petty Sessions in Ireland* (1879), a collection of children's stories with haunting themes, *Under the Sunset* (1881), and his Irish adventure romance, *The Snake's Pass*. While Stoker remained in Irving's employment until the actor's death in 1905, the popularity of Holmes liberated Doyle from a medical career. After stints as a ship's doctor in the Arctic in 1880, on the coast of West Africa in 1881-82, and a brief and unfortunate partnership with a former Edinburgh classmate in Plymouth, Doyle set up his own medical practice in Southsea on the south coast of England.[3] A literary career developed alongside his medical work, and by 1889 he noted in a letter to a friend that he "divide[d] his time between oculism, occultism and . . . writ-

---

[1] Hallam, Lord Tennyson, Letter to Bram Stoker, 25 February 1881, Correspondence and Literary Manuscripts of Bram Stoker.
[2] Irving performed it to celebrate Queen Victoria's Diamond Jubilee in 1897. Stoker remarked that it "sounded the note of the unity of Empire". See *Personal Reminiscences of Henry Irving*, vol. 1 (London: William Heinemann, 1906), p. 251.
[3] See Daniel Stashower, *Teller of Tales: The Life of Arthur Conan Doyle* (London: Penguin, 1999), pp. 33-115.

ing".[1] In 1891, after briefly studying ophthalmology in Vienna, he established a practice in London. It was a failure, but his empty consulting rooms facilitated his fiction and by summer Doyle had abandoned medicine to become a full-time writer.

Doyle's medical studies at Edinburgh University led to his rejection of the ardent Catholicism of his paternal family; Doyle's uncle, Richard, remembered today as a fairy painter, was a cartoonist for *Punch* but resigned in protest in 1850 at the magazine's anti-Catholic stance. When his paternal uncles offered to help Doyle establish himself as a doctor by contacting eminent Catholic families, he refused and informed them that he had lost his faith.[2] He was, of course, a product of the late nineteenth century culture of doubt and shared with many of his contemporaries the quest for other forms of belief on a spectrum from science to the occult. He joined the Portsmouth Literary and Scientific Society in 1883, and was a vice-president of the Hampshire Psychical Society, established in 1888. In 1891, he became a member of the Society for Psychical Research, which was set up to investigate psychical phenomena such as hypnotism and telepathy. Under its auspices he investigated a reputedly haunted house in Dorset in 1894.[3] In 1916, he formally converted to spiritualism, a religious movement promulgating the belief that the dead could communicate with the living. It offered, in short, an empirical religion for an uncertain age. Spiritualism contains, as Ruth Braddon suggests, "a gothic mixture; and this was the age of the gothic, in literature as well as religion."[4]

Biographically, Doyle and Stoker diverge in the former's endorsement of spiritualism and the preoccupation in his latter

---

[1] Arthur Conan Doyle, Letter to Amy Hoare, n.d. Quoted in Jon Lellenberg, Daniel Stashower and Charles Foley, eds., *Arthur Conan Doyle: A Life in Letters* (London: Harper, 2007), p. 267.

[2] Pierre Nordon, *Conan Doyle*, translated by Frances Partridge (1964; London: John Murray, 1966), pp. 29-30.

[3] Catherine Wynne, "Arthur Conan Doyle's Domestic Desires: Mesmerism, Mediumship and the *Femme Fatale*," *Victorian Literary Mesmerism*, edited by Martin Willis and Catherine Wynne (Amsterdam: Rodopi, 2006), pp. 223-225.

[4] Ruth Braddon, *The Spiritualists: The Passion for the Occult in the Nineteenth and Twentieth Centuries* (London: Weidenfeld and Nicolson, 1983), p. 10.

years with piercing this veil between life and death. Where in Stoker, these occult propensities resided solely in his fictions, Doyle, the creator of the rational detective, moved between the real and the unreal, the natural and the spiritual and plundered science, or more specifically, empiricism to substantiate his beliefs. Although Stoker is more celebrated as a Gothic writer, *The Watter's Mou'* is a melodramatic novel and Doyle's *The Parasite*, with its obsession with mesmeric entrapment, operates more closely within a familiar Gothic terrain. Apart from their publishing connection, there is, the reader must be cautioned, no direct association between these texts. In their wider writings, however, both Doyle and Stoker share remarkably similar thematic preoccupations. In *The Parasite* and *The Watter's Mou'* we can identify one constant point of reference: the fear of female sexuality which threatens to criminalize and consume. *The Parasite* is preoccupied with mesmerism and sexual possession, and *The Watter's Mou'* explores sexual desire played out on a grim topography. The protagonists of both texts, Austin Gilroy and Willy Barrow, become victims of females who, in different ways, take possession of them.

The Parasite

The Parasite emerged at a difficult period in Doyle's life, as his wife, Louise, was diagnosed with tuberculosis in 1893. Doyle took her to Davos in Switzerland in an attempt to recover her health, and wrote the tale while in residence there. *The Parasite* combines medical interest with mesmeric inquiry and sexual possession. Prior to his wife's diagnosis, Doyle had some interest in her disease. In a medical article, "Life and Death in the Blood", published in *Good Words* in 1883, he had praised the eminent bacteriologist, Robert Koch, who had discovered the bacillus in 1882: he had demonstrated "the existence of a little rod-like creature in tubercule or consumption, which swarms in the diseased lungs" and the article looked forward to the day when consumption and other diseases "will have ceased to exist".[1] In 1890, when Koch announced that

---

[1] A. Conan Doyle, "Life and Death in the Blood," *Good Words*, xxiv (1883): 180-181. This article, along with Doyle's other medical stories and nonfiction

he would demonstrate a cure for tuberculosis, Doyle travelled to Berlin. In his autobiography, *Memories and Adventures* (1924), he recalls how he believed at the time that the "whole thing was experimental and premature" and noted this in a letter to the *Daily Telegraph*.¹ He was right. By 1894, the Alps still offered Louise the "best chance of killing this accursed microbe".² Andrew Lycett argues that by calling his text *The Parasite*, Doyle "was referring, if only subconsciously, to the bacteria which had invaded his wife's body".³

The Parasite exposes a double fear: the unexplored depths of the unconscious and the colonization of the mind through mesmerism. The theme is equally explicit in Stoker's last novel, *The Lair of the White Worm* (1911), in which Lady Arabella March, like Dracula, has the power of metamorphosis and the ability to induce trance states in her victims. Like *Dracula*, *The Parasite* demonstrates the limits of scientific knowledge, but while in Stoker's text the trance state is associated with or induced by occult powers, Miss Penelosa, for all her quasi-vampiric proclivities, is not supernatural. She probes the boundaries of psychic knowledge, penetrates a scientific community, and in the process destabilizes one of its elite for sexual gain. The novella traces prevailing nineteenth-century tensions concerning the boundaries of orthodox science, as "other" knowledge, ranging from "semi-science" to "charlatanry", threatened medical authority.

Mesmerism, or animal magnetism, entered scientific discourse at the end of the eighteenth century and its influence permeated late nineteenth-century developments in psychology. It derived its name from Franz Anton Mesmer, who attained notoriety when he propounded his theories of magnetic healing. He claimed that the universe was surrounded by invisible fluid, and that bodily illness occurred when an obstacle impeded its flow. Cure resulted

---

writings, is included in the Valancourt Books edition of his *Round the Red Lamp*, edited by Robert Darby (Kansas City: Valancourt, 2007).

¹ Arthur Conan Doyle, *Memories and Adventures* (1924; Oxford: Oxford University Press, 1989), p. 90.
² Ibid., p. 120.
³ Andrew Lycett, *Conan Doyle: The Man Who Created Sherlock Holmes* (London: Weidenfeld & Nicolson, 2007), p. 202.

by magnetizing the body's poles to allow the fluid to move freely. Mesmer's cures, which he practiced in Paris from 1778, were controversial: the ability to mesmerize was not confined to qualified practitioners and thus it had popular and democratic appeal.[1] By 1784, Mesmer's theories were disputed by medical orthodoxy in France after a commission set up to investigate the phenomenon rejected it. Meanwhile Mesmer's cures were conducted in a theatrical vein with their practitioner dressed in silken robes and carrying a wand as he went through his treatment rooms filled with *baquets* or vats of magnetized water, and touched his patients with his wand. Mesmer's feats were translated to the stage and performed for popular entertainment. Of course, mesmerism also provided titillating literary possibilities. By the end of the nineteenth century, the fear grew in popular fiction and stage productions that everyone could be subject to trance.

In Britain, mesmerism entered the medical establishment in the late 1830s under the auspices of John Elliotson, Professor of Physiology at University College London, but its scientific progress was controversial. In 1844, James Braid contested Mesmer's fluidic theory and argued that the trance phenomenon was the result of suggestion. He coined the term hypnotism. By the end of the nineteenth century, key figures in the field were Jean-Marie Charcot, whose experiments on hysteria patients at the Salpêtrière in Paris led him to believe that hypnosis could only be induced in subjects liable to hysteria. His ideas were supplanted by the Nancy School of Ambroise-Auguste Liébeault and Hippolyte Bernheim, who posited that hypnotism works through suggestion. To counter the view that a tendency to be hypnotized was a form of "weakness" associated with women, Bernheim used male subjects in his experiments in the 1880s.[2]

In his 1894 presidential address to the Society for Psychical Research, published in its *Proceedings*, Arthur Balfour commented on the historical reception of Mesmer's theories, arguing that "scientific men have shown in connection with it a bigoted intoler-

---

[1] See Robert Darnton, *Mesmerism and the End of the Enlightenment in France* (Cambridge, Mass.: Harvard University Press, 1968), pp. 83-84.
[2] Robin Waterfield, *Hidden Depths: The Story of Hypnosis* (Basingstoke: Macmillan, 2002), p. 216.

ance", but acknowledging that "deliberate fraud or unconscious deception makes observation doubly and trebly difficult, and throws obstacles in the way of the investigator which his happier brother in the region of material and physical science has not to contend with".[1] The sentiment echoes the early thoughts of Austin Gilroy, Doyle's fictional professor of physiology, as he ponders the psychological research of his colleague, Wilson, in *The Parasite*:

> Physiology is a recognised science. If I add even a brick to the edifice, everyone sees and applauds it. But Wilson is trying to dig the foundations for a science of the future . . . I am filled with wonder and admiration when I think of him, and yet, when he asks me to associate myself with his researches, I am compelled to tell him that, in their present state, they offer little attraction to a man who is devoted to exact science . . . So long as half his subjects are tainted with *charlatanerie* and the other half with hysteria we physiologists must content ourselves with the body and leave the mind to our descendants.

While Gilroy positions himself as a "materialist" devoted to "pure reason", he describes Wilson's research as a "semi-science" in its movement between the study of mesmerism and allied conditions such as clairvoyance. Indeed, the close relationship between mesmerism and spiritualism after 1850 is noted by Janet Oppenheim:

> In both cases, sitters were gathered at meetings known as séances, while the participants often held hands in a linked circle around *baquet* or table to enhance the potency of the invisible forces at work. It takes little effort, furthermore, to see the magnetic trance as the precursor of the similar mediumistic state, especially since some mesmerized subjects became clairvoyant while entranced.[2]

In the same 1894 *Proceedings*, the eminent physicist Oliver Lodge describes the mediumship of Leonora Piper, who, in a trance

---

[1] A. J. Balfour, "Address by the President," *Proceedings of the Society for Psychical Research*, vol. x (London: Kegan Paul, Trench, Trübner, 1894), pp. 4, 6.
[2] Janet Oppenheim, *The Other World: Spiritualism and Psychical Research in England, 1850-1914* (Cambridge: Cambridge University Press, 1985), pp. 217-218.

state, reported conversations with dead people via her spirit-control, Phinuit. Doyle was impressed with Lodge's experiments and wrote to the scientist from Davos to commend his results.[1]

The Parasite, although written at a time when Doyle was receptive to the potentialities of mesmeric phenomena, is nonetheless a cautionary tale about the dangers inherent in mesmeric experimentation. Gilroy's path to enthrallment commences when he agrees to witness the experiments that Wilson is conducting with a new mesmerist in his home. The event, however, is a social one, demonstrating mesmerism's projection across Victorian society. Just as mesmeric performances were enacted on the Victorian stage, mediumship was conducted in the home, compounding the difficulties surrounding the conditions of experimentation. Where does performance end and science begin?

Doyle's fascination with mesmerism is also evident in the short stories that he produced in the 1880s. In a letter to his mother, Doyle's interests are revealed as he speculates on a suitable title for a collection of stories:

> What think you of 'Twilight Tales' for a name. You see it would have a double meaning—not only as being tales suitable for the gloaming, but as treating of the strange twilight land between the natural and the absolutely supernatural (animal magnetism—mesmerism and these other acknowledged powers play a large part in them).[2]

These "twilight tales" include "The Captain of the Pole-Star" (1883), "The Winning Shot" (1883), and "John Barrington Cowles" (1884), stories that demonstrate a correlation between wild and barren landscapes and the occult. In the first of these tales, Captain Craigie pursues what he believes is the spirit of his dead fiancée to his death across the polar icecaps, and, when his shipmates find his corpse, some attest that they see the shape of a woman's body temporarily crystallize from snowflakes to kiss it. Though a supernatural story, it recalls the destructive relationship of *The Watter's Mou'*. In "The Winning Shot", Octavius Gaster, described

---

[1] Lellenberg, Stashower and Foley, pp. 331-332.
[2] Ibid., p. 224.

as a "blood-sucking species of bat", destroys his love rival at a shooting competition.[1] As the innocent Charley Pillar prepares to take a shot, he declares that he sees his double in front of him. Like Dorian Gray's stabbing of his portrait-soul, Pillar's bullet culminates in his own destruction, and his fiancée is mesmerized and kidnapped by Gaster.

"John Barrington Cowles" is a precursor of *The Parasite*. The narrator, Jack Armitage, speculates that Cowles's death is attributable to "preternatural agency". The two men meet as students at Edinburgh University. The son of an army colonel, Cowles, who was born in India, exhibits an "ardent tropical disposition" and "concentrate[s] all his affection" on Armitage but, with his "Velasquez-like face" and "dark, tender eyes", Cowles also attracts women. He shuns their company in order to concentrate on his medical studies until he meets the vampiric Kate Northcott. Northcott's two previous fiancés committed suicide, so when Cowles becomes engaged to her, Armitage investigates her origins and discovers that her uncle was involved in occult practices in India. At a mesmerist's stage show, Northcott reveals to Armitage that her powers are superior to those of Dr. Messinger, who declares that he intends to summon a member of the audience to the stage. However, when Messinger proceeds to experiment with Cowles, Northcott counteracts the performance and Messinger is forced to admit defeat as Cowles remains in his seat. Northcott possesses a terrible secret that she reveals to her fiancés on the eve of marriage which drives them to suicide, and when Cowles becomes party to this mystery, he ends the engagement to avoid what seems to be an undisclosed Faustian pact. He escapes with Armitage to Scotland's remote Isle of May, but on a stormy night, Cowles becomes entranced and declares that he can see Northcott coming for him. Despite Armitage's attempted restraint, Cowles follows the hazy figure to the cliffs. As Armitage and some fishermen search for him, they hear a woman's laugh coming from the sea.

Northcott's defeat of Messinger prefigures Penelosa's victory over Gilroy in *The Parasite*. When Penelosa asks Gilroy if he

---

[1] Arthur Conan Doyle, "The Winning Shot," *Bow Bells: A Magazine of General Literature and Art*, xxxix (11 July 1893), p. 62.

will "admit the mesmeric sleep and the power of suggestion", he replies that "he will admit nothing". Gilroy remains skeptical until Penelosa experiments with Agatha Marden, and under the influence of post-hypnotic suggestion, Agatha breaks her engagement to Gilroy. The note that Penelosa gives him the night before corroborates Agatha's actions. When Gilroy visits Agatha at home she has no recollection of the event and even denies having left her house. In a quasi-Holmesian flourish, Gilroy points to her dusty boots as evidence that she has been outside.

Gilroy, now excited by new scientific possibilities, becomes the subject of Penelosa's mesmerism and increasingly relinquishes his psychological and physical autonomy. Initially, the experiments are conducted in the presence of Wilson and his wife. In the illustration by Howard Pyle for the first American edition of *The Parasite*, Penelosa is presented with her back to the viewer and with her arms raised over the figure of Gilroy, who is slumped in a chair. Wilson is standing at Penelosa's side with an opened notebook and pen poised to record observations. Adjacent to Wilson in the background is the seated figure of his wife. On the wall opposite Penelosa, over Gilroy's chair is the half-figure portrait of a woman, dressed like Penelosa and gazing towards the viewer. Penelosa, it seems to imply, is controlling the gaze.

Complications arise when Gilroy decides to continue the experiments when Wilson is absent, thus allowing greater intimacy between mesmerizer and subject. Two anecdotal accounts from the *Hampshire Telegraph and Sussex Chronicle* from 1887 recall similarities with Gilroy's sexual entrapment: the first story, "No More Pleasant Evenings", details how a Church of England vicar mesmerized his governess for the entertainment of visitors but when one of the guests became appalled that the young woman was instructed while in trance to remove her shoes and stockings, he notified her brother who assaulted the clergyman and removed his sister. In the second story, "Mesmerised into Madness", a young girl became so attached to her French mesmerist that she followed him to France and had to be recovered by her guardians and placed in an asylum.[1]

---

[1] "A Chat About Mesmerism," *Hampshire Telegraph and Sussex Chronicle* (Supplement), Saturday, 10 December 1887, p. 9.

Sexual possession is the hallmark of these late-century mesmeric tales. Penelosa is clearly interested in Gilroy's sexual possibilities: he is a handsome thirty-four year old and Penelosa is middle-aged, insignificant-looking, and disabled. She admits that the scientific aspects of mesmerism are irrelevant to her but manipulates Gilroy's professional interest.

As foreigner, she conforms to the standard representation of the mesmerist in the period's literature. The novel was published in the same year as George du Maurier's more famous representation of mesmeric influence, *Trilby*. Set in bohemian Paris, the novel's titular character Trilby is an artist's model who, under the control of the mesmerizing Svengali, is transformed into a concert singer. Penelosa, Northcott, and Svengali are foreigners and their threat, though explicitly sexual, is also implicitly racial. The representation of the mesmerist is linked to xenophobia: Svengali is an Eastern European Jew; Northcott is associated with India; Penelosa is from the West Indies. In her strange sexual voracity and her threat to English womanhood, Penelosa mirrors *Jane Eyre*'s Bertha Mason. Like Dracula, who mesmerizes his victims to gain their blood, these figures, whether human or supernatural, wield their mesmeric powers for sexual and, in Dracula's case, imperial purposes. In F. Frankfort Moore's shockingly racist *Dr. Koomadhi of Ashantee* (1896), the tenth volume of the Acme Library series, set in Africa's Gold Coast, Koomadhi takes revenge on the white woman who has rejected him for another man by using tribal magic to mesmerize her husband into acting like an ape. Koomadhi's mother compares her sorcery with drawing-room mesmerism in England. In *Dracula*, the vampire creates a psychic connection with Mina so he can read her mind and Professor Van Helsing's triumph is to discover that he can also read Dracula's mind when he puts Mina into a trance. These fictions seem to suggest that the trouble with mesmerism is one of boundaries: once boundaries—imperial, psychological and sexual—are crossed, they remain permeable.

Doyle's mesmeric fictions also suggest that some individuals are more susceptible to mesmerism than others. Armitage believes that Messinger chooses Cowles from the audience for his mesmeric feats because his "dark skin and bright eyes marked him out as a man of a highly nervous temperament". Gilroy describes how his own physical traits such as "black" hair and "dark" eyes, as well as his "thin olive face" are "characteristics" of his "real temperament, and cause experts like Wilson to claim [him] as their own". As his compliment to Stoker's "Celtic imagination" reveals, Doyle subscribed to the period's pseudo-racial stereotypes. The construction of the Celt as mystical also had a political motivation: Celts were both different from but necessary to the rational Anglo-Saxon self.[1] But if Celts were imaginative, they were also susceptible. Likewise Charlotte Brontë's "intense glowing imagination" was attributed by Doyle to her Cornish mother (but not, strangely enough, to her Irish father) because "there is something strange, and weird, and great, lurking down yonder in the great peninsula which juts into the western sea".[2] In an interview with Stoker for the *New York World* in 1907, featured in the appendix to this volume, Doyle attributes his gift for story-telling to his mother's Celtic imagination. In another interview, Doyle declares: "I am half Irish, you know, and my British half has the devil of a job to hold the hot-headed rascal in."[3] Geoffrey Stavert notes that in 1889 Doyle attended a performance for Southsea's professionals by a travelling mesmerist, Milo De Meyer. De Meyer tried to mesmerize Doyle but he failed.[4] No doubt, on this occasion, Doyle's "British half" prevailed. However, *Dracula* and Richard Marsh's *The Beetle* (1897), for instance, also reveal that English middle-class men, especially those like Jonathan Harker and *The Beetle*'s Paul Lessingham, who travel abroad, are equally prone to mesmeric influence and they bring vampires and supernatural beetles back to British women, just as the creature that attacks Agatha is described as a parasite. Sexual disease is manifested through these figures.

---

[1] For Doyle's negotiation of his Irishness, see Catherine Wynne, *The Colonial Conan Doyle: British Imperialism, Irish Nationalism, and the Gothic* (Westport, Conn.: Greenwood Press, 2002).

[2] Arthur Conan Doyle, *Through the Magic Door* (London: Thomas Nelson and Sons, n.d.), p. 88.

[3] See Ralph D. Blumenfeld, "The Father of Sherlock Holmes," *Sir Arthur Conan Doyle: Interviews and Recollections*, edited by Harold Orel (Basingstoke: Macmillan, 1991), p. 229. It seems that Sherlock Holmes's Anglo-Saxon rationalism is tempered by a dash of French blood from his artistic forbears.

[4] Geoffrey Stavert, *A Study in Southsea: The Unrevealed Life of Doctor Arthur Conan Doyle* (Portsmouth: Milestone, 1987), p. 141.

Owen Dudley Edwards and Daniel Stashower connect *The Parasite* with a near-contemporaneous Holmes story, "The Adventure of the Cardboard Box", which was published in *The Strand* in January 1893.[1] When Susan Cushing receives a package with two human ears preserved in salt, Holmes investigates and discovers that the ears belonged to Susan's youngest sister, Mary, and her lover, Alec Fairbairn. Mary's husband, Jim Browner, after discovering that his wife is having an affair with Fairbairn, murders them and cuts off their ears. He had intended to send the ears to the second sister, Sarah Cushing, who, besotted by Jim, had encouraged Mary to have an affair. Browner alleges that Sarah had loved him but when he spurned her advances, her love had turned venomous and she sought revenge through his wife.

A similar love triangle recurs in *The Parasite* as Penelosa is jealous of Agatha, whom she describes as "conventional", and she seeks to sexually compromise Gilroy. When Gilroy gives Penelosa a photograph over which he has written "words of affection", the act recalls the photograph of Irene Adler and the King of Bohemia in "A Scandal in Bohemia" (1892). The king employs Holmes to recover the photograph in order to prevent the affair from damaging his forthcoming nuptials. Just as the photograph has, Holmes admits, compromised the king, Gilroy's photograph, with its amorous message, would compromise the scientist, so when Penelosa's mesmeric power over him temporarily fails, Gilroy seizes the opportunity to destroy the evidence and denounce her:

> "You vile woman," I said, "if I did my duty to society, you would never leave this room alive!"
> "I love you, Austin; I love you!" she wailed.
> "Yes," I cried, "and Charles Sadler before. And how many others before that?"

The final comment is revealing: the sexually repressed Gilroy is obsessed with Penelosa's promiscuity.

The Parasite shares another connection with "The Adventure of the Cardboard Box": Doyle suppressed both texts. The Holmes

---

[1] Stashower, *Teller of Tales*, p. 172; Owen Dudley Edwards, *The Quest for Sherlock Holmes* (Edinburgh: Mainstream, 1983), p. 287.

story was excluded at his request from the first English edition of *The Memoirs of Sherlock Holmes* which was compiled by George Newnes in 1893 and the story did not appear in a collection until *His Last Bow* (1917). The reasons for Doyle's expurgation of the Holmes story are a matter of speculation: it contained an illicit love affair and a horrific double murder.[1] For Anne Cranny-Francis, *The Parasite* expresses Doyle's "sexual frustration", which may have been a reason for its suppression.[2] Contemporaneous medical opinion on tuberculosis dictated that Doyle could not have sexual relations with his wife. The story deals with attempted sexual violation of a male which marks it as different from *Trilby*, for instance. Gilroy reads Alfred Binet and Charles Féré's *Animal Magnetism* (1890) which cautions that "a subject might be violated in the hypnotic state, in which *she* would be unable to offer any resistance" [emphasis added].[3] Of course, Doyle towards the end of his life became enthralled by mesmerism's ally, spiritualism, which offered him the possibility of crossing the boundary between life and death, and this may have been another reason to suppress the text.[4]

The Parasite also deals with an issue of keen interest to the detective canon—the notion of criminal responsibility. Debate on the subject can be located within medico-legal and journalistic discourse from the 1880s. As Mary Elizabeth Leighton notes, the *British Medical Journal* warned of the "dangers of sexual assault" and "enforced criminality" whilst subjects were hypnotized.[5] Fic-

---

[1] Green and Gibson, *A Bibliography of A. Conan Doyle*, p. 76; Christopher Metress, "Thinking the Unthinkable: Reopening Conan Doyle's 'Cardboard Box,'" *Midwest Quarterly: A Journal of Contemporary Thought* 42.2 (Winter 2001): 183.

[2] Anne Cranny-Francis, "Arthur Conan Doyle's *The Parasite*: The Case of the Anguished Author," *Nineteenth-Century Suspense: From Poe to Conan Doyle*, edited by Clive Bloom *et al.* (New York: St. Martin's Press, 1988), p. 105.

[3] Alfred Binet and Charles Féré, *Animal Magnetism* (London: Kegan Paul, Trench, 1887), p. 367. They were acolytes of Charcot who came into conflict with the Nancy School.

[4] See Roger Luckhurst, *The Invention of Telepathy, 1870-1901* (Oxford: Oxford University Press, 2002), p. 206.

[5] Mary Elizabeth Leighton, "Under the Influence: Crime and Hypnotic Fictions of the *fin de siècle*," *Victorian Literary Mesmerism*, p. 208.

tion writers were quick to seize the thematic opportunities: Stuart Cumberland's occult novel *A Fatal Affinity: A Weird Story* (1889) introduces a short account of girl who, in a mesmerized state, murders her parents in their bed. A doctor who hypnotizes her reveals that the "mesmerist had established an influence over his victim, and whilst in a mesmeric state he had impressed upon her the necessity of killing both her father and her mother for the sake of their wealth."[1] Ernest Hart's *Hypnotism, Animal Magnetism and Hysteria* (1893) cautions that "you can induce sentiments of anger, nay even of violent and destructive rage, ecstasy, affection, grief at will, by verbal suggestion".[2]

Penelosa's vengeance commences by reducing Gilroy to ridicule during his lectures which results in his dismissal from the university. Here Doyle may have been drawing on his earlier story, "The Great Keinplatz Experiment" (1885), in which a professor's experimentations in soul transference accidently result in his soul entering the body of a young student and vice versa, with hilarious consequences. Penelosa, however, endeavors to criminalize Gilroy. He attempts to rob a local bank, he assaults Charles Sadler and finally, he awakens from trance in Agatha's private sitting-room with a bottle of sulphuric acid in his hand. Penelosa had planned that Agatha should be the object of this most vicious attack but Agatha has been delayed by a vicar in the drawing-room. Meanwhile Penelosa's death releases Gilroy and saves Agatha from disfigurement and potential blindness. This final attempted assault on the beauty of her rival marks the crime as one of passion and distinguishes Penelosa as a desiring and frustrated female. More troublingly, for a writer celebrated for his neat Holmesian dénouements in which order is restored, Gilroy, though free, remains unresolved about the nature and extent of mesmeric influence and of spiritual intervention.

---

[1] Stuart Cumberland, *A Fatal Affinity: A Weird Story* (London: Spencer Blackett, 1889), p. 34.
[2] Ernest Hart, *Hypnotism, Animal Magnetism and Hysteria: Abstract of an Address Delivered at the Sheffield Philosophical Institute* (London: Smith, Elder, 1893), p. 12.

Doyle and Stoker: Mesmeric Convergences

The Fate of Fenella also links trance states to crimes of passion. In the first three chapters, Fenella, separated from her husband, Lord Francis Onslow, accidentally meets him on holiday in Harrogate. The couple's marriage had ended when they squabbled over Lord Francis's associations with another woman and Fenella, in revenge, flirted with Count De Mürger. In Doyle's chapter Frank's dormant passion for his wife is re-awakened and he regrets his transgression with the passionate Mediterranean beauty, Lucille de Vigny. Lucille has followed him to Harrogate, and reveals that she has seen his estranged wife with De Mürger. Frank forgets Fenella as Lucille's "warm, magnetic hand tighten[s] upon his wrist".[1] Just as he is lulled by her sexual wiles, Fenella, who had intended to forgive her husband, sees him in the arms of her rival. She spurns him but he counters the attack by demanding whether she has seen De Mürger. Her confirmation results in Lucille's triumph. An unreformed flirt, Fenella compounds the marital estrangement by trifling with the affections of a barrister.

The theme of a love triangle, a feature of Doyle's fiction in this period, finds one of its most violent expressions in the non-Holmesian "The Case of Lady Sannox" (1893) in which a husband exacts revenge on his adulterous wife by having her lover, a surgeon, disfigure her lip under the false pretext of extracting poison from it. The instability of female sexuality recurs in Doyle's fiction: in the Holmes canon women, whether alien or native, are often dangerous. For instance, in *The Hound of the Baskervilles*, Stapleton deploys his South American wife as bait to tempt Sir Henry onto the moor, just as he used the English Laura Lyons to decoy Sir Charles to the moor gate, where he fatally encounters the hound. Moreover, Helen Penelosa is invited into the home and the university town by Wilson's West Indian wife.

Meanwhile, in the succeeding chapters of *The Fate of Fenella*,

---

[1] A. Conan Doyle, "Between Two Fires," *The Fate of Fenella*, edited by Andrew Maunder (1892; Kansas City: Valancourt Books, 2008), p. 32. The first three chapters were written by Helen Mathers, Justin McCarthy and Frances Trollope.

De Mürger appears in Harrogate and Frank stabs him after he sees him entering his wife's room at night. He has, however, committed the murder in a trance and has no recollection of it. Having departed the hotel and travelled abroad directly after the murder, he appears on the island of Guernsey in Stoker's chapter ten, with no idea that his wife has been tried and acquitted of De Mürger's murder.[1] Husband and wife meet in misunderstanding as Fenella believes that Frank perceives her as guilty of the murder, but Frank, with no knowledge of it, sees her as guilty of sexual immorality. Lord Castleton, an acquaintance, informs Frank about Fenella's trial, and he reveals that Fenella pleaded that she had stabbed De Mürger to avoid sexual assault. Frank now believes that his wife, though guilty of murder, is—more importantly for him—innocent of sexual misconduct. However, when he starts to read about the trial, he enters a trance and re-enacts the murder in front of the astonished Castleton:

> The hypnotic trance was on him again. Presently he rose, and with stealthy steps approached his sleeping friend. Murmuring "Why did I not kill him?" he struck with the folded paper, as though with a dagger, the form before him. Castleton, who had sunk into a pleasant sleep and whose fat face was wreathed with a smile, was annoyed at the rude awakening. "What the devil!" he began angrily, and then stopped as his eyes met the face of his friend and he realised that he was in some sort of trance. He grew very pale as he saw Frank Onslow stab, and stab, and stab again. There was a sort of grotesqueness in the affair—the man in such terrible earnest in his mind committing murder, whilst his real weapon was but a folded paper.[2]

Castleton believes that he has solved the crime, but Stoker's moral universe is a complicated one, so the chapter ends with Castleton's uncertainty about whether or not he should reveal his knowledge. A revelation could result in Frank's trial for murder, and more importantly, Fenella's heroism in saving her honour would be impugned if it were revealed that her husband had to

---

[1] The chapters were written by May Crommelin, F. C. Phillips, "Rita", Joseph Hatton, and Mrs. Lovett Cameron.
[2] Bram Stoker, *The Fate of Fenella*, p. 73.

intervene with violence in an attempt to save her reputation. As Andrew Maunder argues, Stoker's chapter figures the "unruly woman as dangerous social presence, one troublesome to the stability of the social structure presided over by men."[1] Anxieties surrounding women's unruliness recur in Stoker's fiction.

An influence on Stoker's chapter is Irving's production of *The Bells* which was first staged at the Lyceum in 1871 and performed over eight hundred times in Britain and North America. In *The Bells*, Mathias is a murderer who fears the exposure of his fifteen-year old crime. He dreams that at his trial a mesmerist induces him to confess. As he semi-awakens, he cries for the removal of the hangman's noose and then collapses in death. Stoker returns to the theme of mesmerism in his representation of the degenerate Edgar Caswall in *The Lair of the White Worm*. Caswall has a trunk bequeathed to his ancestors by Mesmer and uses his powers to destroy one of his tenants, Lilla Watford. In his nonfictional 1908 study, *Famous Impostors*, Stoker accuses Mesmer of imposture because of the theatrical manner in which he performed his cures—a strange criticism for an author who spent most of his working life in the theatre.[2] Of course, the correlation of criminality and altered states of consciousness has a famous literary precedent in Wilkie Collins's detective novel, *The Moonstone* (1858). Doyle's second Sherlock Holmes story, *The Sign of Four*, is indebted to Collins's text, and the painted shirt that appears to indict Franklin Blake in the novel resurfaces in *The Parasite* when Gilroy discovers that he must have tried to rob the bank when he sees its door's fresh paint on his house coat. Given the Victorian scientific and social interest in mesmerism, it is unsurprising that a fascination with trance states occurs in the period's cultural output.

The Watter's Mou'

Stoker and Doyle share another Victorian interest: travel. Doyle's travels, which inspired the early Gothic stories from the 1880s, resulted in his photographic essays published in the *British Journal*

---

[1] Andrew Maunder, Introduction, *The Fate of Fenella*, p. xvii.
[2] Bram Stoker, *Famous Impostors* (London: Sidgwick and Jackson, 1910), p. 155.

of Photography. For instance, "After Cormorants with a Camera" (1881) describes the Isle of May off the east coast of Scotland, which is the setting for the dénouement of "John Barrington Cowles"; "Dry Plates on a Wet Moor" (1882) is an essay on Dartmoor, the setting for "The Winning Shot", and, of course, much later for *The Hound of the Baskervilles*. Meanwhile Stoker was stimulated by his travels in Scotland, particularly on the Aberdeenshire coast, where he set his story, and from his duties as Inspector of Petty Sessions which required him to visit Ireland's rural courts in the 1870s. His Irish work produced *The Snake's Pass*, which commences as a travel narrative in the west of Ireland. In H. D. Traill's review of *The Watter's Mou'* in *The Graphic*, Stoker's talent for topographical detail is commended: "[I]ts scene is laid on the Aberdeenshire coast, where I do not remember to have ever met Mr. Bram Stoker before. He seems, however, to be as much at home there as he is in Ireland, and can sketch the wild sea and seaboard of Eastern Scotland with as sure a hand as he does the mountains and moorland scenery of his native isle."[1] In his capacity as the Lyceum's business manager, Stoker was part of the theatrical company's North American tours. Shortly after he produced *The Watter's Mou'*, he published a novel set in America's Rocky Mountains, *The Shoulder of Shasta* (1895). *Dracula*, too, commences as a travel narrative as Jonathan Harker contemplates his journey east but the text quickly becomes a battleground over the control of body and mind, when the Count lands from a boat at Whitby in the north of England.

In *Six Buchan Villages* (1977), Margaret Aitken claims that she "spoke to Dracula's housekeeper", or rather that she spoke to the "niece of the land-lady of Bram Stoker, Dracula's creator, while he holidayed in the village of Whinnyfold".[2] Whinnyfold is located three miles south of the setting of *The Watter's Mou'*. Stoker holidayed in the Cruden Bay area from 1893, and this coastline also provides the setting for *The Mystery of the Sea*. With the extension of the rail network in the nineteenth century, which by 1850 had reached Aberdeen, and Queen Victoria's mid-century development of Balmoral as a royal residence, Scotland became an increas-

---

[1] H. D. Traill, "The World of Letters," *The Graphic*, Saturday, 26 Jan. 1895, p. 88.
[2] Margaret Aitken, *Six Buchan Villages* (Peterhead: Buchan Observer, 1977), p. 53.

ingly popular tourist destination for the wealthier middle-classes. The influence of Walter Scott was central to the development of the country as a cultural destination in the nineteenth century.[1] A famous eighteenth-century traveller, much cited in nineteenth-century guide-books, was Samuel Johnson.

Initially, Stoker stayed at the Kilmarnock Arms Hotel in Cruden, and in subsequent holidays took lodgings in Whinnyfold. The third edition of James Dalgarno's travel guide, *From the Brig O'Balgownie to the Bullers o' Buchan* (1897), features an advertisement for the Kilmarnock Arms Hotel. It boasted "12 bedrooms, two bathrooms (hot and cold water), Sitting rooms, Dining Hall" and promised an "excellent Bathing Beach within seven minutes' walk", "Trout fishing in Cruden Water free of charge" and, of course, golf.[2] A. J. Murray's illustrations which accompany Dalgarno's third edition depict geographical and architectural features of the area such as Slains Castle, a model for Dracula's castle, and the "water's mou". Stoker describes it as being "formerly" the mouth of the Water of Cruden, "a natural cleft—formed by primeval fire or earthquake or some sort of natural convulsion—which runs through the vast mass of red granite which forms a promontory running due south". John B. Pratt's *Buchan* (1858) includes a detailed description of the surrounding area:

> To the north of Whinnyfold is the *Bay of Cruden*. The beautiful beach, which follows the sweep of the bay, extends from the *Scaurs*—a group of prominent rocks running out about half a mile into the sea—to the *Water of Cruden*; a distance of nearly two miles. Near the centre is the *Hawklaw*, a lofty headland ... Below the eye, the sweeping beach, with sands as smooth and firm as the floor of a cathedral ... in the middle distance, Slains Castle towers over the cliffs. These, with its pure and exhilarating air, constitute this one of the most pleasing spots on the coast.[3]

---

[1] John R. Gold and Margaret M. Gold, *Imagining Scotland: Tradition, Representation and Promotion in Scottish Tourism since 1750* (Aldershot, Hampshire: Scolar Press, 1995), pp. 60-85.
[2] James Dalgarno, *From the Brig o' Balgownie to the Buller's o' Buchan*, with illustrations by A. J. Murray, 3rd ed. (1890; Collieston, Aberdeenshire: Caledonian Books, 1986), advertisements.
[3] John B. Pratt, *Buchan* (Aberdeen: Lewis & James Smith, 1858), pp. 31-32.

The coastline with its "creeks and rock shelves" served as "excellent hiding places in the days of smuggling".[1] *The Watter's Mou'* draws inspiration from the area's smuggling history, and the story is about the conflict of duty, love and family loyalty. The area is patrolled by Willy Barrow, a coastguard in the Customs service. Barrow, as a Yorkshire man, is an outsider in this barren and tempestuous locale, but is employed to read the signs of land and sea for the prospect of smuggling. The local inhabitants thwart Barrow's attempts to impede the smuggling activity by hosting a wedding-feast on the same night as illicit cargo is due to land. Barrow, who is instructed to maintain cordial relations with the locals, provides them with rockets to celebrate the wedding but becomes suspicious when he discovers that their direction has been moved in order to operate as a signal to the smuggling vessel at sea.

In order to fully understand this critically neglected text, it is useful to contextualize it in terms of smuggling history in Scotland. Although smuggling existed in the country before the Act of Union between Scotland and England in 1707, increased levels of duty on items such as tea, tobacco, wine, and spirits in the following years meant that the Act of Union was, as Gavin D. Smith notes, "little short of a smuggler's charter in Scotland".[2] In Scotland, smuggling took on a political manifestation as well, as Richard Platt argues: "The taxes were seen by the Scots as oppressive, and resistance to them positively patriotic."[3] Smuggling was associated with the Jacobites, supporters of King James II of the Scottish House of Stuart, who had lost his throne to William of Orange in 1688. During their exile in France, James's supporters often used smugglers to maintain contact with sympathizers in Britain.[4]

In *The Watter's Mou'* an historical episode involving the killing of a smuggler is mentioned as the area's former smuggling activities are contrasted with the state of affairs that exists between Willy Barrow and his adversaries. Pratt's romanticized account of this

---

[1] Dalgarno, p. 38.
[2] Gavin D. Smith, *The Scottish Smuggler* (Edinburgh: Birlinn, 2003), p. 4.
[3] Richard Platt, *Smuggling in the British Isles: A History* (Stroud: Tempus, 2007), p. 102.
[4] Ibid., pp. 125-126.

episode is an indicator of how smuggling activity was perceived. In 1798 there was a fracas between Philip Kennedy, his smuggling companions, and the excise officers. Kennedy, described by Pratt as a "man of undaunted courage and resolution", challenged the officers and held two of them down and called on his companions to help:

> But these, possessing neither courage nor the devotedness of poor Kennedy, decamped, and hid themselves . . . Anderson, the officer still at liberty, attacked Kennedy . . . Anderson was observed to hold up his sword to the moon, as if to ascertain whether he was using the edge, and then, with one desperate stroke, cleft open the poor fellow's skull. Strange to say, Kennedy, streaming with blood, made out to reach Kirkton of Slains, a distance of nearly a quarter of a mile, where, in the course of a few minutes, he expired. His last words were, "If all had been as true as I was, the goods would have been safe, and I should not now have been bleeding to death."[1]

Anderson was acquitted of murder. Stoker would have seen Kennedy's headstone "nearly opposite the bell door" of the churchyard of Slains.[2]

In his description of Tammas Mac's public-house as the focus of smuggling history, the narrator of *The Watter's Mou'* notes:

> It was at this house, in the good old days of smuggling, that the coastguards used to be entertained when a run was on foot, and where they slept off their drunkenness whilst the cargoes were being hidden or taken inland in the ready carts. Of course all this state of things had been altered, and there was as improved a decorum amongst the smugglers as there was a sterner rule and discipline amongst the coastguards. It was many a long year since Philip Kennedy met his death at Kirkton at the hands of the exciseman Anderson.

As a coastguard of the preventive service, Barrow's role represents the modernization and increased efficiency of the customs

---

[1] Pratt, p. 29.
[2] Dalgarno, p. 19.

service from the 1820s. By the 1840s, with the adoption of free trade policies by the government, smuggling activities declined.[1] What is especially interesting, then, about Stoker's text is the conflict between the forces of governmental authority represented by Barrow and a free-trading past, represented by Tammas Mac and his associates. The text is a site of confrontation between the forces of modernity and backwardness, a theme which haunts many of Stoker's fictions, including *Dracula* and *The Snake's Pass*. In Stoker's work women invariably occupy the centre of such conflicts: Lucy and Mina in *Dracula* and Norah Joyce in *The Snake's Pass*. Similarly, in *The Watter's Mou'* Maggie MacWhirter is trapped between her love for Barrow and her duty to her father, who she knows is carrying contraband goods on his fishing vessel, the *Sea Gull*. The scene in which Maggie tempts Barrow from his duty expresses Stoker's ambivalence about female sexuality:

> If her lover could take the matter so much to heart all might yet be well, and in the moment all the womanhood in her awoke to the call. Her fear had broken down the barriers that had kept back her passion, and now the passion came with all the force of a virgin nature. She drew Willy close to her—closer still—and whispered to him in a low sweet voice, that thrilled with emotion—
>
> 'Willy, Willy, darlin'; ye wouldna see harm come to my father—my father, my father!' and in a wave of tumultuous, voluptuous passion she kissed him full in the mouth. Willy felt for the moment half dazed. Love has its opiates that soothe and stun even in the midst of their activity. He clasped Maggie close in his arms, and for a moment their hearts beat together and their mouths breathed the same air.

Stoker's obsession with women's "voluptuous" passions recurs in his female vampires who lure men from their paths of duty: Harker, though engaged to Mina, is tempted by the vampire women at Dracula's castle.[2] In *The Watter's Mou'* Maggie must sacrifice her life at sea in order to atone for her attempted sexual transgression and her father's criminal activity. She washes ashore

---

[1] Platt, pp. 137-139.
[2] Murray, p. 61.

in the Water of Cruden and Willy sees among the wreckage of her boat, "a dead woman, whose white face was set in an aureole of floating hair".

The image recalls John Everett Millais's 1852 painting of the dead Ophelia, suspended in a stream with her dead white face surrounded by her floating hair. Not only was this a famous Victorian painting, but Stoker would have been familiar with it. Elizabeth Siddal, the model who posed for it, was also married to the painter-poet, Dante Gabriel Rossetti. Stoker's friend, the novelist Hall Caine, had worked as Rossetti's secretary and would have known how Rossetti had exhumed his wife's coffin years after her death in order to retrieve poems that he had buried with her. When the coffin was opened, it was alleged that Siddal's hair had grown. This claim may have inspired Stoker's supernatural tale, "The Secret of the Growing Gold" (1892). Here a murderer buries his wife under the floorboards but when he remarries, his dead wife's golden hair grows out through the cracks in the floor. As his wife is transfixed by the sight and gently falls into a death-sleep, Geoffrey Brent is struck dead by the horror and is discovered with golden hair twined about his feet. In *The Watter's Mou'*, Willy rushes into the waves towards Maggie's corpse and the narrative of his subsequent demise is ambiguous as the point of view shifts to a young boy who alerts the villagers to the sight of Maggie's "brown hair floating wide and twined round the neck of Sailor Willy, who held her tight in his dead arms". Caught between the forces of order and disorder, authority and lawlessness Willy Barrow is consumed in death in the "watter's mou'".

"The Coming of Abel Behenna", which was inspired by Stoker's 1892 visit to Boscastle in Cornwall, shares thematic associations with *The Watter's Mou'*. It concerns a woman's destructive potential and has a similar coastal setting. Here two Cornish fishermen vie over the affections of the worthless Sarah Trefusis. As she cannot decide between Abel Behenna and Eric Sanson, her mother proposes that the suitors pool their finances and draw lots for her with the victor taking the combined wealth to trade at sea for a year. Behenna wins Sarah but Sanson warns him that he must return within a year or he will forfeit his claim. One week before the year's end, a ship is wrecked off the coast and Sanson, looking for survivors, hears a cry emanating from a watery cave. He throws a rope but when he discovers that it is his former friend whom he is rescuing, he releases his grasp and Behenna falls back into the sea to his death. Sanson proceeds with the marriage ceremony, but as he returns with Sarah to his cottage, Behenna's corpse with a rope trailing from the waist is seen on the river bed opposite Sanson's door: "The right elbow had fallen in a chink in the rock, leaving the hand outstretched toward Sarah, with the open palm upward as though it were extended to receive hers, the pale drooping finger open to the clasp", and Sanson, faced with a horror that coincides with imminent sexual consummation, realizes that he has paid the "devil's price".

Many of Stoker's stories represent the horrifying implications of female sexuality. In his early supernatural allegory, "The Castle of the King", from *Under the Sunset*, a poet, informed that his wife has died, decides to follow her into the valley of death to the Castle of the King, a journey across gorges, recesses, slimy marshes, cliffs, crevasses and turrets. At the end of this erogenous panorama, he sees his dead wife waiting for him. In "The Crystal Cup" (1872), an artist is imprisoned by a king and separated from his home and his beloved, Aurora, until he can produce a satisfactory work of art. While singing Aurora's song, he crafts a crystal vase, into which he imparts his desire. As he completes it, he feels that his life is ebbing away into the cup but the King decrees that all the competitors, whether dead or alive, must be present at the Feast of Beauty. As Aurora sings the cup smashes into pieces and just before the artist dies, consumed by its "great vortex", he sees the king struck dead on his throne.[1] Written at a time when Stoker was connected to the Wilde family in Dublin, the story conflates sexuality and art in a manner evoking Oscar Wilde's *The Picture of Dorian Gray* (1890); the artist's frustrated desires, embodied in the vase, culminate in self-destruction. *The Watter's Mou'* and "The Coming of Abel Behenna" also invite a homoerotic interpretation. As Barrow waits for Maggie's body to wash up on shore, he finds some comfort from her brother's physical similarity to her. In many of Stoker's

---

[1] Bram Stoker, "The Crystal Cup", *Dracula's Guest and Other Stories*, London: Wordsworth, 2006, p. 157.

fictions men vie or unite over the bodies of women, whether dead or alive. Similarly, Doyle's "John Barrington Cowles", a story of close connections between medical men in Scotland's capital, was published two years before Robert Louis Stevenson's *Strange Case of Dr Jekyll and Mr Hyde*.[1]

In the reviews of *The Watter's Mou'*, critics noted its melodramatic associations. Indeed, the novel is produced like a melodrama, and Stoker, in his role at the Lyceum, would have been familiar with elaborate melodramatic stagings, particularly the works of fellow Irishman Dion Boucicault. In his Irish play, *The Colleen Bawn* (1860), the heroine is saved from murder by drowning through the swift intervention of Myles-na-Coppaleen. Boucicault's staging of the water scene, which was enabled by an elaborate water tank on London's Adelphi stage, drew popular acclaim.[2]

The Watter's Mou' follows the stock conventions of melodrama with its ill-fated heroine saving her father from the machinations of the villain. The thinly drawn villain in this context is, however, a Dutch Jewish trader, Samuel Mendoza, and the text engages in the anti-Semitism displayed throughout the period's mesmeric fictions as discussed above. During Stoker's period at the Lyceum, Irving, also noted for his melodramatic productions, had staged *The Merchant of Venice* and had delivered a sympathetic interpretation of Shylock, but in *The Watter's Mou'* Stoker indulged in negative stereotyping more associated with melodrama. In Irving's *The Bells* Mathias murders a Polish Jew, who visits his tavern on Christmas Eve for his money-belt of gold coins. Whether presented as villain or victim, stereotypes of the Jew in British fiction and drama of the period generally focused upon the issue of money.[3] To further complicate Stoker's interpretation of racial issues, Mendoza exhibits similarities with Black Murdock, the Irish Catholic usurer or "gombeen man" of *The Snake's Pass* who is equally threatening to the heroine's welfare. H. L. Malchow suggests that "there is a hint

---

[1] See Wynne, "Arthur Conan Doyle's Domestic Desires", p. 230.
[2] Nicholas Daly connects *The Snake's Pass* with Boucicault's *The Shaughran* (1874). *Modernism, Romance and the Fin de Siècle: Popular Fiction and British Culture, 1880-1914* (Cambridge: Cambridge University Press, 1999), p. 67.
[3] Edgar Rosenberg, *From Shylock to Svengali: Jewish Stereotypes in English Fiction* (London: Peter Owen, 1961), pp. 262-263.

of Jewish avarice in his portrait of the money-lending Gombeen man."[1]

Given that Stoker had been working at the Lyceum since 1878, it is unsurprising that the *Athenæum*'s reviewer should distinguish the influence of the stage in his story:

> There is some good descriptive writing in this little tale about smuggling and love and duty nobly done. The storm and Maggie's wild sail to save her father's honour are told with much power and excitement, and the coastguardman's victory over temptation is finely conceived. The chief defect of the book, inevitable perhaps from the author's associations, is a tendency to melodramatic and stagey writing in some of the speeches and situations.[2]

The *Nation*'s reviewer also acknowledged its melodramatic effects: "The central incident has a thrill in its heart which loses force by the author's artificial treatment, and never have sky, sea, and wind glowered, raged, and roared with more amazing spectacular effect, not only o'erstepping, but quite putting to shame, the modesty of nature."[3] The *Derby Mercury* praised the "wholesome and entirely excellent way" in which the "conflict between love and duty" was presented and commended the Acme Library for its "handy volumes, plain readable type, and first-class fiction".[4]

The *Dundee Advertiser* was rather more critical of the text's ending, and of Stoker's use of dialect:

> We cannot forgive Mr. Stoker for so wantonly killing two such excellent young persons. Conscious of his weakness in the matter of Scotch dialect, Mr. Stoker has indulged in that luxury as little as possible, but the little that he does introduce is truly awful. He will probably be surprised to learn that Aberdeenshire has a dialect of its own quite distinct from Lowland Scotch.

---

[1] H. L. Malchow, *Gothic Images of Race in Nineteenth-Century Britain* (Stanford: Stanford University Press, 1996), p. 155.

[2] *Athenæum*, 23 February 1895, no. 3513, p. 246.

[3] *The Nation*, 27 February 1896, vol. 62, p. 183. See Carol A. Senf, *The Critical Response to Bram Stoker* (Westport, Conn. and London: Greenwood Press, 1993), p. 56.

[4] *Derby Mercury*, 16 January 1895, p. 6.

"The Watter's Mou'" is somewhat forced and mechanical, but it has at least the great merit of being short and easy to read.[1]

Neither *The Watter's Mou'* nor *The Parasite* represents the finest productions of their respective authors. Both texts have, at the same time, been unfairly neglected. In the review of a rival mesmeric novel, the *Glasgow Herald* argued that "hypnotic suggestion and influence had reached their highest point in the marvellous achievements of Svengali and his feminine counterpart, the heroine of Conan Doyle's 'Parasite'".[2] Although today *The Parasite* remains a largely forgotten text, Du Maurier's mesmerist occupies a place in the English language and popular culture secondary to the most famous creations of Doyle and Stoker. What *The Parasite* and *The Watter's Mou'* reveal, however, is that these two writers share more than the celebrity of Dracula and Sherlock Holmes. In *The Watter's Mou'*, *The Parasite*, their pre-texts "The Coming of Abel Behenna" and "John Barrington Cowles", and even in the chapters they devised for *The Fate of Fenella*, dangerous land and seascapes, criminal femininities, irrational desire, mind control and the occult, variously unveil questions concerning the complex nature of possession: psychological, sexual, and even colonial.

Catherine Wynne
University of Hull

August 15, 2008

---

[1] *Dundee Advertiser*, 10 January 1895, p. 2.
[2] *Glasgow Herald*, Friday, 3 June 1896, p. 8.

A NOTE ON THE TEXTS

The text of *The Parasite* follows the first edition, published as volume one in the Acme Library series by the London publisher Archibald Constable in December 1894. The first American edition was published in New York in 1895 by Harper and Brothers, and illustrations were provided by Howard Pyle. Here Penelosa's name is changed to Penclosa. The text was serialized in *Lloyd's Weekly Newspaper* from 11 November to 2 December 1894 as *The Parasite: A Mesmeric and Hypnotic Story*. *The Watter's Mou'* follows the first edition published in January 1895 by Archibald Constable as volume two in the Acme Library Series. Some copies were printed in New York in 1894 by T. L. De Vinne to safeguard American copyright. It was also published in New York by Appleton in 1895. With thanks to the British Library and the National Library of Ireland for copies of the first editions of *The Parasite* and *The Watter's Mou'*.

ARTHUR CONAN DOYLE

The Parasite

THE PARASITE

March 24th.—The spring is fairly with us now. Outside my laboratory window the great chestnut-tree is all covered with the big glutinous gummy buds, some of which have already begun to break into little green shuttlecocks. As you walk down the lanes you are conscious of the rich silent forces of nature working all around you. The wet earth smells fruitful and luscious. Green shoots are peeping out everywhere. The twigs are stiff with their sap; and the moist heavy English air is laden with a faintly resinous perfume. Buds in the hedges, lambs beneath them—everywhere the work of reproduction going forward!

I can see it without and I can feel it within. We also have our spring when the little arterioles[1] dilate, the lymph flows in a brisker stream, the glands work harder, winnowing and straining. Every year Nature readjusts the whole machine. I can feel the ferment in my blood at this very moment, and as the cool sunshine pours through my window I could dance about in it like a gnat. So I should, only that Charles Sadler would rush upstairs to know what was the matter. Besides, I must remember that I am Professor Gilroy. An old professor may afford to be natural, but when fortune has given one of the first chairs in the university to a man of four-and-thirty he must try and act the part consistently.

What a fellow Wilson is! If I could only throw the same enthusiasm into physiology that he does into psychology, I should become a Claude Bernard[2] at the least. His whole life and soul and energy works to one end. He drops to sleep collating his results of the past day, and he wakes to plan his researches for the coming one. And yet, outside the narrow circle who follow his proceedings he gets so little credit for it. Physiology is a recognised science. If

---

[1] Unless otherwise stated all medical definitions in these footnotes are derived from Robley Dunglison's *Dictionary of Medical Science*, 21st ed. (London: J. & A. Churchill, 1895). Arteriole is defined as a "small artery" (100).
[2] Eminent French physiologist (1813-1878).

I add even a brick to the edifice every one sees and applauds it. But Wilson is trying to dig the foundations for a science of the future.[1] His work is underground and does not show. Yet he goes on uncomplainingly, corresponding with a hundred semi-maniacs in the hope of finding one reliable witness, sifting a hundred lies on the chance of gaining one little speck of truth, collating old books, devouring new ones, experimenting, lecturing, trying to light up in others the fiery interest which is consuming him. I am filled with wonder and admiration when I think of him; and yet, when he asks me to associate myself with his researches I am compelled to tell him that, in their present state they offer little attraction to a man who is devoted to exact science. If he could show me something positive and objective, I might then be tempted to approach the question from its physiological side. So long as half his subjects are tainted with charlatanry and the other half with hysteria,[2] we physiologists must content ourselves with the body and leave the mind to our descendants.

---

[1] The story is saturated in psychological enquiry. Mesmerism or animal magnetism was at the forefront of many of these experiments. It was called mesmerism after its eighteenth-century practitioner, Franz Anton Mesmer, who posited that an invisible fluid flowed through all living things and that bodily illness occurred when the fluid was blocked. Mesmer's cure involved unblocking the fluid by making magnetic passes over a patient's body. A Manchester doctor, James Braid, contested Mesmer's fluidic theory in 1844 and argued that the phenomenon was a product of the subject's imagination, or heightened sensory perception when acted upon by the experimenter. He coined the term hypnotism. The two terms were often used interchangeably after 1850. By the end of the nineteenth century the key medical figures in the field were Jean-Marie Charcot, who used hypnotism to treat hysteria patients at the Salpêtrière in Paris, and the rival Nancy School of Ambroise-Auguste Liébeault and Hippolyte Bernheim. Freud was initially influenced by Charcot but soon allied himself with the Nancy School.

[2] Charcot used hypnotism in his treatment of hysteria patients and believed that the hypnotic trance could only be induced in patients prone to hysteria. Hysteria is defined by Dunglison as a "species of neurosis, so called because reputed to have its seat in the uterus (hysteria) . . . It generally occurs in paroxysms, the chief characters of which consist in alternate fits of laughing and crying . . . loss of consciousness (although the presence of consciousness generally distinguishes it from epilepsy) and convulsions. Hysteria appears to depend upon irregularity of nervous distribution in very impressible persons, and is not confined to women; well-marked cases are occasionally met with in men" (562).

No doubt I am a materialist. Agatha says that I am a rank one. I tell her that is an excellent reason for shortening our engagement, since I am in such urgent need of her spirituality. And yet I may claim to be a curious example of the effect of education upon temperament, for by nature I am, unless I deceive myself, a highly psychic[1] man. I was a nervous, sensitive boy, a dreamer, a somnambulist, full of impressions and intuitions. My black hair, my dark eyes, my thin, olive face, my tapering fingers, are all characteristic of my real temperament, and cause experts like Wilson to claim me as their own.[2] But my brain is soaked with exact knowledge. I have trained myself to deal only with fact and with proof. Surmise and fancy have no place in my scheme of thought. Show me what I can see with my microscope, cut with my scalpel, weigh in my balance, and I will devote a lifetime to its investigation. But when you ask me to study feelings, impressions, suggestions, you ask me to do what is distasteful and even demoralising. A departure from pure reason affects me like an evil smell or a musical discord.

Which is a very sufficient reason why I am a little loth to go to Professor Wilson's to-night. Still, I feel that I could hardly get out of the invitation without positive rudeness—and now that Mrs. Marden and Agatha are going, of course I would not if I could. But I had rather meet them anywhere else. I know that Wilson would draw me into this nebulous semi-science of his if he could. In his enthusiasm he is perfectly impervious to hints or remonstrances. Nothing short of a positive quarrel will make him realise my aversion to the whole business. I have no doubt that he has some new mesmerist, or clairvoyant,[3] or medium, or trickster of some sort whom he is going to exhibit to us, for even his entertainments bear upon his hobby. Well, it will be a treat for Agatha, at any rate. She

---

[1] "Relating to the mind or mental endowments. *Psychological* is not unfrequently used with the like signification" (924).
[2] Susceptibility to mesmerism is racially determined in Doyle's writings.
[3] Dunglison associates clairvoyance with the mesmeric state: "Clearness of sight, said to be communicated by animal magnetism, which not only enables the magnetized person to see in the dark, through stone walls, etc., but even to observe prospects which he has never seen previously, while he may fancy he is flying in the air. It need hardly be said that the possession of such powers is fabulous" (240). Clairvoyance is a type of extra-sensory perception.

is interested in it, as woman usually is in whatever is vague and mystical and indefinite.

10-50 p.m.—This diary-keeping of mine is, I fancy, the outcome of that scientific habit of mind about which I wrote this morning. I like to register impressions while they are fresh. Once a day at least I endeavour to define my own mental position. It is a useful piece of self-analysis, and has, I fancy, a steadying effect upon the character. Frankly, I must confess that my own needs what stiffening I can give it. I fear that after all much of my neurotic temperament survives, and that I am far from that cool, calm precision which characterises Murdoch or Pratt-Haldane. Otherwise, why should the tomfoolery which I have witnessed this evening have set my nerves thrilling so that even now I am all unstrung. My only comfort is that neither Wilson, nor Miss Penelosa,[1] nor even Agatha could have possibly known my weakness.

And what in the world was there to excite me? Nothing, or so little that it will seem ludicrous when I set it down.

The Mardens got to Wilson's before me. In fact I was one of the last to arrive, and found the room crowded. I had hardly time to say a word to Mrs. Marden and to Agatha, who was looking charming in white and pink with glittering wheat-ears in her hair, when Wilson came twitching at my sleeve.

'You want something positive, Gilroy,' said he, drawing me apart into a corner. 'My dear fellow, I have a phenomenon—a phenomenon.'

I should have been more impressed had I not heard the same before. His sanguine spirit turns every firefly into a star.

'No possible question about the bona fides this time,' said he, in answer perhaps to some little gleam of amusement in my eyes. 'My wife has known her for many years. They both come from Trinidad, you know. Miss Penelosa has only been in England a month or two, and knows no one outside the university circle; but I assure you that the things she has told us suffice in themselves to establish clairvoyance upon an absolutely scientific basis. There is nothing like her, amateur or professional. Come and be introduced!'

I like none of these mystery-mongers, but the amateur least

---

[1] In the first American edition the name is changed to Penclosa.

of all. With the paid performer you may pounce upon him and expose him the instant that you have seen through his trick. He is there to deceive you, and you are there to find him out. But what are you to do with the friend of your host's wife? Are you to turn on a light suddenly and expose her slapping a surreptitious banjo?[1] Or are you to hurl cochineal[2] over her evening frock when she steals round with her phosphorus[3] bottle and her supernatural platitude. There would be a scene, and you would be looked upon as a brute. So you have your choice of being that or a dupe. I was in no very good humour as I followed Wilson to the lady.

Any one less like my idea of a West Indian could not be imagined. She was a small, frail creature, well over forty, I should say, with a pale, peaky face, and hair of a very light shade of chestnut. Her presence was insignificant and her manner retiring. In any group of ten women she would have been the last whom one would have picked out. Her eyes were perhaps her most remarkable, and also, I am compelled to say, her least pleasant feature. They were grey in colour—grey with a shade of green—and their expression struck me as being decidedly furtive. I wonder if furtive is the word, or should I have said fierce? On second thoughts, feline

---

[1] The reference here is to the Davenport Brothers, who tied themselves up in a box on stage, within which they allegedly generated spirit manifestations. Banjos and other musical instruments were played but when the box was opened, the brothers were still tied up inside. Although they advertised themselves as mediums, they were, in fact, accomplished conjurors. The actor Henry Irving exposed their tricks in Manchester in 1865. Gilroy is referring to fake mediums who promised to communicate with the spirit world. Spiritualism emerged in America in 1848 and became popular in Britain from the 1850s. Doyle publicly converted to spiritualism in 1916 but his interest in psychic phenomena dates from his time as a doctor in Southsea in the 1880s.
[2] This is a dye. Roger Luckhurst notes an occasion when cochineal was used to identify a fake medium. When cochineal was squirted over the "spirit" at a séance, it was discovered when the lights came back on that the medium was covered with the dye. "Passages in the Invention of the Psyche: Mind-Reading in London, 1881-84," *Transactions and Encounters: Science and Culture in the Nineteenth Century*, ed. Roger Luckhurst and Josephine McDonagh (Manchester: Manchester University Press, 2001), p. 123. With thanks to David Beck.
[3] A chemical compound that glows in the dark. The Davenport Brothers used phosphorus on their musical instruments so that they could see them inside their box.

would have expressed it better. A crutch leaning against the wall told me, what was painfully evident when she rose, that one of her legs was crippled.

So I was introduced to Miss Penelosa, and it did not escape me that as my name was mentioned she glanced across at Agatha. Wilson had evidently been talking. And presently no doubt, thought I, she will inform me by occult means that I am engaged to a young lady with wheat-ears in her hair. I wondered how much more Wilson had been telling her about me.

'Professor Gilroy is a terrible sceptic,' said he; 'I hope, Miss Penelosa, that you will be able to convert him.'

She looked keenly up at me.

'Professor Gilroy is quite right to be sceptical if he has not seen anything convincing,' said she. 'I should have thought,' she added, 'that you would yourself have been an excellent subject.'

'For what, may I ask?' said I.

'Well, for mesmerism, for example.'

'My experience has been, that mesmerists go for their subjects to those who are mentally unsound. All their results are vitiated, as it seems to me, by the fact that they are dealing with abnormal organisms.'[1]

'Which of these ladies would you say possessed a normal organism?' she asked. 'I should like you to select the one who seems to you to have the best-balanced mind. Should we say the girl in pink and white—Miss Agatha Marden, I think the name is?'

'Yes, I should attach weight to any results from her.'

'I have never tried how far she is impressionable. Of course some people respond much more rapidly than others. May I ask how far your scepticism extends? I suppose that you admit the mesmeric sleep and the power of suggestion.'[2]

---

[1] Charcot argued that the hypnotic state could only be induced in subjects prone to hereditary degeneracy.

[2] The Nancy School of Ambroise-Auguste Liébeault and Hippolyte Bernheim supplanted Charcot's theories in the mid-1880s. The emphasis here was on suggestion—everyone was potentially hypnotizable. Freud notes in 1889: "The key to the understanding of hypnosis is offered by Liébeault's theory of normal sleep (or rather, of normal falling asleep), from which hypnosis is distinguished only by the insertion of the relationship between

'I admit nothing, Miss Penelosa.'

'Dear me, I thought science had got further than that. Of course I know nothing about the scientific side of it. I only know what I can do. You see the girl in red, for example, over near the Japanese jar. I shall will that she come across to us.'

She bent forward as she spoke and dropped her fan upon the floor. The girl whisked round and came straight towards us, with an inquiring look upon her face, as if some one had called her.

'What do you think of that, Gilroy?' cried Wilson, in a kind of ecstasy.

I did not dare to tell him what I thought of it. To me it was the most barefaced, shameless piece of imposture that I had ever witnessed. The collusion and the signal had really been too obvious.

'Professor Gilroy is not satisfied,' said she, glancing up at me with her strange little eyes. 'My poor fan is to get the credit of that experiment. Well, we must try something else. Miss Marden, would you have any objection to my putting you off?'

'Oh, I should love it!' cried Agatha.

By this time all the company had gathered round us in a circle, the shirt-fronted men, and the white-throated women, some awed, some critical, as though it were something between a religious ceremony and a conjurer's entertainment. A red velvet arm-chair had been pushed into the centre, and Agatha lay back in it, a little flushed and trembling slightly from excitement. I could see it from the vibration of the wheat-ears. Miss Penelosa rose from her seat and stood over her, leaning upon her crutch.

And there was a change in the woman. She no longer seemed small or insignificant. Twenty years were gone from her age. Her eyes were shining, a tinge of colour had come into her sallow cheeks, her whole figure had expanded. So I have seen a dull-eyed, listless lad change in an instant into briskness and life when given a task of which he felt himself master. She looked down at Agatha with an expression which I resented from the bottom of my soul— the expression with which a Roman empress might have looked at

---

the subject and the person who puts him to sleep. It follows from this theory that everyone is hypnotizable." "Review of Auguste Forel's *Hypnotism*," *The Standard Edition of the Complete Psychological Works*, gen. ed. and trans. James Strachey, vol. 1 (1889; London: The Hogarth Press, 1966), p. 98.

her kneeling slave. Then, with a quick commanding gesture, she tossed up her arms and swept them slowly down in front of her.

I was watching Agatha narrowly. During three passes she seemed to be simply amused. At the fourth I observed a slight glazing of her eyes, accompanied by some dilation of her pupils. At the sixth there was a momentary rigor. At the seventh her lids began to droop. At the tenth her eyes were closed, and her breathing was slower and fuller than usual. I tried as I watched to preserve my scientific calm, but a foolish, causeless agitation convulsed me. I trust that I hid it, but I felt as a child feels in the dark. I could not have believed that I was still open to such weakness.

'She is in the trance,' said Miss Penelosa.

'She is sleeping,' I cried.

'Wake her, then!'

I pulled her by the arm and shouted in her ear. She might have been dead for all the impression that I could make. Her body was there on the velvet chair. Her organs were acting, her heart, her lungs. But her soul! It had slipped from beyond our ken. Whither had it gone? What power had dispossessed it? I was puzzled and disconcerted.

'So much for the mesmeric sleep,' said Miss Penelosa. 'As regards suggestion, whatever I may suggest Miss Marden will infallibly do, whether it be now or after she has awakened from her trance. Do you demand proof of it?'

'Certainly,' said I.

'You shall have it.'

I saw a smile pass over her face as though an amusing thought had struck her. She stopped and whispered earnestly into her subject's ear. Agatha, who had been so deaf to me, nodded her head as she listened.

'Awake!' cried Miss Penelosa, with a sharp tap of her crutch upon the floor. The eyes opened, the glazing cleared slowly away, and the soul looked out once more after its strange eclipse.

We went away early. Agatha was none the worse for her strange excursion, but I was nervous and unstrung, unable to listen to or answer the stream of comments which Wilson was pouring out for my benefit. As I bade her good-night, Miss Penelosa slipped a piece of paper into my hand.

'Pray forgive me,' said she, 'if I take means to overcome your scepticism. Open this note at ten o'clock to-morrow morning. It is a little private test.'

I can't imagine what she means, but there is the note, and it shall be opened as she directs. My head is aching, and I have written enough for to-night. To-morrow I dare say that what seems so inexplicable will take quite another complexion. I shall not surrender my convictions without a struggle.

March 25th.—I am amazed—confounded. It is clear that I must reconsider my opinion upon this matter. But first, let me place on record what has occurred.

I had finished breakfast and was looking over some diagrams with which my lecture is to be illustrated when my housekeeper entered to tell me that Agatha was in my study, and wished to see me immediately. I glanced at the clock, and saw with surprise that it was only half-past nine.

When I entered the room, she was standing on the hearthrug facing me. Something in her pose chilled me, and checked the words which were rising to my lips. Her veil was half down, but I could see that she was pale and that her expression was constrained.

'Austin,' she said, 'I have come to tell you that our engagement is at an end.'

I staggered. I believe that I literally did stagger. I know that I found myself leaning against the bookcase for support.

'But——but——' I stammered, 'this is very sudden, Agatha.'

'Yes, Austin, I have come here to tell you that our engagement is at an end.'

'But surely,' I cried, 'you will give me some reason. This is unlike you, Agatha. Tell me how I have been unfortunate enough to offend you.'

'It is all over, Austin.'

'But why? You must be under some delusion, Agatha. Perhaps you have been told some falsehood about me. Or you may have misunderstood something that I have said to you. Only let me know what it is, and a word may set it all right.'

'We must consider it all at an end.'

'But you left me last night without a hint at any disagreement. What could have occurred in the interval to change you so. It must have been something that happened last night. You have been thinking it over, and you have disapproved of my conduct. Was it the mesmerism? Did you blame me for letting that woman exercise her power over you? You know that at the least sign I should have interfered.'

'It is useless, Austin. All is over.'

Her voice was cold and measured; her manner strangely formal and hard. It seemed to me that she was absolutely resolved not to be drawn into any argument or explanation. As for me, I was shaking with agitation, and I turned my face aside, so ashamed was I that she should see my want of control.

'You must know what this means to me,' I cried. 'It is the blasting of all my hopes and the ruin of my life. You surely will not inflict such a punishment upon me unheard. You will let me know what is the matter. Consider how impossible it would be for me, under any circumstances, to treat you so. For God's sake, Agatha, let me know what I have done.'

She walked past me without a word and opened the door.

'It is quite useless, Austin,' said she. 'You must consider our engagement at an end.' An instant later she was gone, and before I could recover myself sufficiently to follow her I heard the hall-door close behind her.

I rushed into my room to change my coat, with the idea of hurrying round to Mrs. Marden's to learn from her what the cause of my misfortune might be. So shaken was I that I could hardly lace my boots. Never shall I forget those horrible ten minutes.

I had just pulled on my overcoat when the clock upon the mantel-piece struck ten.

Ten! I associated the idea with Miss Penelosa's note. It was lying before me on the table, and I tore it open. It was scribbled in pencil in a peculiarly angular handwriting.

'My dear Professor Gilroy,' it said, 'pray excuse the personal nature of the test which I am giving you. Professor Wilson happened to mention the relations between you and my subject of this evening, and it struck me that nothing could be more convincing to you than if I were to suggest to Miss Marden that she should call upon you at half-past nine to-morrow morning and suspend your engagement for half an hour or so. Science is so exacting that it is difficult to give a satisfying test, but I am convinced that this at least will be an action which she would be most unlikely to do of her own free-will. Forget any thing that she may have said, as she has really nothing whatever to do with it, and will certainly not recollect any thing about it. I write this note to shorten your anxiety, and to beg you to forgive me for the momentary unhappiness which my suggestion must have caused you.—Yours faithfully, Helen Penelosa.'

Really when I had read the note I was too relieved to be angry. It was a liberty. Certainly it was a very great liberty indeed on the part of a lady whom I had only met once. But after all I had challenged her by my scepticism. It may have been, as she said, a little difficult to devise a test which would satisfy me.

And she had done that. There could be no question at all upon the point. For me hypnotic suggestion was finally established. It took its place from now onward as one of the facts of life. That Agatha, who of all women of my acquaintance has the best-balanced mind, had been reduced to a condition of automatism appeared to be certain. A person at a distance had worked her as an engineer on the shore might guide a Brennan torpedo.[1] A second soul had stepped in, as it were, had pushed her own aside, and had seized her nervous mechanism, saying, 'I will work this for half an hour.' And Agatha must have been unconscious as she came and as she returned. Could she make her way in safety through the streets in such a state! I put on my hat and hurried round to see if all was well with her.

Yes. She was at home. I was shown into the drawing-room and found her sitting with a book upon her lap.

'You are an early visitor, Austin,' said she, smiling.

'And you have been an even earlier one,' I answered.

She looked puzzled. 'What do you mean?' she asked.

'You have not been out to-day?'

'No, certainly not.'

'Agatha,' said I seriously. 'Would you mind telling me exactly what you have done this morning?'

---

[1] A missile developed in the late 1870s by Louis Brennan and used for defence purposes in Britain.

She laughed at my earnestness.

'You've got on your professorial look, Austin. See what comes of being engaged to a man of science. However, I will tell you, though I can't imagine what you want to know for. I got up at eight. I breakfasted at half-past. I came into this room at ten minutes past nine and began to read 'The Memoirs of Madame de Rémusat.'[1] In a few minutes I did the French lady the bad compliment of dropping to sleep over her pages, and I did you, sir, the very flattering one of dreaming about you. It is only a few minutes since I woke up.'

'And found yourself where you had been before?'

'Why, where else should I find myself?'

'Would you mind telling me, Agatha, what it was that you dreamed about me? It really is not mere curiosity on my part.'

'I merely had a vague impression that you came into it. I cannot recall any thing definite.'

'If you have not been out to-day, Agatha, how is it that your shoes are dusty?'

A pained look came over her face.

'Really, Austin, I do not know what is the matter with you this morning. One would almost think that you doubted my word. If my boots are dusty, it must be, of course, that I have put on a pair which the maid had not cleaned.'

It was perfectly evident that she knew nothing whatever about the matter, and I reflected that after all perhaps it was better that I should not enlighten her. It might frighten her, and could serve no good purpose that I could see. I said no more about it, therefore, and left shortly afterwards to give my lecture.

But I am immensely impressed. My horizon of scientific possibilities has suddenly been enormously extended. I no longer wonder at Wilson's demoniac energy and enthusiasm. Who would not work hard who had a vast virgin field ready to his hand? Why, I have known the novel shape of a nucleolus,[2] or a trifling peculiarity of striped muscular fibre seen under a 300 diametre lens, fill me with exultation. How petty do such researches seem when com-

---

[1] Madame de Rémusat's memoirs describe the court of Napoleon. She was Josephine's lady-in-waiting.
[2] "Cell nucleus" (305).

pared with this one which strikes at the very roots of life, and the nature of the soul! I had always looked upon spirit as a product of matter. The brain, I thought, secreted the mind, as the liver does the bile. But how can this be when I see mind working from a distance, and playing upon matter as a musician might upon a violin. The body does not give rise to the soul then, but is rather the rough instrument by which the spirit manifests itself. The windmill does not give rise to the wind, but only indicates it. It was opposed to my whole habit of thought, and yet it was undeniably possible and worthy of investigation.

And why should I not investigate it? I see that under yesterday's date I said, 'If I could see something positive and objective I might be tempted to approach it from the physiological aspect.' Well, I have got my test. I shall be as good as my word. The investigation would, I am sure, be of immense interest. Some of my colleagues might look askance at it, for science is full of unreasoning prejudices, but if Wilson has the courage of his convictions, I can afford to have it also. I shall go to him to-morrow morning—to him and to Miss Penelosa. If she can show us so much it is probable that she can show us more.

March 26th.—Wilson was, as I had anticipated, very exultant over my conversion, and Miss Penelosa was also demurely pleased at the result of her experiment. Strange what a silent, colourless creature she is save only when she exercises her power! Even talking about it gives her colour and life. She seems to take a singular interest in me. I cannot help observing how her eyes follow me about the room.

We had the most interesting conversation about her own powers. It is just as well to put her views on record, though they cannot of course claim any scientific weight.

'You are on the very fringe of the subject,' said she, when I had expressed wonder at the remarkable instance of suggestion which she had shown me. 'I had no direct influence upon Miss Marden when she came round to you. I was not even thinking of her that morning. What I did was to set her mind as I might set the alarum of a clock so that at the hour named it would go off of its own accord. If six months instead of twelve hours had been suggested, it would have been the same.'

'And if the suggestion had been to assassinate me?'

'She would most inevitably have done so.'

'But this is a terrible power!' I cried.

'It is, as you say, a terrible power,' she answered gravely. 'And the more you know of it the more terrible will it seem to you.'

'May I ask,' said I, 'what you meant when you said that this matter of suggestion is only at the fringe of it. What do you consider the essential.'

'I had rather not tell you.'

I was surprised at the decision of her answer.

'You understand,' said I, 'that it is not out of curiosity I ask, but in the hope that I may find some scientific explanation for the facts with which you furnish me.'

'Frankly, Professor Gilroy,' said she, 'I am not at all interested in science, nor do I care whether it can or cannot classify these powers.'

'But I was hoping——'

'Ah, that is quite another thing. If you make it a personal matter,' said she, with the pleasantest of smiles, 'I shall be only too happy to tell you any thing you wish to know. Let me see! What was it you asked me? Oh, about the further powers. Professor Wilson won't believe in them, but they are quite true all the same. For example, it is possible for an operator to gain complete command over his subject—presuming that the latter is a good one. Without any previous suggestion he may make him do whatever he likes.'

'Without the subject's knowledge?'

'That depends. If the force were strongly exerted he would know no more about it than Miss Marden did when she came round and frightened you so. Or, if the influence were less powerful, he might be conscious of what he was doing, but be quite unable to prevent himself from doing it.'

'Would he have lost his own will-power, then?'

'It would be overridden by another, stronger, one.'

'Have you ever exercised this power yourself?'

'Several times.'

'Is your own will so strong, then?'

'Well, it does not entirely depend upon that. Many have strong wills which are not detachable from themselves. The thing is to have the gift of projecting it into another person and superseding their own. I find that the power varies with my own strength and health.'

'Practically, you send your soul into another person's body.'
'Well, you might put it that way.'
'And what does your own body do?'
'It merely feels lethargic.'
'Well, but is there no danger to your own health?' I asked.

'There might be a little. You have to be careful never to let your own consciousness absolutely go, otherwise, you might experience some difficulty in finding your way back again. You must always preserve the connection, as it were. I am afraid I express myself very badly, Professor Gilroy, but of course I don't know how to put these things in a scientific way. I am just giving you my own experiences and my own explanations.'

Well, I read this over now at my leisure, and I marvel at myself! Is this Austin Gilroy, the man who has won his way to the front by his hard reasoning power and by his devotion to fact? Here I am gravely retailing the gossip of a woman who tells me how her soul may be projected from her body, and how, while she lies in a lethargy, she can control the actions of people at a distance! Do I accept it? Certainly not. She must prove and re-prove before I yield a point. But if I am still a sceptic, I have at least ceased to be a scoffer. We are to have a sitting this evening and she is to try if she can produce any mesmeric effect upon me. If she can it will make an excellent starting-point for our investigation. No one can accuse me, at any rate, of complicity. If she cannot, we must try and find some subject who will be like Cæsar's wife.[1] Wilson is perfectly impervious.

10 p.m.—I believe that I am on the threshold of an epoch-making investigation. To have the power of examining these phenomena from inside—to have an organism which will respond, and, at the same time, a brain which will appreciate and criticise—that is surely

---

[1] From Plutarch's story that Caesar divorced his wife, Pompeia, because Clodius, disguised as a woman, had profaned the all-female feast of Bona Dea in Caesar's house. Caesar's wife must be above suspicion. As a scientist, Gilroy sees himself as an objective and legitimate subject. The allusion also suggests an illicit relationship.

a unique advantage. I am quite sure that Wilson would give five years of his life to be as susceptible as I have proved myself to be.

There was no one present except Wilson and his wife. I was seated with my head leaning back, and Miss Penelosa, standing in front and a little to the left, used the same long sweeping strokes as with Agatha. At each of them a warm current of air seemed to strike me, and to suffuse a thrill and glow all through me from head to foot. My eyes were fixed upon Miss Penelosa's face, but as I gazed the features seemed to blur and to fade away. I was conscious only of her own eyes looking down at me, grey, deep, inscrutable. Larger they grew and larger, until they changed suddenly into two mountain lakes toward which I seemed to be falling with horrible rapidity. I shuddered, and as I did so some deeper stratum of thought told me that the shudder represented the rigor which I had observed in Agatha. An instant later I struck the surface of the lakes, now joined into one, and down I went beneath the water with a fulness in my head and a buzzing in my ears. Down I went, down, down, and then with a swoop up again until I could see the light streaming brightly through the green water. I was almost at the surface when the word 'Awake!' rang through my head, and with a start I found myself back in the armchair, with Miss Penelosa leaning on her crutch, and Wilson, his note-book in his hand, peeping over her shoulder. No heaviness or weariness was left behind. On the contrary, though it is only an hour or so since the experiment, I feel so wakeful that I am more inclined for my study than my bedroom. I see quite a vista of interesting experiments extending before us, and am all impatience to begin upon them.

March 27.—A blank day, as Miss Penelosa goes with Wilson and his wife to the Suttons'. Have begun Binet and Ferré's 'Animal Magnetism.'[1] What strange, deep waters these are! Results, results, results—and the cause an absolute mystery. It is stimulating to the imagination, but I must be on my guard against that. Let us have no inferences nor deductions, and nothing but solid facts. I know that the mesmeric trance is true, I know that mesmeric sugges-

---

[1] The final chapter of Alfred Binet and Charles Féré's study suggested the moral risks involved in mesmeric experimentation. See *Animal Magnetism* (London: Kegan Paul, Trench, 1887).

tion is true, I know that I am myself sensitive to this force. That is my present position. I have a large new note-book, which shall be devoted entirely to scientific detail.

Long talk with Agatha and Mrs. Marden in the evening about our marriage. We think that the summer vac. (the beginning of it) would be the best time for the wedding. Why should we delay? I grudge even those few months. Still, as Mrs. Marden says, there are a good many things to be arranged.

March 28.—Mesmerized again by Miss Penelosa. Experience much the same as before, save that insensibility came on more quickly. See Note-book A for temperature of room, barometric pressure, pulse, and respiration, as taken by Professor Wilson.

March 29.—Mesmerized again. Details in Note-book A.

March 30.—Sunday, and a blank day. I grudge any interruption of our experiments. At present they merely embrace the physical signs which go with slight, with complete, and with extreme insensibility. Afterwards we hope to pass on to the phenomena of suggestion and of lucidity. Professors have demonstrated these things upon women at Nancy and at the Saltpetrière. It will be more convincing when a woman demonstrates it upon a professor, with a second professor as a witness. And that I should be the subject, I the sceptic, the materialist! At least I have shown that my devotion to science is greater than to my own personal consistency. The eating of our own words is the greatest sacrifice which truth ever requires of us.

My neighbour, Charles Sadler, the handsome young demonstrator of Anatomy, came in this evening to return a volume of Virchow's Archives[1] which I had lent him. I call him young, but, as a matter of fact, he is a year older than I am.

'I understand, Gilroy,' said he, 'that you are being experimented upon by Miss Penelosa.'

'Well,' he went on, when I had acknowledged it, 'if I were you, I should not let it go any further. You will think me very impertinent, no doubt, but none the less I feel it to be my duty to advise you to have no more to do with her.'

---

[1] Rudolf Carl Virchow was a nineteenth-century German pathologist. Virchow's Archives refers to the *Archive of Pathological Anatomy*, a journal he founded in 1847.

Of course I asked him why.

'I am so placed that I cannot enter into particulars as freely as I could wish,' said he. 'Miss Penelosa is the friend of my friend, and my position is a delicate one. I can only say this, that I have myself been the subject of some of the woman's experiments, and that they have left a most unpleasant impression upon my mind.'

He could hardly expect me to be satisfied with that, and I tried hard to get something more definite out of him, but without success. Is it conceivable that he could be jealous at my having superseded him! Or is he one of those men of science who feel personally injured when facts run counter to their preconceived opinions? He cannot seriously suppose that because he has some vague grievance I am therefore to abandon a series of experiments which promise to be so fruitful of results. He appeared to be annoyed at the light way in which I treated his shadowy warnings, and we parted with some little coldness on both sides.

March 31st.—Mesmerised by Miss P.

April 1st.—Mesmerised by Miss P. (Note-book A.)

April 2nd.—Mesmerized by Miss P. (Sphygmographic[1] chart taken by Professor Wilson.)

April 3rd.—It is possible that this course of mesmerism may be a little trying to the general constitution. Agatha says that I am thinner, and darker under the eyes. I am conscious of a nervous irritability which I had not observed in myself before. The least noise, for example, makes me start, and the stupidity of a student causes me exasperation instead of amusement. Agatha wishes me to stop; but I tell her that every course of study is trying, and that one can never attain a result without paying some price for it. When she sees the sensation which my forthcoming paper on 'The Relation between Mind and Matter' may make, she will understand that it is worth a little nervous wear and tear. I should not be surprised if I got my F. R. S. over it.[2]

Mesmerised again in the evening. The effect is produced more rapidly now, and the subjective visions are less marked. I keep full notes of each sitting. Wilson is leaving for town for a week or ten

---

[1] Wilson is noting Gilroy's pulse.

[2] Fellowship of the Royal Society. This is an eminent, peer-elected body of scientists.

days, but we shall not interrupt the experiments, which depend for their value as much upon my sensations as on his observations.

April 4th.—I must be carefully on my guard. A complication has crept into our experiments which I had not reckoned upon. In my eagerness for scientific facts I have been foolishly blind to the human relations between Miss Penelosa and myself. I can write here what I would not breathe to a living soul. The unhappy woman appears to have formed an attachment for me.

I should not say such a thing even in the privacy of my own intimate journal if it had not come to such a pass that it is impossible to ignore it. For some time,—that is, for the last week,—there have been signs, which I have brushed aside and refused to think of. Her brightness when I come, her dejection when I go, her eagerness that I should come often, the expression of her eyes, the tone of her voice. I tried to think that they meant nothing, and were, perhaps, only her ardent West Indian manner. But last night as I awoke from the mesmeric sleep, I put out my hand, unconsciously, involuntarily, and clasped hers. When I came fully to myself, we were sitting with them locked, she looking up at me with an expectant smile. And the horrible thing was that I felt impelled to say what she expected me to say. What a false wretch I should have been! How I should have loathed myself to-day had I yielded to the temptation of that moment! But, thank God, I was strong enough to spring up and hurry from the room. I was rude, I fear, but I could not—no, I could not trust myself another moment. I, a gentleman, a man of honour, engaged to one of the sweetest girls in England—and yet in a moment of reasonless passion I nearly professed love for this woman whom I hardly know! She is far older than myself, and a cripple. It is monstrous—odious,—and yet the impulse was so strong that had I stayed another minute in her presence I should have committed myself. What was it? I have to teach others the workings of our organism, and what do I know of it myself! Was it the sudden upcropping of some lower stratum in my nature—a brutal primitive instinct suddenly asserting itself? I could almost believe the tales of obsession by evil spirits, so overmastering was the feeling.

Well, the incident places me in a most unfortunate position. On the one hand, I am very loth to abandon a series of experiments which have already gone so far, and which promise such brilliant results. On the other, if this unhappy woman has conceived a passion for me—but surely even now I must have made some hideous mistake. She, with her age and her deformity. It is impossible. And then she knew about Agatha. She understood how I was placed. She only smiled out of amusement, perhaps, when in my dazed state I seized her hand. It was my half-mesmerised brain which gave it a meaning, and sprang with such bestial swiftness to meet it. I wish I could persuade myself that it was indeed so. On the whole, perhaps, my wisest plan would be to postpone our other experiments until Wilson's return. I have written a note to Miss Penelosa, therefore, making no allusion to last night, but saying that a press of work would cause me to interrupt our sittings for a few days. She has answered, formally enough, to say that if I should change my mind I should find her at home at the usual hour.

10 p.m.—Well, well, what a thing of straw I am! I am coming to know myself better of late, and the more I know the lower I fall in my own estimation. Surely I was not always so weak as this. At four o'clock I should have smiled had any one told me that I should go to Miss Penelosa's to-night; and yet at eight I was at Wilson's door as usual. I don't know how it occurred. The influence of habit, I suppose. Perhaps there is a mesmeric craze as there is an opium craze, and I am a victim to it. I only know that as I worked in my study I became more and more uneasy. I fidgeted. I worried. I could not concentrate my mind upon the papers in front of me. And then, at last, almost before I knew what I was doing, I seized my hat and hurried round to keep my usual appointment.

We had an interesting evening. Mrs. Wilson was present during most of the time, which prevented the embarrassment which one at least of us must have felt. Miss Penelosa's manner was quite the same as usual, and she expressed no surprise at my having come in spite of my note. There was nothing in her bearing to show that yesterday's incident had made any impression upon her, and so I am inclined to hope that I overrated it.

April 6th (evening).—No, no, I did not overrate it. I can no longer attempt to conceal from myself that this woman has conceived a passion for me. It is monstrous, but it is true. Again, to-night, I awoke from the mesmeric tra[...] hand in hers, and to suffer that odious feeling whi[...] o throw away my honour, my career—everything—for the sake of this creature who, as I can plainly see when I am away from her influence, possesses no single charm upon earth. But when I am near her I do not feel this. She rouses something in me—something evil—something I had rather not think of. She paralyses my better nature, too, at the moment when she stimulates my worse. Decidedly it is not good for me to be near her.

Last night was worse than before. Instead of flying I actually sat for some time with my hand in hers, talking over the most intimate subjects with her. We spoke of Agatha among other things. What could I have been dreaming of! Miss Penelosa said that she was conventional, and I agreed with her. She spoke once or twice in a disparaging way of her, and I did not protest. What a creature I have been!

Weak as I have proved myself to be, I am still strong enough to bring this sort of thing to an end. It shall not happen again. I have sense enough to fly when I cannot fight. From this Sunday night onwards I shall never sit with Miss Penelosa again. Never! Let the experiments go, let the research come to an end, anything is better than facing this monstrous temptation which drags me so low. I have said nothing to Miss Penelosa, but I shall simply stay away. She can tell the reason without any words of mine.

April 7th.—Have stayed away as I said. It is a pity to ruin such an interesting investigation, but it would be a greater pity still to ruin my life, and I know that I cannot trust myself with that woman.

11 p.m.—God help me! What is the matter with me? Am I going mad? Let me try and be calm and reason with myself. First of all I shall set down exactly what occurred.

It was nearly eight when I wrote the lines with which this day begins. Feeling strangely restless and uneasy, I left my rooms and walked round to spend the evening with Agatha and her mother. They both remarked that I was pale and haggard. About nine Professor Pratt-Haldane came in, and we played a game of whist. I tried hard to concentrate my attention upon the cards, but the feeling of restlessness grew and grew until I found it impossible to struggle against it. I simply could not sit still at the table. At last, in the very middle of a hand, I threw my cards down, and, with some sort of an incoherent apology about having an appointment, I rushed from the room. As if in a dream, I have a vague recollection of tearing through the hall, snatching my hat from the stand, and slamming the door behind me. As in a dream, too, I have the impression of the double line of gas-lamps, and my bespattered boots tell me that I must have run down the middle of the road. It was all misty and strange and unnatural. I came to Wilson's house, I saw Mrs. Wilson and I saw Miss Penelosa. I hardly recall what we talked about, but I do remember that Miss Penelosa shook the head of her crutch at me in a playful way, and accused me of being late and of losing interest in our experiments. There was no mesmerism, but I stayed some time and have only just returned.

My brain is quite clear again, now, and I can think over what has occurred. It is absurd to suppose that it is merely weakness and force of habit. I tried to explain it in that way the other night, but it will no longer suffice. It is something much deeper and more terrible than that. Why, when I was at the Mardens' whist-table, I was dragged away as if the noose of a rope had been cast round me. I can no longer disguise it from myself. The woman has her grip upon me. I am in her clutch. But I must keep my head and reason it out, and see what is best to be done.

But what a blind fool I have been! In my enthusiasm over my research I have walked straight into the pit, although it lay gaping before me. Did she not herself warn me? Did she not tell me, as I can read in my own journal, that when she has acquired power over a subject she can make him do her will? And she has acquired that power over me. I am, for the moment, at the beck and call of this creature with the crutch. I must come when she wills it. I must do as she wills. Worst of all, I must feel as she wills. I loathe her and fear her, yet while I am under the spell she can doubtless make me love her.

There is some consolation in the thought, then, that those odious impulses for which I have blamed myself do not really come from me at all. They are all transferred from her, little as I could have guessed it at the time. I feel cleaner and lighter for the thought.

April 8th.—Yes, now in broad daylight, writing coolly and with time for reflection, I am compelled to confirm everything which I find in my journal last night. I am in a horrible position, but, above all, I must not lose my head. I must pit my intellect against her powers. After all, I am no silly puppet to dance at the end of a string. I have energy, brains, courage. For all her devil's tricks I may beat her yet. May! I must, or what is to become of me?

Let me try to reason it out. This woman, by her own explanation, can dominate my nervous organism. She can project herself into my body and take command of it. She has a parasitic soul—yes, she is a parasite, a monstrous parasite. She creeps into my frame as the hermit crab does into the whelk's shell.¹ I am powerless! What can I do? I am dealing with forces of which I know nothing. And I can tell no one of my trouble. They would set me down as a madman. Certainly, if it got noised abroad, the university would say that they had no need of a devil-ridden professor.² And Agatha! No, no, I must face it alone.

I read over my notes of what the woman said when she spoke about her powers. There is one point which fills me with dismay. She implies that when the influence is slight the subject knows what he is doing but cannot control himself, whereas, when it is strongly exerted, he is absolutely unconscious. Now, I have always known what I did, though less so last night than on the previous occasion. That seems to mean that she has never yet exerted her full powers upon me. Was ever a man so placed before! Yes, perhaps there was, and very near me too. Charles Sadler must know something of this! His vague words of warning take a meaning now. Oh, if I had only listened to him then, before I helped by those repeated sittings to forge the links of the chain which binds me. But I will see him to-day. I will apologise to him for having treated his warning so lightly. I will see if he can advise me.

4 p.m.—No, he cannot. I have talked with him, and he showed such surprise at the first words in which I tried to express my unspeakable secret that I went no further. As far as I can gather (by

---

¹ The hermit crab occupies an empty shell and discards it when it no longer fits.
² Alan Gauld notes that Charcot used the language of "demoniacal attack" to describe the convulsions of his hysteria patients. *A History of Hypnotism* (Cambridge: Cambridge University Press, 1992), p. 309.

hints and inferences rather than by any statement), his own experience was limited to some words or looks such as I have myself endured. His abandonment of Miss Penelosa is in itself a sign that he was never really in her toils. Oh, if he only knew his escape! He has to thank his phlegmatic Saxon temperament for it. I am black and Celtic, and this hag's clutch is deep in my nerves.[1] Shall I ever get it out? Shall I ever be the same man that I was just one short fortnight ago?

Let me consider what I had better do. I cannot leave the university in the middle of the term. If I were free my course would be obvious. I should start at once and travel in Persia. But would she allow me to start? And could her influence not reach me in Persia, and bring me back to within touch of her crutch? I can only find out the limits of this hellish power by my own bitter experience. I will fight and fight and fight—and what can I do more?

I know very well that about eight o'clock to-night that craving for her society—that irresistible restlessness, will come upon me. How shall I overcome it? What shall I do? I must make it impossible for me to leave the room. I shall lock the door and throw the key out of the window. But then, what am I to do in the morning? Never mind about the morning. I must at all costs break this chain which holds me.

April 9th.—Victory! I have done splendidly! At seven o'clock last night I took a hasty dinner and then locked myself up in my bedroom and dropped the key into the garden. I chose a cheery novel, and lay in bed for three hours trying to read it, but really in a horrible state of trepidation, expecting every instant that I should become conscious of the impulse. Nothing of the sort occurred, however, and I awoke this morning with the feeling that a black nightmare had been lifted off me. Perhaps the creature realised what I had done, and understood that it was useless to try to influence me. At any rate, I have beaten her once, and if I can do it once, I can do it again.

It was most awkward about the key in the morning. Luckily there was an under-gardener below, and I asked him to throw it up. No doubt he thought I had just dropped it. I will have doors and

---

[1] This reflects Doyle's pseudo-racial theories. See his interview with Bram Stoker in the appendix.

windows screwed up and six stout men to hold me down in my bed before I will surrender myself to be hag-ridden in this way.

I had a note from Mrs. Marden this afternoon asking me to go round and see her. I intended to do so in any case, but had not expected to find bad news waiting for me. It seems that the Armstrongs, from whom Agatha has expectations, are due home from Adelaide in the 'Aurora,' and that they have written to Mrs. Marden and her to meet them in town. They will probably be away for a month or six weeks, and as the 'Aurora' is due on Wednesday, they must go at once—to-morrow if they are ready in time. My consolation is that when we meet again there will be no more parting between Agatha and me.

'I want you to do one thing, Agatha,' said I, when we were alone together. 'If you should happen to meet Miss Penelosa, either in town or here, you must promise me never again to allow her to mesmerise you.'

Agatha opened her eyes.

'Why, it was only the other day that you were saying how interesting it all was, and how determined you were to finish your experiments.'

'I know, but I have changed my mind since then.'

'And you won't have it any more?'

'No.'

'I am so glad, Austin. You can't think how pale and worn you have been lately. It was really our principal objection to going to London now that we did not wish to leave you when you were so pulled down. And your manner has been so strange occasionally—especially that night when you left poor Professor Pratt-Haldane to play dummy.[1] I am convinced that these experiments are very bad for your nerves.'

'I think so too, dear.'

'And for Miss Penelosa's nerves as well. You have heard that she is ill?'

'No.'

'Mrs. Wilson told us so last night. She described it as a nervous fever. Professor Wilson is coming back this week, and of course

---

[1] An imaginary player at whist.

Mrs. Wilson is very anxious that Miss Penelosa should be well again then, for he has quite a programme of experiments which he is anxious to carry out.'

I was glad to have Agatha's promise, for it was enough that this woman should have one of us in her clutch. On the other hand, I was disturbed to hear about Miss Penelosa's illness. It rather discounts the victory which I appeared to win last night. I remember that she said that loss of health interfered with her power. That may be why I was able to hold my own so easily. Well, well, I must take the same precautions to-night and see what comes of it. I am childishly frightened when I think of her.

April 10.—All went very well last night. I was amused at the gardener's face when I had again to hail him this morning and to ask him to throw up my key. I shall get a name among the servants if this sort of thing goes on. But the great point is that I stayed in my room without the slightest inclination to leave it. I do believe that I am shaking myself clear of this incredible bond—or is it only that the woman's power is in abeyance until she recovers her strength? I can but pray for the best.

The Mardens left this morning, and the brightness seems to have gone out of the spring sunshine. And yet it is very beautiful also as it gleams on the green chestnuts opposite my windows, and gives a touch of gaiety to the heavy, lichen-mottled walls of the old colleges. How sweet and gentle and soothing is Nature! Who would think that there lurked in her also such vile forces, such odious possibilities! For of course I understand that this dreadful thing which has sprung out at me is neither supernatural nor even preternatural. No, it is a natural force which this woman can use and society is ignorant of. The mere fact that it ebbs with her strength shows how entirely it is subject to physical laws. If I had time, I might probe it to the bottom and lay my hands upon its antidote. But you cannot tame the tiger when you are beneath his claws. You can but try to writhe away from him. Ah, when I look in the glass and see my own dark eyes and clear-cut Spanish face, I long for a vitriol splash or a bout of the small-pox.[1] One or the other might have saved me from this calamity.

---

[1] He wishes for some type of facial disfigurement. Vitriol or sulphuric acid

I am inclined to think that I may have trouble to-night. There are two things which make me fear so. One is, that I met Mrs. Wilson on the street and that she tells me that Miss Penelosa is better, though still weak. I find myself wishing in my heart that the illness had been her last. The other is, that Professor Wilson comes back in a day or two, and his presence would act as a constraint upon her. I should not fear our interviews, if a third person were present. For both these reasons I have a presentiment of trouble to-night, and I shall take the same precautions as before.

April 10.—No, thank God, all went well last night. I really could not face the gardener again. I locked my door and thrust the key underneath it, so that I had to ask the maid to let me out in the morning. But the precaution was really not needed, for I never had any inclination to go out at all. Three evenings in succession at home! I am surely near the end of my troubles, for Wilson will be home again either to-day or to-morrow. Shall I tell him of what I have gone through or not? I am convinced that I should not have the slightest sympathy from him. He would look upon me as an interesting case, and read a paper about me at the next meeting of the Psychical Society,[1] in which he would gravely discuss the possibility of my being a deliberate liar, and weigh it against the chances of my being in an early stage of lunacy. No, I shall get no comfort out of Wilson.

I am feeling wonderfully fit and well. I don't think I ever lectured with greater spirit. Oh, if I could only get this shadow off my life how happy I should be! Young, fairly wealthy, in the front rank of my profession, engaged to a beautiful and charming girl—have I not everything which a man could ask for? Only one thing to trouble me, but what a thing it is!

Midnight.—I shall go mad. Yes, that will be the end of it. I shall go mad. I am not far from it now. My head throbs as I rest it on my

---

was easy to purchase and would scar the face and could cause blindness. Smallpox was a highly contagious disease that caused pock-marks.

[1] The Society for Psychical Research was established by a group of Cambridge dons in 1882 to investigate hypnotism, thought-transference and similar phenomena. Doyle became a member in 1891 and was reading the society's published *Proceedings* while writing *The Parasite*.

hot hand. I am quivering all over like a scared horse. Oh, what a night I have had! And yet I have some cause to be satisfied also.

At the risk of becoming the laughing-stock of my own servant I again slipped my key under the door, imprisoning myself for the night. Then, finding it too early to go to bed, I lay down with my clothes on and began to read one of Dumas' novels. Suddenly I was gripped—gripped and dragged from the couch. It is only thus that I can describe the overpowering nature of the force which pounced upon me. I clawed at the coverlet. I clung to the woodwork. I believe that I screamed out in my frenzy. It was all useless, hopeless. I must go. There was no way out of it. It was only at the outset that I resisted. The force soon became too overmastering for that. I thank goodness that there were no watchers there to interfere with me. I could not have answered for myself if there had been. And besides the determination to get out, there came to me also the keenest and coolest judgment in choosing my means. I lit a candle and endeavoured, kneeling in front of the door, to pull the key through with the feather-end of a quill pen. It was just too short and pushed it further away. Then with quiet persistence I got a paper-knife out of one of the drawers, and with that I managed to draw the key back. I opened the door, stepped into my study, took a photograph of myself from the bureau, wrote something across it, placed it in the inside pocket of my coat, and then started off for Wilson's.

It was all wonderfully clear, and yet disassociated from the rest of my life, as the incidents of even the most vivid dream might be. A peculiar <u>double consciousness possessed</u> me. There was the predominant alien will, which was bent upon drawing me to the side of its owner, and there was the feebler protesting personality, which I recognised as being myself, tugging feebly at the overmastering impulse as a led terrier might at its chain. I can remember recognising these two conflicting forces, but I recall nothing of my walk, nor of how I was admitted to the house. Very vivid, however, is my recollection of how I met Miss Penelosa. She was reclining on the sofa in the little boudoir in which our experiments had usually been carried out. Her head was rested on her hand, and a tiger-skin rug had been partly drawn over her. She looked up expectantly as I entered, and, as the lamplight fell upon her face, I could see that she was very pale and thin, with dark hollows under her eyes. She smiled at me and pointed to a stool beside her. It was with her left hand that she pointed, and I, running eagerly forward, seized it—I loathe myself as I think of it—and pressed it passionately to my lips. Then, seating myself upon the stool, and still retaining her hand, I gave her the photograph which I had brought with me, and talked, and talked, and talked, of my love for her, of my grief over her illness, of my joy at her recovery, of the misery it was to me to be absent a single evening from her side. She lay quietly looking down at me with imperious eyes and her provocative smile. Once I remember that she passed her hand over my hair as one caresses a dog. And it gave me pleasure, the caress. I thrilled under it. I was her slave, body and soul, and for the moment I rejoiced in my slavery.

And then came the blessed change. Never tell me that there is not a Providence. I was on the brink of perdition. My feet were on the edge. Was it a coincidence that at that very instant help should come! No, no, no, there is a Providence, and its hand has drawn me back. There is something in the universe stronger than this devil woman with her tricks. Ah, what a balm to my heart it is to think so!

As I looked up at her I was conscious of a change in her. Her face, which had been pale before, was now ghastly. Her eyes were dull, and the lids drooped heavily over them. Above all, the look of serene confidence had gone from her features. Her mouth had weakened. Her forehead had puckered. She was frightened and undecided. And, as I watched the change, my own spirit fluttered and struggled, trying hard to tear itself from the grip which held it—a grip which, from moment to moment, grew less secure.

'Austin,' she whispered, 'I have tried to do too much. I was not strong enough. I have not recovered yet from my illness. But I could not live longer without seeing you. You won't leave me, Austin? This is only a passing weakness. If you will only give me five minutes I shall be myself again. Give me the small decanter from the table in the window.'

But I had regained my soul. With her waning strength the influence had cleared away from me and left me free. And I was aggressive—bitterly, fiercely aggressive. For once, at least, I could make this woman understand what my real feelings towards her were. My soul was filled with a hatred as bestial as the love against which it was a reaction. It was the savage, murderous passion of the revolted serf. I could have taken the crutch from her side and beaten her face in with it. She threw her hands up, as if to avoid a blow, and cowered away from me into the corner of the settee.

'The brandy!' she gasped. 'The brandy!'

I took the decanter and poured it over the roots of a palm in the window. Then I snatched the photograph from her hand and tore it into a hundred pieces.

'You vile woman!' I said, 'If I did my duty to society, you would never leave this room alive.'

'I love you, Austin. I love you,' she wailed.

'Yes,' I cried. 'And Charles Sadler before. And how many others before that?'

'Charles Sadler!' she gasped. 'He has spoken to you! So, Charles Sadler, Charles Sadler!' Her voice came through her white lips like a snake's hiss.

'Yes, I know you, and others shall know you too. You shameless creature! You knew how I stood. And yet you used your vile power to bring me to your side. You may perhaps do so again, but at least you will remember that you have heard me say that I love Miss Marden from the bottom of my soul, and that I loathe you, abhor you. The very sight of you and the sound of your voice fill me with horror and disgust. The thought of you is repulsive. That is how I feel towards you, and if it pleases you by your tricks to draw me again to your side as you have done to-night, you will at least, I should think, have little satisfaction in trying to make a lover out of a man who has told you his real opinion of you. You may put what words you will into my mouth, but you cannot help remembering——'

I stopped, for the woman's head had fallen back and she had fainted. She could not bear to hear what I had to say to her. What a glow of satisfaction it gives me to think that come what may in the future she can never misunderstand my true feelings towards her. But what will occur in the future? What will she do next? I dare not think of it. Oh, if only I could hope that she will leave me alone!

But when I think of what I said to her—never mind, I have been stronger than she for once.

April 11.—I hardly slept last night, and found myself in the morning so unstrung and feverish that I was compelled to ask Pratt-Haldane to do my lecture for me. It is the first that I have ever missed. I rose at midday, but my head is aching, my hands quivering, and my nerves in a pitiable state.

Who should come round this evening but Wilson. He has just come back from London, where he has lectured, read papers, convened meetings, exposed a medium, conducted a series of experiments on thought transference, entertained Professor Richet of Paris, spent hours gazing into a crystal, and obtained some evidence as to the passage of matter through matter.[1] All this he poured into my ears in a single gust.

'But you,' he cried at last, 'you are not looking well. And Miss Penelosa is quite prostrated to-day. How about the experiments?'

'I have abandoned them.'

'Tut, tut! Why?'

'The subject seems to me to be a dangerous one.'

Out came his big brown note-book.

'This is of great interest,' said he. 'What are your grounds for saying that it is a dangerous one? Please give your facts in chronological order with approximate dates and names of reliable witnesses with their permanent addresses.'

'First of all,' I asked, 'would you tell me whether you have col-

---

[1] Gilroy is referring to experiments conducted by the Society for Psychical Research. Frederic Myers, a founding member of the Society, coined the term 'telepathy' in 1882. Charles Richet, President of the Society for Psychical Research in 1905, was an eminent physiologist who won the Nobel Prize in 1913 for his discovery of anaphylaxis. He experimented with telepathy and clairvoyance and coined the term 'ectoplasm', the substance that supposedly emanated from a medium in which spirit manifestations were produced. The movement here between orthodox science, crystal-gazing and mediumship demonstrates the fluid boundaries between science and pseudo-science in the late nineteenth century. Richet instituted modern hypnosis in 1875 and his early researches discovered that "magnetization produces an effect like that of hashish or of opium, with a general anæsthesia or analgesia, and a feeling of detachment and happiness" (Gauld, pp. 299-300).

lected any cases where the mesmerist has gained a command over the subject and has used it for evil purposes?'

'Dozens,' he cried exultantly. 'Crime by suggestion——'

'I don't mean suggestion. I mean where a sudden impulse comes from a person at a distance—an uncontrollable impulse.'

'Obsession!' he shrieked, in an ecstasy of delight. 'It is the rarest condition. We have eight cases, five well attested. You don't mean to say——' his exultation made him hardly articulate.

'No, I don't,' said I. 'Good-evening! You will excuse me, but I am not very well to-night.' And so at last I got rid of him, still brandishing his pencil and his note-book. My troubles may be bad to hear, but at least it is better to hug them to myself than to have myself exhibited by Wilson, like a freak at a fair.[1] He has lost sight of human beings. Everything to him is a case and a phenomenon. I will die before I speak to him again upon the matter.

April 12.—Yesterday was a blessed day of quiet, and I enjoyed an uneventful night. Wilson's presence is a great consolation. What can the woman do now? Surely when she has heard me say what I have said she will conceive the same disgust for me which I have for her. She could not—no, she could not—desire to have a lover who had insulted her so. No, I believe I am free from her love—but how about her hate? Might she not use these powers of hers for revenge? Tut, why should I frighten myself over shadows! She will forget about me and I shall forget about her, and all will be well.

April 13.—My nerves have quite recovered their tone. I really believe that I have conquered the creature. But I must confess to living in some suspense. She is well again, for I hear that she was driving with Mrs. Wilson in the High Street in the afternoon.

April 14.—I do wish I could get away from the place altogether. I shall fly to Agatha's side the very day that the term closes. I suppose it is pitiably weak of me, but this woman gets upon my nerves most terribly. I have seen her again, and I have spoken with her.

It was just after lunch, and I was smoking a cigarette in my study when I heard the step of my servant Murray in the passage.

---

[1] The fear of becoming an exhibit recalls the stage performances of mesmerists. Charcot famously experimented on his female hysteria subjects in a theatre full of medical men, journalists, and members of the public.

I was languidly conscious that a second step was audible behind, and had hardly troubled myself to speculate who it might be, when suddenly a slight noise brought me out of my chair with my skin creeping with apprehension. I had never particularly observed before what sort of sound the tapping of a crutch was, but my quivering nerves told me that I heard it now in the sharp wooden clack which alternated with the muffled thud of the footfall. Another instant and my servant had shown her in.

I did not attempt the usual conventions of society, nor did she. I simply stood with the smouldering cigarette in my hand and gazed at her. She in her turn looked silently at me, and at her look I remembered how in these very pages I had tried to define the expression of her eyes, whether they were furtive or fierce. To-day they were fierce—coldly and inexorably so.

'Well,' said she at last, 'are you still of the same mind as when I saw you last?'

'I have always been of the same mind.'

'Let us understand each other, Professor Gilroy,' said she slowly. 'I am not a very safe person to trifle with, as you should realise by now. It was you who asked me to enter into a series of experiments with you, it was you who won my affections, it was you who professed your love for me, it was you who brought me your own photograph with words of affection upon it, and finally, it was you who on the very same evening thought fit to insult me most outrageously, addressing me as no man has ever dared to speak to me yet. Tell me that those words came from you in a moment of passion, and I am prepared to forget and to forgive them. You did not mean what you said, Austin? You do not really hate me?'

I might have pitied this deformed woman—such a longing for love broke suddenly through the menace of her eyes. But then I thought of what I had gone through, and my heart set like flint.

'If ever you heard me speak of love,' said I, 'you know very well that it was your voice which spoke and not mine. The only words of truth which I have ever been able to say to you are those which you heard when last we met.'

'I know. Some one has set you against me. It was he.' She tapped with her crutch upon the floor. 'Well, you know very well that I could bring you this instant crouching like a spaniel to my feet. You will not find me again in my hours of weakness when you can insult me with impunity. Have a care what you are doing, Professor Gilroy. You stand in a terrible position. You have not yet realised the hold which I have upon you.'

I shrugged my shoulders and turned away.

'Well,' said she, after a pause, 'if you despise my love I must see what can be done with fear. You smile, but the day will come when you will come screaming to me for pardon. Yes, you will grovel on the ground before me, proud as you are, and you will curse the day that ever you turned me from your best friend into your most bitter enemy. Have a care, Professor Gilroy.' I saw a white hand shaking in the air, and a face which was scarcely human so convulsed was it with passion. An instant later she was gone, and I heard the quick hobble and tap receding down the passage.

But she has left a weight upon my heart. Vague presentiments of coming misfortune lie heavy upon me. I try in vain to persuade myself that these are only words of empty anger. I can remember those relentless eyes too clearly to think so. What shall I do—ah, what shall I do? I am no longer master of my own soul. At any moment this loathsome parasite may creep into me, and then——? I must tell some one my hideous secret—I must tell it or go mad. If I had some one to sympathise and advise! Wilson is out of the question. Charles Sadler would understand me only so far as his own experience carries him. Pratt-Haldane! He is a well-balanced man, a man of great common sense and resource. I will go to him. I will tell him everything. God grant that he may be able to advise me!

6.45 p.m.—No, it is useless. There is no human help for me; I must fight this out single-handed. Two courses lie before me. I might become this woman's lover, or I must endure such persecutions as she can inflict upon me. Even if none come, I shall live in a hell of apprehension. But she may torture me, she may drive me mad, she may kill me, I will never, never, never give in. What can she inflict which would be worse than the loss of Agatha, and the knowledge that I am a perjured liar, and have forfeited the name of gentleman?

Pratt-Haldane was most amiable, and listened with all politeness to my story. But when I looked at his heavy set features, his slow eyes, and the ponderous study furniture which surrounded him, I could hardly tell him what I had come to say. It was all so substantial, so material. And, besides, what would I myself have said a short month ago if one of my colleagues had come to me with a story of demoniac possession? Perhaps I should have been less patient than he was. As it was, he took notes of my statement, asked me how much tea I drank, how many hours I slept, whether I had been overworking much, had I had sudden pains in the head, evil dreams, singing in the ears, flashes before the eyes—all questions which pointed to his belief that brain congestion was at the bottom of my trouble. Finally he dismissed me with a great many platitudes about open-air exercise and avoidance of nervous excitement. His prescription, which was for chloral and bromide,[1] I rolled up and threw into the gutter.

No, I can look for no help from any human being. If I consult any more, they may put their heads together and I may find myself in an asylum. I can but grip my courage with both hands, and pray that an honest man may not be abandoned.

April 15.—It is the sweetest spring within the memory of man. So green, so mild, so beautiful! Ah, what a contrast between Nature without and my own soul, so torn with doubt and terror! It has been an uneventful day, but I know that I am on the edge of an abyss. I know it, and yet I go on with the routine of my life. The one bright spot is that Agatha is happy and well, and out of all danger. If this creature had a hand on each of us, what might she not do?

April 16.—The woman is ingenious in her torments. She knows how fond I am of my work, and how highly my lectures are thought of. So it is from that point that she now attacks me. It will end, I can see, in my losing my professorship, but I will fight to the finish. She shall not drive me out of it without a struggle.

I was not conscious of any change during my lecture this morning save that for a minute or two I had a dizziness and swimminess which rapidly passed away. On the contrary, I congratu-

---

[1] Prescribed as an "anodyne and soporific, causing extreme muscular relaxation" but in the dose of "ten to twenty grains, or even more, in solution, insomnia, delirium tremens" (223). Bromides have a "therapeutic value" in "exercising remarkable influence in allaying nervous irritation" (159).

lated myself upon having made my subject (the functions of the red corpuscles) both interesting and clear. I was surprised, therefore, when a student came into my laboratory immediately after the lecture and complained of being puzzled by the discrepancy between my statements and those in the textbooks. He showed me his note-book, in which I was reported as having in one portion of the lecture championed the most outrageous and unscientific heresies. Of course I denied it, and declared that he had misunderstood me; but on comparing his notes with those of his companions, it became clear that he was right, and that I really had made some most preposterous statements. Of course I shall explain it away as being the result of a moment of aberration, but I feel only too sure that it will be the first of a series. It is but a month now to the end of the session, and I pray that I may be able to hold out until then.

April 26.—Ten days have elapsed since I have had the heart to make any entry in my journal. Why should I record my own humiliation and degradation! I had vowed never to open it again. And yet the force of habit is strong, and here I find myself taking up once more the record of my own dreadful experiences—in much the same spirit in which a suicide has been known to take notes of the effects of the poison which killed him.

Well, the crash which I had foreseen has come—and that no further back than yesterday. The university authorities have taken my lectureship from me. It has been done in the most delicate way, purporting to be a temporary measure to relieve me from the effects of overwork and to give me the opportunity of recovering my health. None the less it has been done, and I am no longer Professor Gilroy. The laboratory is still in my charge, but I have little doubt that that also will soon go.

The fact is that my lectures had become the laughing-stock of the university. My class was crowded with students who came to see and hear what the eccentric professor would do or say next. I cannot go into the detail of my humiliation. Oh, that devilish woman! There is no depth of buffoonery and imbecility to which she has not forced me. I would begin my lecture clearly and well—but always with the sense of a coming eclipse. Then as I felt the influence I would struggle against it, striving with clenched hands and beads of sweat upon my brow to get the better of it, while the students, hearing my incoherent words and watching my contortions, would roar with laughter at the antics of their professor. And then, when she had once fairly mastered me, out would come the most outrageous things: silly jokes, sentiments as though I were proposing a toast, snatches of ballads, personal abuse even against some member of my class. And then in a moment my brain would clear again and my lecture proceed decorously to the end. No wonder that my conduct has been the talk of the colleges! No wonder that the university senate has been compelled to take official notice of such a scandal. Oh, that devilish woman!

And the most dreadful part of it all is my own loneliness. Here I sit in a commonplace English bow-window, looking out upon a commonplace English street with its garish 'busses and its lounging policemen, and behind me there hangs a shadow which is out of all keeping with the age and place. In the home of knowledge I am weighed down and tortured by a power of which science knows nothing. No magistrate would listen to me. No paper would discuss my case. No doctor would believe my symptoms. My own most intimate friends would only look upon it as a sign of brain derangement. I am out of all touch with my kind. Oh, that devilish woman! Let her have a care! She may push me too far. When the law cannot help a man he may make a law for himself.

She met me in the High Street yesterday evening and spoke to me. It was as well for her, perhaps, that it was not between the hedges of a lonely country road. She asked me with her cold smile whether I had been chastened yet. I did not deign to answer her. 'We must try another turn of the screw,' said she. Have a care, my lady, have a care! I had her at my mercy once. Perhaps another chance may come.

April 28.—The suspension of my lectureship has had the effect also of taking away her means of annoying me, and so I have enjoyed two blessed days of peace. After all, there is no reason to despair. Sympathy pours in to me from all sides, and every one agrees that it is my devotion to science and the arduous nature of my researches which have shaken my nervous system. I have had the kindest message from the council, advising me to travel abroad, and expressing the confident hope that I may be able to resume all my duties by the beginning of the summer term. Nothing could be more flattering than their allusions to my career and to my services to the university. It is only in misfortune that one can test one's own popularity. This creature may weary of tormenting me, and then all may yet be well. May God grant it!

April 29.—Our sleepy little town has had a small sensation. The only knowledge of crime which we ever have is when a rowdy undergraduate breaks a few lamps, or comes to blows with a policeman. Last night, however, there was an attempt made to break into the branch of the Bank of England, and we are all in a flutter in consequence.

Parkinson the manager is an intimate friend of mine, and I found him very much excited when I walked round there after breakfast. Had the thieves broken into the counting-house they would still have had the safes to reckon with, so that the defence was considerably stronger than the attack. Indeed the latter does not appear to have ever been very formidable. Two of the lower windows have marks as if a chisel or some such instrument had been pushed under them to force them open. The police should have a good clue, for the woodwork had been done with green paint only the day before, and from the smears it is evident that some of it has found its way on to the criminal's hands or clothes.

4.30 p.m.—Ah, that accursed woman! That thrice-accursed woman! Never mind! She shall not beat me! No, she shall not! But, oh, the she-devil! She has taken my professorship; now she would take my honour. Is there nothing I can do against her, nothing save—ah, but hard pushed as I am I cannot bring myself to think of that!

It was about an hour ago that I went into my bedroom, and was brushing my hair before the glass when suddenly my eyes lit upon something which left me so sick and cold that I sat down upon the edge of the bed and began to cry. It is many a long year since I shed tears, but all my nerve was gone, and I could but sob and sob in impotent grief and anger. There was my house jacket, the coat I usually wear after dinner, hanging on its peg by the wardrobe, with the right sleeve thickly crusted from wrist to elbow with daubs of green paint.

So this was what she meant by another turn of the screw! She had made a public imbecile of me. Now she would brand me as a criminal. This time she has failed. But how about the next? I dare not think of it—and of Agatha, and my poor old mother! I wish that I were dead!

Yes, this is the other turn of the screw. And this is also what she meant, no doubt, when she said that I had not realised yet the power she has over me. I look back at my account of my conversation with her, and I see how she declared that with a slight exertion of her will her subject would be conscious, and with a stronger one unconscious. Last night I was unconscious. I could have sworn that I slept soundly in my bed without so much as a dream. And yet those stains tell me that I dressed, made my way out, attempted to open the bank windows, and returned. Was I observed? Is it possible that some one saw me do it and followed me home? Ah, what a hell my life has become! I have no peace, no rest. But my patience is nearing its end.

10 p.m.—I have cleaned my coat with turpentine. I do not think that any one could have seen me. It was with my screw-driver that I made the marks. I found it all crusted with paint, and I have cleaned it. My head aches as if it would burst, and I have taken five grains of antipyrine.[1] If it were not for Agatha, I should have taken fifty and had an end of it.

May 3.—Three quiet days. This hell-fiend is like a cat with a mouse. She lets me loose only to pounce upon me again. I am never so frightened as when everything is still. My physical state is deplorable—perpetual hiccough and ptosis of the left eyelid.[2] I have heard from the Mardens that they will be back the day after to-morrow. I do not know whether I am glad or sorry. They were safe in London. Once here they may be drawn into the miserable network in which I am myself struggling. And I must tell them of it. I cannot marry Agatha so long as I know that I am not responsible for my own actions. Yes, I must tell them, even if it brings everything to an end between us.

To-night is the university ball, and I must go. God knows I

---

[1] A "grayish-white soluble crystal powder active antipyretic [to lower fever] and antineuralgic; externally, antiseptic. It is a heart-depressant, and should be prescribed with caution" (76).
[2] This is the "falling down of the upper eyelid over the eye" (927).

never felt less in the humour for festivity, but I must not have it said that I am unfit to appear in public. If I am seen there, and have speech with some of the elders of the university it will go a long way toward showing them that it would be unjust to take my chair away from me.

10 p.m.—I have been to the ball. Charles Sadler and I went together, but I have come away before him. I shall wait up for him, however, for indeed I fear to go to sleep these nights. He is a cheery, practical fellow, and a chat with him will steady my nerves. On the whole, the evening was a great success. I talked to every one who has influence, and I think that I made them realise that my chair is not vacant quite yet. The creature was at the ball—unable to dance, of course, but sitting with Mrs. Wilson. Again and again her eyes rested upon me. They were almost the last things I saw before I left the room. Once as I sat sideways to her I watched her and saw that her gaze was following some one else. It was Sadler, who was dancing at the time with the second Miss Thurston. To judge by her expression it is well for him that he is not in her grip as I am. He does not know the escape he has had. I think I hear his step in the street now, and I will go down and let him in. If he will——

May 4.—Why did I break off in this way last night? I never went downstairs after all—at least I have no recollection of doing so. But, on the other hand, I cannot remember going to bed. One of my hands is greatly swollen this morning, and yet I have no remembrance of injuring it yesterday. Otherwise I am feeling all the better for last night's festivity. But I cannot understand how it is that I did not meet Charles Sadler when I so fully intended to do so. Is it possible—my God, it is only too probable! Has she been leading me some devil's dance again? I will go down to Sadler and ask him.

Midday. The thing has come to a crisis. My life is not worth living. But if I am to die then she shall come also. I will not leave her behind, to drive some other man mad as she has me. No, I have come to the limit of my endurance. She has made me as desperate and dangerous a man as walks the earth. God knows I have never had the heart to hurt a fly, and yet if I had my hands now upon that woman she should never leave this room alive. I shall see her this very day, and she shall learn what she has to expect from me.

I went to Sadler and found him to my surprise in bed. As I entered he sat up and turned a face towards me which sickened me as I looked at it.

'Why, Sadler, what has happened?' I cried, but my heart turned cold as I said it.

'Gilroy,' he answered, mumbling with his swollen lips, 'I have for some weeks been under the impression that you are a madman. Now I know it, and that you are a dangerous one as well. If it were not that I am unwilling to make a scandal in the college you would now be in the hands of the police.'

'Do you mean——?' I cried.

'I mean that as I opened the door last night you rushed out upon me, struck me with both your fists in the face, knocked me down, kicked me furiously in the side, and left me lying almost unconscious in the street. Look at your own hand bearing witness against you.'

Yes, there it was, puffed up with sponge-like knuckles as after some terrific blow. What could I do? Though he put me down as a madman I must tell him all. I sat by his bed and went over all my troubles from the beginning. I poured them out with quivering hands and burning words which might have carried conviction to the most sceptical. 'She hates you and she hates me,' I cried. 'She revenged herself last night on both of us at once. She saw me leave the ball and she must have seen you also. She knew how long it would take you to reach home. Then she had but to use her wicked will. Ah, your bruised face is a small thing beside my bruised soul!'

He was struck by my story. That was evident. 'Yes, yes, she watched me out of the room,' he muttered. 'She is capable of it. But is it possible that she has really reduced you to this? What do you intend to do?'

'To stop it,' I cried. 'I am perfectly desperate. I shall give her fair warning to-day, and the next time will be the last.'

'Do nothing rash,' said he.

'Rash!' I cried. 'The only rash thing is that I should postpone it another hour.' With that I rushed to my room. And here I am on the eve of what may be the great crisis of my life. I shall start at once. I have gained one thing to-day, for I have made one man at least realise the truth of this monstrous experience of mine. And, if the worst should happen, this diary remains as a proof of the goad that has driven me.

Evening.—When I came to Wilson's I was shown up, and found that he was sitting with Miss Penelosa. For half an hour I had to endure his fussy talk about his recent research into the exact nature of the spiritualistic rap,[1] while the creature and I sat in silence looking across the room at each other. I read a sinister amusement in her eyes, and she must have seen hatred and menace in mine. I had almost despaired of having speech with her when he was called from the room, and we were left for a few moments together.

'Well, Professor Gilroy—or is it Mr. Gilroy?' said she, with that bitter smile of hers, 'how is your friend Mr. Charles Sadler after the ball?'

'You fiend!' I cried, 'you have come to the end of your tricks now. I will have no more of them. Listen to what I say.'—I strode across and shook her roughly by the shoulder. 'As sure as there is a God in heaven I swear that if you try another of your devilries upon me I will have your life for it. Come what may, I will have your life. I have come to the end of what a man can endure.'

'Accounts are not quite settled between us,' said she, with a passion that equalled my own. 'I can love and I can hate. You had your choice. You chose to spurn the first, now you must test the other. It will take a little more to break your spirit, I see, but broken it shall be. Miss Marden comes back to-morrow, as I understand.'

'What has that to do with you?' I cried. 'It is a pollution that you should dare even to think of her. If I thought that you would harm her——'

She was frightened I could see, though she tried to brazen it out. She read the black thought in my mind and cowered away from me.

'She is fortunate in having such a champion,' said she. 'He actually dares to threaten a lonely woman. I must really congratulate Miss Marden upon her protector.'

The words were bitter, but the voice and manner were more acid still.

---

[1] In 1848, the Fox sisters attributed the mysterious raps in their home in Hydesville, New York to spirit communications and the movement known as modern spiritualism was founded.

'There is no use talking,' said I. 'I only came here to tell you—and to tell you most solemnly,—that your next outrage upon me will be your last.' With that, as I heard Wilson's step upon the stairs, I walked from the room. Ay, she may look venomous and deadly, but for all that she is beginning to see now that she has as much to fear from me as I can have from her. Murder! It has an ugly sound. But you don't talk of murdering a snake or of murdering a tiger. Let her have a care now.

May 5.—I met Agatha and her mother at the station at eleven o'clock. She is looking so bright, so happy, so beautiful. And she was so overjoyed to see me. What have I done to deserve such love? I went back home with them and we lunched together. All the troubles seem in a moment to have been shredded back from my life. She tells me that I am looking pale, and worried, and ill. The dear child puts it down to my loneliness and the perfunctory attentions of a housekeeper. I pray that she may never know the truth! May the shadow, if shadow there must be, lie ever black across my life and leave hers in the sunshine! I have just come back from them, feeling a new man. With her by my side I think that I could show a bold face to anything which life might send.

5 p.m.—Now let me try to be accurate. Let me try to say exactly how it occurred. It is fresh in my mind, and I can set it down correctly, though it is not likely that the time will ever come when I shall forget the doings of to-day.

I had returned from the Mardens' after lunch, and was cutting some microscopic sections in my freezing microtome,[1] when in an instant I lost consciousness in the sudden hateful fashion which has become only too familiar to me of late.

When my senses came back to me I was sitting in a small chamber very different from the one in which I had been working. It was cosy and bright, with chintz-covered settees, coloured hangings, and a thousand pretty little trifles upon the wall. A small ornamental clock ticked in front of me, and the hands pointed to half-past three. It was all quite familiar to me, and yet I stared about for a moment in a half-dazed way until my eyes fell upon a cabinet photograph of myself upon the top of the piano. At the other side

---

[1] "An instrument for cutting fine sections for microscopical examination" (702).

stood one of Mrs. Marden. Then, of course, I remembered where I was. It was Agatha's boudoir.

But how came I there, and what did I want? A horrible sinking came to my heart. Had I been sent here on some devilish errand? Had that errand already been done? Surely it must, otherwise why should I be allowed to come back to consciousness. Oh, the agony of that moment! What had I done! I sprang to my feet in my despair, and as I did so a small glass bottle fell from my knees on to the carpet.

It was unbroken and I picked it up. Outside was written 'Sulphuric Acid. Fort.' When I drew the round glass stopper a thick fume rose slowly up and a pungent choking smell pervaded the room. I recognised it as one which I kept for chemical testing in my chambers. But why had I brought a bottle of vitriol into Agatha's chamber? Was it not this thick reeking liquid with which jealous women had been known to mar the beauty of their rivals!¹ My heart stood still as I held the bottle to the light. Thank God, it was full! No mischief had been done as yet. But had Agatha come in a minute sooner, was it not certain that the hellish parasite within me would have dashed the stuff on to her—ah! it will not bear to be thought of! But it must have been for that. Why else should I have brought it? At the thought of what I might have done my worn nerves broke down and I sat shivering and twitching, the pitiable wreck of a man. It was the sound of Agatha's voice and the rustle of her dress which restored me. I looked up and saw her blue eyes, so full of tenderness and pity, gazing down at me.

'We must take you away to the country, Austin,' she said. 'You want rest and quiet. You look wretchedly ill.'

'Oh, it is nothing,' said I, trying to smile. 'It was only a momentary weakness. I am all right again now.'

'I am so sorry to keep you waiting. Poor boy, you must have been here quite half an hour. The vicar was in the drawing-room, and, as I knew that you did not care for him I thought it better that Jane should show you up here. I thought the man would never go.'

---

¹ In the Sherlock Holmes story, "The Adventure of the Illustrious Client" (1925), a prostitute who has been helping Holmes throws vitriol at Baron Gruner's face to seek revenge and prevent him from destroying other women through his captivating physical charms.

'Thank God he stayed! Thank God he stayed!' I cried hysterically.

'Why, what is the matter with you, Austin,' she asked, holding my arm as I staggered up from the chair. 'Why are you glad that the vicar stayed? And what is this little bottle in your hand?'

'Nothing,' I cried, thrusting it into my pocket. 'But I must go. I have something important to do.'

'How stern you look, Austin! I have never seen your face like that. You are angry?'

'Yes, I am angry.'

'But not with me?'

'No, no, my darling. You would not understand.'

'But you have not told me why you came.'

'I came to ask you whether you would always love me—no matter what I did or what shadow might fall on my name. Would you believe in me and trust me however black appearances might be against me?'

'You know that I would, Austin.'

'Yes, I know that you would. What I do I shall do for you. I am driven to it. There is no other way out, my darling!' I kissed her and rushed from the room.

The time for indecision was at an end. As long as the creature threatened my own prospects and my honour there might be a question as to what I should do. But now, when Agatha—my innocent Agatha—was endangered, my duty lay before me like a turnpike-road. I had no weapon, but I never paused for that. What weapon should I need when I felt every muscle quivering with the strength of a frenzied man? I ran through the streets, so set upon what I had to do that I was only dimly conscious of the faces of friends whom I met—dimly conscious also that Professor Wilson met me, running with equal precipitance in the opposite direction. Breathless but resolute I reached the house and rang the bell. A white-cheeked maid opened the door, and turned whiter yet when she saw the face that looked in at her.

'Show me up at once to Miss Penelosa,' I demanded.

'Sir,' she gasped, 'Miss Penelosa died this afternoon at half-past three.'

BRAM STOKER

The Watter's Mou'

To my
Dear Mother
in her loneliness[1]

---

[1] Charlotte Stoker (1818-1902). The early development of Stoker's Gothic imagination is generally attributed to his mother's story-telling.

THE WATTER'S MOU'

I

It threatened to be a wild night. All day banks of sea-fog had come and gone, sweeping on shore with the south-east wind, which is so fatal at Cruden Bay,[1] and indeed all along the coast of Aberdeenshire, and losing themselves in the breezy expanses of the high uplands beyond. As yet the wind only came in puffs, followed by intervals of ominous calm; but the barometer had been falling for days, and the sky had on the previous night been streaked with great 'mare's-tails'[2] running in the direction of the dangerous wind. Up to early morning the wind had been south-westerly, but had then 'backed' to south-east; and the sudden change, no less than the backing, was ominous indeed. From the waste of sea came a ceaseless muffled roar, which seemed loudest and most full of dangerous import when it came through the mystery of the driving fog. Whenever the fog-belts would lift or disperse, or disappear inland before the gusts of wind, the sea would look as though swept with growing anger; for though there were neither big waves as during a storm, nor a great swell as after one, all the surface of the water as far as the eye could reach was covered with

---

[1] The area encompasses a two-mile stretch of bay situated in Aberdeenshire on the north-east coast of Scotland. The harbour area is called Port Erroll. According to John B. Pratt, Cruden was formerly called "Invercruden, that is, Cruden near the mouth of a stream. The name is said by some to be derived from *Croch Dain, Croja Dnorum, Corja Dain*, or *Cruchain* which in different languages denote the slaughter of the Danes" after a battle between the victorious Scots and the Danes in 1012. *Buchan* (Aberdeen: Lewis & James Smith 1858), p. 36. From 1893 Stoker frequently holidayed in the area during the Lyceum summer recess. He initially stayed at the Kilmarnock Arms Hotel. The ruins of the nearby Slains Castle, the seat of the Earls of Erroll, allegedly inspired Dracula's Castle.

[2] Cirrus cloud (*OED*).

little waves tipped with white. Closer together grew these waves as the day wore on, the angrier ever the curl of the white water where they broke. In the North Sea it does not take long for the waves to rise; and all along the eastern edge of Buchan it was taken for granted that there would be wild work on the coast before the night was over.

In the little look-out house on the top of the cliff over the tiny harbour of Port Erroll[1] the coastguard on duty was pacing rapidly to and fro. Every now and again he would pause, and, lifting a field-glass from the desk, sweep the horizon from Girdleness at the south of Aberdeen, when the lifting of the mist would let him see beyond the Scaurs, away to the north, where the high cranes of the Blackman quarries at Murdoch Head[2] seemed to cleave the sky like gigantic gallows-trees.

He was manifestly in high spirits, and from the manner in which, one after another, he looked again and again at the Martini-Henry rifle in the rack, the navy revolver stuck muzzle down on a spike, and the cutlass in its sheath hanging on the wall, it was easy to see that his interest arose from something connected with his work as a coastguard. On the desk lay an open telegram smoothed down by his hard hands, with the brown envelope lying beside it. It gave some sort of clue to his excitement, although it did not go into detail. 'Keep careful watch to-night; run expected; spare no efforts; most important.'

William Barrow, popularly known as Sailor Willy, was a very young man to be a chief boatman in the preventive service, albeit that his station was one of the smallest on the coast.[3] He had been

---

[1] The harbour was built by the Earl of Erroll in the 1590s.
[2] Murdoch Head is a headland north-east coast of Cruden Bay and about four miles from Peterhead. Peterhead was an important centre for the whaling industry in the nineteenth century. The Scaurs are a reef of rocks in the sea situated to the south of the beach.
[3] Willy Barrow is a Customs officer whose duties include the prevention of smuggling. The Preventive Waterguard was founded in 1809 using Royal Navy sailors. The service was increasingly professionalized from 1822 when the Coastguard Service was established with officers deployed on land and naval cruisers at sea. The 1856 Coastguard Service Act gave the Admiralty control of the preventive service. See Gavin D. Smith, *The Scottish Smuggler* (Edinburgh: Birlinn, 2003), p. 23.

allowed, as a reward for saving the life of his lieutenant, to join the coast service, and had been promoted to chief boatman as a further reward for a clever capture of smugglers, wherein he had shown not only great bravery, but much ability and power of rapid organisation.

The Aberdeen coast is an important one in the way of guarding on account of the vast number of fishing-smacks which, during the season, work from Peterhead up and down the coast, and away on the North Sea right to the shores of Germany and Holland. This vast coming and going affords endless opportunities for smuggling; and, despite of all vigilance, a considerable amount of 'stuff' finds its way to the consumers without the formality of the Custom House.[1] The fish traffic is a quick traffic, and its returns come all at once, so that a truly enormous staff would be requisite to examine adequately the thousand fishing-smacks which use the harbour of Peterhead, and on Sundays pack its basins with a solid mass of boats. The coast-line for some forty miles south is favourable for this illicit traffic. The gneiss and granite formations broken up by every convulsion of nature, and worn by the strain and toil of ages into every conceivable form of rocky beauty, offers an endless variety of narrow creeks and bays where the daring, to whom the rocks and the currents and the tides are known, may find secret entrance and speedy exit for their craft. This season the smuggling had been chiefly of an overt kind—that is, the goods had been brought into the harbour amongst the fish and nets, and had been taken through the streets under the eyes of the unsuspecting Customs officers. Some of these takes were so large, that the authorities had made up their minds that there must be a great amount of smuggling going on. The secret agents in the German, Dutch, Flemish, and French ports were asked to make extra exertions in discovering the amount of the illicit trade, and their later reports were of an almost alarming nature. They said that really vast amounts of tobacco, brandy, rum, silks, laces, and all sorts of excisable commodities were being secretly shipped in the British fishing-fleet; and as only a very small proportion of this was dis-

---

[1] Contraband goods smuggled into the east coast of Scotland from the Continent chiefly included tea, tobacco, wine,- and brandy.

covered, it was manifest that smuggling to a large extent was once more to the fore. Accordingly precautions were doubled all along the east coast frequented by the fishing-fleets. Not only were the coastguards warned of the danger and cautioned against devices which might keep them from their work at critical times, but they were apprised of every new shipment as reported from abroad. Furthermore, the detectives of the service were sent about to parts where the men were suspected of laxity—or worse.

Thus it was that Sailor Willy, with the experience of two promotions for cause, and with the sense of responsibility which belonged to his office, felt in every way elated at the possibility of some daring work before him. He knew, of course, that a similar telegram had been received at every station on the coast, and that the chance of an attempt being made in Cruden Bay or its surroundings was a small one; but he was young and brave and hopeful, and with an adamantine sense of integrity to support him in his work. It was unfortunate that his comrade was absent, ill in the hospital at Aberdeen, and that the strain at present on the service, together with the men away on annual training and in the naval manœuvres, did not permit of a substitute being sent to him. However, he felt strong enough to undertake any amount of duty—he was strong enough and handsome enough to have a good opinion of himself, and too brave and too sensible to let his head be turned by vanity.

As he walked to and fro there was in the distance of his mind—in that dim background against which in a man's mind a woman's form finds suitable projection—some sort of vague hope that a wild dream of rising in the world might be some time realised. He knew that every precaution in his power had been already taken, and felt that he could indulge in fancies without detriment to his work. He had signalled the coastguard at Whinnyfold[1] on the south side of the Bay, and they had exchanged ideas by means of the signal language. His appliances for further signalling by day or night were in perfect order, and he had been right over his whole boundary since he had received the telegram seeing that all things

---

[1] Stoker holidayed in Whinnyfold in the 1890s. Whinnyfold is three miles south of Cruden Bay.

were in order. Willy Barrow was not one to leave things to chance where duty was concerned.

His day-dreams were not all selfish. They were at least so far unselfish that the results were to be shared with another; for Willy Barrow was engaged to be married. Maggie MacWhirter was the daughter of an old fisherman who had seen days more prosperous than the present. He had once on a time owned a fishing-smack, but by degrees he had been compelled to borrow on her, till now, when, although he was nominal owner, the boat was so heavily mortgaged that at any moment he might lose his entire possession. That such an event was not unlikely was manifest, for the mortgagee was no other than Solomon Mendoza of Hamburg and Aberdeen, who had changed in like manner the ownership of a hundred boats, and who had the reputation of being as remorseless as he was rich. MacWhirter had long been a widower, and Maggie since a little girl had kept house for her father and her two brothers, Andrew and Niel. Andrew was twenty-seven—six years older than Maggie—and Niel had just turned twenty. The elder brother was a quiet, self-contained, hard working man, who now and again manifested great determination, though generally at unexpected times; the younger was rash, impetuous, and passionate, and though in his moments of quiescence more tender to those he cared for than was usual with men of his class, he was a never-ending source of anxiety to his father and his sister. Andrew, or Sandy as he was always called, took him with consistent quietness.

The present year, although a good one in the main, had been but poor for MacWhirter's boat. Never once had he had a good take of fish—not one-half the number of crans[1] of the best boat; and the season was so far advanced, and the supply had been so plentiful, that a few days before the notice had been up at Peterhead that after the following week the buyers would not take any more herring.

This notice naturally caused much excitement, and the whole fishing industry determined to make every effort to improve the

---

[1] A barrel that refers to a measurement of fresh herring (Scots). Information on Scots words is derived from the *Dictionary of the Scots Language*.

shining hours left to them. Exertions were on all sides redoubled, and on sea and shore there was little idleness. Naturally the smuggling interest bestirred itself too; its chance for the year was in the rush and bustle and hurry of the coming and going fleet, and anything held over for a chance had to be ventured now or left over for a year—which might mean indefinitely. Great ventures were therefore taken by some of the boats; and from their daring the authorities concluded that either heavy bribes were given, or else that the goods were provided by others than the fishermen who undertook to run them. A few important seizures, however, made the men wary; and it was understood from the less frequent but greater importance of the seizures, that the price for 'running' had greatly gone up. There was much passionate excitement amongst those who were found out and their friends, and a general wish to discover the informers. Some of the smuggling fishermen at first refused to pay the fines until they were told who had informed. This position being unsupportable, they had instead paid the fines and cherished hatred in their hearts. Some of the more reckless and turbulent spirits had declared their intention of avenging themselves on the informers when they should be known. It was only natural that this feeling of rage should extend to the Customs officers and men of the preventive service, who stood between the unscrupulous adventurers and their harvest; and altogether matters had become somewhat strained between the fishermen and the authorities.

The Port Erroll boats, like those from Collieston,[1] were all up at Peterhead, and of course amongst them MacWhirter's boat the 'Sea Gull' with her skipper and his two sons. It was now Friday night, and the boats had been out for several days, so that it was pretty certain that there would be a full harbour at Peterhead on the Saturday. A marriage had been arranged to take place this evening between Thomas Keith of Boddam[2] and Alice MacDonald, whose father kept the public-house 'The Jamie Fleeman' on the northern edge of the Erroll estate.[3] Though the occasion was to be

---

[1] The area around the fishing village of Collieston is populated with caves which provided useful hiding-places for contraband goods. See Pratt, p. 26.
[2] Fishing village near Peterhead.
[3] Referring to the estate of the Earls of Erroll, whose seat was at Slains

a grand one, the notice of it had been short indeed. It was said by the bride's friends that it had been fixed so hurriedly because the notice of the closing of the fishing season had been so suddenly given out at Peterhead. Truth to tell, some sort of explanation was necessary, for it was only on Wednesday morning that word had been sent to the guests, and as these came from all sorts of places between Peterhead and Collieston, and taking a sweep of some ten miles inland, there was need of some preparation. The affair was to top all that had ever been seen at Port Erroll, and as 'The Jamie Fleeman' was but a tiny place—nothing, in fact, but a wayside public-house—it was arranged that it was to take place in the new barn and storehouses Matthew Beagrie had just built on the inner side of the sandhills, where they came close to the Water of Cruden.

Throughout all the east side of Buchan there had for some time existed a wonder amongst the quiet-going people as to the strange prosperity of MacDonald. His public-house had, of course, a practical monopoly; for as there was not a licensed house on the Erroll estate, and as his was the nearest house of call to the port, he naturally got what custom there was going. The fishermen all along the coast for some seven or eight miles went to him either to drink or to get their liquor for drinking elsewhere; and not a few of the Collieston men on their Saturday journey home from Peterhead and their Sunday journey out there again made a detour to have a glass and a chat and a pipe, if time permitted, with 'Tammas Mac'[1]—for such was his sobriquet. To the authorities he and his house were also sources of interest; for there was some kind of suspicion that some of the excellent brandy and cigars which he dispensed had arrived by a simpler road than that through the Custom House. It was at this house, in the good old days of smuggling, that the coastguards used to be entertained when a run was on foot, and where they slept off their drunkenness whilst the cargoes were being hidden or taken inland in the ready carts. Of

---

Castle. During his 1893 holiday in Cruden Bay, Stoker met the 20th Earl of Erroll, Charles Hay, at Slains Castle. Barbara Belford, *Bram Stoker: A Biography of the Author of* Dracula (1996; London: Phoenix, 1997), p. 234.

[1] Thomas (Scots). Mac is a Gaelic prefix corresponding to the English word son.

course all this state of things had been altered, and there was as improved a decorum amongst the smugglers as there was a sterner rule and discipline amongst the coastguards. It was many a long year since Philip Kennedy met his death at Kirkton at the hands of the exciseman Anderson.[1] Comparatively innocent deception was now the smuggler's only wile.

To-night the whole country-side was to be at the wedding, and the dance which was to follow it; and for this occasion the lion was to lie down with the lamb,[2] for the coastguards were bidden to the feast with the rest. Sailor Willy had looked forward to the dance with delight, for Maggie was to be there, and on the 'Billy Ruffian,' which had been his last ship, he had been looked on as the best dancer before the mast. If there be any man who shuns a dance in which he knows he can shine, and at which his own particular girl is to be present, that man is not to be found in the Royal Naval Marine, even amongst those of them who have joined in the preventive service.

Maggie was no less delighted, although she had a source of grief which for the present she had kept all to herself. Her father had of late been much disturbed about affairs. He had not spoken of them to her, and she did not dare to mention the matter to him; for old MacWhirter was a close-mouthed man, and did not exchange many confidences even with his own children. But Maggie guessed at the cause of the sadness—of the down-bent head when none were looking; the sleepless nights and the deep smothered groans which now and again marked his heavy sleep told the tale loudly enough to reach the daughter's ears. For the last few weeks, whenever her father was at home, Maggie had herself lain awake listening, listening, in increasing agony of spirit,

---

[1] Philip Kennedy was a smuggler who was killed by an excise-man called Anderson in 1798, as he tried to defend his illegal contraband of Dutch gin which had been smuggled from the continent by the *Crooked Mary*. Kennedy's comrades fled and Kennedy was struck on the head with a sword by Anderson. He struggled to the Kirkton (church) of Slains where he died. Kennedy's death was recorded on a stone in the churchyard of Slains.

[2] Cf. Isaiah 11:6: "The wolf also shall dwell with the lamb, and the leopard shall lie down with the kid; and the calf and the young lion and the fatling together; and a little child shall lead them."

for one of these half moans or for the sound of the tossing of the restless man. He was as gentle and kind to his daughter as ever; but on his leaving the last time there had been an omission on his part which troubled her to the quick. For the first time in his life he had not kissed her as he went away.

On the previous day Sailor Willy had said he would come to the wedding and the dance if his duties should permit him; and, when asked if he could spare a few rockets for the occasion, promised that he would let off three Board of Trade[1] rockets, which he could now deal with as it was three months since he had used any. He was delighted at the opportunity of meeting the fisherfolk and his neighbours; for his officers had impressed on him the need of being on good terms with all around him, both for the possibility which it would always afford him of knowing how things were going on, and for the benefit of the rocket-service whenever there might be need of willing hands and hearts to work with him, for in the Board of Trade rocket-service much depends on voluntary aid. That very afternoon he had fixed the rockets on the wall of the barn with staples, so that he could fire them from below with a slow match, which he fixed ready. When he had got the telegram he had called in to Maggie and told her if he did not come to fetch her she was to go on to the wedding by herself, and that he would try to join her later. She had appeared a little startled when he told her he might not be present; but after a pause smiled, and said she would go, and that he was not to lose any time coming when he was free. Now that every arrangement was complete, and as he had between puffs of the sea-fog got a clean sweep of the horizon and saw that there was no sail of any kind within sight, he thought he might have a look through the village and keep in evidence so as not to create any suspicion in the minds of the people. As he went through the street he noticed that nearly every house door was closed—all the women were at the new barn. It was now eight o'clock, and the darkness, which is slow of coming in the North, was closing in. Down by the barn there were quite a number of carts, and the horses had not been taken out, though the wedding

---

[1] Rockets were used by the coastguard service for signaling and for assisting distressed vessels at sea.

was not to be till nine o'clock, or perhaps even later; for Mrs MacDonald had taken care to tell her friends that Keith might not get over from Boddam till late. Willy looked at them carefully—some idea seemed to have struck him. Their lettering shewed them to be from all parts round, and the names mostly of those who had not the best reputation. When his brief survey was finished he looked round and then went swiftly behind the barn so that no one might see him. As he went he muttered reflectively—

'Too many light carts and fast horses—too much silence in the barn—too little liquor going to be all safe. There's something up here to-night.' He was under the lee of the barn and looked up where he had fixed the rockets ready to fire. This gave him a new idea.

'I fixed them low so as to go over the sandhills and not be noticeable at Collieston or beyond. They are now placed up straight and will be seen for fifty miles if the weather be clear.'

It was too dark to see very clearly, and he would not climb up to examine them lest he should be noticed and his purpose of acquiring information frustrated; but then and there he made up his mind that Port Erroll or its neighbourhood had been the spot chosen for the running of the smuggled goods. He determined to find out more, and straightway went round to the front and entered the room.

II

As soon as Sailor Willy was seen to enter, a large part of the gathering looked relieved, and at once began to chat and gabble in marked contrast to their previous gloom and silence. Port Erroll was well represented by its womankind, and by such of its men as were not away at the fishing; for it was the intention to mask the smuggling scheme by an assemblage at which all the respectability would be present. There appeared to be little rivalry between the two shoemakers, MacPherson and Beagrie, who chatted together in a corner, the former telling his companion how he had just been down to the lifeboat-house to see, as one of the Committee, that it was all ready in case it should be wanting before the night was over. Lang[1] John and Lang Jim, the policemen of the place, looked sprucer even than usual, and their buttons shone in the light of the many paraffin lamps as if they had been newly burnished. Mitchell and his companions of the salmon fishery were grouped in another corner, and Andrew Mason was telling Mackay, the new flesher, whose shed was erected on the edge of the burn[2] opposite John Reid's shop, of a great crab which he had taken that morning in a pot opposite the Twa Een.[3]

But these and nearly all the other Port Erroll folk present were quiet, and their talk was of local interest; the main clack of tongues came from the many strange men who stood in groups near the centre of the room and talked loudly. In the midst of them was the bridegroom, more joyous than any, though in the midst of his laughter he kept constantly turning to look at the door. The minister from Peterhead sat in a corner with the bride and her mother and father—the latter of whom, despite his constant laughter, had an anxious look on his face. Sailor Willy was greeted joyously, and the giver of the feast and the bridegroom each rose, and, taking a bottle and glass, offered him a drink.

'To the bride,' said he; but seeing that no one else was drinking, he tapped the bridegroom on the shoulder, 'Come, drink this with me, my lad!' he added. The latter paused an instant and then helped himself from MacDonald's bottle. Willy did not fail to notice the act, and holding out his glass said—

'Come, my lad, you drink with me! Change glasses in old style!' An odd pallor passed quickly across the bridegroom's face, but MacDonald spoke quickly—

'Tak it, mon,[4] tak it!' So he took the glass, crying 'No heeltaps,'[5] threw back his head, and raised the glass. Willy threw back his head too, and tossed off his liquor, but, as he did so, took care to keep a sharp eye on the other, and saw him, instead of swallowing

---

[1] Long (Scots).
[2] A brook or stream (Scots).
[3] Translates as "two eyes" (Scots). Refers in this case to a rock formation with two openings like eyes which is situated near Slains Castle.
[4] Man (Scots).
[5] A drinking direction to drain to the bottom of the glass.

his liquor, pour it into his thick beard. His mind was quite made up now. They meant to keep him out of the way by fair means or foul.

Just then two persons entered the room, one of them, James Cruickshank of the Kilmarnock Arms, who was showing the way to the other, an elderly man with a bald head, keen eyes, a ragged grey beard, a hooked nose, and an evil smile. As he entered MacDonald jumped up and came over to greet him.

'Oh! Mr. Mendoza, this is braw!¹ We hopit tae see ye the nicht,² but we were that feared that ye wadna come.'

'Mein Gott, but why shall I not come—on this occasion of all— the occasion of the marriage of the daughter of mein goot frient, Tam Smack? And moreovers when I bring these as I haf promise. For you, mein frient Keith, this cheque, which one week you cash, and for you, my tear Miss Alice, these so bright necklace, which you will wear, ant which will sell if so you choose.'

As he spoke he handed his gifts to the groom and bride. He then walked to the corner where Mrs. Mac sat, exchanging a keen look with his host as he did so. The latter seemed to have taken his cue and spoke out at once.

'And now, reverend sir, we may proceed—all is ready.' As he spoke the bridal pair stood up, and the friends crowded round.

Sailor Willy moved towards the door, and just as the parson opened his book, began to pass out. Tammas Mac immediately spoke to him—

'Ye're no gangin',³ Sailor Willy? Sure ye'll wait and see Tam Keith marit⁴ on my lass?'

He instantly replied—

'I must go for a while. I have some things to do, and then I want to try to bring Maggie down for the dance!' and before anything could be said, he was gone.

The instant he left the door he slipped round to the back of the barn, and running across the sandhills to the left, crossed the wooden bridge, and hurrying up the roadway by the cottage on the cliff gained the watch-house. He knew that none of the com-

---

[1] Fine or excellent (Scots).
[2] Night (Scots).
[3] Go, depart (Scots).
[4] Married (Scots).

pany in the barn could leave till the service was over, with the minister's eye on them, without giving cause for after suspicion; and he knew, too, that as there were no windows on the south side of the barn, nothing could be seen from that side. Without a moment's delay he arranged his signals for the call for aid; and as the rockets whizzed aloft, sending a white glare far into the sky, he felt that the struggle had entered on its second stage.

The night had now set in with a darkness unusual in August. The swaithes[1] of sea-mist whirled in by the wind came fewer and fainter, and at times a sudden rift through the driving clouds showed that there was starlight somewhere between the driving masses of mist and gloom. Willy Barrow once more tried all his weapons and saw that all his signals were in order. Then he strapped the revolver and the cutlass in his belt, and lit a dark lantern so that it might be ready in case of need. This done, he left the watch-house, locking the door behind him, and, after looking steadily across the Bay to the Scaurs beyond, turned and walked northward towards the Watter's Mou'.[2] Between the cliff on the edge of this and the watch-house there was a crane used for raising the granite boulders quarried below, and when he drew near this he stopped instinctively and called out, 'Who is there?' for he felt, rather than saw, some presence. 'It is only me, Willy,' came a soft voice, and a woman drew a step nearer through the darkness from behind the shaft of the crane.

'Maggie! Why, darling, what brings you here? I thought you were going to the wedding!'

'I knew ye wadna be there, and I wanted to speak wi' ye'—this was said in a very low voice.

'How did you know I wouldn't be there?—I was to join you if I could.'

'I saw Bella Cruickshank hand ye the telegram as ye went by the

---

[1] Swathes (*OED*).
[2] Charles Mackay's *A Dictionary of Lowland Scotch* (London: Whittaker, 1888) notes that in a dispute between John Clerk, Lord Eldin and the Lord Chancellor Eldon, Eldin annoyed the latter by repeating "the word *watter* with a strong Scottish accent. "Mr. Clerk," inquired the lordship, "is it the custom in your country to spell water with two *t's*?" "No, my lord," replied Clerk; "but it's the fashion in *my* country to spell *manners* wi' twa *n's*" (265).

Post Office, and—and I knew there would be something to keep ye. O Willy, Willy! why do ye draw awa frae me?' for Sailor Willy had instinctively loosened his arms which were round her and had drawn back—in the instant his love and his business seemed as though antagonistic. He answered with blunt truthfulness—

'I was thinking, Maggie, that I had no cause to be making love here and now. I've got work, mayhap, to-night!'

'I feared so, Willy—I feared so!' Willy was touched, for it seemed to him that she was anxious for him, and answered tenderly—

'All right, dear! All right! There's no danger—why, if need be, I am armed,' and he slipped his hand on the butt of the revolver in his belt. To his surprise Maggie uttered a deep low groan, and turning away sat on the turf bank beside her, as though her strength was failing her. Willy did not know what to say, so there was a space of silence. Then Maggie went on hurriedly—

'O my God! it is a dreadfu' thing to lift yer han' in sic[1] a deadly manner against yer neighbours, and ye not knowing what woe ye may cause.' Willy could answer this time—

'Ay, lass! it's hard indeed, and that's the truth. But that's the very reason that men like me are put here that can and will do their duty no matter how hard it may be.'

Another pause, and then Maggie spoke again. Willy could not see her face, but she seemed to speak between gasps for breath.

'Ye're lookin' for hard wark[2] the nicht?'

'I am!—I fear so.'

'I can guess that that telegram tellt ye that some boats would try to rin[3] in somewhere the nicht.'

'Mayhap, lass. But the telegrams are secret, and I must not speak of what's in them.'

After a long pause Maggie spoke again, but in a voice so low that he could hardly hear her amid the roar of the breaking waves which came in on the wind—

'Willy, ye're not a cruel man!—ye wadna, if ye could help it, dae harm to them that loved ye, or work woe to their belongin's?'

'My lass! that I wouldn't.' As he answered he felt a horrible

---

[1] Such (Scots).
[2] Work or labour (Scots).
[3] Run (Scots).

sinking of the heart. What did all this mean? Was it possible that Maggie, too, had any interest in the smuggling? No, no! a thousand times no! Ashamed of his suspicion he drew closer and again put his arm around her in a protecting way. The unexpected tenderness overcame her, and, bursting into tears, she threw herself on Willy's neck and whispered to him between her sobs—

'O Willy, Willy! I'm in sic sair[1] trouble, and there's nane that I can speak to. Nae! not ane in the wide warld.'

'Tell me, darling; you know you'll soon be my wife, and then I'll have a right to know all!'

'Oh, I canna! I canna! I canna!'[2] she said, and taking her arms from round his neck she beat her hands wildly together. Willy was something frightened, for a woman's distress touches a strong man in direct ratio to his manliness. He tried to soothe her as though she were a frightened child, and held her tight to him.

'There! there! my darling. Don't cry. I'm here with you, and you can tell me all your trouble.' She shook her head; he felt the movement on his breast, and he went on—

'Don't be frightened, Maggie; tell me all. Tell me quietly, and mayhap I can help ye out over the difficult places.' Then he remained silent, and her sobs grew less violent; at last she raised her head and dashed away her tears fiercely with her hand. She dragged herself away from him: he tried to stop her, but she said—

'Nae, nae, Willy dear; let me speak it in my ain way. If I canna trust ye, wha can I trust? My trouble is not for mysel.' She paused, and he asked—

'Who, then, is it for?'

'My father and my brothers.' Then she went on hurriedly, fearing to stop lest her courage should fail her, and he listened in dead silence, with a growing pain in his heart.

'Ye ken[3] that for several seasons back our boat has had bad luck—we took less fish and lost mair[4] nets than any of the boats; even on the land everything went wrong. Our coo[5] died, and the

---

[1] sore (Scots).
[2] cannot (Scots).
[3] know (Scots).
[4] more (Scots).
[5] cow (Scots).

shed was blawn doon, and then the blight touched the potatoes in our field. Father could dae naething, and had to borrow money on the boat to go on with his wark; and the debt grew and grew, till now he only owns her in name, and we never ken when we may be sold up. And the man that has the mortgage isn't like to let us off or gie time!'[1]

'Who is he? His name?' said Willy hoarsely.

'Mendoza—the man frae Hamburg wha[2] lends to the boats at Peterhead.'

Willy groaned. Before his eyes rose the vision of that hard, cruel, white face that he had seen only a few minutes ago, and again he saw him hand out the presents with which he had bought the man and woman to help in his wicked scheme. When Maggie heard the groan her courage and her hope arose. If her lover could take the matter so much to heart all might yet be well, and in the moment all the womanhood in her awoke to the call. Her fear had broken down the barriers that had kept back her passion, and now the passion came with all the force of a virgin nature. She drew Willy close to her—closer still—and whispered to him in a low sweet voice, that thrilled with emotion—

'Willy, Willy, darlin'; ye wouldna see harm come to my father—my father, my father!' and in a wave of tumultuous, voluptuous passion she kissed him full in the mouth. Willy felt for the moment half dazed. Love has its opiates that soothe and stun even in the midst of their activity. He clasped Maggie close in his arms, and for a moment their hearts beat together and their mouths breathed the same air. Then Willy drew back, but Maggie hung limp in his arms. The silence which hung in the midst of nature's tumult broke its own spell. Willy realised what and where he was: with the waves dashing below his feet and the night wind laden with drifting mist wreathing around him in the darkness, and whistling amongst the rocks and screaming sadly through the ropes and stays of the flag-

---

[1] In Stoker's Irish novel *The Snake's Pass* (1890) Phelim Joyce forfeits his land to the gombeen-man (usurer) Black Murdock because he has not repaid a loan in time. Although Joyce is only a few hours late, Murdock refuses to accept the payment.

[2] Who (Scots).

staff on the cliff. There was a wild fear in his heart and a burning desire to know all that was in his sweetheart's mind.

'Go on, Maggie! go on!' he said. Maggie roused herself and again took up the thread of her story—this time in feverish haste. The moment of passion had disquieted and disturbed her. She seemed to herself to be two people, one of whom was new to her, and whom she feared, but woman-like, she felt that as she had begun so must she go on; and thus her woman's courage sustained her.

'Some weeks ago, father began to get letters frae[1] Mr. Mendoza, and they aye upset him. He wrote answers and sent them away at once. Then Mr. Mendoza sent him a telegram frae Hamburg, and he sent a reply—and a month ago father got a telegram telling him to meet him at Peterhead. He was very angry at first and very low-spirited after; but he went to Peterhead, and when he cam back he was very still and quite pale. He would eat naething, and went to bed although it was only seven o'clock. Then there were more letters and telegrams, but father answered nane o' them—sae far as I ken—and then Mr. Mendoza cam to our hoose. Father got as pale as a sheet when he saw him, and then he got red and angry, and I thocht he was going to strike him; but Mr. Mendoza said not to frichten his daughter, and father got quiet and sent me oot on a message to the Nether Mill. And when I cam back Mr. Mendoza had gone, and father was sitting with his face in his hands, and he didna hear me come in. When I spoke, he started up and he was as white as a sheet, and then he mumbled something and went into his room. And ever since then he hardly spoke to any one, and seemed to avoid me a'thegither. When he went away the last time he never even kissed me. And so, Willy—so, I fear that that awfu' Mr. Mendoza has made him dae something that he didna want to dae, and it's all breaking my heart!' and again she laid her head on her lover's breast and sobbed. Willy breathed more freely; but he could not be content to remain in doubt, and his courage was never harder tried than when he asked his next question.

'Then, Maggie, you don't know anything for certain?'

'Naething, Willy—but I fear.'

---

[1] From (Scots).

'But there may be nothing, after all!' Maggie's hopes rose again, for there was something in her lover's voice which told her that he was willing to cling to any straw, and once again her woman's nature took advantage of her sense of right and wrong.

'Please God, Willy, there may be naething! but I fear much that it may be so; but we must act as if we didna fear. It wadna dae to suspect poor father without some cause. You know, Willy, the Earl has promised to mak him the new harbourmaster. Old Forgie is bedridden now, and when winter comes he'll no even be able to pretend to work, so the Earl is to pension him, and father will get the post and hae the hoose by the harbour, and you know that every one's sae glad, for they a' respect father.'

'Ay, lass,' interrupted Willy, 'that's true; and why, then, should we—you and me, Maggie—think he would do ill to please that damned scoundrel, Mendoza?'

'Indeed, I'm thinkin' that it's just because that he is respeckit that Mendoza wants him to help him. He kens weel that nane would suspeck father, and'—here she clipped her lover close in her arms once again, and her breath came hot in his face till it made him half drunk with a voluptuous[1] intoxication—'he kens that father, my father, would never be harmt by my lover!'

Even then, at the moment when the tragedy of his life seemed to be accomplished, when the woman he loved and honoured seemed to be urging him to some breach of duty, Willy Barrow could not but feel that some responsibility for her action rested on him. That first passionate kiss, which had seemed to unlock the very gates of her soul—in which she had yielded herself to him—had some mysterious bond or virtue like that which abides in the wedding ring. The Maggie who thus acted was his Maggie, and in all that came of it he had a part. But his mind was made up; nothing—not Maggie's kisses or Maggie's fears—would turn him from his path of duty, and strong in this resolution he could afford to be silent to the woman in his arms. Maggie instinctively knew that silence could now be her best weapon, and said no word as they walked towards the guard-house, Willy casting keen looks seawards, and up and down the coast as they went. When they

---

[1] The adjective recurs in Stoker's description of female vampires in *Dracula*.

were so close that in its shelter the roar of the surf seemed muffled, Maggie again nestled close to her lover, and whispered in his ear as he looked out over Cruden Bay—

'The "Sea Gull" comes hame the nicht!' Willy quivered, but said nothing for a time that seemed to be endless. Then he answered—

'They'll find it hard to make the Port to-night. Look! the waves are rolling high and the wind is getting up. It would be madness to try it.' Again she whispered to him—

'Couldna she rin in somewhere else—there are other openings besides Port Erroll in Buchan!' Willy laughed the laugh of a strong man who knew well what he said—

'Other openings! Ay, lass, there are other openings; but the coble[1] isn't built that can run them this night. With a south-east gale, who would dare to try? The Bullers, or Robies Haven, or Dunbuy, or Twa Havens, or Lang Haven, or The Watter's Mou'[2]— why, lass, they'd be in matches on the rocks before they could turn their tiller or slack a sail.'

She interrupted him, speaking with a despairing voice—

'Then ye'll no hae to watch nane o' them the nicht?'

'Nay, Maggie. Port Erroll is my watch to-night; and from it I won't budge.'

'And the Watter's Mou'?' she asked, 'is that no safe wi'oot watch? It's no far frae the Port.' Again Willy laughed his arrogant, masculine laugh, which made Maggie, despite her trouble, admire him more than ever, and he answered—

'The Watter's Mou'? To try to get in there in this wind would be

---

[1] A flat-bottomed fishing boat popular in this part of Scotland.
[2] The Bullers refers to the Bullers of Buchan, possibly from an old Scots word meaning the rushing of water. Pratt describes it as a "circular cavern, or basin, entered through an arch and open to the sky . . . the sides of the cavern are perpendicular walls of rock that in places are less than a couple of yards wide . . . [D]uring storms the sea dashes quite over the lofty sides, and any human being in its way would be swept to destruction" (52); Robies Haven is an inlet of the sea just south of the Bullers; Dunbuy is an island; Twa Havens and Lang Haven are inlets of the sea. This is a rocky coastline with numerous inlets and caves used by smugglers. Most guides refer to Samuel Johnson's *A Journey to the Western Islands of Scotland* (1775) in their descriptions of the Bullers of Buchan.

to court sudden death. Why, lass, it would take a man all he knew to get out from there, let alone get in, in this weather! And then the chances would be ten to one that he'd be dashed to pieces on the rocks beyond,' and he pointed to where a line of sharp rocks rose between the billows on the south side of the inlet.[1] Truly it was a fearful-looking place to be dashed on, for the great waves broke on the rocks with a loud roaring, and even in the semi-darkness they could see the white lines as the waters poured down to leeward in the wake of the heaving wave. The white cluster of rocks looked like a ghostly mouth opened to swallow whatever might come in touch.[2] Maggie shuddered; but some sudden idea seemed to strike her, and she drew away from her lover for a moment, and looked towards the black cleft in the rocks of which they could just see the top from where they stood—the entrance to the Watter's Mou'.

And then with one long, wild, appealing glance skyward, as though looking a prayer which she dared not utter even in her heart, Maggie turned towards her lover once more. Again she drew close to him, and hung around his neck, and said with many gasps and pauses between her words—

'If the "Sea Gull" should come in to the Port the nicht, and if ony[3] attempt that ye feared should tak you away to Whinnyfold or to Dunbuy so that you might be a bit—only a wee bit—late to search when the boat cam in——'

She stopped affrighted, for Willy put her from him to arm's length, not too gently either, and said to her so sternly that each word seemed to smite her like the lash of a whip, till she shrunk and quivered and cowered away from him—

'Maggie, lass! What's this you're saying to me? It isn't fit for you to speak or me to hear! It's bad enough to be a smuggler, but what is it that you would make of me? Not only a smuggler, but a per-

---

[1] The Scaurs which run out to sea from the south of Cruden Bay were notorious for shipwrecks. Pratt describes how "the beautiful beach, which follows the sweep of the bay, extends from the *Scaurs*—a group of prominent rocks running out about half a mile into the sea—to the *Water of Cruden*; a distance of nearly two miles" (31).

[2] Stoker invests topography with monstrous or Gothic associations. In *The Snake's Pass*, for instance, a shifting bog consumes everything within its path.

[3] Any (Scots).

jurer and a traitor too. God! am I mistaken? Is it you, Maggie, that would make this of me? Of me! Maggie MacWhirter, if this be your counsel, then God help us both! you are no fit wife for me!' In an instant the whole truth dawned on Maggie of what a thing she would make of the man she loved, whom she had loved at the first because he was strong and brave and true. In the sudden revulsion of her feelings she flung herself on her knees beside him, and took his hand and held it hard, and despite his efforts to withdraw it, kissed it wildly in the humility of her self-abasement, and poured out to him a passionate outburst of pleading for his forgiveness, of justification of herself, and of appeals to his mercy for her father.

'O Willy, Willy! dinna[1] turn frae me this nicht! My heart is sae fu' o' trouble that I am nigh mad! I dinna ken what to dae nor where to look for help! I think, and think, and think, and everywhere there is nought but dark before me, just as there is blackness oot ower the sea, when I look for my father. And noo when I want ye to help me—ye that are all I hae, and the only ane on earth that I can look tae in my wae[2] and trouble—I can dae nae mair than turn ye frae me! Ye that I love! oh, love more than my life or my soul! I must dishonour and mak ye hate me! Oh, what shall I dae? what shall I dae? what shall I dae?' and again she beat the palms of her hands together in a paroxysm of wild despair, whilst Willy looked on with his heart full of pain and pity, though his resolution never flinched. And then through the completeness of her self-abasement came the pleading of her soul from a depth of her nature even deeper than despair. Despair has its own bravery, but hope can sap the strongest resolution. And the pleadings of love came from the depths of that Pandora's box[3] which we call human nature.

'O Willy, Willy! forgie me—forgie me! I was daft to say what I did! I was daft to think that ye would be so base!—daft to think that I would like you to so betray yoursel! Forgie me, Willy, forgie me, and tak my wild words as spoken not to ye but to the storm that maks me fear sae for my father! Let me tak it a' back, Willy

---

[1] Do not (Scots).

[2] Woe (Scots).

[3] In Greek mythology Pandora was the first mortal woman who was sent to earth by Zeus with a box of evils.

darlin'—Willy, my Willy; and dinna leave me desolate here with this new shadow ower me!' Here, as she kissed his hand again, her lover stooped and raised her in his strong arms and held her to him. And then, when she felt herself in a position of security, the same hysterical emotion came sweeping up in her brain and her blood—the same self-abandonment to her lover overcame her—and the current of her thought once again turned to win from him something by the force of her woman's wile and her woman's contact with the man.

'Willy,' she whispered, as she kissed him on the mouth and then kissed his head on the side of his neck, 'Willy, ye have forgien me, I ken—and I ken that ye'll harm father nae mair than ye can help—but if——'

What more she was going to say she hardly knew herself. As for Willy, he felt that something better left unsaid was coming, and unconsciously his muscles stiffened till he held her from him rather than to him. She, too, felt the change, and held him closer—closer still, with the tenacity induced by a sense of coming danger. Their difficulty was solved for them, for just on the instant when the suggestion of treachery to his duty was hanging on her lips, there came from the village below, in a pause between the gusts of wind, the fierce roar of a flying rocket. Up and up and up, as though it would never stop—up it rose with its prolonged screech, increasing in sound at the first till it began to die away in the aërial heights above, so that when the explosion came it seemed to startle a quietude around it. Up in the air a thousand feet over their heads the fierce glitter of the falling fires of red and blue made a blaze of light which lit up the coast-line from the Scaurs to Dunbuy, and with an instinctive intelligence Willy Barrow took in all he saw, including the many men at the little port below, sheltering under the sea-wall from the sweeping of the waves as they looked out seawards. Instinctively also he counted the seconds till the next rocket should be fired—one, two, three; and then another roar and another blaze of coloured lights. And then another pause, of six seconds this time! and then the third rocket sped aloft with its fiery message. And then the darkness seemed blacker than ever, and the mysterious booming of the sea to grow louder and louder as though it came through silence. By this time the man and the woman were apart no less in spirit than physically. Willy, intent on his work, was standing outside the window of the guard-house, whence he could see all around the Bay and up and down the coast, and at the same time command the whole of the harbour. His feet were planted wide apart, for on the exposed rock the sweep of the wind was strong, and as he raised his arm with his field-glass to search the horizon the wind drove back his jacket and showed the butt of his revolver and the hilt of his cutlass. Maggie stood a little behind him, gazing seawards, with no less eager eyes, for she too expected what would follow. Her heart seemed to stand still though her breath came in quick gasps, and she did not dare to make a sound or to encroach on the business-like earnestness of the man. For full a minute they waited thus, and then far off at sea, away to the south, they saw a faint blue light, and then another and another, till at the last three lights were burning in a row. Instantly from the town a single rocket went up—not this time a great Board of Trade rocket, laden with coloured fire, but one which left a plain white track of light behind it. Willy gazed seawards, but there was no more sign from the far-off ship at sea; the signal, whatever it was, was complete. The coastguard was uncertain as to the meaning, but to Maggie no explanation was necessary. There, away at sea, tossed on the stormy waters, was her father. There was danger round him, but a greater danger on the shore—every way of entrance was barred by the storm—save the one where, through his fatal cargo, dishonour lay in wait for him. She seemed to see her duty clear before her, and come what might she meant to do it: her father must be warned. It was with a faint voice indeed that she now spoke to her lover—

'Willy!'

His heart was melted at the faltering voice, but he feared she was trying some new temptation, so, coldly and hardly enough, he answered—

'What is it, lass?'

'Willy, ye wadna see poor father injured?'

'No, Maggie, not if I could help it. But I'd have to do my duty all the same.'

'And we should a' dae oor¹ duty—whatever it might be—at a' costs?'

---

¹ All do our (Scots).

'Ay, lass—at all costs!' His voice was firm enough now, and there was no mistaking the truth of its ring. Maggie's hope died away. From the stern task which seemed to rise before her over the waste of the black sea she must not shrink. There was but one more yielding to the weakness of her fear, and she said, so timidly that Willy was startled, the voice and manner were so different from those he had ever known—

'And if—mind I say "if," Willy—I had a duty to dae and it was fu' o' fear and danger, and ye could save me frae it, wad ye?' As she waited for his reply, her heart beat so fast and so heavily that Willy could hear it: her very life, she felt, lay in his answer. He did not quite understand the full import of her words and all that they implied, but he knew that she was in deadly earnest, and he felt that some vague terror lay in his answer; but the manhood in him rose to the occasion—Willy Barrow was of the stuff of which heroes are made—and he replied—

'Maggie, as God is above us, I have no other answer to give! I don't know what you mean, but I have a shadow of fear! I must do my duty whatever comes of it!' There was a long pause, and then Maggie spoke again, but this time in so different a voice that her lover's heart went out to her in tenfold love and passion, with never a shadow of doubt or fear.

'Willy, tak me in your arms—I am not unworthy, dear, though for a moment I did falter!' He clasped her to him, and whispered when their lips had met—

'Maggie, my darling, I never loved you like now. I would die for you if I could do you good.'

'Hush, dear, I ken it weel. But your duty is not only for yoursel, and it must be done! I too hae a duty to dae—a grave and stern ane!'

'What is it? Tell me, Maggie dear!'

'Ye maunna[1] ask me! Ye maun never ken! Kiss me once again, Willy, before I go—for oh, my love, my love! it may be the last!'

Her words were lost in the passionate embrace which followed. Then, when he least expected it, she suddenly tore herself away and fled through the darkness across the field which lay between

---

[1] Must not (Scots).

them and her home, whilst he stood doggedly at his watch looking out for another signal between sea and shore.

III

When she got to the far side of the field, Maggie, instead of turning to the left, which would have brought her home, went down the sloping track to the right, which led to the rustic bridge crossing the Back Burn near the Pigeon Tower. Thence turning to the right she scrambled down the bank beside the ruined barley-mill, so as to reach the little plots of sea-grass—islands, except at low tide—between which the tide rises to meet the waters of the stream.

The whole situation of Cruden is peculiar. The main stream, the Water of Cruden, runs in a south-easterly direction, skirts the sandhills, and, swirling under the stone bridge, partly built with the ruins of the old church which Malcolm erected to celebrate his victory over Sueno,[1] turns suddenly to the right and runs to sea over a stony bottom. The estuary has in its wash some dangerous outcropping granite rocks, nearly covered at high tide, and the mouth opens between the most northerly end of the sandhills and the village street, whose houses mark the slope of the detritus from the rocks. Formerly the Water of Cruden, instead of taking this last turn, used to flow straight on till it joined the lesser stream known as the Back Burn, and together the streams ran seawards. Even in comparatively recent years, in times of flood or freshet, the spate broke down or swept over the intervening tongue of land, and the Water of Cruden took its old course seaward. This course is what is known as the Watter's Mou'. It is a natural cleft—formed by primæval fire or earthquake or some sort of natural convulsion—which runs through the vast mass of red granite which forms a promontory running due south. Water has done its work as well as fire in the formation of the gully as it now is, for the drip and flow and rush of water that mark the seasons for countless ages have completed the work of the pristine fire. As one sees this natu-

---

[1] Malcolm II, King of the Scots from 1005-1034, built a chapel to commemorate his victory over the Danish led by Canute, son of Sueno, King of Denmark in 1012.

ral mouth of the stream in the rocky face of the cliff, it is hard to realise that Nature alone has done the work.

At first the cleft runs from west to east, and broadens out into a wide bay of which on one side a steep grassy slope leads towards the new castle of Slains,[1] and on the other rises a sheer bank, with tufts of the thick grass growing on the ledges, where the earth has been blown. From this the cleft opens again between towering rocks like what in America is called a cañon[2] and tends seaward to the south between precipices two hundred feet high, and over a bottom of great boulders exposed at low water towards the northern end. The precipice to the left or eastward side is twice rent with great openings, through which, in time of storm, the spray and spume of the easterly gale piling the great waves into the Castle Bay are swept. These openings are, however, so guarded with masses of rock that the force of the wildest wave is broken before it can leap up the piles of boulders which rise from their sandy floors. At the very mouth the cleft opens away to the west, where the cliff falls back, and seaward of which rise great masses of black frowning rock, most of which only show their presence at high water by the angry patches of foam which even in calm weather mark them—for the current here runs fast. The eastern portal is composed of a giant mass of red granite, which, from its overhanging shape, is known as 'the Ship's Starn.'[3] It lies somewhat lower than the cliff of which it is a part, being attached to it by a great sloping shelf of granite, over which, when the storm is east-

---

[1] In an atmospheric description of the area, Lady Blanche Murphy describes the new Slains Castle as a "giant watchman upon giant cliffs, built up only one story high, on account of the tremendous winds that prevail there in spring and autumn, and cased with the gray Aberdeen granite of the famous quarries nearby. The surrounding country is as bare and uninviting as one could imagine; the road from Aberdeen (twenty miles) is bleak and stony; the young trees near the castle are stunted . . . and a damp veil of mist hangs perpetually over the scene." "Slains Castle," *Lippincott's Magazine of Popular Literature and Science* (June 1873): 646. The old castle located at Collieston was destroyed by James VI of Scotland in revenge for the Earl of Erroll's revolt. The new castle dates from the end of the sixteenth century and was rebuilt in 1836.
[2] Canyon. Stoker is using the Spanish spelling.
[3] A rock formation.

erly, the torrent of spray sent up by the dashing waves rolls down to join the foamy waves in the Watter's Mou'.

Maggie knew that close to the Barley Mill, safe from the onset of the waves—for the wildest waves that ever rise lose their force fretting and churning on the stony sides and bottom of the Watter's Mou'—was kept a light boat belonging to her brother, which he sometimes used when the weather was fine and he wanted to utilise his spare time in line fishing. Her mind was made up that it was her duty to give her father warning of what awaited him on landing—if she could. She was afraid to think of the danger, of the myriad chances against her success; but, woman-like, when once the idea was fixed in her mind she went straight on to its realisation. Truly, thought of any kind would have been an absolute barrier to action in such a case, for any one of the difficulties ahead would have seemed sufficient. To leave the shore at all on such a night, and in such a frail craft, with none but a girl to manage it; then to find a way, despite storm and current, out to the boat so far off at sea; and finally, to find the boat she wanted at all in the fret of such a stormy sea—a wilderness of driving mist—in such a night, when never a star even was to be seen: the prospect might well appal the bravest.

But to think was to hesitate, and to hesitate was to fail. Keeping her thoughts on the danger to her father, and seeing through the blackness of the stormy night his white, woe-laden face before her, and hearing through the tumult of the tempest his sobs as on that night when her fear for him began to be acute, she set about her work with desperate energy. The boat was moored on the northern side of the largest of the little islands of sea-grass, and so far in shelter that she could get all in readiness. She set the oars in their places, stepped the mast, and rigged the sail ready to haul up. Then she took a small spar of broken wood and knotted to it a piece of rope, fastening the other end of the rope, some five yards long, just under the thwarts near the centre of the boat, and just a little forward on the port side. The spar she put carefully ready to throw out of the boat when the sweep of the wind should take her sail—for without some such strain as it would afford, the boat would probably heel over. Then she guided the boat in the shallow water round the little island till it was stern on to the sea side. It was rough work, for the rush and recoil of the waves beat the boat back on the sandy bank or left her now and again dry till a new wave lifted her.

All this time she took something of inspiration from the darkness and the roar of the storm around her. She was not yet face to face with danger, and did not realise, or try to realise, its magnitude. In such a mystery of darkness as lay before, above, and around her, her own personality seemed as nought. Truly there is an instinct of one's own littleness which becomes consciously manifest in the times when Nature puts forth her might. The wind swept up the channel of the Watter's Mou' in great gusts, till the open bay where she stood became the centre of an intermittent whirlwind. The storm came not only from the Mouth itself, but through the great gaps in the eastern wall. It drove across the gully till high amongst the rocks overhead on both sides it seemed now and again to scream as a living thing in pain or anger. Great sheets of mist appeared out of the inky darkness beyond, coming suddenly as though like the great sails of ships driving up before the wind. With gladness Maggie saw that the sheets of fog were becoming fewer and thinner, and realised that so far her dreadful task was becoming possible. She was getting more inspired by the sound and elemental fury around her. There was in her blood, as in the blood of all the hardy children of the northern seas, some strain of those sturdy Berserkers[1] who knew no fear, and rode the very tempest on its wings with supreme bravery. Such natures rise with the occasion, and now, when the call had come, Maggie's brave nature answered it. It was with a strong, almost an eager, heart that she jumped into the boat, and, seizing the oars, set out on her perilous course. The start was difficult, for the boat was bumping savagely on the sand; but, taking advantage of a big wave, two or three powerful strokes took her out into deeper water. Here, too, there was shelter, for the cliffs rose steeply; and when she had entered the elbow of the gully and saw before her the whole length of the Watter's Mou', the drift of the wind took it over her head, and she was able to row in comparative calmness under the shadow of the cliffs. A few minutes took her to the first

---

[1] Norse warriors.

of the openings in the eastern cliff, and here she began to feel the full fury of the storm. The opening itself was sheer on each side, but in the gap between was piled a mass of giant boulders, the work of the sea at its wildest during centuries of stress. On the farther side of these the waves broke, and sent up a white cloud of spume that drove instantly into the darkness beyond. Maggie knew that here her first great effort had to be made, and lending her strength pulled the boat through the turmoil of wind and wave. As she passed the cleft, driven somewhat more out into the middle of the channel, she caught, in a pause between the rush of the waves, a glimpse of the lighted windows of the castle on the cliff. The sight for an instant unnerved her, for it brought into opposition her own dreadful situation, mental and physical, with the happy faces of those clustered round the comforting light. But the reaction was helpful, for the little jealousy which was at the base of the idea was blotted out by the thought of that stern and paramount duty which she had undertaken. Not seldom in days gone by had women like her, in times of test and torment, taken their way over the red-hot ploughshares under somewhat similar stress of mind.

She was now under the shelter of the cliff, and gaining the second and last opening in the rocky wall: as the boat advanced the force of the waves became greater, for every yard up the Watter's Mou' the fretting of the rocky bottom and sides had broken their force. This was brought home to her roughly when the breaking of a coming wave threw a sheet of water over her as she bent to her oars. Chop! chop! went the boat into the trough of each succeeding wave, till it became necessary to bale out the boat or she might never even get started on her way. This done she rowed on, and now came to the second opening in the cliff. This was much wilder than the first, for outside of it, to the east, the waves of the North Sea broke in all their violence, and with the breaking of each a great sheet of water came drifting over the wall of piled-up boulders. Again Maggie kept out in the channel, and, pulling with all her might, passed again into the shelter of the cliff. Here the water was stiller, for the waves were breaking directly behind the sheltering cliff, and the sound of them was heard high overhead in the rushing wind.

Maggie drew close to the rock, and, hugging it, crept on her outward way. There was now only one danger to come, before her final effort. The great shelf of rock inside the Ship's Starn was only saved from exposure by its rise on the outer side; but here, happily, the waves did not break, they swept under the overhanging slope on the outer side, and then passed on their way; the vast depth of the water outside was their protection within. Now and then a wave broke on the edge of the Ship's Starn, and then a great wall of green water rose and rushed down the steep slope, but in the pause between Maggie passed along; and now the boat nestled on the black water, under the shelter of the very outermost wall of rock. The Ship's Starn was now her last refuge. As she hurriedly began to get the sail ready she could hear the whistling of the wind round the outer side of the rock and overhead. The black water underneath her rose and fell, but in some mysterious eddy or back-water of Nature's forces she rested in comparative calm on the very edge of the maelström. By contrast with the darkness of the Watter's Mou' between the towering walls of rock, the sea had some mysterious light of its own, and just outside the opening on the western side she could see the white water pouring over the sunken rocks as the passing waves exposed them, till once more they looked like teeth in the jaws of the hungry sea.

And now came the final struggle in her effort to get out to open water. The moment she should pass beyond the shelter of the Ship's Starn the easterly gale would in all probability drive her straight upon the outer reef of rocks amongst those angry jaws, where the white teeth would in an instant grind her and her boat to nothingness. But if she should pass this last danger she should be out in the open sea and might make her way to save her father. She held in her mind the spot whence she had seen the answering signal to the rockets, and felt a blind trust that God would help her in her difficulty. Was not God pleased with self-sacrifice? What could be better for a maid than to save her father from accomplished sin and the discovery which made sin so bitter to bear? 'Greater love hath no man than this, that a man lay down his life for his friend.'[1] Besides there was Sailor Willy! Had not he—even he—doubted her; and might she not by this wild night's

---

[1] John 15:13.

work win back her old place in his heart and his faith? Strong in this new hope, she made careful preparation for her great effort. She threw overboard the spar and got ready the tiller. Then having put the sheet round the thwart on the starboard side, and laid the loose end where she could grasp it whilst holding the tiller, she hoisted the sail and belayed the rope that held it. In the eddy of the storm behind the sheltered rock the sail hung idly for a few seconds, and in this time she jumped to the stern and held the tiller with one hand and with the other drew the sheet of the sail taut and belayed it. An instant after, the sail caught a gust of wind and the boat sprang, as though a living thing, out toward the channel. The instant the shelter was past the sail caught the full sweep of the easterly gale, and the boat would have turned over only for the strain from the floating spar line, which now did its part well. The bow was thrown round towards the wind, and the boat began rushing through the water at a terrific pace. Maggie felt the coldness of death in her heart; but in that wild moment the bravery of her nature came out. She shut her teeth and jammed the tiller down hard, keeping it in place against her thigh, with the other leg pressed like a pillar against the side of the boat. The little craft seemed sweeping right down on the outer rocks; already she could see the white wall of water, articulated into white lines like giant hairs, rushing after the retreating waves, and a great despair swept over her. But at that moment the rocks on the western side of the Watter's Mou' opened so far that she caught a glimpse of Sailor Willy's lamp reflected through the window of the coastguard hut. This gave her new hope, and with a mighty effort she pressed the tiller harder. The boat sank in the trough of the waves, rose again, the spar caught the rush of the receding wave and pulled the boat's head a point round, and then the outer rock was passed, and the boat, actually touching the rock so that the limpets scraped her side, ran free in the stormy waves beyond.

Maggie breathed a prayer as with trembling hand she unloosed the rope of the floating spar; then, having loosened the sheet, she turned the boat's head south, and, tacking, ran out in the direction where she had seen the signal light of her father's boat.

By contrast with the terrible turmoil amid the rocks, the great waves of the open sea were safety itself. No one to whom the sea is an occupation ever fears it in the open; and this fisher's daughter, with the Viking blood in her veins, actually rejoiced as the cockle-shell of a boat, dipping and jerking like an angry horse, drove up and down the swell of the waves. She was a good way out now, and the whole coast-line east and west was opening up to her. The mist had gone by, or, if it lasted, hung amid the rocks inshore; and through the great blackness round she saw the lights in the windows of the castle, the glimmering lights of the village of Cruden, and far off the powerful light at Girdleness blazing out at intervals. But there was one light on which her eyes lingered fixedly—the dim window of the coastguard's shelter, where she knew that her lover kept his grim watch. Her heart was filled with gladness as she thought that by what she was doing she would keep pain and trouble from him. She knew now, what she had all along in her heart believed, that Sailor Willy would not flinch from any duty however stern and pain-laden to him it might be; and she knew, too, that neither her rugged father nor her passionate young brother would ever forgive him for that duty. But now she would not, could not, think of failing, but gripped the tiller hard, and with set teeth and fixed eyes held on her perilous way.

Time went by hour by hour, but so great was her anxiety that she never noted how it went, but held on her course, tacking again and again as she tried to beat her way to her father through the storm. The eyes of sea folk are not ordinary eyes—they can pierce the darkness wherein the vision of land folk becomes lost or arrested; and the sea and the sky over it, and the coastline, however black and dim—however low-lying or distant—have lessons of their own. Maggie began by some mysterious instinct to find her way where she wanted to go, till little by little the coast-line, save for the distant lights of Girdleness and Boddam,[1] faded out of sight. Lying as she was on the very surface of the water, she had the horizon rising as it were around her, and there is nearly always some slight sign of light somewhere on the horizon's rim. There came now and again rents in the thick clouding of the stormy sky, and at such moments here and there came patches of lesser darkness like oases of light in the desert of the ebon sea. At one such moment

---

[1] Boddam Lighthouse is situated three miles from Peterhead.

she saw far off to the port side the outline of a vessel well known on the coast, the revenue cutter[1] which was the seaward arm of the preventive service. And then a great fear came over poor Maggie's heart; the sea was no longer the open sea, for her father was held in the toils of his enemies, and escape seaward became difficult or would be almost impossible, when the coming morn would reveal all the mysteries that the darkness hid. Despair, however, has its own courage, and Maggie was too far in her venture now to dread for more than a passing moment anything which might follow.

She knew that the 'Sea Gull' lay still to the front, and with a beating heart and a brain that throbbed with the eagerness of hope and fear she held on her course. The break in the sky which had shown her the revenue cutter was only momentary, and all was again swallowed up in the darkness; but she feared that some other such rent in the cloudy night might expose her father to his enemies. Every moment, therefore, became precious, and steeling her heart and drawing the sheet of her sail as tight as she dared, she sped on into the darkness—on for a time that seemed interminable agony. Suddenly something black loomed up ahead of her, thrown out against the light of the horizon's rim, and her heart gave a great jump, for something told her that the Powers which aid the good wishes of daughters had sent her father out of that wilderness of stormy sea. With her sea-trained eyes she knew in a few moments that the boat pitching so heavily was indeed the 'Sea Gull.' At the same moment some one on the boat's deck saw her sail, and a hoarse muffled murmur of voices came to her over the waves in the gale. The coble's head was thrown round to the wind, and in that stress of storm and chopping sea she beat and buffeted, and like magic her way stopped, and she lay tossing. Maggie realised the intention of the manœuvre, and deftly swung her boat round till she came under the starboard quarter of the fishing-boat, and in the shadow of her greater bulk and vaster sail, reefed though it was, found a comparative calm. Then she called out—

'Father! It's me—Maggie! Dinna show a licht,[2] but try to throw me a rope.'

---

[1] Fast, sturdy boats with two head sails. David Phillipson, *Smuggling: A History, 1700-1970* (Newton Abbot: David & Charles, 1973), pp. 32-49.
[2] Light (Scots).

With a shout in which were mingled many strong feelings, her father leaned over the bulwark, and, with seaman's instinct of instant action, threw her a rope. She deftly caught it, and, making it fast to the bows of her boat, dropped her sail. Then someone threw her another rope, which she fastened round her waist. She threw herself into the sea, and, holding tight to the rope, was shortly pulled breathless on board the 'Sea Gull.'

She was instantly the centre of a ring of men. Not only were her father and two brothers on board, but there were no less than six men, seemingly foreigners, in the group.

'Maggie!' said her father, 'in God's name, lass, hoo cam ye oot here? Were ye overta'en by the storm? God be thankit that ye met us, for this is a wild nicht to be oot on the North Sea by yer lanes.'

'Father!' said she, in a hurried whisper in his ear. 'I must speak wi' ye alane. There isna a moment to lose!'

'Speak on, lass.'

'No' before these strangers, father. I must speak alane!' Without a word, MacWhirter took his daughter aside, and, amid a muttered dissatisfaction of the strange men, signed to her to proceed. Then, as briefly as she could, Maggie told her father that it was known that a cargo was to be run that night, that the coastguard all along Buchan had been warned, and that she had come out to tell him of his danger.

As she spoke the old man groaned, and after a pause said—'I maun tell the rest. I'm no' the maister here the noo. Mendoza has me in his grip, an' his men rule here!'

'But, father, the boat is yours, and the risk is yours. It is you 'll be punished if there is a discovery!'

'That may be, lass, but I'm no' free.'

'I feared it was true, father, but I thocht it my duty to come!'

Doubtless the old man knew that Maggie would understand fully what he meant, but the only recognition he made of her act of heroism was to lay his hand heavily on her shoulder. Then stepping forward he called the men round him, and in his own rough way told them of the danger. The strangers muttered and scowled; but Andrew and Niel drew close to their sister, and the younger man put his arm around her and pressed her to him. Maggie felt the comfort of the kindness, and laying her head on her brother's shoulder, cried quietly in the darkness. It was a relief to her pent-up feelings to be able to give way if only so far. When MacWhirter brought his tale to a close, and asked: 'And now, lads, what's to be done?' one of the strangers, a brawny, heavily-built man, spoke out harshly—

'But for why this? Was it not that this woman's lover was of the guard? In this affair the women must do their best too. This lover of the guard——' He was hotly interrupted by Niel—

"Tisna the part of Maggie to tak a hand in this at a'.'

'But I say it is the part of all. When Mendoza bought this man he bought all—unless there be traitors in his house!' This roused Maggie, who spoke out quickly, for she feared her brother's passion might brew trouble—

'I hae nae part in this dreadfu' affair. It's no' by ma wish or ma aid that father has embarked in this—this enterprise. I hae naught to dae wi't o' ony kind.'

'Then for why are you here?' asked the burly man, with a coarse laugh.

'Because ma father and ma brithers are in danger, danger into which they hae been led, or been forced, by ye and the like o' ye. Do ye think it was for pleasure, or, O my God! for profit either, that I cam oot this nicht—an' in that?' and as she spoke she pointed to where the little boat strained madly at the rope which held her. Then MacWhirter spoke out fiercely, so fiercely that the lesser spirits who opposed him were cowed—

'Leave the lass alane, I say! Yon's[1] nane o' her doin'; and if ye be men ye'd honour her that cam oot in sic a tempest for the sake o' the likes o' me—o' us!'

But when the strangers were silent, Niel, whose passion had been aroused, could not be quieted, and spoke out with a growing fury which seemed to choke him—

'So Sailor Willy told ye the danger and then let ye come oot in this nicht! He'll hae to reckon wi' me for that when we get in.'

'He telt me naethin'. I saw Bella Cruickshank gie him the telegram, and I guessed. He doesna ken I'm here—and he maun never ken. Nane must ever ken that a warning cam the nicht to father!'

---

[1] That's (Scots).

'But they'll watch for us comin' in.'

'We maun rin back to Cuxhaven,'[1] said the quiet voice of Andrew, who had not yet spoken.

'But ye canna,' said Maggie; 'the revenue cutter is on the watch, and when the mornin' comes will follow ye; and besides, hoo can ye get to Cuxhaven in this wind?'

'Then what are we to do, lass?' said her father.

'Dae, father? Dae what ye should dae—throw a' this poisonous stuff that has brought this ruin owerboard. Lichten yer boat as ye will lichten yer conscience, and come hame as ye went oot!'

The burly man swore a great oath.

'Nothing overboard shall be thrown. These belongs not to you but to Mendoza. If they be touched he closes on your boat and ruin it is for you!' Maggie saw her father hesitate, and feared that other counsels might prevail, so she spoke out as by an inspiration. There, amid the surges of the perilous seas, the daughter's heroic devotion and her passionate earnestness made a new calm in her father's life—

'Father, dinna be deceived. Wi' this wind onshore, an' the revenue cutter ootside an' the dawn no' far off ye canna escape. Noo in the darkness ye can get rid o' the danger. Dinna lose a moment. The storm is somewhat lesser just enoo. Throw a' owerboard and come back to yer old self! What if we be ruined? We can work; and shall a' be happy yet!'

Something seemed to rise in the old man's heart and give him strength. Without pause he said with a grand simplicity—

'Ye're reet, lass, ye're reet! Haud up the casks, men, and stave[2] them in!'

Andrew and Niel rushed to his bidding. Mendoza's men protested, but were afraid to intervene, and one after another bales and casks were lifted on deck. The bales were tossed overboard, and the heads of the casks stove in till the scuppers[3] were alternately drenched with brandy and washed with the seas.

In the midst of this, Maggie, knowing that if all were to be of

---

[1] German fishing port.
[2] Break them up (Scots).
[3] A hole or opening in the side of a ship.

any use she must be found at home in the morning, quietly pulled her boat as close as she dared, and slipping down the rope managed to clamber into it. Then she loosed the painter;[1] and the wind and waves took her each instant farther and farther away.

The sky over the horizon was brightening every instant, and there was a wild fear in her heart which not even the dull thud of the hammers as the casks were staved in could allay. She felt that it was a race against time, and her over-excited imagination multiplied her natural fear; her boat's head was to home, steering for where she guessed was the dim light on the cliff, towards which her heart yearned. She hauled the sheets close—as close as she dared, for now speed was everything if she was to get back unseen. Well she knew that Sailor Willy on his lonely vigil would be true to his trust, and that his eagle eye could not fail to note her entry when once the day had broken. In a fever of anxiety she kept her eye on the Girdleness light by which she had to steer, and with the rise and fall of every wave as she swept by them, threw the boat's head a point to the wind and let it fall away again.

The storm had nearly spent itself, but there were still angry moments when the mist was swept in masses before fresh gusts. These, however, were fewer and fewer, and in a little while she ceased to heed them or even to look for them, and at last her eager eye began to discern through the storm the flickering lights of the little port. There came a moment when the tempest poured out the lees of its wrath in one final burst of energy, which wrapped the flying boat in a wraith of mist.

And then the tempest swept onward, shoreward, with the broken mist showing white in the springing dawn like the wings of some messenger of coming peace.

IV

Matters looked serious enough on the 'Sea Gull' when the time came in which rather the darkness began to disappear than the light to appear. Night and day have their own mysteries, and their nascence is as distant and as mysterious as the origin of life. The

---

[1] Rope used to secure a boat.

sky and the waters still seemed black, and the circle in which the little craft lived was as narrow as ever; but here and there in sky and on sea were faint streaks perceptible rather than distinguishable, as though swept thither by the trumpet blast of the messenger of the dawn. Mendoza's men did not stint their curses nor their threats, and Niel with passionate violence so assailed them in return that both MacWhirter and Andrew had to exercise their powers of restraint. But blood is hot, and the lives of lawless men are prone to make violence a habit; the two elder men were anxious that there should be no extension of the present bitter bickering. As for MacWhirter, his mind was in a whirl and tumult of mixed emotions. First came his anxiety for Maggie when she had set forth alone on the stormy sea with such inadequate equipment. Well the old fisherman knew the perils that lay before her in her effort to win the shore, and his heart was postively sick with anxiety when every effort of thought or imagination concerning her ended in something like despair. In one way he was happier than he had been for many months; the impending blow had fallen, and though he was ruined it had come in such a time that his criminal intent had not been accomplished. Here again his anxiety regarding Maggie became intensified, for was it not to save him that she had set forth on her desperate enterprise. He groaned aloud as he thought of the price that he might yet have to pay—that he might have paid already, though he knew it not as yet—for the service which had saved him from the after-consequences of his sin. He dared not think more on the subject, for it would, he feared, madden him, and he must have other work to engross his thoughts.

Thus it was that the danger of collision between Niel and Mendoza's men became an anodyne to his pain. He knew that a quarrel among seamen and under such conditions would be no idle thing, for they had all their knives, and with such hot blood on all sides none would hesitate to use them. The whole of the smuggled goods had by now been thrown overboard, the tobacco having gone the last, the bales having been broken up. So heavy had been the cargo that there was a new danger in that the boat was too much lightened. As Mendoza had intended that force as well as fraud was to aid this venture he had not stuck at trifles. There was no pretence of concealment and even the ballast¹ had made way for cask and box and bale. The 'Sea Gull' had been only partially loaded at Hamburg, but when out of sight of port her cargo had been completed from other boats which had followed, till, when she started for Buchan, she was almost a solid mass of contraband goods. Mendoza's men felt desperate at this hopeless failure of the venture; and as Niel, too, was desperate, in a different way, there was a grim possibility of trouble on board at any minute.

The coming of the dawn was therefore a welcome relief, for it united—if only for a time—all on board to try to avert a common danger.

Lighter and lighter grew the expanse of sea and sky, until over the universe seemed to spread a cool, pearly grey, against which every object seemed to stand starkly out. The smugglers were keenly on the watch, and they saw, growing more clearly each instant out of the darkness, the black, low-lying hull, short funnel, and tapering spars of the revenue cutter about three or four miles off the starboard quarter. The preventive men seemed to see them at the same time, for there was a manifest stir on board, and the cutter's head was changed. Then MacWhirter knew it was necessary to take some bold course of action, for the 'Sea Gull' lay between two fires, and he made up his mind to run then and there for Port Erroll.

As the 'Sea Gull' drew nearer in to shore the waves became more turbulent, for there is ever a more ordered succession in deep waters than where the onward rush is broken by the undulations of the shore. Minute by minute the dawn was growing brighter, and the shore was opening up. The 'Sea Gull,' lightened of her load, could not with safety be thrown across the wind, and so the difficulty of her tacks was increased. The dawn was just shooting its first rays over the eastern sea when the final effort to win the little port came to be made.

The harbour of Port Erroll is a tiny haven of refuge won from the jagged rocks that bound the eastern side of Cruden Bay. It is sheltered on the northern side by the cliff which runs as far as the Watter's Mou', and separated from the mouth of the Water of

---

¹ Extra weight on a boat to provide stability.

Cruden, with its waste of shifting sands, by a high wall of concrete. The harbour faces east, and its first basin is the smaller of the two, the larger opening sharply to the left a little way in. At the best of times it is not an easy matter to gain the harbour, for only when the tide has fairly risen is it available at all, and the rapid tide which runs up from the Scaurs makes in itself a difficulty at such times. The tide was now at three-quarters flood, so that in as far as water was concerned there was no difficulty; but the fierceness of the waves which sent up a wall of white water all along the cliffs looked ominous indeed.

As the 'Sea Gull' drew nearer to the shore, considerable commotion was caused on both sea and land. The revenue cutter dared not approach so close to the shore, studded as it was with sunken rocks, as did the lighter draughted coble; but her commander evidently did not mean to let this be to the advantage of the smuggler. A gun was fired to attract the authorities on shore, and signals were got ready to hoist.

The crowd of strangers who thronged the little port had instinctively hidden themselves behind rock and wall and boat, as the revelation of the dawn came upon them, so that the whole place presented the appearance of a warren when the rabbits are beginning to emerge after a temporary scare. There were not wanting, however, many who stood out in the open, affecting, with what nonchalance they could, a simple business interest at the little port.

Sailor Willy was on the cliff between the guard-house and the Watter's Mou', where he had kept his vigil all the night long. As soon as possible after he had sent out his appeal for help the lieutenant had come over from Collieston with a boatman and three men, and these were now down on the quay waiting for the coming of the 'Sea Gull.' When he had arrived, and had learned the state of things, the lieutenant, who knew of Willy Barrow's relations with the daughter of the suspected man, had kindly ordered him to watch the cliff, whilst he himself with the men would look after the port. When he had first given the order in the presence of the other coastguards, Willy had instinctively drawn himself up as though he felt that he, too, had come under suspicion, so the lieutenant took the earliest opportunity when they were alone of saying to Willy—

'Barrow, I have arranged your duties as I have done, not by any means because I suspect that you would be drawn by your sympathies into any neglect of duty—I know you too well for that—but simply because I want to spare you pain in case things may be as we suspect!'

Willy saluted and thanked him with his eyes as he turned away, for he feared that the fulness of his heart might betray him. The poor fellow was much overwrought. All night long he had paced the cliffs in the dull routine of his duty, with his heart feeling like a lump of lead, and his brain on fire with fear. He knew from the wildness of Maggie's rush away from him that she was bent on some desperate enterprise, and as he had no clue to her definite intentions he could only imagine. He thought and thought until his brain almost began to reel with the intensity of his mental effort; and as he was so placed, tied to the stake of his duty, that he could speak with no one on the subject, he had to endure alone, and in doubt, the darkness of his soul, tortured alike by hopes and fears, through all the long night. At last, however, the pain exhausted itself, and doubt became its own anodyne. Despair has its calms—the backwaters of fears—where the tired imagination may rest awhile before the strife begins anew.

With joy he saw that the storm was slackening with the coming of the dawn; and when the last fierce gust had swept by him, screaming through the rigging of the flagstaff overhead, and sweeping inland the broken fragments of the mist, he turned to the sea, now of a cool grey with the light of the coming dawn, and swept it far and wide with his glass. With gladness—and yet with an ache in his heart which he could not understand—he realised that there was in sight only one coble—the 'Sea Gull'—he knew her well—running for the port, and further out the hull and smoke, the light spars and swift lines of the revenue cutter, which was evidently following her. He strolled with the appearance of leisureliness, though his heart was throbbing, towards the cliff right over the little harbour, so that he could look down and see from close quarters all that went on. He could not but note the many strangers dispersed about, all within easy distance of a rush to the quay when the boat should land, or the way in which the lieutenant and his men seemed to keep guard over the whole place. As first the figures, the walls of the port, the cranes, the boats, and the distant headlands were silhouetted in black against the background of grey sea and grey sky; but as the dawn came closer each object began to stand out in its natural proportions. All kept growing clearer and yet clearer and more and more thoroughly outlined, till the moment came when the sun, shooting over the horizon, set every living thing whose eyes had been regulated to the strain of the darkness and the twilight blinking and winking in the glory of the full light of day.

Eagerly he searched the faces of the crowd with his glass for Maggie, but he could not see her anywhere, and his heart seemed to sink within him, for well he knew that it must be no ordinary cause which kept Maggie from being one of the earliest on the look-out for her father. Closer and closer came the 'Sea Gull,' running for the port with a speed and recklessness that set both the smugglers and the preventive men all agog. Such haste and such indifference to danger sprang, they felt, from no common cause, and they all came to the conclusion that the boat, delayed by the storm, discovered by the daylight, and cut off by the revenue cutter, was making a desperate push for success in her hazard. And so all, watchers and watched, braced themselves for what might come about. Amongst the groups moved the tall figure of Mendoza, whispering and pointing, but keeping carefully hidden from the sight of the coastguards. He was evidently inciting them to some course from which they held back.

Closer and closer came the 'Sea Gull,' lying down to the scuppers as she tacked; lightened as she was she made more leeway than was usual to so crank a boat. At last she got her head in the right direction for a run in, and, to the amazement of all who saw her, came full tilt into the outer basin, and, turning sharply round, ran into the inner basin under bare poles. There was not one present, smuggler or coastguard, who did not set down the daring attempt as simply suicidal. In a few seconds the boat stuck on the sandbank accumulated at the western end of the basin and stopped, her bows almost touching the side of the pier. The coastguards had not expected any such manœuvre, and had taken their place on either side of the entrance to the inner basin, so that it took them a few seconds to run the length of the pier and come opposite the boat. The crowd of the smugglers and the smugglers' friends was so great that just as Niel and his brother began to shove out a plank from the bows to step ashore there was so thick a cluster round the spot that the lieutenant as he came could not see what was going on. Some little opposition was made to his passing through the mass of people, which was getting closer every instant, but his men closed up behind, and together they forced a way to the front before any one from the 'Sea Gull' could spring on shore. A sort of angry murmur—that deep undertone which marks the passion of a mass—arose, and the lieutenant, recognising its import, faced round like lightning, his revolver pointed straight in the faces of the crowd, whilst the men with him drew their cutlasses.

To Sailor Willy this appearance of action gave a relief from almost intolerable pain. He was in feverish anxiety about Maggie, but he could do nothing—nothing; and to an active and resolute man this feeling is in itself the worst of pain. His heart was simply breaking with suspense, and so it was that the sight of drawn weapons, in whatever cause, came like an anodyne to his tortured imagination. The flash of the cutlasses woke in him the instinct of action, and with a leaping heart he sprang down the narrow winding path that led to the quay.

Before the lieutenant's pistol the crowd fell back. It was not that they were afraid—for cowardice is pretty well unknown in Buchan—but authority, and especially in arms, has a special force with law-breakers. But the smugglers did not mean going back altogether now that their booty was so close to them, and the two bodies stood facing each other when Sailor Willy came upon the scene and stood beside the officers. Things were looking pretty serious when the resonant voice of MacWhirter was heard—

'What d'ye mean, men, crowdin' on the officers. Stand back, there, and let the coastguards come aboard an[1] they will. There's naught here that they mayn't see.'

The lieutenant turned and stepped on the plank—which Niel had by this time shoved on shore—and went on board, followed by two of his men, the other remaining with the boatman and Willy Barrow on the quay. Niel went straight to the officer, and said—

---

[1] If (Scots).

'I want to go ashore at once! Search me an ye will!' He spoke so rudely that the officer was angered, and said to one of the men beside him—

'Put your hands over him and let him go,' adding, sotto voce, 'He wants a lesson in manners!' The man lightly passed his hands over him to see that he had nothing contraband about him, and, being satisfied on the point, stood back and nodded to his officer, and Niel sprang ashore, and hurried off towards the village.

Willy had, by this time, a certain feeling of relief, for he had been thinking, and he knew that MacWhirter would not have been so ready to bring the coastguards on board if he had any contraband with him. Hope did for him what despair could not, for as he instinctively turned his eyes over the waste of angry sea, for an instant he did not know if it were the blood in his eyes or, in reality, the red of the dawn which had shot up over the eastern horizon.

Mendoza's men having been carefully searched by one of the coastguards came sullenly on shore and went to the back of the crowd, where their master, scowling and white-faced, began eagerly to talk with them in whispers. MacWhirter and his elder son busied themselves with apparent nonchalance in the needful matters of the landing, and the crowd seemed holding back for a spring. The suspense of all was broken by the incoming of a boat sent off from the revenue cutter, which, driven by four sturdy oarsmen, and steered by the commander himself, swept into the outer basin of the harbour, tossing amongst the broken waves. In the comparative shelter of the wall it turned, and driving into the inner basin pulled up on the slip beyond where the 'Sea Gull' lay. The instant the boat touched, six bluejackets[1] sprang ashore, followed by the commander, and all seven men marched quietly but resolutely to the quay opposite the 'Sea Gull's' bow. The oarsmen followed, when they had hauled their boat up on the slip. The crowd now abandoned whatever had been its intention, and fell back looking and muttering thunder.

By this time the lieutenant was satisfied that the coble contained nothing that was contraband, and, telling its master so,

---

[1] An informal term describing a sailor in the British navy whose standard uniform after 1858 was a blue jacket.

stepped on shore just as Niel, with his face white as a sheet, and his eyes blazing, rushed back at full speed. He immediately attacked Sailor Willy—

'What hae ye dune wi' ma sister Maggie?'

He answered as quietly as he could, although there shot through his heart a new pain, a new anxiety—

'I know naught of her. I haven't seen her since last night, when Alice MacDonald was being married. Is she not at home?'

'Dinna ye ken damned weel that she's no'. Why did ye send her oot?' And he looked at him with the menace of murder in his eyes. The lieutenant saw from the looks of the two men that something was wrong, and asked Niel shortly—

'Where did you see her last?' Niel was going to make some angry reply, but in an instant Mendoza stepped forward, and in a loud voice gave instruction to one of his men who had been on board the 'Sea Gull' to take charge of her, as she was his under a bill of sale. This gave Niel time to think, and his answer came sullenly—

'Nane o' ye're business—mind yer ain affairs!' MacWhirter, when he had seen Niel come running back, had realised the worst, and leaned on the taffrail of the boat groaning. Mendoza's man sprang on board, and, taking him roughly by the shoulder, said—

'Come, clear out here. This boat is to Mendoza; get away!' The old man was so overcome with his feelings regarding Maggie that he made no reply, but quietly, with bent form, stepped on the plank and gained the quay. Willy Barrow rushed forward and took him by the hand and whispered to him—

'What does he mean?'

'He means,' said the old man in a low, strained voice, 'that for me an' him, an' to warn us she cam oot last nicht in the storm in a wee bit boat, an' that she is no' to her hame!' and he groaned. Willy was smitten with horror. This, then, was Maggie's high and desperate purpose when she left him. He knew now the meaning of those despairing words, and the darkness of the grave seemed to close over his soul. He moaned out to the old man: 'She did not tell me she was going. I never knew it. O my God!' The old man, with the protective instinct of the old to the young, laid his hand on his shoulder, as he said to him in a broken voice—

'A ken it, lad! A ken it weel! She tell't me sae hersel! The sin is a' wi' me, though you, puir lad, must e'en bear yer share o' the pain!' The commander said quietly to the lieutenant—

'Looks queer, don't it—the coastguard and the smuggler whispering?'

'All right,' came the answer, 'I know Barrow; he is as true as steel, but he's engaged to the old man's daughter. But I gather there's something queer going on this morning about her. I'll find out. Barrow,' he added, calling Willy to him, 'what is it about Mac-Whirter's daughter?'

'I don't know for certain, sir; but I fear she was out at sea last night.'

'At sea,' broke in the commander; 'at sea last night—how?'

'She was in a bit fishin'-boat,' broke in MacWhirter. 'Neighbours, hae ony o' ye seen her this mornin'? 'Twas ma son Andra's boat, that he keeps i' the Downans!'—another name for the Watter's Mou'. A sad silence that left the angry roar of the waves as they broke on the rocks and on the long strand in full possession was the only reply.

'Is the boat back in the Watter's Mou'?' asked the lieutenant sharply.

'No,' said a fisherman. 'A cam up jist noo past the Barley Mill, an' there's nae boat there.'

'Then God help her, an' God forgie me,' said MacWhirter, tearing off his cap and holding up his hands, 'for A've killed her—her that sae loved her auld father, that she went oot alane in a bit boat i' the storm i' the nicht to save him frae the consequence o' his sin.' Willy Barrow groaned, and the lieutenant turned to him: 'Heart, man, heart! God won't let a brave girl like that be lost. That's the lass for a sailor's wife. 'Twill be all right—you'll be proud of her yet!'

But Sailor Willy only groaned despite the approval of his conscience; his words of last night came back to him. 'Ye're no fit wife for me!' Now the commander spoke out to MacWhirter:

'When did you see her last?'

'Aboot twa o'clock i' the mornin'.'

'Where?'

'Aboot twenty miles off the Scaurs.'

'How did she come to leave you?'

'She pulled the boat that she cam in alongside the coble, an' got in by hersel—the last I saw o' her she had hoisted her sail an' was running nor'west . . . But A'll see her nae mair—a's ower wi' the puir, brave lass—an' wi' me, tae, that killed her—a's ower the noo—a's ower!' and he covered his face with his hands and sobbed. The commander said kindly enough, but with a stern gravity that there was no mistaking—

'Do I take it rightly that the girl went out in the storm to warn you?'

'Ay! Puir lass—'twas an ill day that made me put sic a task on her—God forgie me!' and there and then he told them all of her gallant deed.

The commander turned to the lieutenant, and spoke in the quick, resolute, masterful accent of habitual command—

'I shall leave you the bluejackets to help—send your men all out, and scour every nook and inlet from Kirkton to Boddam. Out with all the lifeboats on the coast! And you, men!' he turned to the crowd, 'turn out, all of you, to help! Show that there's some man's blood in you, to atone if you can for the wrong that sent this young girl out in a storm to save her father from you and your like!' Here he turned again to the lieutenant, 'Keep a sharp eye on that man—Mendoza, and all his belongings. We'll attend to him later on: I'll be back before night.'

'Where are you off to, Commander?'

'I'm going to scour the sea in the track of the storm where that gallant lass went last night. A brave girl that dared what she did for her father's sake is not to be lost without an effort; and, by God, she shan't lack it whilst I hold Her Majesty's command! Boatswain,[1] signal the cutter full steam up—no, you! We mustn't lose time, and the boatswain comes with me. To your oars, men!'

The seamen gave a quick, sharp 'Hurrah!' as they sprang to their places, whilst the man of the shore party to whom the order had been given climbed the sea-wall and telegraphed the needful orders; the crowd seemed to catch the enthusiasm of the moment, and scattered right and left to make search along the shore. In a

---

[1] A ship's officer.

few seconds the revenue boat was tossing on the waves outside the harbour, the men laying to their work as they drove her along, their bending oars keeping time to the swaying body of the commander, who had himself taken the tiller. The lieutenant said to Willy with thoughtful kindness—

'Where would you like to work on the search? Choose which part you will!' Willy instinctively touched his cap as he answered sadly—

'I should like to watch here, sir, if I may. She would make straight for the Watter's Mou'!'

V

The search for the missing girl was begun vigorously, and carried on thoroughly and with untiring energy. The Port Erroll lifeboat was got out and proceeded up coast, and a telegram was sent to Kirkton to get out the lifeboat there, and follow up the shore to Port Erroll. From either place a body of men with ropes followed on shore keeping pace with the boat's progress. In the meantime the men of each village and hamlet all along the shore of Buchan from Kirkton to Boddam began a systematic exploration of all the openings on the coast. Of course there were some places where no search could at present be made. The Bullers, for instance, was well justifying its name with the wild turmoil of waters that fretted and churned between its rocky walls, and the neighbourhood of the Twa Een was like a seething caldron. At Dunbuy, a great sheet of foam, perpetually renewed by the rush and recoil of the waves among the rocks, lay like a great white blanket over the inlet, and effectually hid any flotsam or jetsam that might have been driven thither. But on the high cliffs around these places, on every coign of vantage, sat women and children, who kept keen watch for aught that might develop. Every now and again a shrill cry would bring a rush to the place and eager eyes would follow the pointing hand of the watcher who had seen some floating matter; but in every case a few seconds and a little dispersing of the shrouding foam put an end to expectation.

Throughout that day the ardour of the searchers never abated. Morning had come rosy and smiling over the waste of heaving waters, and the sun rose and rose till its noonday rays beat down oppressively. But Willy Barrow never ceased from his lonely vigil on the cliff. At dinner-time a good-hearted woman brought him some food, and in kindly sympathy sat by him in silence, whilst he ate it. At first it seemed to him that to eat at all was some sort of wrong to Maggie, and he felt that to attempt it would choke him. But after a few mouthfuls the human need in him responded to the occasion, and he realised how much he wanted food. The kindly neighbour then tried to cheer him with a few words of hope, and a many words of Maggie's worth, and left him, if not cheered, at least sustained for what he had to endure.

All day long his glass ranged the sea in endless, ever-baffled hope. He saw the revenue boat strike away at first towards Girdleness, and then turn and go out to where Maggie had left the 'Sea Gull;' and then under full steam churn her way north-west through the fretted seas. Now and again he saw boats, far and near, pass on their way; and as they went through that wide belt of sea where Maggie's body might be drifting with the wreckage of her boat, his heart leaped and fell again under stress of hope and despair. The tide fell lower and ever lower, till the waves piling into the estuary roared among the rocks that paved the Watter's Mou'. Again and again he peered down from every rocky point in fear of seeing amid the turmoil—what, he feared to think. There was ever before his eyes the figure of the woman he loved, spread out rising and falling with the heaving waves, her long hair tossing wide and making an aureole round the upturned white face. Turn where he would, in sea or land, or in the white clouds of the summer sky, that image was ever before him, as though it had in some way burned into his iris.

Late in the afternoon, as he stood beside the crane, where he had met Maggie the night before, he saw Niel coming towards him, and instinctively moved from the place, for he felt that he would not like to meet on that spot, for ever to be hallowed in his mind, Maggie's brother with hatred in his heart. So he moved slowly to meet him, and when he had got close to the flagstaff waited till he should come up, and swept once again the wide horizon with his glass—in vain. Niel, too, had begun to slow his steps as he drew nearer. Slower and slower he came, and at last stood close to the man whom in the morning he had spoken to with hatred and murder in his heart.

All the morning Niel had worked with a restless, feverish activity, which was the wonder of all. He had not stayed with the searching party with whom he had set out; their exhaustive method was too slow for him, and he soon distanced them, and alone scoured the whole coast as far as Murdoch Head. Then in almost complete despair, for his mind was satisfied that Maggie's body had never reached that part of the shore, he had retraced his steps almost at a run, and, skirting the sands of Cruden Bay, on whose wide expanse the breakers still rolled heavily and roared loudly, he glanced among the jagged rocks that lay around Whinnyfold and stretched under the water away to the Scaurs. Then he came back again, and the sense of desolation complete upon him moved his passionate heart to sympathy and pity. It is when the soul within us feels the narrow environments of our selfishness that she really begins to spread her wings.

Niel walked over the sandhills along Cruden Bay like a man in a dream. With a sailor's habit he watched the sea, and now and again had his attention attracted by the drifting masses of seaweed torn from its rocky bed by the storm. In such tossing black masses he sometimes thought Maggie's body might lie, but his instinct of the sea was too true to be long deceived. And then he began to take himself to task. Hitherto he had been too blindly passionate to be able to think of anything but his own trouble; but now, despite what he could do, the woe-stricken face of Sailor Willy would rise before his inner eye like the embodiment or the wraith of a troubled conscience. When once this train of argument had been started, the remorseless logic which is the mechanism of the spirit of conscience went on its way unerringly. Well he knew it was the ill-doing of which he had a share, and not the duty that Willy owed, that took his sister out alone on the stormy sea. He knew from her own lips that Willy had neither sent her nor even knew of her going, and the habit of fair play which belonged to his life began to exert an influence. The first sign of his change of mind was the tear which welled up in his eye and rolled down his cheek. 'Poor Maggie! Poor Willy!' he murmured to himself, half unconsciously, 'A'll gang to him an' tak it a' back!' With this impulse on him he quickened his steps, and never paused till he saw Willy Barrow before him, spy-glass to eye, searching the sea for any sign of his lost love. Then his fears, and the awkwardness which a man feels at such a moment, no matter how poignant may be the grief which underlies it, began to trip him up. When he stood beside Willy Barrow, he said, with what bravery he could—

'I tak it a' back, Sailor Willy! Ye werena to blame! It was oor daein'! Will ye forgie me?' Willy turned and impulsively grasped the hand extended to him. In the midst of his overwhelming pain this was some little gleam of sunshine. He had himself just sufficient remorse to make the assurance of his innocence by another grateful. He knew well that if he had chosen to sacrifice his duty Maggie would never have gone out to sea, and though it did not even occur to him to repent of doing his duty, the mere temptation—the mere struggle against it, made a sort of foothold where flying remorse might for a moment rest. When the eyes of the two men met, Willy felt a new duty rise within his. He had always loved Niel, who was younger than himself, and was Maggie's brother, and he could not but see the look of anguish in the eyes that were so like Maggie's. He saw there something which in one way transcended his own pain, and made him glad that he had not on his soul the guilt of treachery to his duty. Not for the wide world would he have gazed into Maggie's eyes with such a look as that in his own. And yet—and yet—there came back to him with an overpowering flood of anguish the thought that, though the darkness had mercifully hidden it, Maggie's face, after she had tempted him, had had in it something of the same expression.

It is a part of the penalty of being human that we cannot forbid the coming of thoughts, but it is a glory of humanity that we can wrestle with them and overcome them. Quick on the harrowing memory of Maggie's shame came the thought of Maggie's heroic self-devotion: her true spirit had found a way out of shame and difficulty, and the tribute of the lieutenant, 'That's the lass for a sailor's wife!' seemed to ring in Willy's ears. As far as death was concerned, Willy Barrow did not fear it for himself, and how could he feel the fear for another. Such semblance of fear as had been in his distress was based on the selfishness which is a part of man's love, and in this wild hour of pain and distress became a thing of naught. All this reasoning, all this sequence of emotions, passed in a few seconds, and, as it seemed to him all at once, Willy Barrow broke out crying with the abandon which marks strong men when spiritual pain breaks down the barriers of their pride. Men of Willy's class seldom give way to their emotions. The prose of life is too continuous to allow of any habit of prolonged emotional indulgence; the pendulum swings back from fact to fact and things go on as before. So it was with Sailor Willy. His spasmodic grief was quick as well as fierce, like an April shower; and in a few seconds he had regained his calm. But the break, though but momentary, had relieved his pent-up feelings, and his heart beat more calmly for it. Then some of the love which he had for Maggie went out to her brother, and as he saw that the pain in his face did not lessen, a great pity overcame him and he tried to comfort Niel.

'Don't grieve, man. Don't grieve. I know well you'd give your heart's blood for Maggie'—he faltered as he spoke her name, but with a great gulp went on bravely: 'There's your father—her father, we must try and comfort him. Maggie,' here he lifted his cap reverently, 'is with God! We, you and I, and all, must so bear ourselves that she shall not have died in vain.' To Sailor Willy's tear-blurred eyes, as he looked upward, it seemed as if the great white gull which perched as he spoke on the yard of the flagstaff over his head was in some way an embodiment of the spirit of the lost girl, and, like the lightning phantasmagoria of a dream, there flitted across his mind many an old legend and eerie belief gained among the wolds and barrows of his Yorkshire home.[1]

There was not much more to be said between the men, for they understood each other, and men of their class are not prone to speak more than is required. They walked northwards, and for a long time they stood together on the edge of the cliff, now and again gazing seawards, and ever and anon to where below their feet and falling tide was fretting and churning amongst the boulders at the entrance of the Watter's Mou'.

Niel was unconsciously watching his companion's face and fol-

---

[1] Iona Opie and Moira Tatem locate superstitions regarding seagulls in the Scottish Highlands, one of which identifies them with the souls of the dead. *A Dictionary of Superstitions* (Oxford and New York: Oxford University Press, 1989), pp. 345-346. With thanks to Veronica O'Mara and Ian Blyth.

lowing his thoughts, and presently said, as though in answer to something that had gone before: 'Then ye think she'll drift in here, if onywhere?' Willy started as though he had been struck, for there seemed a positive brutality in the way of putting his own secret belief. He faced Niel quickly, but there was nothing in his face of any brutal thought. On the contrary, the lines of his face were so softened that all his likeness to his sister stood out so markedly as to make the heart of her lover ache with a fresh pang—a new sense, not of loss, but of what he had lost. Niel was surprised at the manner of his look, and his mind working back gave him the clue. All at once he broke out—

'O Willy mon, we'll never see her again! Never! never! till the sea gies up its dead;[1] what can we dae, mon? what can we dae? what can we dae?'

Again there was a new wrench to Sailor Willy's heart. Here were almost Maggie's very words of the night before, spoken in the same despairing tone, in the same spot, and by one who was not only her well-beloved brother, but who was, as he stood in this abandonment of his grief, almost her living image. However, he did not know what to say, and he could do nothing but only bear in stolid patient misery the woes that came upon him. He did all that could be done—nothing—but stood in silent sympathy and waited for the storm in the remorseful young man's soul to pass. After a few minutes Niel recovered somewhat, and, pulling himself together, said to Willy with what bravery he could—

'A'll gang look after father. A've left him ower lang as 't is!' The purpose of Maggie's death was beginning to bear fruit already.

He went across the field straight towards where his father's cottage stood under the brow of the slope towards the Water of Cruden. Sailor Willy watched him go with sadness, for anything that had been close to Maggie was dear to him, and Niel's presence had been in some degree an alleviation of his pain.

During the hours that followed he had one gleam of pleasure—something that moved him strangely in the midst of his pain. Early

---

[1] From *The Book of Common Prayer* which refers to resurrection of the body "when the sea shall give up her dead". See James Cornford, *The Book of Common Prayer, with Historical Notes* (London: Eyre and Spottiswoode, 1880), p. 311.

in the morning the news of Maggie's loss had been taken to the Castle, and all its household had turned out to aid vigorously in the search. In his talk with the lieutenant and his men, and from the frequent conversation of the villagers, the Earl had gathered pretty well the whole truth of what had occurred. Maggie had been a favourite with the ladies of the Castle, and it was as much on her account as his own that the Mastership of the Harbour had been settled prospectively on MacWhirter. That this arrangement was to be upset since the man had turned smuggler was taken for granted by all, and already rumour and surmise were busy in selecting a successor to the promise. The Earl listened but said nothing. Later on in the day, however, he strolled up the cliff where Willy paced on guard, and spoke with him. He had a sincere regard and liking for the fine young fellow, and when he saw his silent misery his heart went out to him. He tried to comfort him with hopes, but, finding that there was no response in Willy's mind, confined himself to praise of Maggie. Willy listened eagerly as he spoke of her devotion, her bravery, her noble spirit, that took her out on such a mission; and the words fell like drops of balm on the seared heart of her lover. But the bitterness of his loss was too much that he should be altogether patient, and he said presently—

'And all in vain! All in vain! she lost, and her father ruined, his character gone as well as all his means of livelihood—and all in vain! God might be juster than to let such a death as hers be in vain!'

'No, not in vain!' he answered solemnly, 'such a deed as hers is never wrought in vain. God sees and hears, and His hand is strong and sure. Many a man in Buchan for many a year to come will lead an honester life for what she has done; and many a woman will try to learn her lesson in patience and self-devotion. God does not in vain put such thoughts into the minds of His people, or into their hearts the noble bravery to carry them out.'

Sailor Willy groaned. 'Don't think me ungrateful, my lord,' he said, 'for your kind words—but I'm half wild with trouble, and my heart is sore. Maybe it is as you say—and yet—and yet the poor lass went out to save her father and here he is, ruined in means, in character, in prospects—for who will employ him now just when he most wants it. Everything is gone—and she gone too that could have helped and comforted him!'

As he spoke there shot through the mind of his comforter a thought followed by a purpose not unworthy of that ancestor, whose heroism and self-devotion won an earldom with an ox-yoke as its crest, and the circuit of a hawk's flight as its dower.[1] There was a new tone in the Earl's voice as he spoke—

'You mean about the harbour-mastership! Don't let that distress you, my poor lad. MacWhirter has lapsed a bit, but he has always borne an excellent character, and from all I hear he was sorely tempted. And, after all, he hasn't done—at least completed—any offence. Ah!' and here he spoke solemnly, 'poor Maggie's warning did come in time. Her work was not in vain, though God help us all! she and those that loved her paid a heavy price for it. But even if MacWhirter had committed the offence, and it lay in my power, I should try to prove that her noble devotion was not without its purpose—or its reward. It is true that I might not altogether trust MacWhirter until, at least, such time as by good service he had re-established his character. But I would and shall trust the father of Maggie MacWhirter, that gave her life for him; and well I know that there isn't an honest man or woman in Buchan that won't say the same. He shall be the harbour-master if he will. We shall find in time that he has reared again the love and respect of all men. That will be Maggie's monument; and a noble one too in the eyes of God and of men!'

He grasped Willy's hand in his own strong one, and the hearts of both men, the gentle and the simple, went out each to the other, and became bound together as men's hearts do when touched with flame of any kind.

When he was alone Willy felt somehow more easy in his

---

[1] James II of Scotland conferred the Earldom on Sir William Hay in 1452. He was descended from William de la Haya, principal butler to the court of King Malcolm IV. Hay had assisted in the defeat of the Danes in 980 under the reign of Kenneth III. The Danes had ravaged the Aberdeenshire coast to Perth. According to tradition the Scots fled until they encountered a farmer and his two sons armed with the yokes of their ploughs. They rallied the army and the Scots turned on the Danes and defeated them. The king awarded the farmer with as much land as a falcon could fly over, raised him to the ranks of nobility and assigned him armorial bearings to commemorate his service. Willliam Anderson, *The Scottish Nation* (Edinburgh: Fullarton, 1862), p. 141.

mind—the bitterest spirit of all his woe—the futility of Maggie's sacrifice—was gone, exorcised by the hopeful words and kind act of the Earl, and the resilience of his manhood began to act.

And now there came another distraction to his thoughts—an ominous weather change. It had grown colder as the day went on, but now the heat began to be oppressive, and there was a deadly stillness in the air; it was manifest that another storm was at hand. The sacrifice of the night had not fully appeased the storm-gods. Somewhere up in that Northern Unknown, where the Fates weave their web of destiny, a tempest was brewing which would soon boil over. Darker and darker grew the sky, and more still and silent and oppressive grew the air, till the cry of a sea-bird or the beating of the waves upon the rocks came as distinct and separate things, as though having no counterpart in the active world. Towards sunset the very electricity in the air made all animate nature so nervous that men and women could not sit quiet, but moved restlessly. Susceptible women longed to scream out and vent their feelings, as did the cattle in the meadows with their clamorous lowing, or the birds wheeling restlessly aloft with articulate cries. Willy Barrow stuck steadfastly to his post. He had some feeling—some presentiment, that there would soon be a happening—what, he knew not; but, as all his thoughts were of Maggie, it must surely be of her. It might have been that the thunderous disturbance wrought on a system overtaxed almost beyond human endurance, for it was two whole nights since he had slept. Or it may have been that the recoil from despair was acting on his strong nature in the way that drives men at times to desperate deeds, when they rush into the thick of battle, and, fighting, die. Or it may simply have been that the seaman in him spoke through all the ways and offices of instinct and habit, and that with the foreknowledge of coming stress woke the power that was to combat with it. For great natures of the fighting kind move with their surroundings, and the spirit of the sailor grew with the storm pressure whose might he should have to brave.

Down came the storm in one wild, frenzied burst. All at once the waters seemed to rise, throwing great sheets of foam from the summit of the lifting waves. The wind whistled high and low, and screamed as it swept through the rigging of the flagstaff. Flashes of lightning and rolling thunderclaps seemed to come together, so swift their succession. The rain fell in torrents, so that within a few moments the whole earth seemed one filmy sheet, shining in the lightning flashes that rent the black clouds, and burn and rill and runlet roared with rushing water. All through the hamlet men and women, even the hardiest, fled to shelter—all save the one who paced the rocks above the Watter's Mou', peering as he had done for many an hour down into the depths below him in the pauses of his seaward glance. Something seemed to tell him that Maggie was coming closer to him. He could feel her presence in the air and the sea; and the memory of that long, passionate kiss, which had made her his, came back, not as a vivid recollection, but as something of the living present. To and fro he paced between the flagstaff and the edge of the rocks; but each turn he kept further and further from the flagstaff, as though some fatal fascination was holding him to the Watter's Mou'. He saw the great waves come into the cove tumbling and roaring; dipping deep under the lee of the Ship's Starn in wide patches of black, which in the dark silence of their onward sweep stood out in strong contrast to the white turmoil of the churning waters under his feet. Every now and again a wave greater than all its fellows—what fishermen call the 'sailor's wave'—would ride in with all the majesty of resistless power, shutting out for a moment the jagged whiteness of the submerged rocks, and sweeping up the cove as though the bringer of some royal message from the sea.

As one of these great waves rushed in, Willy's heart beat loudly, and for a second he looked around as though for some voice, from whence he knew not, which was calling to him. Then he looked down and saw, far below him, tossed high upon the summit of the wave, a mass that in the gloom of the evening and the storm looked like a tangle of wreckage—spar and sail and rope—twirling in the rushing water round a dead woman, whose white face was set in an aureole of floating hair.

Without a word, but with the bound of a panther, Willy Barrow sprang out on the projecting point of rock, and plunged down into the rushing wave whence he could meet that precious wreckage and grasp it tight.

. . . .

Down in the village the men were talking in groups as the chance of the storm had driven them to shelter. In the rocket-house opposite the Salmon Fisher's store had gathered a big cluster, and they were talking eagerly of all that had gone by. Presently one of them said—

'Men, oughtn't some o' us to gang abeen[1] the rocks and bide a wee wi' Sailor Willy? The puir lad is nigh daft wi' his loss, an a wee bit companionship wouldna be bad for him.' To which a sturdy youth answered as he stepped out—

'A'll go bide wi' him. It must be main lonely for him in the guard-house the nicht. An' when he's relieved, as A hear he is to be, by Michael Watson ower frae Whinnyfold, A'll gang wi' him or tak him hame wi' me. Mither'll[2] be recht glad to thole[3] for him!' and drawing his oilskin closer round his neck he went out in the storm. As he walked up the path to the cliff the storm seemed to fade away—the clouds broke, and through the wet mist came gleams of fading twilight; and when he looked eastwards from the cliff the angry sea was all that was of storm, for in the sky was every promise of fine weather to come. He went straight to the guard-house and tried to open the door, but it was locked; then he went to the side and looked in. There was just sufficient light to see that the place was empty. So he went along the cliff looking for Willy. It was now light enough to see all round, for the blackness of the sky overhead had passed, the heavy clouds being swept away by the driving wind; but nowhere could he see any trace of the man he sought. He went all along the cliff up the Watter's Mou', till, following the downward trend of the rock, and plashing a way through the marsh—now like a quagmire, so saturated was it with the heavy rainfall—he came to the shallows opposite the Barley Mill. Here he met a man from The Bullers, who had come along by the Castle, and him he asked if he had seen Willy Barrow on his way. The decidedly negative answer 'A've seen nane. It's nae a night for ony to be oot that can bide wi'in!' made him think that

---

[1] To go above (Scots).
[2] Mother (Scots).
[3] Suffer or endure (Scots).

all might not be well with Sailor Willy, and so he went back again on his search, peering into every hole and cranny as he went. At the flagstaff he met some of his companions, who, since the storm had passed, had come to look for weather signs and to see what the sudden tempest might have brought about. When they heard that there was no sign of the coastguard they separated, searching for him, and shouting lest he might have fallen anywhere and could hear their voices.

All that night they searched, for each minute made it more apparent that all was not well with him; but they found no sign. The waves still beat into the Watter's Mou' with violence, for though the storm had passed the sea was a wide-stretching mass of angry waters, and curling white crowned every wave. But with the outgoing tide the rocky bed of the cove broke up the waves, and they roared sullenly as they washed up the estuary.

In the grey of the morning a fisher-boy rushed up to a knot of men who were clustered round the guard-house and called to them—

'There's somethin' wollopin' aboot i' the shallows be the Barley Mill! Come an' get it oot! It looks like some ane!' So there was a rush made to the place. When they got to the islands of sea-grass the ebbing tide had done its work, and stranded the 'something' which had rolled amid the shallows.

There, on the very spot whence the boat had set sail on its warning errand, lay its wreckage, and tangled in it the body of the noble girl who had steered it—her brown hair floating wide and twined round the neck of Sailor Willy, who held her tight in his dead arms.

The requiem of the twain was the roar of the breaking waves and the screams of the white birds that circled round the Watter's Mou'.

Appendix A: Arthur Conan Doyle, "John Barrington Cowles"[1]

It might seem rash of me to say that I ascribe the death of my poor friend, John Barrington Cowles, to any preternatural agency. I am aware that in the present state of public feeling a chain of evidence would require to be strong indeed before the possibility of such a conclusion could be admitted.

I shall therefore merely state the circumstances which led up to this sad event as concisely and as plainly as I can, and leave every reader to draw his own deductions. Perhaps there may be some one who can throw light upon what is dark to me.

I first met Barrington Cowles when I went up to Edinburgh University to take out medical classes there. My landlady in Northumberland Street had a large house, and, being a widow without children, she gained a livelihood by providing accommodation for several students.

Barrington Cowles happened to have taken a bedroom upon the same floor as mine, and when we came to know each other better we shared a small sitting-room, in which we took our meals. In this manner we originated a friendship which was unmarred by the slightest disagreement up to the day of his death.

Cowles' father was the colonel of a Sikh regiment and had remained in India for many years. He allowed his son a handsome income, but seldom gave any other sign of parental affection—writing irregularly and briefly.

My friend, who had himself been born in India, and whose whole disposition was an ardent tropical one, was much hurt by this neglect. His mother was dead, and he had no other relation in the world to supply the blank.

Thus he came in time to concentrate all his affection upon me, and to confide in me in a manner which is rare among men. Even when a stronger and deeper passion came upon him, it never infringed upon the old tenderness between us.

Cowles was a tall, slim young fellow, with an olive, Velasquez-

---

[1] Doyle's story was first published in *Cassell's Saturday Journal* in April 1884 as "John Barrington Cowles: The Story of a Medical Student".

like[1] face, and dark, tender eyes. I have seldom seen a man who was more likely to excite a woman's interest, or to captivate her imagination. His expression was, as a rule, dreamy, and even languid; but if in conversation a subject arose which interested him he would be all animation in a moment. On such occasions his colour would heighten, his eyes gleam, and he could speak with an eloquence which would carry his audience with him.

In spite of these natural advantages he led a solitary life, avoiding female society, and reading with great diligence. He was one of the foremost men of his year, taking the senior medal for anatomy, and the Neil Arnott prize for physics.

How well I can recollect the first time we met her! Often and often I have recalled the circumstances, and tried to remember what the exact impression was which she produced on my mind at the time. After we came to know her my judgment was warped, so that I am curious to recollect what my unbiassed instincts were. It is hard, however, to eliminate the feelings which reason or prejudice afterwards raised in me.

It was at the opening of the Royal Scottish Academy in the spring of 1879. My poor friend was passionately attached to art in every form, and a pleasing chord in music or a delicate effect upon canvas would give exquisite pleasure to his highly-strung nature. We had gone together to see the pictures, and were standing in the grand central *salon*, when I noticed an extremely beautiful woman standing at the other side of the room. In my whole life I have never seen such a classically perfect countenance. It was the real Greek type—the forehead broad, very low, and as white as marble, with a cloudlet of delicate locks wreathing round it, the nose straight and clean cut, the lips inclined to thinness, the chin and lower jaw beautifully rounded off, and yet sufficiently developed to promise unusual strength of character.

But those eyes—those wonderful eyes! If I could but give some faint idea of their varying moods, their steely hardness, their feminine softness, their power of command, their penetrating intensity suddenly melting away into an expression of womanly weakness—but I am speaking now of future impressions!

---

[1] Diego Velasquez (1599-1660) was a leading Spanish painter and portraitist.

There was a tall, yellow-haired young man with this lady, whom I at once recognised as a law student with whom I had a slight acquaintance.

Archibald Reeves—for that was his name—was a dashing, handsome young fellow, and had at one time been a ringleader in every university escapade; but of late I had seen little of him, and the report was that he was engaged to be married. His companion was, then, I presumed, his *fiancée*. I seated myself upon the velvet settee in the centre of the room, and furtively watched the couple from behind my catalogue.

The more I looked at her the more her beauty grew upon me. She was somewhat short in stature, it is true; but her figure was perfection, and she bore herself in such a fashion that it was only by actual comparison that one would have known her to be under the medium height.

As I kept my eyes upon them, Reeves was called away for some reason, and the young lady was left alone. Turning her back to the pictures, she passed the time until the return of her escort in taking a deliberate survey of the company, without paying the least heed to the fact that a dozen pair of eyes, attracted by her elegance and beauty, were bent curiously upon her. With one of her hands holding the red silk cord which railed off the pictures, she stood languidly moving her eyes from face to face with as little self-consciousness as if she were looking at the canvas creatures behind her. Suddenly, as I watched her, I saw her gaze become fixed, and, as it were, intense. I followed the direction of her looks, wondering what could have attracted her so strongly.

John Barrington Cowles was standing before a picture—one, I think, by Noel Paton[1]—I know that the subject was a noble and ethereal one. His profile was turned towards us, and never have I seen him to such advantage. I have said that he was a strikingly handsome man, but at that moment he looked absolutely magnificent. It was evident that he had momentarily forgotten his surroundings, and that his whole soul was in sympathy with the picture before him. His eyes sparkled, and a dusky pink shone

---

[1] Noel Paton (1821-1901) was a Scottish painter noted for his fairy paintings and illustrations.

through his clear olive cheeks. She continued to watch him fixedly, with a look of interest upon her face, until he came out of his reverie with a start, and turned abruptly round, so that his gaze met hers. She glanced away at once, but his eyes remained fixed upon her for some moments. The picture was forgotten already, and his soul had come down to earth once more.

We caught sight of her once or twice before we left, and each time I noticed my friend look after her. He made no remark, however, until we got out into the open air, and were walking arm-in-arm along Princes Street.

"Did you notice that beautiful woman, in the dark dress, with the white fur?" he asked.

"Yes, I saw her," I answered.

"Do you know her?" he asked eagerly. "Have you any idea who she is?"

"I don't know her personally," I replied. "But I have no doubt I could find out all about her, for I believe she is engaged to young Archie Reeves, and he and I have a lot of mutual friends."

"Engaged!" ejaculated Cowles.

"Why, my dear boy," I said, laughing, "you don't mean to say you are so susceptible that the fact that a girl to whom you never spoke in your life is engaged is enough to upset you?"

"Well, not exactly to upset me," he answered, forcing a laugh. "But I don't mind telling you, Armitage, that I never was so taken by any one in my life. It wasn't the mere beauty of the face— though that was perfect enough—but it was the character and the intellect upon it. I hope, if she is engaged, that it is to some man who will be worthy of her."

"Why," I remarked, "you speak quite feelingly. It is a clear case of love at first sight, Jack. However, to put your perturbed spirit at rest, I'll make a point of finding out all about her whenever I meet any fellow who is likely to know."

Barrington Cowles thanked me, and the conversation drifted off into other channels. For several days neither of us made any allusion to the subject, though my companion was perhaps a little more dreamy and distraught than usual. The incident had almost vanished from my remembrance, when one day young Brodie, who is a second cousin of mine, came up to me on the university steps with the face of a bearer of tidings.

"I say," he began, "you know Reeves, don't you?"

"Yes. What of him?"

"His engagement is off."

"Off!" I cried. "Why, I only learned the other day that it was on."

"Oh, yes—it's all off. His brother told me so. Deucedly mean of Reeves, you know, if he has backed out of it, for she was an uncommonly nice girl."

"I've seen her," I said; "but I don't know her name."

"She is a Miss Northcott, and lives with an old aunt of hers in Abercrombie Place.[1] Nobody knows anything about her people, or where she comes from. Anyhow, she is about the most unlucky girl in the world, poor soul!"

"Why unlucky?"

"Well, you know, this was her second engagement," said young Brodie, who had a marvellous knack of knowing everything about everybody. "She was engaged to Prescott—William Prescott, who died. That was a very sad affair. The wedding day was fixed, and the whole thing looked as straight as a die when the smash came."

"What smash?" I asked, with some dim recollection of the circumstances.

"Why, Prescott's death. He came to Abercrombie Place one night, and stayed very late. No one knows exactly when he left, but about one in the morning a fellow who knew him met him walking rapidly in the direction of the Queen's Park. He bade him good night, but Prescott hurried on without heeding him, and that was the last time he was ever seen alive. Three days afterwards his body was found floating in St. Margaret's Loch, under St. Anthony's Chapel.[2] No one could ever understand it, but of course the verdict brought it in as temporary insanity."

"It was very strange," I remarked.

"Yes, and deucedly rough on the poor girl," said Brodie. "Now

---

[1] A wealthy area of Victorian Edinburgh.

[2] St. Margaret's Loch is a man-made loch lying beneath the ruins of the fifteenth-century chapel.

that this other blow has come it will quite crush her. So gentle and ladylike she is too!"

"You know her personally, then!" I asked.

"Oh, yes, I know her. I have met her several times. I could easily manage that you should be introduced to her."

"Well," I answered, "it's not so much for my own sake as for a friend of mine. However, I don't suppose she will go out much for some little time after this. When she does I will take advantage of your offer."

We shook hands on this, and I thought no more of the matter for some time.

The next incident which I have to relate as bearing at all upon the question of Miss Northcott is an unpleasant one. Yet I must detail it as accurately as possible, since it may throw some light upon the sequel. One cold night, several months after the conversation with my second cousin which I have quoted above, I was walking down one of the lowest streets in the city on my way back from a case which I had been attending. It was very late, and I was picking my way among the dirty loungers who were clustering round the doors of a great gin-palace,[1] when a man staggered out from among them, and held out his hand to me with a drunken leer. The gaslight fell full upon his face, and, to my intense astonishment, I recognised in the degraded creature before me my former acquaintance, young Archibald Reeves, who had once been famous as one of the most dressy and particular men in the whole college. I was so utterly surprised that for a moment I almost doubted the evidence of my own senses; but there was no mistaking those features, which, though bloated with drink, still retained some of their former comeliness. I was determined to rescue him, for one night at least, from the company into which he had fallen.

"Holloa, Reeves!" I said. "Come along with me. I'm going in your direction."

He muttered some incoherent apology for his condition, and took my arm. As I supported him towards his lodgings I could see that he was not only suffering from the effects of a recent debauch,

---

[1] A public house with elaborate decorations dating from the 1830s in Britain. The consumption of gin was associated with degradation.

but that a long course of intemperance had affected his nerves and his brain. His hand when I touched it was dry and feverish, and he started from every shadow which fell upon the pavement. He rambled in his speech, too, in a manner which suggested the delirium of disease rather than the talk of a drunkard.

When I got him to his lodgings I partially undressed him and laid him upon his bed. His pulse at this time was very high, and he was evidently extremely feverish. He seemed to have sunk into a doze; and I was about to steal out of the room to warn his landlady of his condition, when he started up and caught me by the sleeve of my coat.

"Don't go!" he cried. "I feel better when you are here. I am safe from her then."

"From her!" I said. "From whom?"

"Her! her!" he answered peevishly. "Ah! you don't know her. She is the devil! Beautiful—beautiful; but the devil!"

"You are feverish and excited," I said. "Try and get a little sleep. You will wake better."

"Sleep!" he groaned. "How am I to sleep when I see her sitting down yonder at the foot of the bed with her great eyes watching and watching hour after hour? I tell you it saps all the strength and manhood out of me. That's what makes me drink. God help me—I'm half drunk now!"

"You are very ill," I said, putting some vinegar to his temples; "and you are delirious. You don't know what you say."

"Yes, I do," he interrupted sharply, looking up at me. "I know very well what I say. I brought it upon myself. It is my own choice. But I couldn't—no, by heaven, I couldn't—accept the alternative. I couldn't keep my faith to her. It was more than man could do."

I sat by the side of the bed, holding one of his burning hands in mine, and wondering over his strange words. He lay still for some time, and then, raising his eyes to me, said in a most plaintive voice:

"Why did she not give me warning sooner? Why did she wait until I had learned to love her so?"

He repeated this question several times, rolling his feverish head from side to side, and then he dropped into a troubled sleep. I crept out of the room, and, having seen that he would be properly cared for, left the house. His words, however, rang in my ears for days afterwards, and assumed a deeper significance when taken with what was to come.

My friend, Barrington Cowles, had been away for his summer holidays, and I had heard nothing of him for several months. When the winter session came on, however, I received a telegram from him, asking me to secure the old rooms in Northumberland Street for him, and telling me the train by which he would arrive. I went down to meet him, and was delighted to find him looking wonderfully hearty and well.

"By the way," he said suddenly, that night, as we sat in our chairs by the fire, talking over the events of the holidays, "you have never congratulated me yet!"

"On what, my boy?" I asked.

"What! Do you mean to say you have not heard of my engagement?"

"Engagement! No!" I answered. "However, I am delighted to hear it, and congratulate you with all my heart."

"I wonder it didn't come to your ears," he said. "It was the queerest thing. You remember that girl whom we both admired so much at the Academy?"

"What!" I cried, with a vague feeling of apprehension at my heart. "You don't mean to say that you are engaged to her?"

"I thought you would be surprised," he answered. "When I was staying with an old aunt of mine in Peterhead, in Aberdeenshire, the Northcotts happened to come there on a visit, and as we had mutual friends we soon met. I found out that it was a false alarm about her being engaged, and then—well, you know what it is when you are thrown into the society of such a girl in a place like Peterhead. Not, mind you," he added, "that I consider I did a foolish or hasty thing. I have never regretted it for a moment. The more I know Kate the more I admire her and love her. However, you must be introduced to her, and then you will form your own opinion."

I expressed my pleasure at the prospect, and endeavoured to speak as lightly as I could to Cowles upon the subject, but I felt depressed and anxious at heart. The words of Reeves and the unhappy fate of young Prescott recurred to my recollection, and though I could assign no tangible reason for it, a vague, dim fear and distrust of the woman took possession of me. It may be that this was foolish prejudice and superstition upon my part, and that I involuntarily contorted her future doings and sayings to fit into some half-formed wild theory of my own. This has been suggested to me by others as an explanation of my narrative. They are welcome to their opinion if they can reconcile it with the facts which I have to tell.

I went round with my friend a few days afterwards to call upon Miss Northcott. I remember that, as we went down Abercrombie Place, our attention was attracted by the shrill yelping of a dog—which noise proved eventually to come from the house to which we were bound. We were shown upstairs, where I was introduced to old Mrs. Merton, Miss Northcott's aunt, and to the young lady herself. She looked as beautiful as ever, and I could not wonder at my friend's infatuation. Her face was a little more flushed than usual, and she held in her hand a heavy dog-whip, with which she had been chastising a small Scotch terrier, whose cries we had heard in the street. The poor brute was cringing up against the wall, whining piteously, and evidently completely cowed.

"So Kate," said my friend, after we had taken our seats, "you have been falling out with Carlo again."

"Only a very little quarrel this time," she said, smiling charmingly. "He is a dear, good old fellow, but he needs correction now and then." Then, turning to me, "We all do that, Mr. Armitage, don't we? What a capital thing if, instead of receiving a collective punishment at the end of our lives, we were to have one at once, as the dogs do, when we did anything wicked. It would make us more careful, wouldn't it?"

I acknowledged that it would.

"Supposing that every time a man misbehaved himself a gigantic hand were to seize him, and he were lashed with a whip until he fainted"—she clenched her white fingers as she spoke, and cut out viciously with the dog-whip—"it would do more to keep him good than any number of high-minded theories of morality."

"Why, Kate," said my friend, "you are quite savage to-day."

"No, Jack," she laughed. "I'm only propounding a theory for Mr. Armitage's consideration."

The two began to chat together about some Aberdeenshire reminiscence, and I had time to observe Mrs. Merton, who had remained silent during our short conversation. She was a very strange-looking old lady. What attracted attention most in her appearance was the utter want of colour which she exhibited. Her hair was snow-white, and her face extremely pale. Her lips were bloodless, and even her eyes were of such a light tinge of blue that they hardly relieved the general pallor. Her dress was a grey silk, which harmonised with her general appearance. She had a peculiar expression of countenance, which I was unable at the moment to refer to its proper cause.

She was working at some old-fashioned piece of ornamental needlework, and as she moved her arms her dress gave forth a dry, melancholy rustling, like the sound of leaves in the autumn. There was something mournful and depressing in the sight of her. I moved my chair a little nearer, and asked her how she liked Edinburgh, and whether she had been there long.

When I spoke to her she started and looked up at me with a scared look on her face. Then I saw in a moment what the expression was which I had observed there. It was one of fear—intense and overpowering fear. It was so marked that I could have staked my life on the woman before me having at some period of her life been subjected to some terrible experience or dreadful misfortune.

"Oh, yes, I like it," she said, in a soft, timid voice; "and we have been here long—that is, not very long. We move about a great deal." She spoke with hesitation, as if afraid of committing herself.

"You are a native of Scotland, I presume?" I said.

"No—that is, not entirely. We are not natives of any place. We are cosmopolitan, you know." She glanced round in the direction of Miss Northcott as she spoke, but the two were still chatting together near the window. Then she suddenly bent forward to me, with a look of intense earnestness upon her face, and said—

"Don't talk to me any more, please. She does not like it, and I shall suffer for it afterwards. Please, don't do it."

I was about to ask her the reason for this strange request, but when she saw I was going to address her, she rose and walked slowly out of the room. As she did so I perceived that the lovers had ceased to talk, and that Miss Northcott was looking at me with her keen, grey eyes.

"You must excuse my aunt, Mr. Armitage," she said; "she is old, and easily fatigued. Come over and look at my album."

We spent some time examining the portraits. Miss Northcott's father and mother were apparently ordinary mortals enough, and I could not detect in either of them any traces of the character which showed itself in their daughter's face. There was one old daguerreotype, however, which arrested my attention. It represented a man of about the age of forty, and strikingly handsome. He was clean shaven, and extraordinary power was expressed upon his prominent lower jaw and firm, straight mouth. His eyes were somewhat deeply set in his head, however, and there was a snake-like flattening at the upper part of his forehead, which detracted from his appearance. I almost involuntarily, when I saw the head, pointed to it, and exclaimed—

"There is your prototype in your family, Miss Northcott."

"Do you think so?" she said. "I am afraid you are paying me a very bad compliment. Uncle Anthony was always considered the black sheep of the family."

"Indeed," I answered; "my remark was an unfortunate one, then."

"Oh, don't mind that," she said; "I always thought myself that he was worth all of them put together. He was an officer in the Forty-first Regiment, and he was killed in action during the Persian War[1]—so he died nobly, at any rate."

"That's the sort of death I should like to die," said Cowles, his dark eyes flashing, as they would when he was excited; "I often wish I had taken to my father's profession instead of this vile pill-compounding drudgery."

"Come, Jack, you are not going to die any sort of death yet," she said, tenderly taking his hand in hers.

I could not understand the woman. There was such an extraordinary mixture of masculine decision and womanly tenderness about her, with the consciousness of something all her own in

---

[1] This occurred at the end of the Crimean War in 1856 after the shah seized a disputed area of Afghanistan.

the background, that she fairly puzzled me. I hardly knew, therefore, how to answer Cowles when, as we walked down the street together, he asked the comprehensive question—

"Well, what do you think of her?"

"I think she is wonderfully beautiful," I answered guardedly.

"That, of course," he replied irritably. "You knew that before you came!"

"I think she is very clever too," I remarked.

Barrington Cowles walked on for some time, and then he suddenly turned on me with the strange question—

"Do you think she is cruel? Do you think she is the sort of girl who would take a pleasure in inflicting pain?"

"Well, really," I answered, "I have hardly had time to form an opinion."

We then walked on for some time in silence.

"She is an old fool," at length muttered Cowles. "She is mad."

"Who is?" I asked.

"Why, that old woman—that aunt of Kate's—Mrs. Merton, or whatever her name is."

Then I knew that my poor colourless friend had been speaking to Cowles, but he never said anything more as to the nature of her communication.

My companion went to bed early that night, and I sat up a long time by the fire, thinking over all that I had seen and heard. I felt that there was some mystery about the girl—some dark fatality so strange as to defy conjecture. I thought of Prescott's interview with her before their marriage, and the fatal termination of it. I coupled it with poor drunken Reeves' plaintive cry, "Why did she not tell me sooner?" and with the other words he had spoken. Then my mind ran over Mrs. Merton's warning to me, Cowles' reference to her, and even the episode of the whip and the cringing dog.

The whole effect of my recollections was unpleasant to a degree, and yet there was no tangible charge which I could bring against the woman. It would be worse than useless to attempt to warn my friend until I had definitely made up my mind what I was to warn him against. He would treat any charge against her with scorn. What could I do? How could I get at some tangible conclusion as to her character and antecedents? No one in Edinburgh knew them except as recent acquaintances. She was an orphan, and as far as I knew she had never disclosed where her former home had been. Suddenly an idea struck me. Among my father's friends there was a Colonel Joyce, who had served a long time in India upon the staff, and who would be likely to know most of the officers who had been out there since the Mutiny. I sat down at once, and, having trimmed the lamp, proceeded to write a letter to the Colonel. I told him that I was very curious to gain some particulars about a certain Captain Northcott, who had served in the Forty-first Foot, and who had fallen in the Persian War. I described the man as well as I could from my recollection of the daguerreotype, and then, having directed the letter, posted it that very night, after which, feeling that I had done all that could be done, I retired to bed, with a mind too anxious to allow me to sleep.

PART II.

I GOT an answer from Leicester, where the Colonel resided, within two days. I have it before me as I write, and copy it verbatim.

"DEAR BOB," it said, "I remember the man well. I was with him at Calcutta, and afterwards at Hyderabad. He was a curious, solitary sort of mortal; but a gallant soldier enough, for he distinguished himself at Sobraon,[1] and was wounded, if I remember right. He was not popular in his corps—they said he was a pitiless, cold-blooded fellow, with no geniality in him. There was a rumour, too, that he was a devil-worshipper, or something of that sort, and also that he had the evil eye,[2] which, of course, was all nonsense. He had some strange theories, I remember, about the power of the human will and the effects of mind upon matter.

---

[1] The refers to the Battle of Sobraon (1846) in which the British defeated the Sikhs.
[2] The notion that an evil glance can cause injury or death exists in many cultures and is quite prevalent in Celtic folklore. Lady Wilde describes the evil eye as generating a "poisonous atmosphere which chills and blights everything within its reach" and renders individuals "utterly paralyzed". *Ancient Legends, Mystic Charms and Superstitions of Ireland*, vol. 1 (London: Ward and Downey, 1887), p. 43.

"How are you getting on with your medical studies? Never forget, my boy, that your father's son has every claim upon me, and that if I can serve you in any way I am always at your command.—Ever affectionately yours, EDWARD JOYCE.

"P.S.—By the way, Northcott did not fall in action. He was killed after peace was declared in a crazy attempt to get some of the eternal fire from the sun-worshippers' temple. There was considerable mystery about his death."

I read this epistle over several times—at first with a feeling of satisfaction, and then with one of disappointment. I had come on some curious information, and yet hardly what I wanted. He was an eccentric man, a devil-worshipper, and rumoured to have the power of the evil eye. I could believe the young lady's eyes, when endowed with that cold, grey shimmer which I had noticed in them once or twice, to be capable of any evil which human eye ever wrought; but still the superstition was an effete one. Was there not more meaning in that sentence which followed—"He had theories of the power of the human will and of the effect of mind upon matter"? I remember having once read a quaint treatise, which I had imagined to be mere charlatanism at the time, of the power of certain human minds, and of effects produced by them at a distance. Was Miss Northcott endowed with some exceptional power of the sort? The idea grew upon me, and very shortly I had evidence which convinced me of the truth of the supposition.

It happened that at the very time when my mind was dwelling upon this subject, I saw a notice in the paper that our town was to be visited by Dr. Messinger, the well-known medium and mesmerist. Messinger was a man whose performance, such as it was, had been again and again pronounced to be genuine by competent judges. He was far above trickery, and had the reputation of being the soundest living authority upon the strange pseudo-sciences of animal magnetism[1] and electro-biology.[2] Determined, therefore, to

---

[1] More frequently termed mesmerism.
[2] A practice introduced into Britain from America in 1850. "A coin made up of a core of copper, surrounded by zinc, would produce an electric circuit through the air that would suspend an individual's will while leaving him

see what the human will could do, even against all the disadvantages of glaring footlights and a public platform, I took a ticket for the first night of the performance, and went with several student friends.

We had secured one of the side boxes, and did not arrive until after the performance had begun. I had hardly taken my seat before I recognised Barrington Cowles, with his *fiancée* and old Mrs. Merton, sitting in the third or fourth row of the stalls. They caught sight of me at almost the same moment, and we bowed to each other. The first portion of the lecture was somewhat commonplace, the lecturer giving tricks of pure legerdemain,[1] with one or two manifestations of mesmerism, performed upon a subject whom he had brought with him. He gave us an exhibition of clairvoyance too, throwing his subject into a trance, and then demanding particulars as to the movements of absent friends, and the whereabouts of hidden objects, all of which appeared to be answered satisfactorily. I had seen all this before, however. What I wanted to see now was the effect of the lecturer's will when exerted upon some independent member of the audience.

He came round to that as the concluding exhibition in his performance. "I have shown you," he said, "that a mesmerised subject is entirely dominated by the will of the mesmeriser. He loses all power of volition, and his very thoughts are such as are suggested to him by the master-mind. The same end may be attained without any preliminary process. A strong will can, simply by virtue of its strength, take possession of a weaker one, even at a distance, and can regulate the impulses and the actions of the owner of it. If there was one man in the world who had a very much more highly-developed will than any of the rest of the human family, there is no reason why he should not be able to rule over them all, and to reduce his fellow-creatures to the condition of automatons. Happily there is such a dead level of mental power, or rather of mental weakness, among us that such a catastrophe is not likely to occur; but still within our small compass there are variations which pro-

---

or her conscious and fully cognizant of all that transpired." Alison Winter, *Mesmerized: Powers of Mind in Victorian Britain* (Chicago and London: University of Chicago Press, 1998), p. 281.

[1] Sleight of hand; trickery.

duce surprising effects. I shall now single out one of the audience, and endeavour 'by the mere power of will' to compel him to come upon the platform, and do and say what I wish. Let me assure you that there is no collusion, and that the subject whom I may select is at perfect liberty to resent to the uttermost any impulse which I may communicate to him."

With these words the lecturer came to the front of the platform, and glanced over the first few rows of the stalls. No doubt Cowles' dark skin and bright eyes marked him out as a man of a highly nervous temperament, for the mesmerist picked him out in a moment, and fixed his eyes upon him. I saw my friend give a start of surprise, and then settle down in his chair, as if to express his determination not to yield to the influence of the operator. Messinger was not a man whose head denoted any great brainpower, but his gaze was singularly intense and penetrating. Under the influence of it Cowles made one or two spasmodic motions of his hands, as if to grasp the sides of his seat, and then half rose, but only to sink down again, though with an evident effort. I was watching the scene with intense interest, when I happened to catch a glimpse of Miss Northcott's face. She was sitting with her eyes fixed intently upon the mesmerist, and with such an expression of concentrated power upon her features as I have never seen on any other human countenance. Her jaw was firmly set, her lips compressed, and her face as hard as if it were a beautiful sculpture cut out of the whitest marble. Her eyebrows were drawn down, however, and from beneath them her grey eyes seemed to sparkle and gleam with a cold light.

I looked at Cowles again, expecting every moment to see him rise and obey the mesmerist's wishes, when there came from the platform a short, gasping cry as of a man utterly worn out and prostrated by a prolonged struggle. Messinger was leaning against the table, his hand to his forehead, and the perspiration pouring down his face. "I won't go on," he cried, addressing the audience. "There is a stronger will than mine acting against me. You must excuse me for to-night." The man was evidently ill, and utterly unable to proceed, so the curtain was lowered, and the audience dispersed, with many comments upon the lecturer's sudden indisposition.

I waited outside the hall until my friend and the ladies came out. Cowles was laughing over his recent experience.

"He didn't succeed with me, Bob," he cried triumphantly, as he shook my hand. "I think he caught a Tartar[1] that time."

"Yes," said Miss Northcott, "I think that Jack ought to be very proud of his strength of mind; don't you, Mr. Armitage?"

"It took me all my time, though," my friend said seriously. "You can't conceive what a strange feeling I had once or twice. All the strength seemed to have gone out of me—especially just before he collapsed himself."

I walked round with Cowles in order to see the ladies home. He walked in front with Mrs. Merton, and I found myself behind with the young lady. For a minute or so I walked beside her without making any remark, and then I suddenly blurted out, in a manner which must have seemed somewhat brusque to her:

"You did that, Miss Northcott."

"Did what?" she asked sharply.

"Why, mesmerised the mesmeriser—I suppose that is the best way of describing the transaction."

"What a strange idea!" she said, laughing. "You give me credit for a strong will then?"

"Yes," I said. "For a dangerously strong one."

"Why dangerous?" she asked, in a tone of surprise.

"I think," I answered, "that any will which can exercise such power is dangerous—for there is always a chance of its being turned to bad uses."

"You would make me out a very dreadful individual, Mr. Armitage," she said; and then looking up suddenly in my face—"You have never liked me. You are suspicious of me and distrust me, though I have never given you cause."

The accusation was so sudden and so true that I was unable to find any reply to it. She paused for a moment, and then said in a voice which was hard and cold—

"Don't let your prejudice lead you to interfere with me, how-

---

[1] To encounter someone who is more than your equal. The Tartars refer to the people of central Asia who, under the leadership of Genghis Khan (1162-1227), founded a huge empire.

ever, or say anything to your friend, Mr. Cowles, which might lead to a difference between us. You would find that to be very bad policy."

There was something in the way she spoke which gave an indescribable air of a threat to these few words.

"I have no power," I said, "to interfere with your plans for the future. I cannot help, however, from what I have seen and heard, having fears for my friend."

"Fears!" she repeated scornfully. "Pray what have you seen and heard. Something from Mr. Reeves, perhaps—I believe he is another of your friends?"

"He never mentioned your name to me," I answered, truthfully enough. "You will be sorry to hear that he is dying." As I said it we passed by a lighted window, and I glanced down to see what effect my words had upon her. She was laughing—there was no doubt of it; she was laughing quietly to herself. I could see merriment in every feature of her face. I feared and mistrusted the woman from that moment more than ever.

We said little more that night. When we parted she gave me a quick, warning glance, as if to remind me of what she had said about the danger of interference. Her cautions would have made little difference to me could I have seen my way to benefiting Barrington Cowles by anything which I might say. But what could I say? I might say that her former suitors had been unfortunate. I might say that I believed her to be a cruel-hearted woman. I might say that I considered her to possess wonderful, and almost preternatural powers. What impression would any of these accusations make upon an ardent lover—a man with my friend's enthusiastic temperament? I felt that it would be useless to advance them, so I was silent.

And now I come to the beginning of the end. Hitherto much has been surmise and inference and hearsay. It is my painful task to relate now, as dispassionately and as accurately as I can, what actually occurred under my own notice, and to reduce to writing the events which preceded the death of my friend.

Towards the end of the winter Cowles remarked to me that he intended to marry Miss Northcott as soon as possible—probably some time in the spring. He was, as I have already remarked, fairly well off, and the young lady had some money of her own, so that there was no pecuniary reason for a long engagement. "We are going to take a little house out at Corstorphine,"[1] he said, "and we hope to see your face at our table, Bob, as often as you can possibly come." I thanked him, and tried to shake off my apprehensions, and persuade myself that all would yet be well.

It was about three weeks before the time fixed for the marriage, that Cowles remarked to me one evening that he feared he would be late that night. "I have had a note from Kate," he said, "asking me to call about eleven o'clock to-night, which seems rather a late hour, but perhaps she wants to talk over something quietly after old Mrs. Merton retires."

It was not until after my friend's departure that I suddenly recollected the mysterious interview which I had been told of as preceding the suicide of young Prescott. Then I thought of the ravings of poor Reeves, rendered more tragic by the fact that I had heard that very day of his death. What was the meaning of it all? Had this woman some baleful secret to disclose which must be known before her marriage? Was it some reason which forbade her to marry? Or was it some reason which forbade others to marry her? I felt so uneasy that I would have followed Cowles, even at the risk of offending him, and endeavoured to dissuade him from keeping his appointment, but a glance at the clock showed me that I was too late.

I was determined to wait up for his return, so I piled some coals upon the fire and took down a novel from the shelf. My thoughts proved more interesting than the book, however, and I threw it on one side. An indefinable feeling of anxiety and depression weighed upon me. Twelve o'clock came, and then half-past, without any sign of my friend. It was nearly one when I heard a step in the street outside, and then a knocking at the door. I was surprised, as I knew that my friend always carried a key—however, I hurried down and undid the latch. As the door flew open I knew in a moment that my worst apprehensions had been fulfilled. Barrington Cowles was leaning against the railings outside with his face sunk upon his breast, and his whole attitude expressive of the

---

[1] A village situated to the west of Edinburgh.

most intense despondency. As he passed in he gave a stagger, and would have fallen had I not thrown my left arm around him. Supporting him with this, and holding the lamp in my other hand, I led him slowly upstairs into our sitting-room. He sank down upon the sofa without a word. Now that I could get a good view of him, I was horrified to see the change which had come over him. His face was deadly pale, and his very lips were bloodless. His cheeks and forehead were clammy, his eyes glazed, and his whole expression altered. He looked like a man who had gone through some terrible ordeal, and was thoroughly unnerved.

"My dear fellow, what is the matter?" I asked, breaking the silence. "Nothing amiss, I trust? Are you unwell?"

"Brandy!" he gasped. "Give me some brandy!"

I took out the decanter, and was about to help him, when he snatched it from me with a trembling hand, and poured out nearly half a tumbler of the spirit. He was usually a most abstemious man, but he took this off at a gulp without adding any water to it. It seemed to do him good, for the colour began to come back to his face, and he leaned upon his elbow.

"My engagement is off, Bob," he said, trying to speak calmly, but with a tremor in his voice which he could not conceal. "It is all over."

"Cheer up!" I answered, trying to encourage him. "Don't get down on your luck. How was it? What was it all about?"

"About?" he groaned, covering his face with his hands. "If I did tell you, Bob, you would not believe it. It is too dreadful—too horrible—unutterably awful and incredible! O Kate, Kate!" and he rocked himself to and fro in his grief; "I pictured you an angel and I find you a——"

"A what?" I asked, for he had paused.

He looked at me with a vacant stare, and then suddenly burst out, waving his arms: "A fiend!" he cried. "A ghoul from the pit! A vampire soul behind a lovely face! Now, God forgive me!" he went on in a lower tone, turning his face to the wall; "I have said more than I should. I have loved her too much to speak of her as she is. I love her too much now."

He lay still for some time, and I had hoped that the brandy had

had the effect of sending him to sleep, when he suddenly turned his face towards me.

"Did you ever read of wehr-wolves?" he asked.

I answered that I had.

"There is a story," he said thoughtfully, "in one of Marryat's books, about a beautiful woman who took the form of a wolf at night and devoured her own children. I wonder what put that idea into Marryat's head?"[1]

He pondered for some minutes, and then he cried out for some more brandy. There was a small bottle of laudanum[2] upon the table, and I managed, by insisting upon helping him myself, to mix about half a drachm with the spirits. He drank it off, and sank his head once more upon the pillow. "Anything better than that," he groaned. "Death is better than that. Crime and cruelty; cruelty and crime. Anything is better than that," and so on, with the monotonous refrain, until at last the words became indistinct, his eyelids closed over his weary eyes, and he sank into a profound slumber. I carried him into his bedroom without arousing him; and making a couch for myself out of the chairs, I remained by his side all night.

In the morning Barrington Cowles was in a high fever. For weeks he lingered between life and death. The highest medical skill of Edinburgh was called in, and his vigorous constitution slowly got the better of his disease. I nursed him during this anxious time; but through all his wild delirium and ravings he never let a word escape him which explained the mystery connected with Miss Northcott. Sometimes he spoke of her in the tenderest words and most loving voice. At others he screamed out that she was a fiend, and stretched out his arms, as if to keep her off. Several times he cried that he would not sell his soul for a beautiful face, and then he would moan in a most piteous voice, "But I love her—I love her for all that; I shall never cease to love her."

When he came to himself he was an altered man. His severe illness had emaciated him greatly, but his dark eyes had lost none of their brightness. They shone out with startling brilliancy from

---

[1] In Frederick Marryat's *The Phantom Ship* (1839) a widower marries a woman who transforms into a werewolf and murders his children.

[2] Generally used in the Victorian period for pain relief or as a sedative.

under his dark, overhanging brows. His manner was eccentric and variable—sometimes irritable, sometimes recklessly mirthful, but never natural. He would glance about him in a strange, suspicious manner, like one who feared something, and yet hardly knew what it was he dreaded. He never mentioned Miss Northcott's name—never until that fatal evening of which I have now to speak.

In an endeavour to break the current of his thoughts by frequent change of scene, I travelled with him through the highlands of Scotland, and afterwards down the east coast. In one of these peregrinations of ours we visited the Isle of May, an island near the mouth of the Firth of Forth, which, except in the tourist season, is singularly barren and desolate. Beyond the keeper of the lighthouse there are only one or two families of poor fisher-folk, who sustain a precarious existence by their nets, and by the capture of cormorants and solan geese.[1] This grim spot seemed to have such a fascination for Cowles that we engaged a room in one of the fishermen's huts, with the intention of passing a week or two there. I found it very dull, but the loneliness appeared to be a relief to my friend's mind. He lost the look of apprehension which had become habitual to him, and became something like his old self. He would wander round the island all day, looking down from the summit of the great cliffs which gird it round, and watching the long green waves as they came booming in and burst in a shower of spray over the rocks beneath.

One night—I think it was our third or fourth on the island—Barrington Cowles and I went outside the cottage before retiring to rest, to enjoy a little fresh air, for our room was small, and the rough lamp caused an unpleasant odour. How well I remember every little circumstance in connection with that night! It promised to be tempestuous, for the clouds were piling up in the northwest, and the dark wrack was drifting across the face of the moon, throwing alternate belts of light and shade upon the rugged surface of the island and the restless sea beyond.

We were standing talking close by the door of the cottage, and I was thinking to myself that my friend was more cheerful

---

[1] Doyle published his photographic essay about the Isle of May, "After Cormorants with a Camera", in the *British Journal of Photography* in 1881.

than he had been since his illness, when he gave a sudden, sharp cry, and looking round at him I saw, by the light of the moon, an expression of unutterable horror come over his features. His eyes became fixed and staring, as if riveted upon some approaching object, and he extended his long thin forefinger, which quivered as he pointed.

"Look there!" he cried. "It is she! It is she! You see her there coming down the side of the brae."[1] He gripped me convulsively by the wrist as he spoke. "There she is, coming towards us!"

"Who?" I cried, straining my eyes into the darkness.

"She—Kate—Kate Northcott!" he screamed. "She has come for me. Hold me fast, old friend. Don't let me go!"

"Hold up, old man," I said, clapping him on the shoulder. "Pull yourself together; you are dreaming; there is nothing to fear."

"She is gone!" he cried, with a gasp of relief. "No; by heaven! there she is again, and nearer—coming nearer. She told me she would come for me, and she keeps her word."

"Come into the house," I said. His hand, as I grasped it, was as cold as ice.

"Ah, I knew it!" he shouted. "There she is, waving her arms. She is beckoning to me. It is the signal. I must go. I am coming, Kate; I am coming!"

I threw my arms around him, but he burst from me with superhuman strength, and dashed into the darkness of the night. I followed him, calling to him to stop, but he ran the more swiftly. When the moon shone out between the clouds I could catch a glimpse of his dark figure, running rapidly in a straight line, as if to reach some definite goal. It may have been imagination, but it seemed to me that in the flickering light I could distinguish a vague something in front of him—a shimmering form which eluded his grasp and led him onwards.[2] I saw his outlines stand out hard against the sky behind him as he surmounted the brow of a little hill, then he disappeared, and that was the last ever seen by mortal eye of Barrington Cowles.

---

[1] Brow of a hill (Scots).
[2] Doyle uses a similar dénouement in "The Captain of the 'Pole-star'" as the doctor-narrator is unable to prevent Captain Craigie from pursuing a nebulous form over the polar ice-caps.

The fishermen and I walked round the island all that night with lanterns, and examined every nook and corner without seeing a trace of my poor lost friend. The direction in which he had been running terminated in a rugged line of jagged cliffs overhanging the sea. At one place here the edge was somewhat crumbled, and there appeared marks upon the turf which might have been left by human feet. We lay upon our faces at this spot, and peered with our lanterns over the edge, looking down on the boiling surge two hundred feet below. As we lay there, suddenly, above the beating of the waves and the howling of the wind, there rose a strange wild screech[1] from the abyss below. The fishermen—a naturally superstitious race—averred that it was the sound of a woman's laughter, and I could hardly persuade them to continue the search. For my own part I think it may have been the cry of some sea-fowl startled from its nest by the flash of the lantern. However that may be, I never wish to hear such a sound again.

And now I have come to the end of the painful duty which I have undertaken. I have told as plainly and as accurately as I could the story of the death of John Barrington Cowles, and the train of events which preceded it. I am aware that to others the sad episode seemed commonplace enough. Here is the prosaic account which appeared in the *Scotsman* a couple of days afterwards:

"*Sad Occurrence on the Isle of May.*—The Isle of May has been the scene of a sad disaster. Mr. John Barrington Cowles, a gentleman well known in University circles as a most distinguished student, and the present holder of the Neil Arnott prize for physics, has been recruiting his health in this quiet retreat. The night before last he suddenly left his friend, Mr. Robert Armitage, and he has not since been heard of. It is almost certain that he has met his death by falling over the cliffs which surround the island. Mr. Cowles' health has been failing for some time, partly from over-study and partly from worry connected with family affairs. By his death the University loses one of her most promising alumni."

I have nothing more to add to my statement. I have unbur-

---

[1] The banshee of Irish and Scottish folklore is a supernatural creature whose cry prefigures death.

dened my mind of all that I know. I can well conceive that many, after weighing all that I have said, will see no ground for an accusation against Miss Northcott. They will say that, because a man of a naturally excitable disposition says and does wild things, and even eventually commits self-murder after a sudden and heavy disappointment, there is no reason why vague charges should be advanced against a young lady. To this, I answer that they are welcome to their opinion. For my own part, I ascribe the death of William Prescott, of Archibald Reeves, and of John Barrington Cowles to this woman with as much confidence as if I had seen her drive a dagger into their hearts.

You ask me, no doubt, what my own theory is which will explain all these strange facts. I have none, or, at best, a dim and vague one. That Miss Northcott possessed extraordinary powers over the minds, and through the minds over the bodies, of others, I am convinced, as well as that her instincts were to use this power for base and cruel purposes. That some even more fiendish and terrible phase of character lay behind this—some horrible trait which it was necessary for her to reveal before marriage—is to be inferred from the experience of her three lovers, while the dreadful nature of the mystery thus revealed can only be surmised from the fact that the very mention of it drove those from her who had loved her so passionately. Their subsequent fate was, in my opinion, the result of her vindictive remembrance of their desertion of her, and that they were forewarned of it at the time was shown by the words of both Reeves and Cowles. Above this, I can say nothing. I lay the facts soberly before the public as they came under my notice. I have never seen Miss Northcott since, nor do I wish to do so. If by the words I have written I can save any one human being from the snare of those bright eyes and that beautiful face, then I can lay down my pen with the assurance that my poor friend has not died altogether in vain.

Appendix B: Bram Stoker, "The Coming of Abel Behenna"

THE little Cornish port of Pencastle[1] was bright in the early April, when the sun had seemingly come to stay after a long and bitter winter. Boldly and blackly the rock stood out against a background of shaded blue, where the sky fading into mist met the far horizon. The sea was of true Cornish hue—sapphire, save where it became deep emerald green in the fathomless depths under the cliffs, where the seal caves opened their grim jaws. On the slopes the grass was parched and brown. The spikes of furze bushes were ashy grey, but the golden yellow of their flowers streamed along the hillside, dipping out in lines as the rock cropped up, and lessening into patches and dots till finally it died away all together where the sea winds swept round the jutting cliffs and cut short the vegetation as though with an ever-working aerial shears. The whole hillside, with its body of brown and flashes of yellow, was just like a colossal yellow-hammer.

The little harbour opened from the sea between towering cliffs, and behind a lonely rock, pierced with many caves and blow-holes through which the sea in storm time sent its thunderous voice, together with a fountain of drifting spume. Hence, it wound westwards in a serpentine course, guarded at its entrance by two little curving piers to left and right. These were roughly built of dark slates placed endways and held together with great beams bound with iron bands. Thence, it flowed up the rocky bed of the stream whose winter torrents had of old cut out its way amongst the hills. This stream was deep at first, with here and there, where it widened, patches of broken rock exposed at low water, full of holes where crabs and lobsters were to be found at the ebb of the tide. From amongst the rocks rose sturdy posts, used for warping in the little coasting vessels which frequented the port. Higher up, the stream still flowed deeply, for the tide ran far inland, but always calmly for all the force of the wildest storm was broken below.

---

[1] Pencastle is the fictional name for Boscastle in Cornwall, which Stoker visited shortly before Easter in 1892. Harry Ludlam, *A Biography of Dracula: The Life Story of Bram Stoker* (London: W. Foulsham, 1962), p. 83.

Some quarter mile inland the stream was deep at high water, but at low tide there were at each side patches of the same broken rock as lower down, through the chinks of which the sweet water of the natural stream trickled and murmured after the tide had ebbed away. Here, too, rose mooring posts for the fishermen's boats. At either side of the river was a row of cottages down almost on the level of high tide. They were pretty cottages, strongly and snugly built, with trim narrow gardens in front, full of old-fashioned plants, flowering currants, coloured primroses, wallflower, and stonecrop. Over the fronts of many of them climbed clematis and wisteria. The window sides and door posts of all were as white as snow, and the little pathway to each was paved with light coloured stones. At some of the doors were tiny porches, whilst at others were rustic seats cut from tree trunks or from old barrels; in nearly every case the window ledges were filled with boxes or pots of flowers or foliage plants.

Two men lived in cottages exactly opposite each other across the stream. Two men, both young, both good-looking, both prosperous, and who had been companions and rivals from their boyhood. Abel Behenna was dark with the gypsy darkness which the Phœnician mining wanderers left in their track; Eric Sanson—which the local antiquarian said was a corruption of Sagamanson—was fair, with the ruddy hue which marked the path of the wild Norseman. These two seemed to have singled out each other from the very beginning to work and strive together, to fight for each other and to stand back to back in all endeavours. They had now put the coping-stone on their Temple of Unity[1] by falling in love with the same girl. Sarah Trefusis was certainly the prettiest girl in Pencastle, and there was many a young man who would gladly have tried his fortune with her, but that there were two to contend against, and each of these the strongest and most resolute man

---

[1] Stoker is possibly alluding to the New Testament here. Ephesians 2:20: "And [ye] are built upon the foundation of the apostles and the prophets, Jesus Christ himself being the chief corner stone: [21] in whom all the building fitly framed together growth unto an holy temple in the Lord." Ephesians is concerned with the notion of unity. See Ephesians 2:16: "That he might reconcile both [Jews and Gentiles] unto God in one body of the cross, having slain the enmity thereby." With thanks to David Bagchi for his help with this.

in the port—except the other. The average young man thought that this was very hard, and on account of it bore no good will to either of the three principals: whilst the average young woman who had, lest worse should befall, to put up with the grumbling of her sweetheart, and the sense of being only second best which it implied, did not either, be sure, regard Sarah with friendly eye. Thus it came, in the course of a year or so, for rustic courtship is a slow process, that the two men and woman found themselves thrown much together. They were all satisfied, so it did not matter, and Sarah, who was vain and something frivolous, took care to have her revenge on both men and women in a quiet way. When a young woman in her "walking out" can only boast one not-quite-satisfied young man, it is no particular pleasure to her to see her escort cast sheep's eyes at a better-looking girl supported by two devoted swains.

At length there came a time which Sarah dreaded, and which she had tried to keep distant—the time when she had to make her choice between the two men. She liked them both, and, indeed, either of them might have satisfied the ideas of even a more exacting girl. But her mind was so constituted that she thought more of what she might lose, than of what she might gain; and whenever she thought she had made up her mind she became instantly assailed with doubts as to the wisdom of her choice. Always the man whom she had presumably lost became endowed afresh with a newer and more bountiful crop of advantages than had ever arisen from the possibility of his acceptance. She promised each man that on her birthday she would give him his answer, and that day, the 11th of April, had now arrived. The promises had been given singly and confidentially, but each was given to a man who was not likely to forget. Early in the morning she found both men hovering round her door. Neither had taken the other into his confidence, and each was simply seeking an early opportunity of getting his answer, and advancing his suit if necessary. Damon, as a rule, does not take Pythias[1] with him when making a proposal; and in the heart of each man his own affairs had a claim far

---

[1] The legend from the 4th century B.C. relates to the friendship between Damon and Pythias. Damon was willing to sacrifice his life for Pythias, but Pythias returned in time to settle his debts and both lives were spared.

above any requirements of friendship. So, throughout the day, they kept seeing each other out. The position was doubtless somewhat embarrassing to Sarah, and though the satisfaction of her vanity that she should be thus adored was very pleasing, yet there were moments when she was annoyed with both men for being so persistent. Her only consolation at such moments was that she saw, through the elaborate smiles of the other girls when in passing they noticed her door thus doubly guarded, the jealousy which filled their hearts. Sarah's mother was a person of commonplace and sordid ideas, and, seeing all along the state of affairs, her one intention, persistently expressed to her daughter in the plainest words, was to so arrange matters that Sarah should get all that was possible out of both men. With this purpose she had cunningly kept herself as far as possible in the background in the matter of her daughter's wooings, and watched in silence. At first Sarah had been indignant with her for her sordid views; but, as usual, her weak nature gave way before persistence, and she had now got to the stage of acceptance. She was not surprised when her mother whispered to her in the little yard behind the house:

"Go up the hillside for a while; I want to talk to these two. They're both red-hot for ye, and now's the time to get things fixed!" Sarah began a feeble remonstrance, but her mother cut her short.

"I tell ye, girl, that my mind is made up! Both these men want ye, and only one can have ye, but before ye choose it'll be so arranged that ye'll have all that both have got! Don't argy, child! Go up the hillside, and when ye come back I'll have it fixed—I see a way quite easy!" So Sarah went up the hillside through the narrow paths between the golden furze, and Mrs. Trefusis joined the two men in the living-room of the little house.

She opened the attack with the desperate courage which is in all mothers when they think for their children, howsoever mean the thoughts may be.

"Ye two men, ye're both in love with my Sarah!"

Their bashful silence gave consent to the barefaced proposition. She went on.

"Neither of ye has much!" Again they tacitly acquiesced in the soft impeachment.

"I don't know that either of ye could keep a wife!" Though neither said a word their looks and bearing expressed distinct dissent. Mrs. Trefusis went on:

"But if ye'd put what ye both have together ye'd make a comfortable home for one of ye—and Sarah!" She eyed the men keenly, with her cunning eyes half shut, as she spoke; then satisfied from her scrutiny that the idea was accepted she went on quickly, as if to prevent argument:

"The girl likes ye both, and mayhap it's hard for her to choose. Why don't ye toss up for her? First put your money together—ye've each got a bit put by, I know. Let the lucky man take the lot and trade with it a bit, and then come home and marry her. Neither of ye's afraid, I suppose! And neither of ye'll say that he won't do that much for the girl that ye both say ye love!"

Abel broke the silence:

"It don't seem the square thing to toss for the girl! She wouldn't like it herself, and it doesn't seem—seem respectful like to her—" Eric interrupted. He was conscious that his chance was not so good as Abel's in case Sarah should wish to choose between them:

"Are ye afraid of the hazard?"

"Not me!" said Abel, boldly. Mrs. Trefusis, seeing that her idea was beginning to work, followed up the advantage.

"It is settled that ye put yer money together to make a home for her, whether ye toss for her or leave it for her to choose?"

"Yes," said Eric quickly, and Abel agreed with equal sturdiness. Mrs. Trefusis' little cunning eyes twinkled. She heard Sarah's step in the yard, and said:

"Well! here she comes, and I leave it to her." And she went out.

During her brief walk on the hillside Sarah had been trying to make up her mind. She was feeling almost angry with both men for being the cause of her difficulty, and as she came into the room said shortly:

"I want to have a word with you both—come to the Flagstaff Rock, where we can be alone." She took her hat and went out of the house up the winding path to the steep rock crowned with a high flagstaff, where once the wreckers' fire basket[1] used to burn.

---

[1] Ships were lured to their destruction by false lights.

This was the rock which formed the northern jaw of the little harbour. There was only room on the path for two abreast, and it marked the state of things pretty well when, by a sort of implied arrangement, Sarah went first, and the two men followed, walking abreast and keeping step. By this time, each man's heart was boiling with jealousy. When they came to the top of the rock, Sarah stood against the flagstaff, and the two young men stood opposite her. She had chosen her position with knowledge and intention, for there was no room for anyone to stand beside her. They were all silent for a while; then Sarah began to laugh and said:

"I promised the both of you to give you an answer to-day. I've been thinking and thinking and thinking, till I began to get angry with you both for plaguing me so; and even now I don't seem any nearer than ever I was to making up my mind." Eric said suddenly:

"Let us toss for it, lass!" Sarah showed no indignation whatever at the proposition; her mother's eternal suggestion had schooled her to the acceptance of something of the kind, and her weak nature made it easy to her to grasp at any way out of the difficulty. She stood with downcast eyes idly picking at the sleeve of her dress, seeming to have tacitly acquiesced in the proposal. Both men instinctively realising this pulled each a coin from his pocket, spun it in the air, and dropped his other hand over the palm on which it lay. For a few seconds they remained thus, all silent; then Abel, who was the more thoughtful of the men, spoke:

"Sarah! is this good?" As he spoke he removed the upper hand from the coin and placed the latter back in his pocket. Sarah was nettled.

"Good or bad, it's good enough for me! Take it or leave it as you like," she said, to which he replied quickly:

"Nay lass! Aught that concerns you is good enow for me. I did but think of you lest you might have pain or disappointment hereafter. If you love Eric better nor me, in God's name say so, and I think I'm man enow to stand aside. Likewise, if I'm the one, don't make us both miserable for life!" Face to face with a difficulty, Sarah's weak nature proclaimed itself; she put her hands before her face and began to cry, saying:

"It was my mother. She keeps telling me!" The silence which

followed was broken by Eric, who said hotly to Abel: "Let the lass alone, can't you? If she wants to choose this way, let her. It's good enough for me—and for you, too! She's said it now, and must abide by it!" Hereupon Sarah turned upon him in sudden fury, and cried:

"Hold your tongue! what is it to you, at any rate?" and she resumed her crying. Eric was so flabbergasted that he had not a word to say, but stood looking particularly foolish, with his mouth open and his hands held out with the coin still between them. All were silent till Sarah, taking her hands from her face laughed hysterically and said:

"As you two can't make up your minds, I'm going home!" and she turned to go.

"Stop," said Abel, in an authoritative voice. "Eric, you hold the coin, and I'll cry. Now, before we settle it, let us clearly understand: the man who wins takes all the money that we both have got, brings it to Bristol and ships on a voyage and trades with it. Then he comes back and marries Sarah, and they two keep all, whatever there may be, as the result of the trading. Is this what we understand?"

"Yes," said Eric.

"I'll marry him on my next birthday," said Sarah. Having said it the intolerably mercenary spirit of her action seemed to strike her, and impulsively she turned away with a bright blush. Fire seemed to sparkle in the eyes of both men. Said Eric: "A year so be! The man that wins is to have one year."

"Toss!" cried Abel, and the coin spun in the air. Eric caught it, and again held it between his outstretched hands.

"Heads!" cried Abel, a pallor sweeping over his face as he spoke. As he leaned forward to look Sarah leaned forward too, and their heads almost touched. He could feel her hair blowing on his cheek, and it thrilled through him like fire. Eric lifted his upper hand; the coin lay with its head up. Abel stepped forward and took Sarah in his arms. With a curse Eric hurled the coin far into the sea. Then he leaned against the flagstaff and scowled at the others with his hands thrust deep into his pockets. Abel whispered wild words of passion and delight into Sarah's ears, and as she listened she began to believe that fortune had rightly interpreted the wishes of her secret heart, and that she loved Abel best.

Presently Abel looked up and caught sight of Eric's face as the last ray of sunset struck it. The red light intensified the natural ruddiness of his complexion, and he looked as though he were steeped in blood. Abel did not mind his scowl, for now that his own heart was at rest he could feel unalloyed pity for his friend. He stepped over meaning to comfort him, and held out his hand, saying:

"It was my chance, old lad. Don't grudge it me. I'll try to make Sarah a happy woman, and you shall be a brother to us both!"

"Brother be damned!" was all the answer Eric made, as he turned away. When he had gone a few steps down the rocky path he turned and came back. Standing before Abel and Sarah, who had their arms round each other, he said:

"You have a year. Make the most of it! And be sure you're in time to claim your wife! Be back to have your banns up in time to be married on the 11th April. If you're not, I tell you I shall have my banns up,[1] and you may get back too late."

"What do you mean, Eric? You are mad!"

"No more mad than you are, Abel Behenna. You go, that's your chance! I stay, that's mine! I don't mean to let the grass grow under my feet. Sarah cared no more for you than for me five minutes ago, and she may come back to that five minutes after you're gone! You won by a point only—the game may change."

"The game won't change!" said Abel shortly. "Sarah, you'll be true to me? You won't marry till I return?"

"For a year!" added Eric, quickly, "that's the bargain."

"I promise for the year," said Sarah. A dark look came over Abel's face, and he was about to speak, but he mastered himself and smiled.

"I mustn't be too hard or get angry to-night! Come, Eric! we played and fought together. I won fairly. I played fairly all the game

---

[1] Banns were read for three consecutive Sundays in churches to announce a forthcoming marriage. In Henry Irving's 1890 production of *Ravenswood* based on Walter Scott's *The Bride of Lammermoor*, Lucy Ashton promises to marry Edgar Ravenswood when he returns from a year in France. However, Lucy is tricked by her mother into marrying another man. When Edgar returns on the wedding day, Lucy dies consumed by grief and Edgar rides his horse into quicksand.

of our wooing! You know that as well as I do; and now when I am going away, I shall look to my old and true comrade to help me when I am gone!"

"I'll help you none," said Eric, "so help me God!"

"It was God helped me," said Abel simply.

"Then let Him go on helping you," said Eric angrily. "The Devil is good enough for me!" and without another word he rushed down the steep path and disappeared behind the rocks.

When he had gone Abel hoped for some tender passage with Sarah, but the first remark she made chilled him.

"How lonely it all seems without Eric!" and this note sounded till he had left her at home—and after.

Early on the next morning Abel heard a noise at his door, and on going out saw Eric walking rapidly away: a small canvas bag full of gold and silver lay on the threshold; on a small slip of paper pinned to it was written:

"Take the money and go. I stay. God for you! The Devil for me! Remember the 11th of April.—Eric Sanson." That afternoon Abel went off to Bristol, and a week later sailed on the *Star of the Sea* bound for Pahang. His money—including that which had been Eric's—was on board in the shape of a venture of cheap toys. He had been advised by a shrewd old mariner of Bristol whom he knew, and who knew the ways of the Chersonese, who predicted that every penny invested would be returned with a shilling to boot.

As the year wore on Sarah became more and more disturbed in her mind. Eric was always at hand to make love to her in his own persistent, masterful manner, and to this she did not object. Only one letter came from Abel, to say that his venture had proved successful, and that he had sent some two hundred pounds to the bank at Bristol, and was trading with fifty pounds still remaining in goods for China, whither the *Star of the Sea* was bound and whence she would return to Bristol. He suggested that Eric's share of the venture should be returned to him with his share of the profits. This proposition was treated with anger by Eric, and as simply childish by Sarah's mother.

More than six months had since then elapsed, but no other letter had come, and Eric's hopes which had been dashed down by the letter from Pahang, began to rise again. He perpetually assailed Sarah with an "if!" If Abel did not return, would she then marry him? If the 11th April went by without Abel being in the port, would she give him over? If Abel had taken his fortune, and married another girl on the head of it, would she marry him, Eric, as soon as the truth were known? And so on in an endless variety of possibilities. The power of the strong will and the determined purpose over the woman's weaker nature became in time manifest. Sarah began to lose her faith in Abel and to regard Eric as a possible husband; and a possible husband is in a woman's eye different to all other men. A new affection for him began to arise in her breast, and the daily familiarities of permitted courtship furthered the growing affection. Sarah began to regard Abel as rather a rock in the road of her life, and had it not been for her mother's constantly reminding her of the good fortune already laid by in the Bristol Bank she would have tried to have shut her eyes altogether to the fact of Abel's existence.

The 11th April was Saturday, so that in order to have the marriage on that day it would be necessary that the banns should be called on Sunday, 22nd March. From the beginning of that month Eric kept perpetually on the subject of Abel's absence, and his outspoken opinion that the latter was either dead or married began to become a reality to the woman's mind. As the first half of the month wore on Eric became more jubilant, and after church on the 15th he took Sarah for a walk to the Flagstaff Rock. There he asserted himself strongly:

"I told Abel, and you too, that if he was not here to put up his banns in time for the eleventh, I would put up mine for the twelfth. Now the time has come when I mean to do it. He hasn't kept his word"—here Sarah struck in out of her weakness and indecision:

"He hasn't broken it yet!" Eric ground his teeth with anger.

"If you mean to stick up for him," he said, as he smote his hands savagely on the flagstaff, which sent forth a shivering murmur, "well and good. I'll keep my part of the bargain. On Sunday I shall give notice of the banns, and you can deny them in the church if you will. If Abel is in Pencastle on the eleventh, he can have them cancelled, and his own put up; but till then, I take my course, and woe to anyone who stands in my way!" With that he flung himself down the rocky pathway, and Sarah could not but admire his Viking strength and spirit, as, crossing the hill, he strode away along the cliffs towards Bude.

During the week no news was heard of Abel, and on Saturday Eric gave notice of the banns of marriage between himself and Sarah Trefusis. The clergyman would have remonstrated with him, for although nothing formal had been told to the neighbours, it had been understood since Abel's departure that on his return he was to marry Sarah; but Eric would not discuss the question.

"It is a painful subject, sir," he said with a firmness which the parson, who was a very young man, could not but be swayed by. "Surely there is nothing against Sarah or me. Why should there be any bones made about the matter?" The parson said no more, and on the next day he read out the banns for the first time amidst an audible buzz from the congregation. Sarah was present, contrary to custom, and though she blushed furiously enjoyed her triumph over the other girls whose banns had not yet come. Before the week was over she began to make her wedding dress. Eric used to come and look at her at work and the sight thrilled through him. He used to say all sorts of pretty things to her at such times, and there were to both delicious moments of love-making.

The banns were read a second time on the 29th, and Eric's hope grew more and more fixed though there were to him moments of acute despair when he realised that the cup of happiness might be dashed from his lips at any moment, right up to the last. At such times he was full of passion—desperate and remorseless—and he ground his teeth and clenched his hands in a wild way as though some taint of the old Berserker fury of his ancestors still lingered in his blood. On the Thursday of that week he looked in on Sarah and found her, amid a flood of sunshine, putting finishing touches to her white wedding gown. His own heart was full of gaiety, and the sight of the woman who was so soon to be his own so occupied, filled him with a joy unspeakable, and he felt faint with languorous ecstasy. Bending over he kissed Sarah on the mouth, and then whispered in her rosy ear—

"Your wedding dress, Sarah! And for me!" As he drew back to admire her she looked up saucily, and said to him—

"Perhaps not for you. There is more than a week yet for Abel!"

and then cried out in dismay, for with a wild gesture and a fierce oath Eric dashed out of the house, banging the door behind him. The incident disturbed Sarah more than she could have thought possible, for it awoke all her fears and doubts and indecision afresh. She cried a little, and put by her dress, and to soothe herself went out to sit for a while on the summit of the Flagstaff Rock. When she arrived she found there a little group anxiously discussing the weather. The sea was calm and the sun bright, but across the sea were strange lines of darkness and light, and close in to shore the rocks were fringed with foam, which spread out in great white curves and circles as the currents drifted. The wind had backed, and came in sharp, cold puffs. The blow-hole, which ran under the Flagstaff Rock, from the rocky bay without to the harbour within, was booming at intervals, and the seagulls were screaming ceaselessly as they wheeled about the entrance of the port.

"It looks bad," she heard an old fisherman say to the coastguard. "I seen it just like this once before, when the East Indiaman *Coromandel* went to pieces in Dizzard Bay!" Sarah did not wait to hear more. She was of a timid nature where danger was concerned, and could not bear to hear of wrecks and disasters. She went home and resumed the completion of her dress, secretly determined to appease Eric when she should meet him with a sweet apology—and to take the earliest opportunity of being even with him after her marriage. The old fisherman's weather prophecy was justified. That night at dusk a wild storm came on. The sea rose and lashed the western coasts from Skye to Scilly and left a tale of disaster everywhere. The sailors and fishermen of Pencastle all turned out on the rocks and cliffs and watched eagerly. Presently, by a flash of lightning, a "ketch" was seen drifting under only a jib about half-a-mile outside the port. All eyes and all glasses were concentrated on her, waiting for the next flash, and when it came a chorus went up that it was the *Lovely Alice*, trading between Bristol and Penzance, and touching at all the little ports between. "God help them!" said the harbour-master, "for nothing in this world can save them when they are between Bude and Tintagel and the wind on shore!" The coastguards exerted themselves, and, aided by brave hearts and willing hands, they brought the rocket apparatus up on the summit of the Flagstaff Rock. Then they burned blue lights so that those on board might see the harbour opening in case they could make any effort to reach it. They worked gallantly enough on board; but no skill or strength of man could avail. Before many minutes were over the *Lovely Alice* rushed to her doom on the great island rock that guarded the mouth of the port. The screams of those on board were faintly borne on the tempest as they flung themselves into the sea in a last chance for life. The blue lights were kept burning, and eager eyes peered into the depths of the waters in case any face could be seen; and ropes were held ready to fling out in aid. But never a face was seen, and the willing arms rested idle. Eric was there amongst his fellows. His old Icelandic origin was never more apparent than in that wild hour. He took a rope, and shouted in the ear of the harbour-master:

"I shall go down on the rock over the seal cave. The tide is running up, and someone may drift in there!"

"Keep back, man!" came the answer. "Are you mad? One slip on that rock and you are lost: and no man could keep his feet in the dark on such a place in such a tempest!"

"Not a bit," came the reply. "You remember how Abel Behenna saved me there on a night like this when my boat went on the Gull Rock. He dragged me up from the deep water in the seal cave, and now someone may drift in there again as I did," and he was gone into the darkness. The projecting rock hid the light on the Flagstaff Rock, but he knew his way too well to miss it. His boldness and sureness of foot standing to him, he shortly stood on the great round-topped rock cut away beneath by the action of the waves over the entrance of the seal cave, where the water was fathomless. There he stood in comparative safety, for the concave shape of the rock beat back the waves with their own force, and though the water below him seemed to boil like a seething cauldron, just beyond the spot there was a space of almost calm. The rock, too, seemed here to shut off the sound of the gale, and he listened as well as watched. As he stood there ready, with his coil of rope poised to throw, he thought he heard below him, just beyond the whirl of the water, a faint, despairing cry. He echoed it with a shout that rang into the night. Then he waited for the flash of lightning, and as it passed flung his rope out into the darkness where he had seen a face rising through the swirl of the foam. The rope was caught, for he felt a pull on it, and he shouted again in his mighty voice:

"Tie it round your waist, and I shall pull you up." Then when he felt that it was fast he moved along the rock to the far side of the sea cave, where the deep water was something stiller, and where he could get foothold secure enough to drag the rescued man on the overhanging rock. He began to pull, and shortly he knew from the rope taken in that the man he was now rescuing must soon be close to the top of the rock. He steadied himself for a moment, and drew a long breath, that he might at the next effort complete the rescue. He had just bent his back to the work when a flash of lightning revealed to each other the two men—the rescuer and the rescued.

Eric Sanson and Abel Behenna were face to face—and none knew of the meeting save themselves; and God.

On the instant a wave of passion swept through Eric's heart. All his hopes were shattered, and with the hatred of Cain his eyes looked out. He saw in the instant of recognition the joy in Abel's face that his was the hand to succour him, and this intensified his hate. Whilst the passion was on him he started back, and the rope ran out between his hands. His moment of hate was followed by an impulse of his better manhood, but it was too late.

Before he could recover himself, Abel, encumbered with the rope that should have aided him, was plunged with a despairing cry back into the darkness of the devouring sea.

Then, feeling all the madness and the doom of Cain upon him, Eric rushed back over the rocks, heedless of the danger and eager only for one thing—to be amongst other people whose living noises would shut out that last cry which seemed to ring still in his ears. When he regained the Flagstaff Rock the men surrounded him, and through the fury of the storm he heard the harbour-master say:—

"We feared you were lost when we heard a cry! How white you are! Where is your rope? Was there anyone drifted in?"

"No one," he shouted in answer, for he felt that he could never explain that he had let his old comrade slip back into the sea, and at the very place and under the very circumstances in which that comrade had saved his own life. He hoped by one bold lie to set the matter at rest for ever. There was no one to bear witness—and if he should have to carry that still white face in his eyes and that despairing cry in his ears for evermore—at least none should know of it. "No one," he cried, more loudly still. "I slipped on the rock, and the rope fell into the sea!" So saying he left them, and, rushing down the steep path, gained his own cottage and locked himself within.

The remainder of that night he passed lying on his bed—dressed and motionless—staring upwards, and seeming to see through the darkness a pale face gleaming wet in the lightning, with its glad recognition turning to ghastly despair, and to hear a cry which never ceased to echo in his soul.

In the morning the storm was over and all was smiling again, except that the sea was still boisterous with its unspent fury. Great pieces of wreck drifted into the port, and the sea around the island rock was strewn with others. Two bodies also drifted into the harbour—one the master of the wrecked ketch, the other a strange seaman whom no one knew.

Sarah saw nothing of Eric till the evening, and then he only looked in for a minute. He did not come into the house, but simply put his head in through the open window.

"Well, Sarah," he called out in a loud voice, though to her it did not ring truly, "is the wedding dress done? Sunday week, mind! Sunday week!"

Sarah was glad to have the reconciliation so easy; but, womanlike, when she saw the storm was over and her own fears groundless, she at once repeated the cause of offence.

"Sunday so be it," she said without looking up, "if Abel isn't there on Saturday!" Then she looked up saucily, though her heart was full of fear of another outburst on the part of her impetuous lover. But the window was empty; Eric had taken himself off, and with a pout she resumed her work. She saw Eric no more till Sunday afternoon, after the banns had been called the third time, when he came up to her before all the people with an air of proprietorship which half-pleased and half-annoyed her.

"Not yet, mister!" she said, pushing him away, as the other girls giggled. "Wait till Sunday next, if you please—the day after Saturday!" she added, looking at him saucily. The girls giggled again, and the young men guffawed. They thought it was the snub that touched him so that he became as white as a sheet as he turned away. But Sarah, who knew more than they did, laughed, for she saw triumph through the spasm of pain that overspread his face.

The week passed uneventfully; however, as Saturday drew nigh Sarah had occasional moments of anxiety, and as to Eric he went about at night-time like a man possessed. He restrained himself when others were by, but now and again he went down amongst the rocks and caves and shouted aloud. This seemed to relieve him somewhat, and he was better able to restrain himself for some time after. All Saturday he stayed in his own house and never left it. As he was to be married on the morrow, the neighbours thought it was shyness on his part, and did not trouble or notice him. Only once was he disturbed, and that was when the chief boatman came to him and sat down, and after a pause said:

"Eric, I was over in Bristol yesterday. I was in the ropemaker's getting a coil to replace the one you lost the night of the storm, and there I saw Michael Heavens of this place, who is a salesman there. He told me that Abel Behenna had come home the week ere last on the *Star of the Sea* from Canton, and that he had lodged a sight of money in the Bristol Bank in the name of Sarah Behenna. He told Michael so himself—and that he had taken passage on the *Lovely Alice* to Pencastle. Bear up, man," for Eric had with a groan dropped his head on his knees, with his face between his hands. "He was your old comrade, I know, but you couldn't help him. He must have gone down with the rest that awful night. I thought I'd better tell you, lest it might come some other way, and you might keep Sarah Trefusis from being frightened. They were good friends once, and women take these things to heart. It would not do to let her be pained with such a thing on her wedding day!" Then he rose and went away, leaving Eric still sitting disconsolately with his head on his knees.

"Poor fellow!" murmured the chief boatman to himself; "he takes it to heart. Well, well! right enough! They were true comrades once, and Abel saved him!"

The afternoon of that day, when the children had left school, they strayed as usual on half-holidays along the quay and the paths by the cliffs. Presently some of them came running in a state of great excitement to the harbour, where a few men were unloading a coal ketch, and a great many were superintending the operation. One of the children called out:

"There is a porpoise in the harbour mouth! We saw it come through the blow-hole! It had a long tail, and was deep under the water!"

"It was no porpoise," said another; "it was a seal; but it had a long tail! It came out of the seal cave!" The other children bore various testimony, but on two points they were unanimous—it, whatever "it" was, had come through the blow-hole deep under the water, and had a long, thin tail—a tail so long that they could not see the end of it. There was much unmerciful chaffing of the children by the men on this point, but as it was evident that they had seen something, quite a number of persons, young and old, male and female, went along the high paths on either side of the harbour mouth to catch a glimpse of this new addition to the fauna of the sea, a long-tailed porpoise or seal. The tide was now coming in. There was a slight breeze, and the surface of the water was rippled so that it was only at moments that anyone could see clearly into the deep water. After a spell of watching a woman called out that she saw something moving up the channel, just below where she was standing. There was a stampede to the spot, but by the time the crowd had gathered the breeze had freshened, and it was impossible to see with any distinctness below the surface of the water. On being questioned the woman described what she had seen, but in such an incoherent way that the whole thing was put down as an effect of imagination; had it not been for the children's report she would not have been credited at all. Her semi-hysterical statement that what she saw was "like a pig with the entrails out" was only thought anything of by an old coastguard, who shook his head but did not make any remark. For the remainder of the daylight this man was seen always on the bank, looking into the water, but always with disappointment manifest on his face.

Eric arose early on the next morning—he had not slept all night, and it was a relief to him to move about in the light. He shaved himself with a hand that did not tremble, and dressed himself in his wedding clothes. There was a haggard look on his face, and he seemed as though he had grown years older in the last few days. Still there was a wild, uneasy light of triumph in his eyes, and he kept murmuring to himself over and over again:

"This is my wedding-day! Abel cannot claim her now—living or dead!—living or dead! Living or dead!" He sat in his arm-chair, waiting with an uncanny quietness for the church hour to arrive. When the bell began to ring he arose and passed out of his house, closing the door behind him. He looked at the river and saw the tide had just turned. In the church he sat with Sarah and her mother, holding Sarah's hand tightly in his all the time, as though he feared to lose her. When the service was over they stood up together, and were married in the presence of the entire congregation; for no one left the church. Both made the responses clearly—Eric's being even on the defiant side. When the wedding was over Sarah took her husband's arm, and they walked away together, the boys and younger girls being cuffed by their elders into a decorous behaviour, for they would fain have followed close behind their heels.

The way from the church led down to the back of Eric's cottage, a narrow passage being between it and that of his next neighbour. When the bridal couple had passed through this the remainder of the congregation, who had followed them at a little distance, were startled by a long, shrill scream from the bride. They rushed through the passage and found her on the bank with wild eyes, pointing to the river bed opposite Eric Sanson's door.

The falling tide had deposited there the body of Abel Behenna stark upon the broken rocks. The rope trailing from its waist had been twisted by the current round the mooring post, and had held it back whilst the tide had ebbed away from it. The right elbow had fallen in a chink in the rock, leaving the hand outstretched toward Sarah, with the open palm upward as though it were extended to receive hers, the pale drooping fingers open to the clasp.

All that happened afterwards was never quite known to Sarah Sanson. Whenever she would try to recollect there would become a buzzing in her ears and a dimness in her eyes, and all would pass away. The only thing that she could remember of it all—and this she never forgot—was Eric's breathing heavily, with his face whiter than that of the dead man, as he muttered under his breath:

"Devil's help! Devil's faith! Devil's price!"

Appendix C: Bram Stoker, "Sir Arthur Conan Doyle Tells of his Career and Work, his Sentiments towards America, and his Approaching Marriage"[1]

"My first book! That was written when I was six years of age! But if I am to tell you about myself, I suppose I had better begin at the beginning."

The speaker was lying on a chintz covered sofa in the pretty drawing-room of his house at Hindhead, down in Surrey.[2] The forenoon sun was streaming through one of the mullioned windows, of which the bars were softened by the delicate fringe of green of the creepers which spread along them. The whole room was full of soft light, which showed the fine old furniture and the multitude of dainty knick-knacks to perfection. Even the many quaint and pretty pictures seemed to stand out from the walls.

From where I sat the whole of the lovely valley, at the very head of which the house stands, lay before me. Due south it falls away, spreading wider as it goes, till its lines are lost in distance, an endless sea of greenery. Far away there are ranges of hills piling up, one behind the other, in undulations of varying blue. Even the whole sweep of the horizon visible from our altitude is like a wavy sea. Nearer at hand the wonderful green of the valley is articulated by the minor curves and slopes, the trend of surrounding hills. The mighty carpet of green is of the fresh young bracken, whose shoots seem close, are like little crosiers wrought in emer-

---

[1] This interview was published in the *New York World* on 28 July 1907 (Editorial Section, p. 1). A shorter version ("Sir Arthur Conan Doyle Tells of His Work and Career) appeared in the *Daily Chronicle* on 14 February 1908, p. 8. The American interview included a photograph of Doyle and Jean Leckie and the British publication included photographs of Doyle in his "campaigning kit", in his study, a photograph of his wife and a view of Undershaw from the rear.

[2] Doyle had the house built after his first wife, Louise, was diagnosed with tuberculosis. The writer Grant Allen advised Doyle that the air in this part of Surrey was beneficial. Doyle employed his friend, the architect Stanley Ball, to design the house. See Pierre Nordon, *Conan Doyle*, translated by Frances Partridge (1964; London: John Murray, 1966), p. 41.

ald. Against this the rising pine trees seem like dark masses. Close to us, beyond the vivid patch of tennis lawn, are some masses of color which are simply gorgeous amid the expanse of green. Great shrubs of yellow broom, clumps of purple rhododendron, luxuriant alder, with masses of snowy flowers starred in their own peculiar green. An expanse which, whether seen from near or far, in unity or detail, simply ravishes the eye with its myriad beauties.

We had motored up the previous afternoon from Guildford, some twelve miles distant. The last seven miles of the journey up the steep, winding road shows one of the loveliest scenes in England—a scene that brings at every new phase fresh memories of Turner. Indeed, Turner himself loved this piece of the old Portsmouth road. Is not one of the weirdest pictures in Liber Studiorum, "Gallows Hill,"[1] taken from it? But here was the crown of it all—that wide expanse seen beyond this foreground of idyllic beauty.

Undershaw Home at Hindhead

Conan Doyle built his house Undershaw in the western angle at the joining of the road from Haslemere with the Portsmouth road, just below the very top of the hill. It stands on a little platform lying below the road. As north and east of it is a thick grove of trees and shrubs, it is completely sheltered from stranger eyes except from down the valley. It is so sheltered from cold winds that the architect felt justified in having lots of windows, so that the whole place is full of light. Nevertheless, it is cozy and snug to a remarkable degree, and has everywhere that sense of "home" which is so delightful to occupant and stranger alike. Throughout it is full of interesting things got together for their interesting association with the author's life and adventures, for their prettiness, or as curios, or works of art.

The owner of this almost fairy pleasure is a big man, massive and burly, and of great strength. His head and face are broad, and strong, his eyes are blue with a peculiar effect in light, for they

---

[1] One of seventy landscape prints that the English artist J.M.W. Turner (1775-1851) undertook between 1806 and 1819. They were called the *Liber Studiorium*. The print that Stoker is referring to features a gibbet on the summit of Hindhead hill.

seem to have two shades of blue in the iris. His voice is strong and resonant—a very masculine voice.

The "interview" which followed was the result of many questions. The subject of it was most kind and amenable, thoroughly understanding everything and willing to enlighten me as I required. But he is not naturally a pushing man or an egotist, and it was necessary to keep him resolutely to the point of his own identity. I say this as his various statements were so lucid and illuminative that I think it better to give them in his own words in the sequence of a direct narrative. After all, there is nothing like a man's *ipsissima verba* to show the reality of the individual through the mistiness of words. I omit questions except where necessary, and only venture to add comment or description where such may add to the reader's enlightenment.

Doyle's Imaginative Forbears

"My people on my father's side," said the creator of "Sherlock Holmes," "were all artists of a peculiarly imaginative line. My father, Charles Doyle, was in truth a great unrecognized genius. He drifted to Edinburgh from London in his early youth, and so he lost the chance of living before the public eye. His wild and strange fancies alarmed, I think, rather than pleased the stolid Scotchmen of the 50's and 60's. His mind was on strange moonlight effects, done with extraordinary skill in water colours; dancing witches, drowning seamen, death coaches on lonely moors at night, and goblins chasing children across church-yards."

All these pictures were in the room, or in some of those adjacent. With them were a host of others, delicate fancies and weird flights of imagination. There was one tiny picture of a little fairy carrying a branch and leading a beetle by a string, which was daintily sweet.[1]

---

[1] Charles Doyle was institutionalized for alcoholism in 1876 and died in Crighton Royal Institution, Dumfries in October 1893. In 1977 Michael Baker published a sketchbook that Doyle produced in 1889 with images of fairies similar to those described by Stoker. Charles's brother, Richard, was a noted fairy painter and illustrator. Conan Doyle had an ambivalent relationship with his father.

"I have myself no turn for this form of art at all beyond a very keen color sense which makes a discord of shades perfectly painful to my eye. I suppose, however, that there is a metabolism in these things, and that any sense I have for dramatic effects corresponds, or is an equivalent, in some degree, to the artistic nature of my father, whom, by the way, I in no degree resemble physically. But my real love for letters, my instinct for storytelling, springs, I believe, from my mother, who is of Anglo-Celtic stock, with the glamour and romance of the Celt very strongly marked. Her I do resemble physically, and also in character, so that I take my leanings toward romance rather from her side than my father's. In my early childhood, as far back as I can remember anything at all, the vivid stories which she would tell me stand out so clearly that they obscure the real facts of my life. It is not only that she was—is still—a wonderful story-teller, but she had, I remember, an art of sinking her voice to a horror-stricken whisper when she came to a crisis in her narrative, which makes me goose-fleshy now when I think of it. I am sure, looking back, that it was in attempting to emulate these stories of my childhood that I began weaving dreams myself.

A Six-Year-Old Author

"When I was six I wrote a book of adventure—doubtless my mother has it yet. I illustrated it myself. It must have be an absurd production, but still it showed the set of my mind. When I went to school I carried the characteristic with me. There I was in some demand as a story-teller. I could start a hero off from home and carry him through an interminable succession of wayside happenings which would, if necessary, last through the spare hours of a whole term. This faculty remained with me all my school days, and the only scholastic success I can ever remember lay in the direction of English essays and poetry. I was no good at either classics or mathematics; even my English I wrote as pleasure, not as work.

At School in Germany

"After leaving Stonyhurst I was sent to a 'finishing' school in Germany, the Tyrol. There again my tendency to letters asserted itself. I started and edited a school magazine. Although the German acquired was indifferent, I think I had great benefit from the small but select English library. Macaulay and Scott, I remember, were my favorite authors. But I was and am still an omnivorous reader, with very catholic sympathies. There is hardly anything which does not interest me. I have sometimes tested myself by going into a large library and noting which of the books I am tempted to take down. I think that if let loose in such a place on a wet day my first choice would be military memoirs: but I am deeply interested also in criminology, in all sides of history, in science—so far as I can follow it—in comparative theology—if not ruined by the heavy touch of the writer—in travel—if the author has the skill to keep a glamour over his picture—in any form of fiction. Indeed, it would be difficult to name any form of true literature which does not give me intense pleasure.

Studying Medicine in Auld Edinboro'

"In 1876 I drifted into the study of medicine. The reason largely was that my people lived in Edinburgh—he pronounces the word in the Scottish fashion, "Edinboro"—and there is a famous medical school there. For four years I went through the curriculum. My people were not at that time wealthy, and it was a struggle to keep me at college. So I compressed my classes into the winter, and devoted each summer to serving as a medical assistant, and so earning a little money to help to pay the fees. I served in this way in Sheffield, in the country districts of Shropshire, and finally in Birmingham—a billet to which I returned three times. The practice lay mostly in the slums of that great city, and I certainly saw a large variety of character and of life, such as I could hardly have known so intimately in any other way.

"The one trouble to me in this arrangement of my life was that I had no means of gratifying the love of athletics which was very strong within me. I used to box a good deal, for that consumed little time; but my cricket and football were neglected. I can say, however, that I have played for my university in both cricket and Rugby football. I had then no time or chance of being a constant player; I feel justified, therefore, in taking it out at the other end.

I played a heavy match at football when I was forty-two years of age, and I still, at the age of forty-eight, play cricket twice a week. So I claim now the debts which were not paid me in my youth.

Surgeon to an Arctic Whaler

"When I was nearly twenty-one a friend of mine who had been surgeon to a whaler in the Arctic seas told me that he was unable to return that summer, and offered me the billet. I was away for seven months in the Greenland ocean. I came of age in 80 degrees north latitude.

"This was a delightful period of my life. There are eight boats to a whaler, and the eighth, which is kept as a sort of emergency boat, is manned by the so-called 'idlers' of the ship. These consisted in this case, of myself, the steward, the second engineer and an old seaman. But it happened that, with the exception of the veteran, we were all young and strong and keen; and I think our boat was as good as any."

As he spoke he could not fail to remember the harpoons hanging on the staircase wall. They seemed to account for his enthusiasm. He went on:

"One of the truest compliments ever paid me in my life was when the captain offered to make me the harpooner as well as surgeon if I would come for another year. When you think that a whale was then worth some £2,000 and that hit or miss depends on the nerve of the harpooner, I am proud to think that the skipper, old John Grey, should have offered me such a post.

"On returning home from the Arctic I took my degree, having been thrown back one year by the fact of going North. I was twenty-two when I qualified, and, thanks to my numerous assistantships, had a very varied experience behind me."

Down the West African Coast

"Almost immediately afterward I was offered the post of surgeon to a steamer going down the west coast of Africa. I was again most fortunate in my captain, and the voyage was a delightful one. We were away four months and the pleasure of my experience was only marred by my getting the rather virulent fever which prevails on that coast. Two of us got it, and the other man died, so that I suppose I may call myself lucky.

"On my return to England I settled in practice, first in Plymouth and then, after a few months, at Southsea, the fashionable suburb of Portsmouth. My adventures in that rather romantic period, and all my mental and spiritual aspirations, are written down in *The Stark Munro Letters*, a book which, with the exception of one chapter, is a very close autobiography.

"In this period my literary tendencies had slowly developed. During the years of my studentship my life was so full of work that, though I read a great deal, I had little time to cultivate writing. After starting in practice, however, I had much—too much—time on my hands; and then I began to write voluminously.

"Most of it was, I think, pretty poor stuff; but it was apprentice work, and I always hoped that with practice I might learn to use my tools.

"Finding Himself" in Literature

"Every writer is imitative at first. I think that it is an absolute rule; though sometimes he throws back on some model which is not easily traced. My early work, as I look back on it, was a sort of debased composite photograph in which five or six different styles were contending for the mastery. Stevenson was a strong influence; so was Bret Harte; so was Dickens; so were several others.

"Eventually, however, a man 'finds himself,' or rather perhaps it is that he grows more deft in concealing the influences which blend with one another until they form what means a new and constant style.

"I suppose that during those early years I wrote not less than fifty short stories. The first appeared in 1878 while I was still a student. It was in *Chamber's Journal* and was called 'The Mystery of Sassassa [sic] Valley.' I had three guineas for it. After receiving that little check I was a beast that has once tasted blood, for I knew that whatever rebuffs I might receive—and God knows I had plenty—I had once proved I would earn gold, and the spirit was in me to do it again. It was a delightful opportunity for carrying into actuality the dreams of my youth. I had to earn money by some form of work, and that was the sort of work I longed to do.

Ten Years of Anonymity

"For ten years I wrote short stories; roughly, from 1877 to 1887. During that time I do not think that I ever earned £50 in any year by my pen, though I worked incessantly. Nearly all the magazines published the stories anonymously—a most iniquitous fashion by which all chance of promotion is barred to young writers. The best of these stories have since been published in the volume called *The Captain of the Pole Star*. Sometimes I saw my stories praised by critics, but the criticism never came to my address. The *Cornhill Magazine*, *Temple Bar* and *London Society* were the chief magazines in which my stories appeared.

"Finally in 1887 I wrote *A Study in Scarlet*, the first book which introduced Sherlock Holmes. I don't know how I got that name. I was looking the other day at a bit of paper on which I had scribbled 'Sherrinford Holmes' and 'Sherrington Hope' and all sorts of other combinations. Finally, at the bottom of the paper I had written 'Sherlock Holmes.' 'A Study in Scarlet' appeared in a Christmas number of *Beeton's Annual*. The book had no particular success at the time, though many people have been good enough to read it since.

Micah Clarke and *The White Company*

"My next book was *Micah Clarke*, a historical novel. This met with a good reception from the critics and the public; and from that time onward I had no further difficulty in disposing of my manuscripts. When two years later I wrote *The White Company* I felt that my position was strong enough to enable me to give up practice. I still clung to my profession, for I came to London and started as an oculist. After six months, however, this also seemed unnecessary, and I finally retired. I have not indulged in my profession since, except when I went campaigning."

That he did good service in that noble profession in the South African war is attested not only by his book on the record of that

Langman Hospital, but by a noble silver bowl which stands at a corner of his house in Hindhead, on which is inscribed:

"To Arthur Conan Doyle, who in a great crisis—in word and deed—served his country."[1]

When he had come to the part in his history where he had started his bark on the sea of literature, I think he considered that his duty with regard to the interview was done. In obedience to my request, however, he went on. I wished that the American people might hear some special comment on their own affairs.

Doyle's American Tour

"In 1894 I went on a lecturing tour to America. I had no hopes of any success in the matter; my idea was simply to see a country in which I took a deep interest, and to pay my expenses while I was so doing. Major Pond,[2] however, in his enthusiastic way fixed up a considerable programme for me, so that I was forced to do rather more than to pay my expenses, and rather less in the way of seeing the country. I was there, all told, between four and five months, and the fact that I was lecturing had the one advantage that it took me into some of the byways, smaller towns that I should not have otherwise visited.

"I came away from America with a deep admiration for both the country and the people, and much touched by all the kindness and even affection which I had encountered. It has left a lasting impression on my mind which the lapse of thirteen years has in no way effaced. I want to go again without having any work to do, and I want to go out West and Southwest. One feels that society with its highly organized life is to some degree that same everywhere throughout the world, but that the real distinctive America is that portion which is still finding itself, as it were, and has not yet set into its final form.

"I read Wells's book[3] on the subject the other day; it seemed to me to be very deep and very suggestive. I should think that Ameri-

---

[1] The *Daily Chronicle* version ends here.
[2] An agent who organized lecture tours for writers.
[3] H. G. Wells published *The Future in America* in 1906 after a tour of the country.

cans need not mind frank criticism from such a man as he, for his own mind is essentially democratic and American.

"But the fact is that these various dangers and drawbacks which one sees—the dangers of the great trusts—the dangers of violent labor unions—the dangers of the multi-millionaire—the dangers of individual character and violence becoming too strong for the organized legal machinery of the community—all these things are probably prominent problems to be solved by the human race, and only showing up in America because things move faster there and are on a large scale. But always behind the turmoil are ranked the millions of steady, solid, law-supporting citizens; and one knows that in the end all will be well.

"As I am speaking of America, I remember one incident that comes back vividly to mind. When I was there a strong wave of anti-British feeling was passing over the country. It was not shown offensively to the stranger within their gates, but one could hardly pick up any sort of newspaper without reading what was painful and usually untrue about one's country. On one occasion at Detroit this feeling showed on the surface. A small supper was given to me by some kind and hospitable friends at a club there. We looked upon the wine when it was red, and at a late stage in the evening, politics having come up, one of the company made a speech in which he made a severe attack upon Great Britain. I asked my friend Robert Barr,[1] who was in the chair, to allow me to answer the attack. This I did, speaking my mind out of the fullness of heart. I think no one who was present could fail to have been surprised at the way in which the events bore out my remarks. What I said practically was:

"'You Americans have lived, up to now, with a ring fence of your own. Your country has become so vast, and you have had so much to do in peopling it and opening it out, that you have never had to think seriously of outside international politics, and you have lived to some extent in a world of prejudice and of dreams. This period is now drawing swiftly to an end. Your country is filling up, and

---

[1] Robert Barr (1849-1912) was a Scottish-born writer, journalist and co-founder of the *Idler* magazine. He accompanied Doyle on his 1894 North American tour.

soon you will have surplus energies which will lead you on into world politics and bring you into closer actual relations with other powers. Then your friendships and your enmities will be guided, not by prejudice nor by hereditary dislikes, but by actual practical issues. When that day comes and it is coming soon—you will find that the only people who will understand you—who will see what your aims are and who will heartily sympathize with you in them, are your own people, the men from whom you are sprung. In a great world-crisis you will find that you have no natural friend among the nations save your own kin; and to the last they will always be at your side!'

"Well, within three years came the Spanish war[1]—the suggested European coalition against America—the strong attitude of Great Britain upon the subject. It was as good an illustration as one could desire of the prediction which I had made in my speech.

"We know very well on this side that if the case were reversed and we ourselves had to look for sympathy and understanding, all minor contentions would vanish in an instant and we should find a strong and true friend by our side!"

A Happy Announcement

One little personal piece of information was given by Sir Arthur Conan Doyle which may make a fitting conclusion to this interview. It was the news of his approaching marriage. Sir Arthur is engaged to a young lady, Miss Jean Leckie, of Crowborough, to whom he is to be married in September.[2] His face lit up as he finished: "I am the most lucky of men. May I be worthy of my good fortune."

---

[1] The Spanish-American War (1898) resulted in Spain relinquishing power in Cuba and the U.S. extending control over the Caribbean.
[2] Bram and Florence Stoker were guests at the wedding.

Lightning Source UK Ltd.
Milton Keynes UK
30 September 2009

144366UK00001B/161/P

NOTA DA AUTORA

Aos que dizem que as religiões de matriz africana pertencem ao diabo por que não são cristãs (errado, são sim), gostaria de propor a seguinte reflexão: considerando que o termo Cristão foi criado pelo evangelista São Lucas para identificar os seguidores de Jesus Cristo, entende-se que cristão é todo aquele que segue os ensinamentos do Cristo.

Os que atacam com virulência a Umbanda, respondam a si mesmos:

Tudo quanto, pois, quereis que os homens vos façam, assim fazei-o vós também a eles; porque esta é a Lei e os Profetas *(Mateus 7.12)*. Você pensa primeiro em si e nos seus e só depois no próximo, como por exemplo, nos irmãos em Cristo que escolheram religião diferente da sua? E quando insulta e agride, ou se cala e não reage, sendo omisso às agressões impostas aos que professam religião diversa, está sendo cristão?

Se teu irmão pecar [contra ti], vai argui-lo entre ti e ele só. Se ele te ouvir, ganhaste a teu irmão *(Mateus 18.15)*. Você tem humildade e amor quando é alcançado pelo que considera erro ou maledicência? Ou se cala apenas perante má língua contra os que praticam religião diferente da tua? Assume os enganos ou coloca a responsabilidade sobre o outro? E sendo chamado a mediar conflito procura apaziguar os ânimos sem dar palpite e fazer fofoca? Quando se cala perante o caluniador você está sendo cristão ou você pertence ao diabo?

Não acumuleis para vós outros tesouros sobre a terra, onde a traça e a ferrugem corroem e onde ladrões escavam e roubam *(Mateus 6.19)*. Quanta energia você desprende para ter, possuir, acumular dinheiro, propriedades móveis, imóveis? Será a mesma que dedica para o crescimento espiritual? Está sendo cristão quando condena os pobres Terreiros, geralmente dirigidos por pessoas simplicíssimas que dedicam para a caridade o pouco tempo que lhes sobra para o descanso, quando os teus templos e igrejas são cobertos de luxo e riqueza, e os dirigentes se prostituem nos porões do poder?

Aos que agridem nossos Terreiros, ofendem irmãos em Cristo porque "ousam" escolher caminho diferente para chegar ao Pai, proponho aqui uma última reflexão:

A candeia do corpo são os olhos; de sorte que, se os teus olhos forem bons, todo o teu corpo terá luz; Se, porém, os teus olhos forem maus, o teu corpo será tenebroso. Se, portanto, a luz que em ti há são trevas, quão grandes serão tais trevas! *(Mateus 6:22-23)*.

Saravá!

A RELIGIÃO DE UMBANDA

O QUE EU DEVO LEVAR EM CONTA QUANDO FOR ESCOLHER UM TERREIRO PARA FREQUENTAR? Se o comportamento do Dirigente se enquadra rigorosamente dentro das normas éticas, se os médiuns são pessoas que se comportam com seriedade dentro e fora do Terreiro, se há afinidade com as regras que norteiam a Casa, e se há identificação com o conjunto de ritos e atitudes através dos quais se presta reverência aos Guias e Orixás.

COMO SABER SE O TERREIRO É SÉRIO? Em primeiro lugar desconfie de lugares que cobram porque Umbanda é caridade e não deve haver cobrança. Assim como também não deve ser um templo de adivinhação porque esse não é o propósito, como toda religião a Umbanda busca tão somente trazer a evolução moral e espiritual para seus seguidores. Preste atenção à postura dos que ali trabalham, desde o Dirigente até os médiuns, porque no Terreiro deve reinar a paz e a fraternidade, deboches e fofocas falam muito do lugar e dos participantes. Conversas sobre outros assuntos durante a Gira e "risadinhas" são sinais claros de falta de comprometimento com a espiritualidade. Atenção ao comportamento das Entidades incorporadas principalmente em Gira de Esquerda porque é normal que Exus e Pombogiras façam uso do fumo e da bebida como ferramentas úteis aos seus trabalhos, mas havendo bebedeira deve-se redobrar a atenção porque excessos não fazem parte do ritual de Umbanda. Avalie os conselhos recebidos dos Guias. Ouça com atenção as letras dos pontos cantados e se houver referência ao diabo, satanás e outras figuras esdrúxulas saiba que não fazem parte da realidade umbandista, e caso ocorra verifique se trata de sincretismo com a religião católica ou se faz parte do fundamento do Terreiro. Os trabalhos espirituais podem e devem ser feitos às vistas de todos e explicado o que está sendo feito, sem que haja promessas de milagres, porque na Umbanda como na vida tudo acontece pela força da fé, e episódios maravilhosos não são oferecidos em Terreiros sérios. Se houver menção para que se realizem vários trabalhos com a finalidade de afastar maus espíritos ou trazer sorte, marido, esposa, desconfie. Por fim é importante dizer que assim como a maioria das igrejas é boa, também a maioria dos Terreiros é bom, e os procedimentos aqui descritos não são praticados em Casas de Umbanda.

EU ESTOU COM DIFICULDADE FINANCEIRA. SE FREQUENTAR TERREIRO DE UMBANDA E PEDIR AJUDA AOS GUIAS CONSEGUIREI BOAS OPORTUNIDADES PARA GANHAR DINHEIRO? Os Guias não dão nada a ninguém, essa não é a finalidade de uma religião. Os Guias dão os instrumentos e mostram a direção, mas cada um caminha com suas próprias pernas. Umbanda não é balcão de troca onde a pessoa dá 10% de seu rendimento em troca de vida financeira melhor. Se umbandista sugerir isso a qualquer dos Guias eles vão mandar estudar e trabalhar para melhorar de vida.

ESTOU DOENTE FISICAMENTE. A UMBANDA É INDICADA PARA MINHA CURA? Não. A indicação é que procure um médico ou um hospital. Umbanda é religião! A finalidade de uma religião é curar os males da alma, do corpo físico cuidam os médicos e enfermeiros. Aos Guias se pede iluminação para os profissionais que tratarão a doença, esperança e coragem para enfrentar a moléstia.

ESTOU DESEMPREGADO. A UMBANDA É INDICADA PARA EU CONSEGUIR UM EMPREGO? Não se pode confundir Terreiro de Umbanda com consultoria de recursos humanos. Ao que está desempregado aconselhamos procurar uma agência de empregos. Umbanda é religião! Ninguém consegue um bom emprego se não estiver preparado para disputar a vaga com outros que também a querem.

SE EU SAIR DA UMBANDA MEUS GUIAS FECHARÃO MEUS CAMINHOS? Não se pode perder de vista que quem abre e fecha caminhos é engenheiro civil. As Entidades que trabalham na Umbanda respeitam o livre arbítrio e tem mais o que fazer. Os Guias são Espíritos de Luz que só querem o bem, não castigam ninguém nem fecham caminhos.

"QUERIA PARAR DE FREQUENTAR O TERREIRO, MAS NÃO POSSO PORQUE AS PESSOAS NECESSITAM MUITO DE MINHA AJUDA ESPIRITUAL." Quem pensa assim é bom que reflita que cada um é somente mais um trabalhador de uma corrente mediúnica, cujo trabalho continuará sem sua presença. No Terreiro o médium está sendo mais ajudado do que está ajudando. É preciso cuidar para que a caridade não dê lugar à fascinação por si mesmo.

"TENHO MEDIUNIDADE MAIS FORTE DO QUE A MAIORIA E MEUS GUIAS TEM MUITA FORÇA." Não existe medida de intensidade e grandeza da mediunidade, nem existe Guia fraco, forte e mais ou menos. O que existe é médium presunçoso, vaidoso e fútil.

"ENCONTREI NA UMBANDA UMA FORMA DE AUXILIAR O MEU PRÓXIMO". A prática da caridade é a finalidade da Umbanda e abençoado é aquele que faz da compaixão o seu propósito. E se servindo a Deus através da doação o filho de fé encontrar amor, saúde, bom emprego e caminhos abertos, é certo que lhes foram adicionados por merecimento.

A UMBANDA É UMA RELIGIÃO QUE CULTUA O SOBRENATURAL? Depende do que se entende por sobrenatural. Entendendo-se como milagroso, não é sobrenatural porque não existe milagre. Entendendo-se por divino, então sim porque a Umbanda cultua as forças da natureza criadas por Deus. Também tem que considerar que o ser humano chama de sobrenatural tudo o que não entende e não conhece.

POR QUE A MAIORIA CHAMA DE "TERREIRO" O ESPAÇO ONDE É REALIZADO O CULTO DE UMBANDA?

Por herança do Candomblé, cujos templos são chamados de Casas, Roças ou Terreiros. Alguns também denominam Centro como legado do Espiritismo que influenciou a religião em seus primórdios.

É VERDADE QUE SE ENTRAR NA UMBANDA DEPOIS NÃO PODE SAIR PORQUE ATRASA A VIDA?

Pode sair quando quiser que nada de mal acontecerá, a vida não atrasa e nem vai pra frente porque se escolhe frequentar uma religião ou desistir dela. Quando uma pessoa se identifica com os ensinamentos de uma religião a tendência é se tranquilizar, se harmonizar com o mundo espiritual, e isso com certeza é um fator que auxilia o progresso em todos os sentidos. Se estiver em desarmonia consigo até mesmo as questões mais triviais ficam pendentes, sem resolução, então certamente a vida "atrasa". Depois há que se considerar que a pessoa deixa o Terreiro, mas não deixa de ser médium, continua recebendo influência do astral e resta saber se do astral superior ou inferior. Muitos umbandistas vestem branco, vão ao Terreiro e quase nunca faltam, mas grande parte só faz isso. É impaciente com a própria família, não sabe ouvir, adora criticar, não tem boas palavras para os que com ele convivem, e se dentro de casa não tem compaixão certamente fora do lar também não terá. Esses que nunca doam, apenas recebem, não tem a metade da proteção daqueles que não vão a Terreiro nem igreja, não tem nenhuma religião, mas têm a caridade pelo próximo como meta na vida.

NÃO QUERIA SER UMBANDISTA, MAS AÍ COMECEI A RECEBER MEUS GUIAS NA RUA. O QUE FAÇO? Alguém pode pensar que um Guia, um Protetor ou Entidade de Luz possa "tomar" o médium em lugares públicos, expondo-o ao ridículo? A mediunidade desamparada e embrutecida deixa a pessoa à mercê de espíritos trevosos. Ser médium não é um carma a ser resgatado como muitos afirmam, é um dom que todos têm e para alguns uma oportunidade que foi concedida a fim de expurgar maus hábitos. Negar a existência da mediunidade ou fugir dela além de não adiantar ainda não ajuda em nada. Antes de se revoltar é mais inteligente aprender a conviver com ela. Fazer parte de uma corrente em um Terreiro de Umbanda facilita a comunhão com Deus e com os Guias que são espíritos com a missão de nos amparar. Porém se o médium estiver dentro da corrente contrariado, será inútil porque ser umbandista deve ser opção e jamais imposição. Aquele que se mantém harmonizado com o Alto através de orações, vida equilibrada, pensamentos elevados e conduta correta nada de mal pode lhe acontecer, independente da religião que escolha para si.

Como Surgiu A Umbanda

COMO DEVO DEFINIR A UMBANDA QUANDO PERGUNTAM SOBRE MINHA RELIGIÃO? A Umbanda é uma religião estruturada em três princípios básicos que são "Fraternidade, Caridade e Amor ao Próximo"; que acredita em um

Deus único; que reverencia os Orixás entendidos como as vibrações de Deus através da natureza; e que recebe orientação de espíritos denominados Guias que nos ajudam a seguir por um caminho melhor.

UMBANDA E CANDOMBLÉ SÃO AS MESMAS RELIGIÕES? Não. A Umbanda foi fundada pelo Caboclo das Sete Encruzilhadas incorporado no médium Zélio Fernandino de Moraes no começo do século 20 (1908), e o Candomblé criado no Brasil pelos africanos aqui trazidos como escravos ao longo de mais de três séculos (1525-1851). Na Umbanda quem dá consultas, passes e aconselhamentos são entidades espirituais através de incorporação em seus médiuns, e no Candomblé a consulta acontece apenas por meio do jogo de búzios através dos Pais e Mães de Santo. No Candomblé incorporam-se somente os Orixás e na Umbanda jamais se incorporam Orixás. No Candomblé há o sacrifício de animais para obrigação dos médiuns e festas em louvor aos Orixás, e na Umbanda não há sacrifício nem os médiuns fazem obrigações. No Candomblé é preciso que sejam cumpridas várias obrigações para que seja requerido o título de Babalorixá ou Ialorixá (pai e mãe de santo, respectivamente). Na Umbanda o médium pode a qualquer momento ser consagrado sacerdote e tornar-se dono de seu Terreiro, de acordo com a espiritualidade ou sua vontade. São duas religiões diferentes.

ALGUNS PENSAM QUE RELIGIÕES DE MATRIZ AFRICANA COMO O CANDOMBLÉ DEVERIAM SER PROIBIDAS PORQUE NÃO SÃO CRISTÃS! Os que pensam assim certamente gostariam também de proibir o pensamento, porque toda religião quando exteriorizada é uma manifestação do pensamento. Todos têm a liberdade de escolher sua religião, de mudar de religião, de não aderir a nenhuma religião e de ser ateu. Os fanáticos religiosos que agridem com palavras ou atos os que não compartilham de sua crença, nada mais são que meros delinquentes que cometem crime de ódio e pessoas execráveis que ferem a dignidade humana.

UMBANDA E ESPIRITISMO SÃO AS MESMAS RELIGIÕES? Não. O Espiritismo nasceu na França, em Paris, quando em 18 de Abril de 1857 Allan Kardec publicou o "Livro dos Espíritos". A Umbanda nasceu em 16 de Novembro de 1908, quando o primeiro culto foi realizado na casa do médium Zélio de Moraes, em São Gonçalo, no Rio. Mais de 50 anos marcam o advento do Espiritismo do surgimento da Umbanda. São duas religiões diferentes.

A UMBANDA DESAPROVA OS ENSINAMENTOS DE KARDEC? Pelo contrário, os umbandistas devem estudar a doutrina espírita e as obras de Allan Kardec para entender as questões relacionadas aos processos de evolução espiritual, reencarnação, os fenômenos mediúnicos etc.

OS FUNDADORES ESPIRITUAIS DA UMBANDA FORAM O CABOCLO E O PRETO VELHO? Sim, os dois espíritos Caboclo das Sete Encruzilhadas e Preto Velho Pai Antônio foram os iniciadores do que conhecemos hoje como religião de

Umbanda. O Caboclo considerado o criador da Umbanda e o Preto Velho responsável pelos processos de curas das doenças. Posteriormente a Entidade denominada "Orixá Mallet", da vibratória de Ogun, seria o responsável pelos trabalhos de desobsessão (descarrego) e desmanche de magias negras.

É VERDADE QUE O PRIMEIRO MÉDIUM DA UMBANDA FOI UM MENINO DE 17 ANOS? Sim. Seu nome era Zélio Fernandino de Morais, nascido em 10 de abril de 1891, no distrito de Neves, município de São Gonçalo, no Rio de Janeiro. Aos 17 anos incorporou os fundadores da religião de Umbanda, o Caboclo das Sete Encruzilhadas e o Preto Velho Pai Antônio.

É VERDADE QUE OS MÉDICOS DOS HOSPÍCIOS MANDAVAM LISTA COM OS NOMES DOS PACIENTES PARA AS PRIMEIRAS ENTIDADES DE UMBANDA APONTAR QUEM ERA DOENTE MENTAL E QUEM ESTAVA PERTURBADO ESPIRITUALMENTE? Sim, é verdade. Algumas testemunhas contam que médicos de alguns manicômios, como o de Jurujuba em Niterói, enviavam relação com os nomes dos internos para Orixá Mallet, que incorporado em Zélio, indicasse os que tinham distúrbio mental e os que estavam atormentados pelos malefícios da baixa magia ou simplesmente eram perseguidos por obsessores. Contam às testemunhas que no caso dos afligidos por atormentadores a cura era imediata, graças aos procedimentos ritualísticos preconizados pelo Caboclo das Sete Encruzilhadas.

POR QUE AS OUTRAS RELIGIÕES TÊM TEMPLOS E IGREJAS SUNTUOSOS E A UMBANDA QUASE SEMPRE É MUITO SIMPLES? Caboclo das Sete Encruzilhadas preconizou que Casa de "Umbanda só tem sentido se for para a prática da caridade, e para isto basta a copa de uma árvore".

POR QUE NÃO FORAM DITADAS PELO FUNDADOR DA UMBANDA CABOCLO DAS SETE ENCRUZILHADAS REGRAS RELATIVAS À UMBANDA A FIM DE UNIFORMIZAR A RELIGIÃO? SE ELE VEIO COM A MISSÃO DE ANUNCIAR A NOVA RELIGIÃO, ORGANIZÁ-LA E EVANGELIZAR NÃO TERIA SIDO ÚTIL? Não foram ditadas regras talvez para permitir que aquele que seja dotado de mediunidade e afeito a outras crenças possa se tornar um trabalhador sem ter que abandonar seus ideais. A única lei fundamental é que os filhos de Umbanda devem se pautar na humildade, no amor e na caridade. A Umbanda é uma religião que incorpora os elementos de todos os povos que formam nosso país, em especial o índio, o negro e o branco europeu, e nasceu por ordem do astral superior principalmente para a prática da caridade. Mais que isso nós só saberemos quando estivermos preparados para entender.

O QUE É PRECISO FAZER QUEM QUISER SERVIR DE FATO À RELIGIÃO? Ter pureza no coração, cultivar a fé que é a maior alavanca e jamais esquecer de que Umbanda sempre será baseada na simplicidade, no amor, na caridade e na humildade.

O CABOCLO DAS SETE ENCRUZILHADAS SE MANIFESTOU PELA PRIMEIRA VEZ EM UM CENTRO ESPÍRITA? Não. Manifestou-se na casa da benzedeira dona Eva. Dias depois, ao ser levado a Federação Espírita de Niterói (RJ), Zélio foi convidado a participar da sessão e determinou-se que ele sentasse à mesa juntamente com outros médiuns. De repente, tomado por uma força estranha e alheia a sua vontade, ele disse "Aqui está faltando uma flor", e saiu da sala indo ao jardim, de onde voltou com uma flor. Então se deu grande tumulto não só pela atitude inédita de Zélio, mas principalmente porque, ao mesmo tempo em que isso acontecia, ocorreram várias e surpreendentes manifestações de Índios (Caboclos) e Pretos Velhos em todos os médiuns da Mesa de Trabalho. O Dirigente da sessão espírita achou aquilo tudo um absurdo e advertiu-os, com aspereza, citando o "atraso espiritual" em que se encontravam, e convidando-os a se retirarem. Estava evidenciado, desde aquele instante e que perdura até hoje, o preconceito e a empáfia de muitos ditos Espíritas.

ZÉLIO DE MORAES SABIA QUE ELE ESTAVA DESTINADO A SER PRECURSOR DE UMA NOVA RELIGIÃO? Não, muito ao contrário. O choque fica evidente no trecho que transcrevemos em seguida: *"Minha família estava apavorada. Eu mesmo não sabia explicar o que se passava comigo. Surpreendia-me haver dialogado com aqueles austeros senhores de cabeça branca, em volta de uma mesa onde se praticava um trabalho, para mim desconhecido. Como poderia, aos 17* *anos, organizar um culto? No entanto, eu mesmo falara, sem saber o que dizia e porque dizia. Era uma sensação estranha, uma força superior que me impelia a fazer e a dizer o que nem sequer se passava pelo meu pensamento".*

A UMBANDA TEM FUNDAMENTO, É PRECISO PREPARAR!

O QUE É FUNDAMENTO? Fundamento é o princípio sobre o qual se apoia e se desenvolve a religião de Umbanda. O conjunto de regras básicas de organização e funcionamento da religião se chama **Fundamento**.

O QUE É RITUAL? Toda religião possui um conjunto de gestos, palavras e formalidades utilizados de maneira simbólica, aos quais se dá o nome de **Ritual**. Na Umbanda os rituais variam de Terreiro para Terreiro na forma, mas são iguais no conteúdo. O fundamental, ou seja, o básico é igual em todos. Por exemplo, em todos existem pontos cantados e pontos riscados, todos usam velas e defumação, banhos de ervas, fumo e bebida, oferendas, enfim, todos esses elementos fazem parte dos **Fundamentos da Umbanda** e a eles nenhum Dirigente ou Guia Chefe pode se opor, e se assim o fizer estará praticando outra religião e não a Umbanda.

QUAL É O NOME CORRETO PARA REFERIR-SE AO LOCAL ONDE SE CULTUA A UMBANDA? CENTRO DE UMBANDA, TERREIRO, TEMPLO, CASA, TENDA? Todos eles são corretos.

A UMBANDA FAZ SACRIFÍCIO DE ANIMAIS? Não, a Umbanda não faz e não admite que se faça em seus Terreiros, pois não é parte do fundamento da religião. Também não aceita maus tratos de nenhuma espécie com os animais porque entende que os animais são nossos semelhantes no quesito da *senciência,* que é a capacidade de sofrer ou sentir prazer e felicidade, e possuem o interesse em permanecer vivos. E por não ser fundamento, quem sacrifica uma vida na religião de Umbanda estará matando para saciar a sede por tônus vital de espíritos malignos. E o retorno será desesperador.

CONHEÇO ALGUNS TERREIROS DE UMBANDA QUE FAZEM USO DE ANIMAIS EM SEUS TRABALHOS! Terreiro que pratica sacrifício de animais para descarrego, oferenda, iniciação ou qualquer outro rito não é Umbanda sob nenhum ponto de vista. A Umbanda anunciada e fundada como religião pelo Caboclo das Sete Encruzilhadas não tem essa prática.

NÃO ESTOU DE ACORDO COM ALGUMAS NORMAS IMPOSTAS PELO DIRIGENTE DO TERREIRO QUE FREQUENTO. COMO DEVO FAZER PARA TENTAR MUDÁ-LAS? O filho de fé deve se adaptar as normas da Casa que frequenta e não pretender que a Casa mude para atender às suas expectativas. Se não está de acordo, deve procurar outra que mais corresponda ao seu ponto de vista. E fazê-lo em silêncio, com sinceridade e sem maledicência.

ALGUNS DIZEM QUE A UMBANDA ASSIM COMO AS RELIGIÕES DE MATRIZ AFRICANA NÃO É RELIGIÃO, E SIM SEITA! É a ignorância dando voz ao preconceito: "Religião é a minha, seita a dos outros". Embora não seja nada fácil distinguir religião de seita, considera-se religião a crença organizada hierarquicamente, com normas claras de orientação e culto, assim como acontece na Umbanda. Seita sempre é usada no sentido pejorativo para diminuir a crença alheia. Os argumentos usados pelos preconceituosos, além de não resistirem à luz do conhecimento, ainda são vergonhosos e tornam infames os que os proferem.

COMO DEVO AGIR QUANDO SOU AGREDIDO POR PESSOAS DE OUTRAS RELIGIÕES? Ignore-os. São pobres atrasados que não conseguem ver Deus além dos limites impostos pelo seu reduzido entendimento da religião. Quem agride sabe da doutrina, mas nada sabe do Amor. Nem desconfiam o quanto estão distantes do Cristo. São merecedores de compaixão, pois perdem a oportunidade de se encontrar com o Criador que Se comunica por vários caminhos e fala por diferentes mensageiros.

É DIFÍCIL OUVIR DIRETORES DE OUTRAS RELIGIÕES ATACANDO A MINHA RELIGIÃO IMPUNEMENTE EM NOME DA LIBERDADE DE EXPRESSÃO! Para julgar outras religiões é preciso saber julgar a sua, para julgar os homens é preciso ter a grandeza de primeiro saber julgar a si mesmo, mas há muitos que tomam a sua opinião por medida exclusiva do bom e do mau. O que parece bom a essa pobre pessoa automaticamente vira verdadeiro, e o que não corresponde a sua opinião é definido como falso. Contradizem-se suas ideias, sua maneira de ver as coisas, o sistema que conceberam e adotaram, e os que não compartilham julgam pecaminosos aos olhos de Deus. Tudo o que esses mendigos espirituais não concordam precisa ser exterminado. A tais pessoas, em sua maioria autodenominada cristã, falta a primeira qualidade para uma justa apreciação: ser integro no julgamento. Mas disso sequer suspeitam, pois a vaidade não lhes permite e a vaidade é o pecado preferido do maligno.

O QUE É FANÁTICO RELIGIOSO? Fanático é aquele incapaz de admitir o mundo a partir de ponto de vista diferente do que elegeu como absoluto para sua vida. Deste modo seu universo se divide entre o bem e o mal, sendo que o bem são as suas escolhas e preferências, e o mal é a escolha dos outros que não são iguais as suas. Tenha-se sempre em mente que o fanático religioso jamais admitirá que é obsecado, para ele doido são sempre os outros.

POR QUE OS FANÁTICOS RELIGIOSOS CRITICAM TANTO A RELIGIÃO ALHEIA? Porque a crença deles não pode ser questionada ou abalada no intercâmbio com outras formas de crença. O fanático coloca todas as esperanças em sua visão particular, e outras formas de visão abalam suas pequenas certezas.

O QUE É VIOLÊNCIA RELIGIOSA? Não é só a violência física como os terroristas que atacaram o World Trade Center em Nova York, ou a destruição de símbolos históricos e religiosos como faz o Estado Islâmico e seus psicopatas "soldados sagrados de Alá". A violência aparece também na insistente tentativa de desqualificar o outro como alguns "evangélicos" fazem com a Umbanda e o Candomblé. Eles espancam, depredam, humilham em nome de Deus. E justificam a falta de amor ao próximo (que é o primeiro e mais importante ensinamento do Cristo) como atos de fidelidade à sua fé. Daí não é errado afirmar que o fanático religioso deixou de cultuar Deus e passou a cultuar a igreja.

O QUE É SINCRETISMO RELIGIOSO? A religião dos negros que vieram escravizados da África era considerada pelos seus senhores e pelo clero heresia e bruxaria, e foram obrigados a cultuar os santos católicos, porque essa era a religião predominante trazida pelos brancos de origem portuguesa. Quando demonstravam a fé que tinham nos Orixás eram surrados e até mortos. Os escravos acreditavam que as forças divinas se manifestavam na natureza, e cada uma dessas forças era representada por elementos da própria natureza, como as pedras (otás), por exemplo. A maneira que encontraram para reverenciar seus deuses era dispor sobre um altar as imagens dos santos católicos e, sob as imagens (ou dentro delas), assentar as pedras que representavam seus Orixás sagrados. Identificaram os Orixás com os santos de acordo com alguma similitude entre eles e, secretamente, quando rezavam em sua língua nativa para Santa

Bárbara estavam cultuando Iansã, quando se dirigiam a Nossa Senhora da Conceição em seus corações estavam falando com Iemanjá. Esse processo foi chamado de sincretismo religioso até hoje respeitado pela Umbanda.

ALGUNS DE OUTRAS RELIGIÕES DIZEM QUE A UMBANDA É INFERIOR PRINCIPALMENTE PORQUE SE VALE DE SINCRETISMO EM SEUS CULTOS. DIZEM TAMBÉM QUE OS TERREIROS DE UMBANDA E AS CASAS DE CANDOMBLÉ SÃO "ANTROS DE MENTIRA E ENGANAÇÃO" E ONDE SE MANIFESTAM DEMÔNIOS. Sincretismo é o acréscimo de práticas rituais de uma religião à outra, práticas que a Umbanda herdou do Candomblé, de cultos indígenas e do catolicismo. Na Umbanda e no Candomblé, que são as duas religiões mais ultrajadas por quem não tendo nada a dizer fala demais, não se fazem desafios para prosperidade financeira, não vendem objetos para quebra de maldição, não há vigília a meia noite onde todos rodam histericamente até cair de cansaço e excitação. Os Guias da Umbanda e os Orixás do Candomblé não sugerem comportamentos que demonstram desajuste emocional nem desarranjo mental, ninguém fica "loucamente" possuído pelo espírito santo, não há "unção dos animais" onde as pessoas rugem como leão ou cantam como galo ou relincham como cavalo (os Filhos de Fé e o Povo do Santo não expõem seus Guias e Orixás ao ridículo). De forma alguma fazem "unção do riso" porque os umbandistas e os candomblecistas sabem que há "tempo de rir" e "tempo de saltar de alegria", mas não durante os cultos. Nem nos pesadelos mais terríveis umbandista algum jamais pensou em chamar sua Gira de "striptease para zambi" para atrair público pagante. Nas Casas de Umbanda e de Candomblé não há globo espelhado nem canhões de luz estroboscópica e nem fumaça, nunca DJs e MCs embalaram seus praticantes para louvar Oxalá ao som do street dance e heavy metal. Os Dirigentes e Pais e Mães do Santo não desejam dominar o país nem se infiltram na política, não lutam entre si buscando arregimentar rebanho maior que lhes dê mais dinheiro e poder. Nos Terreiros há assistência onde ficam as pessoas que não fazem parte da corrente mediúnica, mas jamais teve nem nunca terá auditório nem tablado porque os Guias e Orixás não se apresentam em picadeiro para divertimento do público. Também ninguém presenciou nessas duas respeitáveis religiões seus adeptos pisarem em tapetes mágicos. E se um descontrolado grita feito demente até cair desfalecido no chão, na Umbanda não é conduzido para acalentar emoções e espíritos, é encaminhado a um psiquiatra. Por tudo o que se expos aqui é preciso perguntar, portanto, qual é o endereço do "antro de mentira e enganação", e onde é que o demônio se manifesta de fato.

É JUSTO NOS TERREIROS HAVER COBRANÇA PELOS ATENDIMENTOS ESPIRITUAIS? Não é justo na medida em que os Guias, que são quem de fato tem a faculdade de auxiliar aos necessitados, nada cobram. Os médiuns e Dirigentes não tem o direito de fazer da caridade objeto de comércio e nem meio de vida. Se as pessoas que buscam auxílio quiserem contribuir, que seja com velas e outros objetos de uso litúrgico, ou materiais de uso comum como sabonete ou copos descartáveis. Se os assistidos tiverem vontade de ir adiante com o auxílio que seja na colaboração com o aluguel que muitos Terreiros pagam, mas que jamais sirva como especulação financeira.

OS ORIXÁS NA UMBANDA

Para conhecer mais sobre os Orixás sugerimos a leitura do livro
"Os Orixás na Umbanda - Para Leigos"

O QUE É ORIXÁ? Orí significa Cabeça e Xá quer dizer Rei ou Senhor, deste modo Orixá quer dizer Senhor da Cabeça. "Qualquer definição que façamos dos Orixás, assim como de Deus, será sempre uma definição incompleta decorrente da pobreza da linguagem humana. Os Orixás estão acima não só da linguagem, mas também da nossa compreensão. É a 'fonte' mais evoluída criada e emanada do astral superior que interage conosco e que se manifesta através das forças da natureza. Buscamos entender e explicar a manifestação dos Orixás através das forças da natureza porque esse é o nosso limite e não temos entendimento nem evolução para avançar mais, pois foge da nossa compreensão".

OS UMBANDISTAS INCORPORAM OS ORIXÁS? Não. Na Umbanda não se incorporam Orixás porque não são entendidos como alguém que teve vida corpórea na Terra, mas sim como manifestações da consciência divina ou energias emanadas da própria natureza. Os umbandistas incorporam seus enviados ou representantes chamados **"Falangeiros"**, por exemplo, Baianos, Boiadeiros, Pretos Velhos. São espíritos que mantêm forte ligação missionária e fluídica com a força original com a qual está ligado, ou seja, com o Orixá. São esses enviados de Orixá que os médiuns incorporam nas Giras de Umbanda.

É CERTO AFIRMAR QUE OS ORIXÁS SÃO OS PRÓPRIOS REINOS DA NATUREZA QUE REPRESENTA?

Não, Oxum não é a cachoeira nem Xangô é a pedreira. Eles representam as forças da natureza, mas não é a natureza que representam.

O QUE SIGNIFICA DIZER QUE "NÃO HÁ BRIGA ENTRE OS ORIXÁS" PORQUE TODOS "TRABALHAM EM ABSOLUTA HARMONIA ENTRE SI E COMPLEMENTAM-SE NA SUSTENTAÇÃO DA CRIAÇÃO DIVINA"?

Quer dizer que não há um Orixá com posição mais elevada que outro ou um Orixá mais importante que outro. Quer dizer que nenhum atua sozinho. Todos os Guias sempre trazem consigo os elementos que se harmonizam na natureza, como o exemplo dos Caboclos: todos os Caboclos trazem consigo a manifestação da energia das matas, portanto todo Caboclo está ligado ao elemento de Oxóssi (que é o Orixá das matas). Mas há Caboclo que traz consigo a vibração de Ogun. Neste caso as duas energias se "misturam", se complementam, e combinadas dão origem aos Caboclos Arranca Toco, ou seja, uma terceira vibração com características próprias. Oxóssi não perdeu sua essência assim como Ogun também não perdeu e ambas as energias geraram uma terceira (Caboclos Arranca Toco). Para ficar bem entendido citemos outro exemplo, sempre considerando a Linha de Caboclo: Oxóssi (1ª. vibração ou energia) vibrando conjuntamente com Omulu (2ª. vibração ou energia) são gerados os Caboclos Flecheiros e Caboclos Bugres (3ª. vibração ou energia). Oxóssi e Omulu se desdobraram em uma terceira energia que deu origem aos Caboclos Flecheiros. Lembrando que todo Caboclo é ligado a Oxóssi, se desdobrado com Yemanjá são originados as Caboclas e Caboclos do Mar. Combinando as vibrações de Oxóssi e Oxum são principiados os Caboclos e Caboclas dos Rios, das Cachoeiras. Com Iansã surgem os Caboclos do Vento. Assim é explicado quando se diz que os Orixás se complementam (ou se desdobram) em outras energias que dão origem a outras manifestações. Erram os que dizem que os Orixás estão "brigando pela cabeça do filho".

QUAL A IMPORTÂNCIA DO ORIXÁ NA PERSONALIDADE DAS PESSOAS? Todos os indivíduos têm suas próprias características de personalidade herdadas de seus Orixás, e a cada Orixá está associada uma tendência de comportamento diante do mundo. Assim a pessoa recebe as emanações próprias de seus Orixás e que influenciam cada aspecto de sua vida.

PODE-SE DIZER QUE OS ORIXÁS SÃO SANTOS? Não. Os Orixás participam da natureza dos anjos enquanto os santos foram espíritos de luz que encarnaram e tiveram uma existência terrena. São entidades espirituais diferentes.

ORIXÁS SÃO DEUSES AFRICANOS? Não. A Umbanda não está baseada em lendas do panteão africano. Não entende Orixás como deuses, semideuses ou divindades. Entende como complexos energéticos e vibratórios.

AQUELES QUE NÃO CREEM TAMBÉM TÊM ORIXÁS? Orixás são as Vibrações de Deus manifestadas por amor à humanidade, ou em outras palavras, são energias emitidas e direcionadas aos seres pela caridade de Deus. Orixá não é propriedade de nenhuma religião, é Força Divina emanada do Criador Deus/Olorun. A eles todos estão ligados, independente de acreditar ou não, de conhecer ou não.

É POSSÍVEL INCORPORAR OS ORIXÁS NO TERREIRO? Não se incorpora Orixás na Umbanda. É importante que se entenda que não existe um espírito chamado Ogun, e que não é um ser que tenha existido como homem porque está além do estágio humano, nem tampouco é um ser sobrenatural. **Trata-se de um grupo de espíritos trabalhando numa determinada faixa energética chamada de Ogun.** Da mesma forma, Oxum, Oxóssi, Yemanjá não são espíritos, mas sim faixas vibratórias onde vários espíritos se agrupam por afinidades, e trabalham numa função específica que recebe a vibração de um determinado Orixá.

OS ORIXÁS AGEM DE MANEIRA INDIVIDUAL OU ESTÃO INTERLIGADOS UNS COM OS OUTROS? Estão profundamente interligados. Agem e interagem de forma absolutamente harmônica e perfeita entre si. Para ilustrar podemos pensar no ciclo das águas. Imagine a água nascendo em uma mina (Nanã, Senhora das Águas Originais), rolando pelas pedras (Xangô, regente das Pedras) até despencar em queda livre na cachoeira (Oxum, Regente das Águas Doces), então corre pela terra (Omulu/Obaluaiê, Regente da Terra) germinando essa terra para o nascimento dos vegetais e árvores (Oxóssi, Regente das Matas) até desaguar no mar (Yemanjá, Regente das Águas Salgadas), o sol aquecendo a água (Ogun, Orixá da Forja) provocando a evaporação e precipitação na terra em forma de chuva (Iansã, Regente das Chuvas e Tempestades) reiniciando assim o processo. **E o culto a essas forças chama-se Umbanda.**

O QUE É AYABÁ? Ayabá, iabá ou iyabá traduzido do iorubá significa "Mãe Rainha", e o termo é usado para referir-se aos Orixás de polaridade feminina. As ayabás cultuadas na Umbanda são Oxum, Iansã, Yemanjá e Nanã.

O QUE SÃO REINOS DOS ORIXÁS? Todo ser vivo sobrevive na natureza deste planeta e interage com animais, vegetais, minerais, tendo todos – homens, bichos, plantas – o mesmo valor, embora muitos arrogantes pensem em si como a criação mais importante de Deus. A energia do Criador vibra em tudo e em toda parte, sejam nos reinos específicos como os rios e cachoeiras, mares, pedreiras, matas e camadas internas e externas do globo, seja nos reinos não específicos como o ar com subdivisões em tempestades, chuvas e ventos. Para as energias que vibram em cada um desses reinos dá-se o nome de Orixás.

Portanto, Orixá é um ser imaterial, ou seja, não tem existência palpável, e é dotado da Essência Divina que se propaga no planeta a fim de direcionar as criaturas encarnadas. **Orixá é Deus em nós, é Deus em toda natureza, é a oportunidade de encontrar Deus através da Sua Obra.**

SE A UMBANDA NÃO ENTENDE OS ORIXÁS COMO ANCESTRAIS DIVINIZADOS QUE VIVERAM E MORRERAM NA TERRA, MAS SIM COMO ENERGIAS QUE EMANAM DA NATUREZA, ENTÃO COMO HÁ HISTÓRIAS SOBRE ELES? Não são histórias, são narrativas simbólicas que objetivam explicar acontecimentos que contêm um sentido oculto. Fala-se dos Orixás como personagens, e às vezes seres que incorporam as forças da natureza com características humanas para que homens e mulheres possam entender. Não se podem conceber os Orixás pela razão, então se usam mitos tentando explicar a realidade através de histórias sagradas.

COMO SE PODE PEDIR A SUSTENTAÇÃO DOS ORIXÁS? Manifestando no cotidiano as qualidades e bons sentimentos ligados aos Orixás. Por exemplo, quanto maior a sintonia com a vibração de amor de Oxum, maior será seu amparo e irradiação.

PRECISO AGRADAR AOS ORIXÁS PARA MINHA VIDA NÃO ANDAR PARA TRÁS? Orixás são seres de pura luz, não fazem o mal e não precisam de agrado. Os seres humanos não tem nada de necessário aos Orixás ao ponto de fazer a "vida andar para trás" se não receberem.

SE EU NÃO FIZER AS OBRIGAÇÕES O ORIXÁ PODE ME COBRAR? Orixá não é Deus, porém foi criado a partir d´Ele, portanto tem caráter divino. Nada que é emanado de Deus pode fazer mal. E na Umbanda não tem "obrigações" e nem fazem parte de seu ritual.

O ORIXÁ PODE SE REVOLTAR SE EU NÃO ATENDER AO QUE ME PEDIU? Orixá, na Umbanda, nada pede.

Os Orixás e Suas Vibrações
Oxalá

QUAL É A VIBRAÇÃO DE OXALÁ? É considerado o Orixá Maior e vibra em todos os elementos através dos outros Orixás. Busca-se entrar em contato com sua irradiação durante os Rituais da Umbanda principalmente quando é preciso reequilibrar tanto o espírito quanto o corpo físico. As irradiações da Fé de Oxalá estimulam a religiosidade. É representado em duas formas: Oxaguian jovem, e Oxalufan velho.

QUEM É OXALÁ? Oxalá é o maior Orixá da Umbanda, abaixo apenas de Olorum, Deus Supremo. É o Criador do Universo, dos animais, vegetais e do homem. É Oxalá quem rege o destino humano. Suas vibrações estimulam a fé individual e geram sentimentos de religiosidade sem fanatismo. É aquele que de¬termina o fim da vida de cada ser humano. Representa o amor, bondade, pureza espiritual, e tudo que indica positividade. Oxalá é o Grande Orixá conhecido como Rei do Pano Branco. Chamado Orixá Funfun que significa branco em iorubá, sua vibração dá maturidade, sabedoria, paz e tranquilidade aos seres criados.

Ogun

QUAL É A VIBRAÇÃO DE OGUN? É a vibração que atua no ferro e nas estradas e corresponde à necessidade de energia, defesa, determinação, perseverança. É quem dá a força ao ser humano quando este precisa criar novos caminhos que acrescente sentido à vida. As irradiações da Lei de Ogun estimulam a ordem. Nos trilhos dos trens são depositadas as suas oferendas.

QUEM É OGUN? Orixá do ferro e da forja, da guerra, do bom combate, das invenções, engenharia e tecnologia. Todas as estradas são guardadas pela vibração de Ogun. Ele está em todos os caminhos ligados à Linha dos Guardiões (Exus). Tem a coragem, a força e a impetuosidade como atributos. Orixá da energia que produz a atitude, perseverança, vencedor de demandas. Ogun está associado ao renascimento no sentido de dar a volta por cima mediante capacidade de se reerguer. Ogun rege todo início de movimento, é a energia que possibilita o início do que quer que seja, abre os caminhos e encruzilhadas junto com Exu. Este Orixá abre os caminhos e vence as lutas agindo pelo instinto para defender e proteger os mais fracos. A vibração de Ogun traz potência e força de seguir em frente.

POR QUE OGUN É CONSIDERADO O SENHOR DOS CAMINHOS? Por herança da cultura africana. Considere-se que, no entendimento do Candomblé, os Orixás são semelhantes aos homens, inclusive tiveram vida humana na Terra. Deste modo Ogun foi, na mitologia da cultura iorubá, o primeiro ferreiro, o descobridor da fundição e inventor de todas as ferramentas que existem. Com a foice entende-se que Ogun abriu os primeiros caminhos para o resto do mundo e assim como abriu também tem o poder de fechar. Inventou o ancinho com o qual arou as terras e plantou os alimentos. Com a tesoura cortou a pele dos animais para aquecer o corpo que, juntamente com o machado para cortar árvores e o martelo para unir os troncos com pregos possibilitou a construção dos necessários abrigos, proteção contra as intempéries e animais selvagens. Com a faca Ogun fez o primeiro sacrifício ritual e por essa razão no Candomblé sempre se louva Ogun durante esses rituais. Também forjou a espada para vencer os inimigos e conquistar território para seu povo. A mitologia mostra que não há um só caminho que Ogun não tenha percorrido em suas guerras de conquista. Na Umbanda costuma-se chamar por seu auxílio em situações gravíssimas, de extrema dificuldade, e quando o inimigo é muito mais forte. É importante esclarecer que na Umbanda não há ritual que envolva animais e os que assim o fazem não tem base religiosa para fazê-lo, portanto não são umbandistas.

Oxóssi

QUAL É A VIBRAÇÃO DE OXÓSSI? É a vibração que atua nas matas e animais e corresponde à necessidade de saúde, nutrição, crescimento através do conhecimento, energia necessária à vida, equilíbrio fisiológico. É quem auxilia na cura. As irradiações do Conhecimento de Oxóssi estimulam o raciocínio.

As matas são os santuários de Oxóssi e seu altar são os bosques.

QUEM É OXÓSSI? Orixá da caça e da fartura alimentar, abundância e prosperidade. Senhor das matas, da verdade e do conhecimento. O grande caçador de almas perdidas, grande curador e grande doutrinador. Senhor das florestas, dos Caboclos de Pena, da caça, da fortuna, da agricultura, da ecologia, da saúde. Oxóssi é o chefe, o patrono dos Caboclos na Umbanda.

POR QUE OXÓSSI TEM DIVERSOS NOMES? Não é apenas Oxóssi que tem diversos nomes, são todos os Orixás. Dependendo do local da África de onde vieram os escravos, trouxeram consigo seus costumes e dialetos. Assim Oxóssi é denominação entre os nagôs, Abê ou Agbê entre os jejes, e Tauamim, Matalumbô ou Congombira entre os escravos bantos.

O QUE SIGNIFICA NAGÔ, JEJE E BANTO? São denominações dos diferentes povos que habitavam o continente africano e que foram trazidos como escravos ao Brasil. Bantos são os que habitavam o litoral da África e falavam diversas línguas como o quicongo, o quimbundo e o umbundo. Nagô era o nome que se dava ao iorubano ou a todo negro da Costa dos Escravos que falava ou entendia o iorubá. Os Jejes foram milhares de negros vindos de várias partes da África e falavam fon, mahi e ewe. A palavra Jeje vem do iorubá adjeje que significa estrangeiro, forasteiro, portanto, nunca existiu uma nação Jeje, o nome era dado de forma pejorativa pelos iorubás. No Brasil, nagôs, jejes e bantos originam os Candomblés e a Umbanda.

AO DIZER QUE "OXÓSSI É CAÇADOR" QUER DIZER QUE ELE ESTIMULA A CAÇA DE ANIMAIS? Não estimula a matança em hipótese alguma. Diz-se que é caçador no sentido de perseguir o conhecimento. Caçar é um ato que exige profunda paciência e quietude, e no silêncio de sua alma o caçador pensa e consegue entender, seja por meio da inteligência, da razão ou da experiência.

OXÓSSI É A DIVINIZAÇÃO DAS MATAS E DAS FLORESTAS. MAS E OS ANIMAIS QUE MORAM NELAS? Ele também reina sobre os animais, porém os selvagens. Diz a lenda que Oxóssi os conhece profundamente e com eles partilha o conhecimento da natureza, além de possuir todas as suas virtudes. Por exemplo, Oxossi é sagaz como o Leopardo, forte como o leão, leve como o pássaro, silencioso como o tigre, observador como a coruja, esconde-se como um tatu, é vaidoso como um pavão, corre como os coelhos, que sobe em árvores como macacos etc. O fundamento de Oxóssi é atingir um objetivo fixando o alvo ao modo do Caçador. É considerado o Orixá que dá de comer as pessoas porque sob seus domínios estão os animais e os vegetais. Todo aquele que tem responsabilidade de alimentar a família está sob a vibração de Oxóssi. Quando se precisa atingir uma meta para prover o sustento, deve-se evocar a energia desse Orixá. Também se apela a Oxóssi quando é preciso encontrar o remédio apropriado para uma doença, embora seja Ossaîn quem determina se o remédio fará ou não efeito. Na mitologia Oxóssi, com apenas uma flecha, conseguiu matar a perigosa feiticeira africana (ajé) chamada Ìyàmì Oxorongá, que se transformou em pássaro e atacou pessoas e cidades espalhando doenças e miséria, enquanto todos os outros caçadores já haviam perdido todas as suas flechas tentando em vão matar o pássaro, por isso é chamado de "Guerreiro de uma única flecha", e por isso é costume pedir a Oxóssi que destrua feitiços ou energias maléficas. Certo dia, enquanto caçava Oxossi conheceu Oxum, a deusa das águas doces e do ouro, por quem se apaixonou e com ela teve um filho, Logun-Edé. Filho da floresta com as águas dos rios, Logun-Edé é considerado o Orixá da riqueza e da fartura, herdeiro dos domínios de seus pais.

Xangô

QUAL É A VIBRAÇÃO DE XANGÔ? É a vibração que atua nas pedras, fogo, trovões e corresponde a necessidade de discernimento, estudo, raciocínio concreto e método. É o que direciona o ser humano quando este precisa de justiça e equilíbrio. As irradiações da Justiça de Xangô estimulam a razão. A montanha é o santuário natural de Xangô e seu altar é a pedra, onde é oferendado.

QUEM É XANGÔ? Orixá do trovão e do fogo, dos estudos, da sabedoria, dos contratos, das demandas judiciais, do magma e de todas as atividades vulcânicas. Este Orixá é advogado dos injustiçados e considerado executor da justiça de Deus, simboliza a lei de causa e efeito responsável por dar a quem merece o devido castigo e a vitória aos que foram oprimidos. É quem dá solução às pendências.

A DEFINIÇÃO DE XANGÔ É MUITO SEMELHANTE A DIVINDADES DE OUTRAS RELIGIÕES E CULTURAS, PORÉM COM NOMES DIFERENTES. POR QUE NA UMBANDA SE CHAMA XANGÔ? Porque a Umbanda fundamentou-se na religião iorubá, por isso denominou o Orixá da Justiça de Xangô. A essência divina que rege a Justiça é apenas uma, mas manifesta-se de forma diferente para as diversas religiões, povos e culturas. Por isso há vários nomes para a mesma divindade.

XANGÔ É ORIXÁ APENAS DA JUSTIÇA? Não, na mitologia africana Xangô é a força representada pelo som do trovão. É também o poder em todas as suas dimensões, seja poder da inteligência, da sedução, da riqueza, da força física etc. O mito diz que é Orixá muito competitivo, tendo roubado a mulher de seu irmão Ogun (Iansã) e também a esposa de seu irmão Oxóssi (Oxum). Em suas lutas dispõe da coragem e impetuosidade de Iansã, da vidência e magia de Oxum, e da força bruta de uma terceira esposa, Obá, guerreira poderosa. Xangô mora num palácio nos céus, onde prepara as chuvas para Yemanjá, sua mãe. Segundo a lenda o barulho dos trovões é o machado de Xangô caindo do céu para fazer justiça.

<u>Yemanjá</u>

QUAL É A VIBRAÇÃO DE YEMANJÁ? É a vibração que atua nos mares e oceanos também chamados de "calunga grande" (grande cemitério) e corresponde a necessidade de segurança familiar e de amor fraternal. É a vibração de consolo e esperança. O mar é o santuário de Yemanjá e seu altar é a praia.

QUEM É YEMANJÁ? É a grande mãe da Umbanda e dos Orixás. Rainha dos mares, dos oceanos, das águas salgadas, representa a geração em todos os sentidos, fecundidade, gestação e maternidade. Senhora da purificação, da família, da harmonia, da saúde mental. Responsável pelos bens materiais e grande mãe e provedora. Orixá dos mares e oceanos, do casamento e da vida em família. Recebe vários nomes como Iemanjá, Janaína, Rainha do Mar, Dona Janaína, Inaê, Maria, Princesa do Aioká, Mãe D'Água, Dandalunda, Ísis, Marabô, Mucunã, Sereia do Mar, Senhora da Coroa Estrelada, Senhora da Calunga Grande (mar). O maior ponto de força da natureza é o mar e pertence à Yemanjá, chamado de *"calunga grande"* (o cemitério é "calunga pequena"). Esse ponto de força natural é grande absorvedor de energias negativas, é um santuário natural para onde é levado tudo o que precisa ser purificado e depois devolvido. Os Guias de Umbanda fazem uso da energia dos mares e oceanos em seus lindos trabalhos de curas. Para o mar são levados muitos espíritos sombrios cujas vibrações densas os impedem de chegar a planos mais sutis. No mar são tratados pelos trabalhadores da Linha de Yemanjá.

POR QUE SE DIZ QUE YEMANJÁ É A MÃE DE TODOS?
Yemanjá é saudada como a Grande Mãe porque, segundo a tradição do candomblé Ketú, esse Orixá é quem maternalmente pega pela mão a alma que vai reencarnar e entrega ao seu respectivo anjo de guarda. Leva, como uma mãe cuidadosa, até o Orixá que vai acompanhar durante a encarnação. Deste modo se diz que Yemanjá é a mãe de todos, e assim é reverenciada e muito respeitada.

TEM FUNDAMENTO A PRÁTICA DE UMBANDA QUE ENSINA FAZER ENTREGAS PARA YEMANJÁ ENCHENDO BARQUINHOS COM PRESENTES? Nenhum fundamento além da tradição.

YEMANJÁ ATENDE AOS PEDIDOS DOS QUE LHES DÃO PRESENTES? Orixá é a energia da natureza. Que utilidade teria para Yemanjá pentes de plástico, vidros de perfume e espelhinhos? Qual sentido espiritual pode haver em matar e mutilar os animais marítimos com o plástico das oferendas jogadas ao mar? Alguém pode acreditar que para garantir um ano novo cheio de axé e boas energias, para que todos os sonhos se realizem é preciso envenenar peixes, tartarugas, baleias, golfinhos que confundem isopor e plástico com alimento? O que há de sagrado em poluir os mares e matar os animais?

POR QUE MUITOS UMBANDISTAS ENSINAM QUE QUANDO O BARQUINHO NAVEGA MAR ADENTRO É PORQUE YEMANJÁ ACEITOU A OFERENDA? Porque desconhecem que os presentes pretensamente "aceitos" por Yemanjá ameaçam o ecossistema marinho e os que ela "devolve" poluem a praia.

O QUE PENSAM AS PESSOAS QUANDO VEEM AS TONELADAS DE LIXO DEIXADAS NAS PRAIAS PELOS UMBANDISTAS? O que pensaria qualquer pessoa se cortasse o pé com o caco de vidro de uma garrafa de champagne "presenteada" a Yemanjá e que foi largada na praia. Imagine o que passa pela cabeça de quem vê o prego do barquinho de Yemanjá fincado no pé de uma criança. Qualquer pessoa evoluída intelectualmente quando contempla as toneladas de vidros, madeiras com pregos, plásticos, comidas, embalagens, fitas, maços e pontas de cigarro, garrafas pet, largados nas praias provavelmente pensa que os umbandistas são porcalhões e pouco civilizados. É um absurdo que religião que cultua a natureza adote práticas de total desrespeito com o meio ambiente.

O QUE OFERENDAR À YEMANJÁ SEM AGREDIR A NATUREZA? Não só à Yemanjá, mas a todos os Orixás porque ninguém gosta de ter sua casa maculada, há opção de flores naturais e frutas que não agridem a natureza e tem seus fundamentos preservados. Velas de parafina podem ser substituídas pelas de cera de abelha. Importante que se jogue apenas o líquido do perfume ao mar e nunca o vidro. O umbandista que for à mata e quiser deixar uma bebida deve colocar o líquido em cuia de coco e recolher a garrafa. Material de plástico deve ser substituído por folha de bananeira. Uso de velas, cigarros e charutos podem provocar acidentes e incêndios em áreas de vegetação principalmente perto de raízes de árvores, de folhas secas e de materiais inflamáveis causando danos irreversíveis à natureza. Nas festas na praia todos são responsáveis pelo recolhimento e destino dos materiais usados nas oferendas, deste modo junto com os atabaques, barracas e demais apetrechos é **dever** levar sacos de lixo e **obrigação** recolher todas as sobras, não deixando na natureza nem mesmo um palito de fósforo. O mesmo em todos os reinos da natureza. Todo umbandista precisa definitivamente substituir os materiais sintéticos por orgânicos, de rápida decomposição e absorção pela natureza. **Não é favor, é responsabilidade e acima de tudo compromisso com a natureza e com a espiritualidade.**

O QUE É CALUNGA GRANDE? O mar é chamado de *"calunga grande"* (o cemitério é "calunga pequena"). O maior ponto de força da natureza é o mar e pertence à Yemanjá. Esse ponto de força natural é grande absorvedor de energias negativas, é um santuário natural para onde é levado tudo o que precisa ser purificado e depois devolvido. Os Guias de Umbanda fazem uso da energia dos mares e oceanos em seus lindos trabalhos de curas. Para o mar são levados muitos espíritos sombrios cujas vibrações densas os impedem de chegar a planos mais sutis. No mar são tratados pelos trabalhadores da Linha de Yemanjá.

Oxum

QUAL É A VIBRAÇÃO DE OXUM? É a vibração que atua nas águas doces (nascentes, lagos, cachoeiras e rios) e corresponde a necessidade de equilíbrio emocional, concórdia, amor, complacência e reprodução. Suas emanações propiciam ao ser humano riqueza material, amor, fertilidade e união entre as pessoas através do amor, pois as irradiações do Amor de Oxum estimulam as uniões. Os rios são os santuários de Oxum e seu altar são as cachoeiras, onde ela é oferendada.

QUEM É OXUM? Orixá do amor puro e verdadeiro, da alegria e da união, regente da fertilidade, dos recém-nascidos, protetora das crianças. A gravidez está sob sua proteção inclusive após o nascimento da criança, até que ela venha a falar e comece a adquirir conhecimentos. Yabá da feminilidade, do mel, da beleza, da vaidade feminina, do encanto e também do jogo de Ifá (jogo de búzios). Oxum é regente das águas doces desde a sua nascente até o seu encontro com o mar. As emanações fluídicas deste Orixá dão grandeza espiritual e material, espalha harmonia e concórdia. Vibra nas águas doces gerando fartura e riqueza. É a dona do ouro, fruto das entranhas da terra. Orixá das cascatas, rios, cachoeiras, grotas, seixos e fontes, sem ela (água) não há vida.

POR QUE SE DIZ QUE OXUM É YIALODÊ? O QUE QUER DIZER YIALODÊ? É um título africano concedido à pessoa que ocupa o lugar mais importante entre as mulheres da cidade. Na mitologia, Oxum é a rainha de todos os rios e exerce seu poder sobre as águas doces, sem a qual a vida na terra seria impossível.

POR QUE OXUM É ASSOCIADA À MATERNIDADE? Porque Oxum representa a força dos rios, cujas águas vão a todos os cantos do mundo. É ela quem nutre as folhas de Ossaîn, são suas águas que arrefecem o aço forjado por Ogum, águas de Oxum que lavam as feridas de Obaluaiê e compõe a luz do arco-íris de Oxumarê. É a água quem dá vida aos animais de Oxossi. Considerando que as águas de Oxum correm sempre adiante e é o rio que a leva e distribui pelo mundo matando a sede, e que nas águas doces moram os peixes que matam a fome, Oxum foi associada à maternidade, igual à Yemanjá.

POR QUE OXUM É ASSOCIADA À FEMINILIDADE?
Não só à feminilidade, mas também a sensualidade, sendo considerada o Orixá do amor. Ninguém pode segurar a água em suas mãos, ela sempre escapa pelos dedos, igual à mulher quando faz uso de sua astúcia feminina.

Oyá - Iansã

QUAL É A VIBRAÇÃO DE IANSÃ? É a vibração que atua nos raios, ventos, tempestades e corresponde à necessidade de mudança, induz ao desapego de coisas e pessoas, impulsiona a transformações materiais, físicas e morais, avanços tecnológicos e intelectuais. É Iansã quem dá força e coragem para dar outra direção à vida. Iansã é o único Orixá que não tem um santuário natural porque o vento está em todos os lugares, ao mesmo tempo em que não está em lugar nenhum.

QUEM É OYÁ-IANSÃ? É Orixá dos ventos e das tempestades que lavam e varrem a atmosfera. A mudança é uma característica forte deste Orixá que com seus ventos modifica toda a estrutura que toca. A vibração de Iansã dá força na busca de melhores condições de vida, é responsável pelas transformações e mudanças ligadas às coisas materiais, fluidez de raciocínio e verbal. Suas irradiações direcionam pra o movimento e a caminhada. Comanda a falange dos Boiadeiros.

IANSÃ E OYÁ SÃO ORIXÁS DIFERENTES? Não, são dois nomes para o mesmo Orixá. De acordo com a mitologia africana, Iansã é um título que Oyá recebeu de Xangô, que dizia ser ela radiante como o entardecer. Assim o nome Iansã pode ser traduzido como "A Mãe do Céu Rosado" ou "A Mãe do Entardecer".

O QUE QUER DIZER "SENHORA DOS EGUNS"? Iansã é considerada a Senhora dos Eguns porque é como os espíritos dos mortos são conhecidos no Candomblé. E é Iansã que os conduz. Por isso, da mesma forma que no campo santo deve-se saudar Omulu/Obaluaiê, também se saúda Iansã.

IANSÃ É ORIXÁ DOS VENTOS E TEMPESTADES NO SENTIDO DAS SITUAÇÕES QUE DEVASTAM A VIDA HUMANA? Também desta forma quando é comparada com a força dos furacões, ou ainda das tempestades que arruínam a existência, mas também é a brisa que arrefece as paixões e os amores momentâneos. Iansã ensina que tudo passa como o vento.

OMULU/OBALUAIÊ

QUAL É A VIBRAÇÃO DE OMULU/OBALUAIÊ? É a vibração que atua na terra, nos cemitérios - também chamados de campo santo ou calunga pequena -, na luz que transforma a ignorância em consciência e corresponde a necessidade de maturidade. Omulu é o Orixá que rege a morte ou o instante da passagem do plano material para o plano espiritual (desencarne). Sua vibração dá saúde para o corpo e a alma. A terra é o santuário natural de Omulu e seu altar é o cemitério.

QUEM É OMULU/OBALUAIÊ? É Orixá Guardião dos mortos e das almas, senhor da terra, senhor da cura, da evolução e da passagem. Orixá da saúde cuja vibração atua sobre os doentes, hospitais e cemitérios. Omulu é a manifestação idosa de Obaluaiê. Rege a morte, o desencarne, o instante da passagem do corpo material para o espiritual. Em alguns Terreiros Omulu e Obaluaiê são cultuados como Orixás distintos e em outros como um desdobramento diferenciado da seguinte forma: Obaluaiê representa a força jovem, o início da vida; Omulu representa a força velha, ou seja, cansada pela vida, Obaluaiê é a manifestação jovem de Omulu, ou seja, vibrando em forma mais jovem. Omulu é quem rege a morte, o desencarne, é quem comanda o instante da morte que é passagem do plano material de volta para o plano espiritual. Conduz cada um a seu devido lugar de acordo com o merecimento. Omulu/Obaluaiê aponta o caminho que o espírito, após o desencarne, irá trilhar de acordo com seus merecimentos, mas importante dizer que não julga ninguém, apenas acompanha, por isso é chamado Orixá da Passagem. É o guardião das almas que ainda não se libertaram da matéria. Na hora do desencarne são os Falangeiros de Omulu que ajudam o ser a desatar os "cordões" que ligam o perispírito ao corpo material. Seus Capangueiros são diretamente responsáveis pelos lugares onde ocorrem as mortes físicas, como cemitérios, necrotérios, hospitais, casas de saúde, ambulatórios, clínicas. Estão sempre próximos aos leitos e envolvem estes lugares com poderosos campos de força a fim de que os vampiros astrais não sorvam as energias dos corpos físicos em vias de morrer ou recém-falecidos. Sua Linha também pode ser denominada "Yorimá", conhecida como a Linha das Almas, que é constituída, além de Pretos Velhos, de espíritos de médicos e cientistas, Exus e Pombogiras. Geralmente médiuns que trabalham sob a vibração deste Orixá são grandes curadores.

É VERDADE QUE OMULU/OBALUAIÊ É UM ORIXÁ TERRÍVEL QUE TRAZ A VARÍOLA E AS DOENÇAS CONTAGIOSAS? Não é verdade. Falta entendimento entre os próprios umbandistas acerca de Omulu/Obaluaiê. Por considerá-lo senhor da doença muitos Terreiros não desenvolvem o médium que tem esse maravilhoso Orixá como regente. Levam em consideração, literalmente, as lendas contadas sobre ele e desconhecem sua extrema força e valor dentro da religião de Umbanda. Como podem pensar que Deus criaria vibrações da natureza para distribuir doenças infecciosas? Esse mito ensina que o mal existe e que pode ser curado, porém é preciso ter consciência do momento em que ele terminou para recomeçar, mesmo após um violento sofrimento.

NANÃ BURUQUÊ

QUAL É A VIBRAÇÃO DE NANÃ BURUQUE? É a vibração que atua nos pântanos, charcos e manguezais, é a senhora da lama dos rios com seu encontro com o mar, do lodo da vida e da morte, e corresponde ao último estágio do desenvolvimento emocional e espiritual. Vibra sobre o ser auxiliando o esquecimento de mágoas, rancor, dor. É Orixá mais velho de todos, e, por isso, muito respeitada. Os pântanos são o santuário natural de Nanã e o seu altar é o mangue.

QUEM É NANÃ BURUQUÊ? É Orixá Senhora das águas paradas, do barro e da sabedoria. Orixá mais antigo do mundo. Senhora dos mistérios, da morte e reencarnação, da memória, protetora dos idosos e doentes. É quem faz a ligação entre o plano espiritual e o plano material no nascimento e na morte. Nanã socorre nos momentos de dor e de pranto. É Nanã quem acompanha os seres durante fim do aprendizado no mundo da matéria. É o Orixá do fim das coisas. Faz o caminho inverso de Oxum. É ela quem reconduz ao terreno do astral as almas que Oxum depositou no "mundo da carne". Também vibra sobre os espíritos que vão reencarnar, purificando-lhes os sentimentos, mágoas e conceitos, e adormecendo suas memórias de modo a prepará-los para a nova vida no plano físico. É o Orixá dos pântanos, o ponto de contato das águas com a terra, vibra nas águas paradas da natureza.

POR QUE NANÃ É CONSIDERADA A LAMA PRIMORDIAL? O QUE ISSO SIGNIFICA? Na mitologia africana Nanã é a lama primordial, o barro, a argila da qual foram feitos os homens. Diz à lenda que Oxalá tentou criar os homens com o ar, mas a criação se dissipou antes de adquirir forma. Tentou com o fogo, mas o homem logo foi queimado. Os criados da pedra não conseguiram se dobrar e nem curvar. Com a madeira ficaram rígidos e não conseguiram se movimentar. Experimentou com água, óleo, azeite e nada deu certo. Então Nanã se ofereceu a Oxalá para que com ela os homens fossem criados, porém impôs a condição de que, sendo criados com sua essência (o barro), a ela fossem devolvidos depois da morte. Por isso Nanã está sempre no começo de tudo. É associada ao limo que atua como fertilizante natural do solo e, portanto, dá vida, e ao mesmo tempo ao limo lodoso que fica nas águas estagnadas, portanto representa a putrefação e morte.

Ossaîn

QUAL É A VIBRAÇÃO DE OSSAÎN? Está relacionado com as matas, as plantas, o verde, é dono do mistério das folhas e de seu emprego medicinal e utilização mágica. Seus pontos de força são as florestas e os lugares onde nascem as plantas selvagens. Ossaîn vibra na saúde, na capacidade para controlar os próprios sentimentos e emoções, sua vibração traz paz em casa e no trabalho, intuição para saber lidar liturgicamente com as ervas.

QUEM É OSSAÎN? É Orixá protetor dos animais, Senhor das ervas medicinais e das ervas litúrgicas, Orixá da cura e das medicinas alternativas, detentor do axé. As folhas estão relacionadas com a cura por isso Ossaîn é o Orixá da medicina. Guarda escondida na floresta a magia da cura para todas as doenças dos homens, contida nas virtudes de todas as folhas. *"Kó si ewé, kó sí Òrìsà"* (pronuncia-se "Côssí eu ê, côssí orixá) significa *"Sem folhas não tem Orixá"*, pois elas são imprescindíveis aos rituais. Cada Orixá possui suas próprias folhas, mas só Ossaîn conhece o axé (força, poder, fundamento) existente nas folhas e ervas, e somente ele sabe os segredos e as palavras (ofó) que despertam o poder e força contidos nelas. Ossaîn tem um auxiliar que se responsabiliza por causar o terror em pessoas que entram na floresta sem a devida permissão, cujo nome é Aroni.

O QUE É MÃO DE OFÁ? Também chamado Mão de Folhas, é o médium preparado especialmente para fazer a colheita e a quinagem (maceração) das ervas usadas para amacís, assim como para remédios e banhos de descarga. Em alguns Terreiros de Umbanda também há um médium, geralmente não incorporante, incumbido de colher e quinar folhas para rituais. Quinar uma erva significa esmagá-la com as mãos dentro da água, de modo a deixá-la picadinha, quase esfarelada. A quinagem permite que as substâncias da planta passem para a água sem precisar de fervura.

OSSAÎN É O SENHOR DAS FOLHAS OU O SENHOR DOS REMÉDIOS? De ambos. Entende-se esse orixá como a própria energia curativa das folhas porque tem consigo o poder da força sagrada que envolve a natureza e seus elementais. As folhas são misteriosas e mágicas porque o mesmo princípio que cura, também mata. *"A diferença entre um remédio e um veneno está só na dosagem" (Paracelso).*

QUEM É ARONI? Segundo a mitologia iorubá, há espíritos que moram na "essência" da floresta (ou no fundo da floresta), chamados de Ajáà. Um desses espíritos é Aroni, que habita na parte mais escura da floresta onde mesmo a luz do sol não consegue penetrar. Diz-se que seu conhecimento acerca das propriedades mágicas das folhas é tão imenso que até os Orixás o temem. Embora Aroni tenha elevado conhecimento das ervas medicinais, só Ossaîn tem o poder da cura. O aspecto físico de Aroni é de gnomo africano ou duende, representado com gorro vermelho enfeitado com búzios, fuma cachimbo de barro ou feito com a casca do ìgbín (caracol), o qual usa para potencializar as propriedades das folhas e encantar as pessoas que se deparam com ele. Anda com uma perna só, semelhante ao Saci-Pererê, e talvez seja a origem do personagem do folclore brasileiro.

Exu

QUAL É A VIBRAÇÃO DE EXU? É relacionado à força da comunicação, da palavra, do sexo, da procriação. Seu ponto de força é a encruzilhada por ser o encontro de dois caminhos. Mas Exu está em todos os caminhos, em todos os lugares e passagens, e não apenas na encruzilhada de rua. Todos os pontos que marcam a entrada e a saída de uma realidade são pontos de firmeza e de manifestação de Exu.

POR QUE AS OFERENDAS PARA EXU SÃO FEITAS EM ENCRUZILHADA? Porque é seu ponto de força, e porque ela é um símbolo de indecisão, é onde se deve obrigatoriamente fazer uma escolha e enfrentar o medo de tomar o caminho errado ou fazer a pior opção. O que aflige o ser humano não é o caminho errado e nem a pior opção, mas sim o momento da escolha. Estar parado no ponto onde dois caminhos se cruzam é Exu.

POR QUE EXU FOI SINCRETIZADO COM O DIABO CRISTÃO? Primordialmente foi entendido como diabo pelos colonizadores, senhores de engenho, traficantes de escravos, missionários, bispos, párocos etc., devido ao seu estilo irreverente, brincalhão e a forma como era representado no culto africano: um falo (pênis) humano ereto, simbolizando a fertilidade. Um Orixá que contrariava as regras mais comuns de conduta aceitas socialmente levaram os primeiros missionários a ligar Exu ao diabo, e fizeram dele o *"símbolo de tudo o que é maldade, perversidade, abjeção e ódio, em oposição à bondade, pureza, elevação e amor de deus"*. Exu jamais se livrou dessa nódoa e foi condenado a ser o Orixá mais incompreendido e caluniado do panteão afro-brasileiro.

POR QUE EXU É REPRESENTADO POR UM FALO (PÊNIS) ERETO? Nas sociedades africanas o poder estava nas mãos dos mais velhos e só o parentesco por parte de pai criava vínculos familiares. Assim, quanto mais parentes, dependentes, agregados e filhos o chefe da família tivesse, maior era seu poder. O homem se casava com uma mulher e podia ter outras esposas e concubinas, inclusive ter várias mulheres era sinal de prestígio, quanto mais poderoso um chefe mais esposas tinha, e quanto mais mulheres pudesse ter mais amplos seriam os laços de solidariedade e fidelidade, pois os casamentos garantiam alianças entre os grupos familiares. Aquele que "possuísse" muitas mulheres, além de ter laços com diversas linhagens teria uma descendência maior porque nascida de suas várias consortes. E quanto mais filhos, mais mão de obra para arar a terra, cuidar do gado e defender a propriedade, sem contar que as mulheres eram as responsáveis pela produção de grãos e mantimentos. Com esse olhar fica fácil entender porque, sendo Exu o protetor dos lares, era representado com um falo ereto. Porém, para os europeus que se relacionavam com as sociedades africanas a poligamia era algo a ser combatido, hábito ligado a formas de vida atrasada e condenada pela religião. Os padres católicos, vendo a representação de um pênis, não viram mais nada além de uma Entidade sexualizada e demoníaca. E até hoje Exu é o diabo.

O QUE É EXU DE DUAS CABEÇAS? Exu é um Orixá de natureza dual (dupla), pois ao mesmo tempo em que é movido pelas necessidades também é movido pelos interesses, por isso o dizer que Exu tem duas cabeças. Suas duas essências são cantadas no ponto que diz *"Exu que tem duas cabeças, ele faz sua Gira com fé, uma é satanás do inferno outra é de Jesus Nazaré"*. Considerando que todo ser humano tem em si a sombra e a luz, no ponto cantado *"satanás do inferno"* representa o lado desconhecido e escuro de si mesmo, os aspectos destrutivos e as projeções sombrias. O oposto é *Jesus de Nazaré*, o bem que também há em cada indivíduo.

ORIXÁ DE FRENTE, ADJUNTÓ E ANCESTRAL

O QUE SIGNIFICA COROA DO MÉDIUM? É a parte de cima da cabeça, chamada também Orí. A Coroa funciona como uma antena de TV capaz de sintonizar todas as transmissões. Coroa é o topo da cabeça (comparada à antena de TV), onde se acredita que os Orixás depositam sua vibração ou essência (as imagens da TV). As duas vibrações melhor sintonizadas são dos chamados Orixás donos da coroa, também conhecidos por "Pai e Mãe de Cabeça". Normalmente a vibração de um dos Orixás de Coroa (ou de Cabeça) é mais forte que a outra, ou seja, é mais atuante que a outra. Esse Orixá, que atua mais fortemente é chamado de "Orixá de Frente" e pode ser o masculino ou o feminino, independentemente do sexo do médium, e lhe determinará algumas características predominantes. O outro é chamado "Adjuntó" que é aquele que auxilia.

O QUE É ORIXÁ DE FRENTE OU ORIXÁ REGENTE?
Também chamado de Orixá da Cabeça ou Orí (cabeça em yorubá), é aquele que acompanha a pessoa na presente encarnação e lhe dá uma direção na vida, é quem guia o ser humano no caminho de sua missão. **Embora todos sejam filhos de todos os Orixás**, o chamado Orixá de Frente é a energia fundamental da atual encarnação, é aquele que dá as características principais da pessoa e marca as particularidades que se sobressaem em sua forma de pensar, sentir e agir.

O QUE É ORIXÁ ADJUNTÓ OU JUNTÓ? O Orixá Adjuntó, Ajuntó ou simplesmente Juntó é um segundo Orixá, formando um par. Este termo quer dizer "junto de" ou ao "lado de". Se o Orixá de Frente é aquele que guiará a pessoa enquanto ela estiver encarnada, o Adjuntó será o seu auxiliar, interferindo e amparando quando houver um desequilíbrio. Sempre que o ser se desequilibra nas qualidades do Orixá de Frente, passa a ser amparado pelas qualidades do seu Orixá de Juntó. Na atual encarnação a pessoa tem no Orixá de Frente as qualidades que é sua missão aprender, e tem no Orixá Juntó a vibração que lhe dará o equilíbrio íntimo e crescimento interior permanentemente. Pode-se dizer que o Adjuntó é a balança da coroa do médium, reequilibrando a ação do Orixá de Frente.

CADA UM DOS SERES HUMANOS TEM UM ORIXÁ REGENTE E UM ADJUNTÓ? Todo ser humano tem TODOS os Orixás. A maioria já ouviu a expressão "Sou filho de Ogun" ou "Sou filha de Oxum" e essa definição já basta. Mas há aí um erro conceitual, porque **cada pessoa** tem TODOS os Orixás influenciando sua existência na medida em que **cada Orixá** é regente em um sentido da vida, e irradia suas forças de forma a equilibrar os diversos aspectos da existência. Por exemplo, uma pessoa que seja filha de Iansã também tem influência de Oxóssi a incentivando a adquirir conhecimento, recebe as irradiações de Oxum regendo suas emoções etc.

O QUE É ORIXÁ ANCESTRAL OU ANCESTRE? O Orixá Ancestral ou Ancestre é aquele que acolheu cada ser humano em seu primeiro momento de existência, no exato momento em que foi criado como espírito muito antes de tornar-se humano e entrar no ciclo reencarnacionista. Desde o princípio e para sempre acompanhará aquele espírito. Ele dá ao ser sua natureza mais íntima, que diz quem é na essência, no mais íntimo e secreto de sua alma. Por exemplo, quem foi criado na "fôrma" de Iansã sempre será Iansã, mesmo que em diversas reencarnações tenha outro Orixá de Frente distinto. Por exemplo, usa-se a expressão *"Made in"* juntamente com o nome do país onde determinada mercadoria é fabricada como forma de identificação, e como o Orixá Ancestral influenciará sempre na característica básica da personalidade da pessoa por todas as reencarnações pelas quais passar, ele será sempre o *"Made in"* daquele espírito.

OS ORIXÁS DÃO ÀS PESSOAS TAMBÉM SUAS CARACTERÍSTICAS NEGATIVAS? Evidentemente que não. Jamais se poderá atribuir ao Orixá a falta de caráter ou tendência à desonestidade. Que fique bem claro que as características negativas de personalidade nunca são do Orixá e sim da pessoa que usa o seu livre arbítrio. Como poderia a emanação do amor de Deus manifestada através das forças da natureza vibrar na Coroa de um "filho" tendência ao roubo ou o gosto à mentira?

TODOS OS FILHOS DE UM DETERMINADO ORIXÁ VÃO SE COMPORTAR DE MANEIRA IGUAL? Não se comportam de maneira igual. Em algumas questões podem no máximo se assemelhar. Um filho de Ogun, por exemplo, tendo seu Adjuntó Nanã terá ímpeto para a guerra, mas terá Nanã para lhe acalmar. Ao contrário do filho de Ogun com Iansã cujo ímpeto para a guerra não será abrandado, pois ambos os Orixás são guerreiros. É importante entender que guerra nesse sentido não é luta armada com o fim de impor supremacia, mas sim à defesa de uma ideia, um valor, um ideal.

POR QUE É CHAMADO ORIXÁ DE FRENTE OU DA CABEÇA? E POR QUE SE DIZ QUE REGE A COROA DO MÉDIUM? Orixá de Frente porque ele regerá a atual encarnação da pessoa e influenciará durante toda a sua vida terrena, pois estará sempre à frente. Estar à frente é encabeçar, chefiar, comandar. Orixá da Cabeça é porque rege a Coroa do médium (chamada Orí), que fica no topo da cabeça, e por onde se recebe todas as irradiações provenientes dos mundos visíveis e invisíveis (espiritual) para o bem e para o mal. É por essa razão inclusive que vários rituais concentram-se nessa parte do corpo, como o Amací e Coroação na Umbanda e o Bori no Candomblé. Os umbandistas são ensinados a preparar ervas e derramar sobre a cabeça pedindo aos Guias de Luz e aos Mestres Amparadores que lancem a energia benfazeja armazenada nas nelas para o equilíbrio espiritual do ser humano.

UM HOMEM SEMPRE VAI TER UM ORIXÁ DE FRENTE MASCULINO E A MULHER TEM NECESSARIAMENTE QUE TER UM ORIXÁ DE FRENTE FEMININO? Não, qualquer Orixá pode estar de frente e qualquer Orixá pode estar de Juntó, apenas deve formar um casal. Homem pode ter Orixá de Frente feminino e de Juntó vai ser masculino. Mulher pode ter Orixá de Frente masculino, logo de Juntó vai ser feminino.

ORIXÁ DE FRENTE E O ORIXÁ DE JUNTÓ SÃO AQUELES QUE REGEM A ATUAL ENCARNAÇÃO? Sim. Em cada encarnação se tem um par de Orixás diferentes.

POR QUE OS ORIXÁS DE FRENTE E ADJUNTÓ GERALMENTE TEM POLARIDADE DIFERENTE? Na maior parte dos casos os Orixás principais que regem formam um par (masculino e o feminino) porque o espírito não tem gênero, e se será homem ou mulher é determinado no momento da programação de sua reencarnação, de modo que poderá encarnar em um corpo de homem ou de mulher diante da sua necessidade de aprendizado. Ocorre que todos tem a memória espiritual onde estão guardados os registros das experiências nos diversos corpos com os quais já reencarnou, e desta forma todo ser humano tem um lado feminino e um lado masculino. Daí justifica-se a atuação do par de Orixás Regentes na coroa dos seus filhos.

DIZ-SE QUE ORIXÁ DE FRENTE E ADJUNTÓ FORMAM UM PAR. É PRECISO NECESSARIAMENTE QUE UM SEJA FEMININO E OUTRO MASCULINO? Sim. Entenda-se masculino e feminino como polaridades do mesmo modo que o Yin e Yang, positivo e negativo e não como gênero (homem e mulher). Polaridade do espírito e o sexo do corpo físico são coisas diferentes, um espírito de polaridade fêmea pode encarnar em um corpo de homem da mesma forma como um espírito de polaridade macho pode encarnar num corpo de mulher de acordo com o planejamento reencarnatório.

ORIXÁ DE FRENTE É SEMPRE APENAS UM ORIXÁ OU PODE SER VÁRIOS ORIXÁS? Enquanto encarnado nesta dimensão espiritual o ser humano recebe influência de todos os Orixás, porém apenas um o direciona na presente encarnação e influencia diretamente a sua personalidade, dando-lhe características próprias como o modo de pensar e o jeito de agir. A este damos o nome de Orixá Regente do Orí (cabeça) ou Orixá de Frente.

DE QUE MODO O ORIXÁ REGENTE PODE INFLUENCIAR A PERSONALIDADE DE UMA PESSOA? Dando características próprias aos seus filhos, por exemplo, pode-se distinguir uma filha de Oxum de uma filha de Iansã sem sombra de dúvida.

É VERDADE QUE SE O MÉDIUM FOR UM HOMEM O ORIXÁ DE CABEÇA TEM QUE SER MASCULINO E O ADJUNTÓ SERÁ FEMININO E SE FOR MULHER SERÁ O INVERSO? Não. Geralmente homem tem Orixá de cabeça de polaridade masculina e mulher de polaridade feminina. Embora muitos Dirigentes de Umbanda entendam que o homem tem necessariamente que ter o Orixá de Frente de polaridade masculina, e a mulher de polaridade feminina, se vê exceções na Coroa de vários filhos de fé.

COMO SABER QUAL É O MEU ORIXÁ? É o Dirigente do Terreiro que identifica os Orixás de cada um dos filhos da Casa. Ocorre que não é incomum a pessoa ir a um Terreiro e ouvir que é de Oxóssi, vai a outro e ouve que é filho de Xangô e a pessoa fica sem saber em quem acreditar. Para ter certeza sobre qual é o seu Orixá, o ideal é o umbandista conhecer as qualidades de todos os Orixás de modo a se identificar com elas. O melhor caminho é estudar, conhecer as características, suas vibrações, e ver com qual se identifica.

POSSO IDENTIFICAR MEU ORIXÁ ATRAVÉS DA DATA DE NASCIMENTO? Não. Orixás não são signos do zodíaco e nem são identificados desta forma. Embora haja semelhança entre as características do signo de Câncer com Oxum, por exemplo, não quer dizer que todos os cancerianos sejam filhos desse Orixá. Os geminianos têm características de Oxóssi, mas não são necessariamente filhos deste Orixá. Os que usam a data de nascimento para determinar o Orixá de Frente e Juntó apenas perdem tempo.

POR QUE ALGUNS DIZEM QUE OS ORIXÁS ESTÃO BRIGANDO PELA COROA DO FILHO?

Essa ideia é inconcebível. Os Orixás não brigam, apenas se manifestam quando a pessoa está precisando de outra energia além daquela do próprio Orixá para reestabelecer seu equilíbrio. Por exemplo, uma pessoa que seja filha de Yemanjá e que esteja sofrendo com emoções reprimidas que lhe causam dor emocional e doenças físicas e que não consegue desabafar os sentimentos, Iansã toma a frente para proporcionar o dinamismo e o extravasamento destas emoções contidas, mesmo não sendo seu Orixá de Frente nem Juntó. É preciso que se entenda que **TODOS** carregam consigo **TODOS** os Orixás harmoniosamente divididos para auxiliar o indivíduo em sua vida. Quando um sensitivo percebe a vibração de Iansã do nosso exemplo, pensa que há briga pela cabeça do filho porque naquele momento há mais de um Orixá de frente. Porém é apenas um ato de misericórdia Divina e não briga. Haverá situações no decorrer da vida em que outro Orixá tomará a frente para ajudar o ser a resolver um problema de difícil solução, mas isso não quer dizer que há briga pelo filho, na verdade é um ato de amor.

POR QUE SE DIZ QUE CADA PESSOA É FILHA DE TODOS OS ORIXÁS? As pessoas não recebem influências apenas de um ou dois Orixás da mesma forma que a educação de uma criança não está sob responsabilidade apenas dos pais, ela também recebe cuidados dos professores, dos avós, tios. Por exemplo, quem tem Ogun de frente não deixa de ter todos os outros Orixás e há momentos, circunstâncias e situações na vida em que outros Orixás tomam a frente para ajudar a pessoa a resolver situações difíceis com as quais ela não sabe lidar. Todos são filhos de todos os Orixás.

ORIXÁS DO PANO BRANCO (FUNFUN)
OXAGUIAN , OXALUFAN, OBATALÁ, ORIXALÁ, OXALÁ

QUEM SÃO OS ORIXÁS DO PANO BRANCO? Os chamados Orixás do Pano Branco são todos aqueles relacionados com a criação do universo, considerados ancestrais espirituais e designados genericamente por *Orixá Funfun* que significa *branco* em yorubá. A cor branca configura-se da criação, pois guarda a essência de todas as demais cores, entendendo-se, portanto, que os Orixás que vestem branco trazem em si os poderes dos demais Orixás. Sendo emanações diretas do próprio Deus (Olorun), os Orixás Funfun são os seres mais elevados da escala da existência.

O QUE É ORIXÁ FUNFUN? Funfun em iorubá significa branco, então Orixá funfun é o Orixá que veste branco como Oxalá, Oxalufan, Oxaguian. Na África todos os Orixás que participaram da criação são chamados de Funfun.

QUEM SÃO OXAGUIAN E OXALUFAN? São duas formas que Oxalá assume quando incorpora no Candomblé. Oxaguian jovem e guerreiro e Oxalufan velho e paciente, este último apoiado no Opaxorô que é um tipo de cajado. Na Umbanda não se cultua essa forma de Oxalá.

QUEM É OXALUFAN? Oxalufan foi o primeiro Orixá criado por Oxalá, tendo idade de imensa antiguidade, por isso apresenta-se com movimentos lentos. É o representante maior das divindades funfun e no Candomblé "desce" nas cabeças dos seus iniciados, diferente de **Oxalá, que é uma força tão imensa que não pode ser medida, e com um poder tão grande que seria perigoso ao orí (coroa/cabeça) do ser humano.** É quem determina o que cada pessoa merece receber, mas deixa que o livre arbítrio exista e seja sempre supervisionado pelo Orixá de cada um.

QUEM É OXAGUIAN? É o mais novo dos Orixás do panteão do branco (funfun), mas isto não o transforma em um jovem, pois nenhuma divindade integrante deste grupo é considerada jovial porque são pertencentes à época da criação, o que os tornam possuidores de idade apagada da memória pelo tempo. Oxaguian só é menos ancião que seu pai, Oxalufan. Representa o nascer do dia, simboliza o primeiro raio de Sol que esquenta a terra fria da madrugada. Ele é a claridade vencendo e cortando a escuridão da noite, "acordando" o dia e ajudando o ser a criar um novo ciclo de vida.

QUEM É OBATALÁ? Dentre os Orixás do Pano Branco o mais importante é Obatalá, o Senhor ou Rei das Vestes Brancas, também conhecido como Orixalá.

QUEM É ORIXALÁ? É o nome do mais importante Orixá funfun, também cultuado como Obatalá (Obàtálá). O nome Orixalá (Òrìsànlá) foi contraído e deu origem à palavra Oxalá, e com esse nome passou a ser conhecido no Brasil e na Europa. No Xirê (sequência de danças feitas aos Orixás no Candomblé, semelhante a Gira na Umbanda) Oxalá é homenageado por último porque ele representa a totalidade, o único Orixá que, igual Exu, reside em todos os seres humanos. Todos são seus filhos já que a humanidade vive sob o mesmo teto.

QUEM É OXALÁ? Dizem os ìtàn (lendas) que Olodumarê/Olorum (O Eterno, O Onipotente, O Criador do mundo) junto com a criação do céu e da terra trouxe para a existência as outras divindades Orixás a fim de ajudá-lo a administrar sua criação. Oxalá foi o primeiro a ser concebido e encarregado de criar não só o universo, como todos os seres e todas as coisas que existiriam no mundo. Oxalá é considerado e cultuado como o maior de todos os Orixás. A ele pertencem os olhos que tudo veem!

ZAMBI, OLORUN, OLODUMÁRE, TUPÃ

QUEM SÃO ZAMBI, OLORUN, OLODUMÁRE, TUPÃ? O maior fundamento da Umbanda é a crença em um Deus único, que é denominado Zambi ou Olorun. Zambi é o nome que Deus recebe no Candomblé da nação de Angola. Na nação Ketú o Ser

Supremo é chamado **Olodumáre ou Olodumaré**, que vive numa dimensão paralela à nossa, conhecida como Orun (pronuncia-se *ôrún*) e por isso também aclamado como Olorun ou o Senhor do Orun. Dependendo da Linha de Trabalho das Entidades que se manifestam nos Terreiros de Umbanda usam a palavra **Zambi ou Olorun** para se referir ao Criador, sem que isso signifique se tratar de divindades distintas. Em razão das influências indígenas na Umbanda também é chamado de Tupã ou, pela influência católica, chamado simplesmente de Deus. Olorun é o Todo e os Orixás são as partes desse Todo, cuja missão é sustentar a criação divina. Uma imagem para se entender essa relação é a fruta (Olorun) e seus gomos (Orixás). São irradiações divinas que amparam homens e mulheres durante o processo de evolução espiritual. Olorun ou Zambi não possui representações em imagens e nem templo próprio, pois na Umbanda entende-se que seu templo está em todos os lugares da natureza (rios, mares, matas etc.).

FORAM ADÃO E EVA OS PRIMEIROS SERES A HABITAREM O PLANETA? A palavra Adão vem do hebraico A-dam, significando ser humano ou humanidade, portanto não é referência a um homem específico. Da mesma forma a palavra Eva também não representa uma mulher em especial, pois ela vem do hebraico "HaVVaH" que significa mãe dos viventes associada a palavra "HaYaH" cuja interpretação é existir ou ser (no sentido de viver). Adão não foi o primeiro e nem o único a povoar a Terra, e não foram Adão e Eva que geraram a humanidade. Essas duas figuras apenas simbolizaram as raízes do povoamento da Terra em linguagem alegórica, de forma que o tempo pudesse trazer condições para as devidas interpretações desse texto. O surgimento do homem no planeta ocorreu de forma coletiva, tanto assim que deixaram registros de sua passagem em todas as épocas e em várias partes do planeta.

LINHAS DE TRABALHO

Para conhecer mais sobre as Linhas de Trabalho sugerimos a leitura do livro "Descomplicando os Guias de Umbanda - Para Leigos"

POR QUE SURGIRAM AS LINHAS DE TRABALHO? As Linhas surgiram para que mentores do astral pudessem se manifestar dentro dos Terreiros de Umbanda em benefício dos necessitados, integrados a uma esfera de trabalho sob a responsabilidade de um determinado Orixá. Os Guias espirituais fortalecem em si as qualidades desse Orixá e passam a ser os intermediadores no mundo dos encarnados. Por exemplo, os trabalhadores espirituais que atuam sob a vibração de Ogun contém em si o sentido da persistência, que é uma característica do Orixá, e desta forma traz inspiração aos seres humanos encarnados para perseguir com firmeza seus objetivos. Muitas entidades que trabalham na Umbanda são figuras simbólicas, como por exemplo, o Preto Velho que se mostra como um escravo que viveu em condições degradantes e que a tudo superou com fé, amor e determinação, e ensina as pessoas a vencer as adversidades através de seus exemplos. Porém isso não significa que aquela Entidade que se chama Preto Velho tenha sido escravo em vidas passadas.

A QUE SE REFERE QUANDO SE FALA DAS LINHAS DE TRABALHO DA UMBANDA? Às Linhas que se apresentam nos Terreiros sob a roupagem de Caboclos, Pretos Velhos, Boiadeiros, Baianos, Exus etc., e que foram pensadas e organizadas de modo que os umbandistas as pudessem entender. Cada Linha está sob a direção de um Orixá, que emite Sua Luz e Força para aquela corrente específica. Essa "força viva" tem a finalidade de equilibrar e harmonizar o padrão vibratório de quem a recebe, alterando seus sentimentos mais íntimos e estimulando pensamentos e ações mais nobres e virtuosos.

Os Guias

QUEM SÃO OS GUIAS ESPIRITUAIS NA UMBANDA? Também chamados Catiços ou Capangueiros, os Guias são protetores e mentores espirituais entendidos como mensageiros. São trabalhadores da Luz dispostos a guiar, intuir e proteger por uma ou mais encarnação, auxiliando o ser humano em sua evolução espiritual. São espíritos humanos que já viveram no plano físico, passaram por várias encarnações e adquiriram conhecimento e sabedoria e são, portanto, nossos ancestrais. Apresentam-se com roupagens variadas como Preto Velho, Caboclo ou Boiadeiro etc., com modo de falar e gestual característicos da Linha de Trabalho, sempre motivados pela firme vontade de ajudar aos irmãos necessitados. Os Capangueiros são os enviados dos **Orixás Menores chamados também de "Falangeiros"**. Atuam em suas respectivas Linhas de Trabalho procurando orientar a humanidade em auxílio a sua evolução espiritual.

POR QUE OS GUIAS NÃO TÊM NOMES PRÓPRIOS QUE OS IDENTIFIQUEM? Que proveito teria se os Guias de Umbanda, tão criticados pelos preconceituosos, se apresentassem como Dr. Fulano de Tal, prodígio em matemática ou Dr. Beltrano, mestre nas leis da dinâmica química ou Dr. Sicrano, laureado com o Nobel de Física? Umbanda é religião e não ciência, os Guias não se apresentam como doutores ou com nomes pomposos, famosos, com a finalidade de causar excessiva impressão na mente das pessoas porque os Guias de Umbanda não precisam disso, são desprovidos do ego.

OS ESPÍRITOS TRABALHADORES SÃO AGREGADOS POR CULTURA OU RELIGIÃO? Os espíritos são agregados através da afinidade mental e emocional, pois no mundo espiritual não há barreira da língua, religião, cultura, etc. Todas as Linhas de Trabalho da Umbanda surgiram como forma de ordenar grupos numerosos de trabalhadores espirituais com característica comuns entre si, e dispostos a atuar no movimento umbandista. Seus obreiros têm atributos e qualidades semelhantes, porém não iguais porque, encarnados ou não, todos mantemos nossa individualidade. Unem-se, portanto, em egrégoras espirituais os trabalhadores que tem gostos e personalidades semelhantes, compondo as Linhas de Caboclo, Pretos Velho, Baiano etc. **Os espíritos de Caboclos, Pretos Velhos e todos os outros Guias de Lei de Umbanda ganham roupagens energéticas que simbolizam a força espiritual (chamada *egrégora*), o modelo como se apresen-**

tarão para serem entendidos (chamado *arquétipo*) e a vibração que dá sustentação ao trabalho por eles realizado (chamado *Orixá*).

Os Guias de Umbanda - Cláudia A. Argoud

TODOS OS GUIAS SÃO MUITO EVOLUÍDOS? Não. Tem variados graus de conhecimento e progresso e continuam estudando, trabalhando e se aprimorando. Como os seres encarnados também os Guias prosseguem nas suas evoluções.

COMO SABER QUAL O GRAU DE EVOLUÇÃO DE UM GUIA? Não nos cabe perguntar sobre o grau de evolução dos trabalhadores que vem por amor nos ajudar porque isso é assunto pessoal de cada mensageiro.

OS GUIAS TEM PLENO CONHECIMENTO DE TODOS OS ASSUNTOS? Os espíritos incorporantes em todas as religiões desse orbe são almas dos homens e mulheres que aqui viveram, assim sendo não possuem nem a plena sabedoria nem a ciência integral. O saber de que qualquer um de nós dispõe, estando encarnados ou desencarnados, se limita ao grau que alcançamos de adiantamento. A opinião do espírito só tem o valor de uma opinião pessoal e por isso deve-se ter sempre em mente que não são infalíveis. Não é incomum dois Guias distintos de um mesmo médium emitir opiniões contrárias a respeito de um único tema. Porém a simples comunicação com essas Entidades, independente do que digam os céticos, prova a existência do mundo espiritual, da vida em um mundo paralelo invisível aos nossos olhos e que aos poucos vai se revelando aos que quiserem acreditar.

SE OS GUIAS NÃO TEM A RESPOSTA DEFINITIVA PARA NOSSAS DÚVIDAS, ENTÃO POR QUE SE DÃO

AO TRABALHO DE VIR AO TERREIRO E CONVERSAR CONOSCO? Qual outra forma os encarnados poderiam conhecer a existência do mundo espiritual, seus costumes e a natureza desse mundo? E além do mais em uma Gira de Pretos Velhos, por exemplo, as pessoas encontram vovôs e vovós com uma humildade emocionante e que com suas boas palavras, rezas e benzimentos incitam o ser humano a melhorar, a ter uma postura mais amorosa com a humanidade e consigo mesmo. Em uma Gira de Caboclo os Guias ensinam a alcançar a cura espiritual ou material através da força de vontade, plantam no ser humano a semente da energia do guerreiro e todos sentem a motivação renovada. Os Baianos incitam a firmeza nos vários campos da vida, no trabalho, nas relações humanas, firmeza na própria fé na vida para poder alcançar os objetivos. E nenhum deles fala verdades incontestáveis.

POR QUE NÃO SE APROPRIAM DE NOMES CONHECIDOS E RESPEITADOS COMO EM OUTRAS RELIGIÕES? Na Umbanda não existe espírito de doutor Fulano ou doutor Beltrano, na Umbanda é Caboclo tal pertencente à Falange tal e ponto final porque a missão dessas Entidades é trazer a simplicidade e a fraternidade. Para os umbandistas não importa quem ele é (ou foi) e sim a mensagem. Esses trabalhadores a todos abrem os braços e estão sempre prontos para ouvir e ajudar. Quando perguntado sobre quem foi em vida, respondem simplesmente *"Não importa quem fui, hoje sou apenas um Caboclo"*, pois não precisam que se preste loa a seu nome.

MUITAS PESSOAS PEDEM AOS GUIAS PARA PARAR COM UM VÍCIO COMO O DA BEBIDA, POR EXEMPLO, OU ADQUIRIR AUTOESTIMA. OS GUIAS PODEM ATENDER? Os Guias não podem jamais interferir no livre arbítrio. E também cabe a cada um valorizar a si mesmo. Os Guias não são mágicos que vão dar jeito na vida de ninguém, é dever de cada um assumir a responsabilidade de sua vida. Os Guias apontam os recursos que a pessoa tem para mudar, mas não carregam ninguém no colo.

MAS SE OS GUIAS NÃO PODEM MUDAR A VIDA, O QUE PODEM FAZER EM BENEFÍCIO DA PESSOA? Ensinar que somente ela tem o poder de modificar sua vida é um dos benefícios. Também podem ajudar com conselhos e sugestões. Podem encorajar a mudança, mas coragem e ação para fazer mudanças profundas é responsabilidade de cada um consigo mesmo.

OS GUIAS AJUDAM AS PESSOAS SOMENTE QUANDO ESTÃO NO TERREIRO? Não. Ajudam o tempo todo sugerindo atitudes misericordiosas, inspirando palavras de consolo e esperança, sugestionando pensamentos positivos que estimulam o ser humano a buscar com serenidade as soluções.

COMO SABER SE QUEM ESTÁ FALANDO CONOSCO É MESMO UM GUIA DE LUZ? Usando de bom senso saberá se é ou não um mistificador. Perceba se o que os Guias dizem despertam bons sentimentos.

O GUIA PODE FAZER PREVISÕES PARA MINHA VIDA? Não é papel do Guia de Umbanda predizer o futuro nem dizer certos fatos que em nada beneficiam a pessoa conhecer. Os espíritos de luz podem pressentir um acontecimento futuro quando esse conhecimento for útil, mas jamais precisar datas, por exemplo, e esse é um indicativo de fraude e mistificação. Também é importante saber que nenhum Guia de Umbanda, assim como todo espírito incorporante em qualquer religião, tem o monopólio da verdade porque todos somos seres em evolução.

QUAL É UM FORTE INDICATIVO DE QUE NÃO ESTAMOS LIDANDO COM UM GUIA DE UMBANDA E SIM COM UM MISTIFICADOR? Linguagem ridícula, vulgar, pretensiosa usando o que se convencionou chamar de "falar difícil", ou quando procura estimular a vaidade e orgulho com elogios desproporcionais e exagerados. Os bons espíritos não aconselham nada além das coisas racionais.

Desconfie se estiver ingerindo álcool em demasia porque o espírito não precisa beber, e se ele bebe é para amortecer o médium.

Baforar charuto na cara das pessoas é um forte indicativo de mistificação, porque uma Entidade sábia e com um mínimo de esclarecimento entende que isso prejudica a saúde, e sabe que há outros meios de limpar os miasmas espirituais.

Espírito que para transmitir energia fica apalpando o assistido demonstra claramente falta de conhecimento e, na maior parte das vezes, é intromissão e despreparo do médium, porque a Entidade sabe o limite do perispírito que é onde devem ser depositadas as energias curadoras.

Os que mandam acender velas de outras Linhas, por exemplo, um Caboclo mandar acender vela de Exu, ou Boiadeiro mandar acender vela de Preto Velho, é forte indicativo de mistificação porque cada Entidade, caso seja necessário, manda acender a vela para sua Linha, e no máximo vai sugerir que a pessoa consulte em outra Linha, mesmo assim sem compromisso com qualquer médium em especial, inclusive o seu.

Falar em outras línguas é forte indicativo, pois os Guias podem acessar as informações pertencentes ao médium e deste modo também podem falar o seu idioma.

Jamais um médium pode conversar sobre vidas passadas, pois isso impressiona perigosamente a mente do assistido e ninguém tem acesso a tais informações, e em nada pode ser útil tal conversa.

Guias que mandam acender vela em igrejas ou usar água benta é tão absurdo que nem há palavras para classificar.

A ENTIDADE ESPIRITUAL PODE PREDIZER O DIA DA MORTE DE ALGUÉM? Jamais dirá mesmo que saiba. Todo ser humano, até o último minuto da vida, tem chance de aprender e mudar. Se souber que o prazo está se encerrando ou se desespera ou simplesmente desiste.

ENTIDADES COM O MESMO NOME SÃO AS MESMAS? Não. São espíritos diferentes que assumiram nome idêntico em função de haverem se integrado à mesma falange. Um Caboclo ou Preto Velho com nome igual, por exemplo, indica apenas que tem características, ou especialidades, ou missões parecidas. Não há nenhum problema em, no mesmo Terreiro e na mesma Gira, ter dois ou mais Guias atuantes com o mesmo nome. Ademais, não é o nome do Guia que deve interessar, e sim o grau de compromisso que o médium tem com a espiritualidade.

POR QUE ALGUMAS ENTIDADES ALGUMAS VEZES CHORAM? As Entidades não choram. As Sereias, por exemplo, são trabalhadoras da Linha das Águas que fazem a limpeza energética nos Terreiros e proferem cânticos que se confundem com choro. Mas quando o médium de fato chora é porque o tipo de energia do Guia pode comovê-lo, daí o choro. Também pode acontecer, devido ao impacto vibratório da Entidade, que nem sempre o médium está com o mental preparado para compartilhar. Mas geralmente não ocorre em médiuns mais equilibrados porque o choro não tem ligação com nenhum Guia de Umbanda.

POR QUE ALGUNS MÉDIUNS DESRESPEITAM AS PESSOAS ALEGANDO QUE "O SANTO NÃO BATEU"? Porque se não é dado conhecimento sobre a religião de Umbanda ele desenvolve opiniões e ideias insignificantes construídas sobre o alicerce da ignorância. E muitos médiuns justificam as próprias falta de cordialidade e educação usando o nome do "santo".

POR QUE ASSIM QUE INCORPORAM ALGUMAS ENTIDADES LOGO EXIGEM CIGARRO E BEBIDA? Por que já está aprofundada na Umbanda a ideia de que o Guia, principalmente de Esquerda, precisa ingerir litros de bebida alcoólica e fumar um cigarro atrás do outro. Isso, infelizmente, é fruto de desequilíbrio do médium e descontrole do Dirigente. O Guia não precisa de nada disso.

AO SER PERGUNTADO SOBRE SEU NOME, O CABOCLO DAS SETE ENCRUZILHADAS, INCORPORADO EM ZÉLIO DE MORAES, RESPONDEU "SE É PRECISO QUE EU TENHA UM NOME, ME CHAME DE CABOCLO DAS SETE ENCRUZILHADAS PORQUE NÃO HAVERÁ CAMINHOS FECHADOS PARA MIM". POR QUE O NÚMERO SETE? Porque sete é um número mágico e todos os Caboclos que levam Sete no nome representam em si mesmos todos os caminhos para se chegar a Deus, não havendo caminhos fechados para eles. Todo Guia que tem Sete no nome trabalha nos sete caminhos e nas sete esferas de ação.

COMO ENTENDER OS SETE CAMINHOS PARA CHEGAR A DEUS DOS GUIAS QUE TEM SETE NO NOME? Os sete caminhos para se chegar a Deus são os sete padrões vibratórios de sete Orixás que desvendam os sete sentidos da Vida. Fé de Oxalá, Amor de Oxum, Conhecimento de Oxossi, Justiça de Xangô, Lei de Ogun e Iansã, Evolução de Omulu/Obaluaiê, Geração (Vida) de Yemanjá. Esses são os sete caminhos que se entrecruzam nas encruzilhadas de Exu.

QUAIS SÃO AS SETE ESFERAS DE AÇÃO QUE OS GUIAS QUE TEM SETE NO NOME TRABALHAM? A esfera de ação de Yemanjá que corresponde à necessidade de acolhimento familiar e de amor fraternal. A esfera de ação de Ogun que corresponde à necessidade de energia, defesa, determinação e tenacidade. A esfera de ação de Xangô que corresponde à necessidade do discernimento, justiça, estudo, raciocínio concreto e metódico. A esfera de ação de Iansã que corresponde à necessidade de mudança, deslocamentos, transformações materiais, avanços tecnológicos e intelectivos. A esfera de ação de Oxóssi que corresponde à necessidade de saúde, nutrição, expansão, energia vital, equilíbrio fisiológico. A esfera de ação de Oxum que corresponde à necessidade de equilíbrio emocional, concórdia, amor, complacência e reprodução. A esfera de ação de Omulu que corresponde à necessidade de compreensão do carma, de regeneração, de evolução, transformações e transmutações cármicas. Oxalá é a união de todos eles, traz em si as vibrações de todas as esferas de ação.

FALANGEIROS E CAPANGUEIROS

O QUE SÃO FALANGEIROS E CAPANGUEIROS? FALANGEIROS, também chamados de **ORIXÁS MENORES,** são os chefes espirituais das Falanges que para efeito de entendimento vamos comparar a uma tropa do exército, onde Ogun é o marechal, os Falangeiros são os generais e abaixo deles estão os trabalhadores aos quais se dá a denominação de Capangueiros, e que, em nosso exemplo, obedecem a uma hierarquia de comando onde tem coronéis, majores, capitães, tenentes, sargentos e soldados. Nada há de belicoso nos Capangueiros e Falangeiros, aqui foram comparados a um esquadrão militar apenas para efeito de entendimento.

QUAL A DIFERENÇA ENTRE ORIXÁ, FALANGEIRO E CAPANGUEIRO? Orixás são as forças da natureza, portanto não incorporam na Umbanda. **Falangeiros** são os representantes diretos de cada um dos Orixás, são Entidades que se afinizam com a vibração de um Orixá. **Capangueiros** são espíritos desencarnados dotados de luz e sabedoria, e atuam sob as ordens dos Falangeiros.

COMO DISTINGUIR O FALANGEIRO DO CAPANGUEIRO? O **Falangeiro** carrega o nome do Orixá em seu próprio nome. Exemplo: Ogun Rompe-Mato. O **Capangueiro** não carrega o nome do Orixá. Exemplo: Caboclo Rompe-Mato.

COMO SABER QUEM SÃO OS FALANGEIROS E OS CAPANGUEIROS NO TERREIRO? Os **Falangeiros dos Orixás** não falam, não utilizam bebida e nem fumo nos trabalhos, não dão consultas. Trabalham na harmonização do Terreiro afastando fluídos pesados e no desenvolvimento e equilíbrio dos médiuns. Já os Guias **Capangueiros dos Orixás** dão consultas e utilizam a bebida e o fumo como instrumentos de trabalho, e interagem com as pessoas, isto é, conversam.

SÓ OS CABOCLOS SÃO CAPANGUEIROS? Não, todos os Guias como Pretos Velhos, Caboclos, Crianças, Boiadeiros, Marinheiros, Baianos, Exus e Pombogiras Guardiões que trabalham sob a vibração de um Orixá também podem ser considerados Capangueiros.

O QUE É FALANGE? Pode-se entender Falange como um grupo de seres espirituais que trabalham dentro de uma mesma Linha comandada por um Falangeiro cujo saber é superior.

OGUM ROMPE-MATO É O MESMO QUE CABOCLO ROMPE-MATO? Não, são duas entidades diferentes. Ogun Rompe-Mato é um Falangeiro, isto é, o intermediador de Ogun e Oxóssi. Caboclo Rompe-Mato é um Capangueiro, ou seja, uma Entidade de Luz que trabalha na Linha de Ogun sob a orientação do Falangeiro Ogun Rompe-Mato. Alguns não colocam a palavra **"Caboclo"** na frente do nome do Capangueiro e por isso há confusão de alguns médiuns que pensam estar trabalhando com um Falangeiro.

GUIA CHEFE

QUEM É O GUIA CHEFE? Guia Chefe, também chamado de Guia de Frente, Guia de Cabeça, Mentor ou Espírito Ancestral, é aquele que acompanha o médium desde o nascimento e será aquele que o acolherá na morte do corpo físico. São espíritos que, ao contrário dos Orixás, já viveram nesse plano de existência, e por evolução espiritual conquistada a partir das experiências obtidas em suas passagens terrenas, ocupam hoje a posição de Mestres ou Mentores. Guias Chefes normalmente são Caboclos, Pretos Velhos, mas podem ser também qualquer outro Guia de Luz que trabalha nos campos da caridade com seu médium. Na Umbanda há mais de um Guia ligado ao médium e todos fazem parte de uma *"equipe"*, onde existe hierarquia e cujo chefe é o espírito mais puro e experiente, ou seja, o Guia Chefe.

CADA TRABALHADOR DA UMBANDA TEM UM GUIA QUE O ACOMPANHA. MAS QUEM É ESSE GUIA? COMO SE DEFINE QUEM VAI SER GUIA DE QUEM? Esse Guia pode ser um grande amigo de muitas vidas, companheiros no amor, irmãos que se amam, assim como também pode ser um carrasco em vidas passadas, um agressor, opressor, torturador, pode ser um atormentador que busca corrigir atos desumanos. **Os Guias não são escolhidos ao acaso, sempre são espíritos que tem um elo cármico fortíssimo com o médium**, seja do amor ou da dor. Os que não frequentam a Umbanda também têm seus Guias, porém eles os chamam de Anjo de Guarda.

COMO SE RECONHECE O GUIA CHEFE? É no processo de desenvolvimento mediúnico que vão surgindo às primeiras manifestações desse Guia, que por serem muito intensas ou muito brandas destoam totalmente das manifestações dos outros. Na fase do desenvolvimento mediúnico, que é aquela em que o médium ainda está conhecendo a incorporação, o Guia Chefe se comporta de forma diferenciada, cuidando muito mais de sintonizar a energia do médium.

OS GUIAS CONVERSAM COM SEUS PROTEGIDOS? Mais do que se imagina.

Caboclos

QUAL FOI A PRIMEIRA ENTIDADE A SE MANIFESTAR NA UMBANDA? O Caboclo foi o primeiro a se manifestar na Umbanda através de Zélio de Moraes, e nomeou-se Caboclo das Sete Encruzilhadas.

DE QUE FORMA SE MANIFESTAM OS CABOCLOS? Nos Terreiros manifestam-se como indígenas embora não necessariamente tenham sido índios em vidas passadas. Apresentam-se com uma postura vigorosa e conhecedores das forças da natureza, as quais manipulam para auxiliar o ser humano em questões que o aflige como saúde e a luta diária pela sobrevivência.

QUAL É O MAIOR ENSINAMENTO DOS CABOCLOS? Ensinam o valor da coragem e persistência para conquistar o que se quer desde que seja bom e justo para todos.

CABOCLO É IGUAL A OXÓSSI? Não. Oxóssi é Orixá. Os Caboclos são Guias de Umbanda e conhecedor das matas e de toda a vida que ela abriga. A mata é associada com Oxóssi, o Senhor das Florestas, e por isso entende-se que **TODO CABOCLO ESTÁ LIGADO À VIBRAÇÃO DE OXÓSSI**, mas não é Oxóssi.

TODOS OS CABOCLOS SÃO DE OXÓSSI? Existem Caboclos e Caboclas de todos os Orixás, mas a Linha de Trabalho sempre é sustentada por Oxóssi. Por exemplo, existem os Caboclos da Praia, do Mar e das Ondas que recebem a vibração de Yemanjá. Há Caboclos que recebem a vibração de Xangô, como o Caboclo da Montanha. Tem os que recebem vibração de Oxum, como os Caboclos da Cachoeira ou dos Rios. Deste modo diz-se que todo Caboclo trabalha na Linha de Oxóssi, mas são regidos (recebem vibração) por seus respectivos Orixás.

QUAL É A DIFERENÇA ENTRE CABOCLO DE PENA E CABOCLO DE COURO? Caboclo de Pena é aquele que os umbandistas identificam com a roupagem fluídica dos ancestrais indígenas e o Caboclo de Couro é aquele que na Umbanda chama-se Boiadeiro.

COMO É A SAUDAÇÃO QUE SE FAZ AOS CABOCLOS?
Saúdam-se os Caboclos dizendo *Okê, Caboclo!*

QUAL É O DIA DA SEMANA E A COR DOS CABOCLOS?
O dia da semana é quinta feira e a cor é verde.

MÉDIUNS QUE RECEBEM CABOCLOS CHEFES DE FALANGE OU CUJOS NOMES SÃO MAIS CONHECIDOS TEM MAIS FORÇA NOS TRABALHOS? Isso só é verdade para médiuns vaidosos que demonstram ignorância se vangloriando. Observe que quando estão no Terreiro os Caboclos tratam uns aos outros como iguais, pois a eles o que importa é o trabalho espiritual e a caridade que se propuseram a fazer.

POR QUE OS CABOCLOS GRITAM? Os caboclos não gritam, quem grita é o médium mal orientado que em algum momento viu outros fazendo um escândalo e acreditou que é assim que se comporta o Caboclo quando incorporado. Terreiro em que se acredita que Caboclo bom é "Caboclo Gritador" parece hospício. Esses excessos afastam muita gente da religião. O brado do Caboclo é lindo, discreto.

POR QUE OS CABOCLOS ASSOBIAM? São representações, na incorporação, dos sons da natureza. Simbolicamente tem a mesma função dos defumadores, charutos e cachimbos, ou seja, preparar o ambiente para os trabalhos que ali serão realizados.

O CABOCLO TEVE AO MENOS UMA ENCARNAÇÃO COMO ÍNDIO? Não necessariamente. O índio representa a Linha de Caboclo porque foi o primeiro habitante desta terra. Tem trabalhadores dessa Linha que nunca tiveram encarnação como índio, mas ao adentrarem a Umbanda assumem a roupagem perispiritual de índio.

QUAL É A FUNÇÃO DOS CABOCLOS NAS GIRAS? São chamados para todo tipo de trabalho, tanto material como espiritual, e por isso diz-se que constituem o braço forte da Umbanda. Os Passes dos Caboclos são poderosos e os resultados de seus trabalhos aparecem muito rapidamente.

O QUE SIGNIFICA CABOCLO QUIMBANDEIRO? É aquele que não trabalha necessariamente somente dentro do Terreiro, e que trabalha bastante com os Exus. São os que, juntamente com os chamados "Exus Quimbandeiros", combatem os espíritos trevosos. São os Caboclos que atuam no astral inferior, os que resgatam os espíritos que estão em sofrimento nesses círculos espirituais tenebrosos. Dentre os Caboclos Quimbandeiros os mais conhecidos são Caboclo Pantera Negra, Caboclo Pantera Vermelha, Caboclo Jiboia, Caboclo Mata de Fogo, Caboclo Águia Valente, Caboclo Corcel Negro e Caboclo do Monte.

O QUE SIGNIFICA CABOCLO QUEBRADOR DE DE-

MANDA? Primeiramente é preciso entender o que é "demanda". A demanda é o instrumento de uma irradiação de fluídos perversos vindo de pessoa ou grupo, repleta de raiva, rancor, mágoa, inveja, ciúme, sentimento de competição, quase sempre movidos pela ideia de vingança e tomados pelo ódio. Esses sentimentos ocupam de tal forma a mente e o coração que cega à pessoa, tornando obcecado aquele que por essas emoções se deixa influenciar. Tomado pelo ódio irracional, irradia intensamente fluídos negativos para atingir aquele que é o alvo de sua insanidade. O Caboclo quebrador de demanda trabalha arduamente para eliminar ou pelo menos minimizar os efeitos deletérios de tais irradiações e combater os emissários, quase sempre espíritos tomados pela insanidade devido a ódio e revolta.

O QUE É DEMANDA? É a irradiação de fluídos perversos emanados por pensamentos de ódio e vingança, e também pelos que optaram por trabalhar com as forças negativas do astral inferior. Demanda são as "batalhas espirituais". Alguns pontos cantados falam sobre ela, cuja finalidade é lembrar aos filhos de fé que há Entidades espirituais que trabalham sob as leis divinas para proteger os que são vítimas de sentimento de profunda inimizade e desejo de destruição. Um exemplo é o ponto cantado *"Rei da demanda é Ogum Megê / Quem rola as pedras é Xangô, Kaô / Flecha de Oxossi é certeira / É Oxalá, é meu Senhor / Sete linhas da Umbanda, sete linhas pra vencer / É a lei de Oxalá: ninguém pode perecer / Tem Oxum nas cachoeiras / Iemanjá deusa do mar/ Iansã pra defender / Cosme e Damião para ajudar (ou Pai Ogum pra demandar)".*

A DEMANDA SE DÁ SOMENTE A PARTIR DE TRABALHOS DE BAIXA MAGIA? Não. Também de pensamentos dirigidos à vítima de maneira intensa, permanente, com o objetivo de causar dor e sofrimento, de forma a impedir que tenha êxito em seus intentos ou mesmo que nada de positivo aconteça, inclusive ocasionando doença física ou mental. Alguns já reencarnam trazendo tais sentimentos na bagagem, frutos de questões de vidas passadas não resolvidas, hostil em relação a uma pessoa às vezes dentro da própria família como missão de resgate. Quase sempre aquele que é alvo da ira alheia nem mesmo sabe o que o está atingindo, e fragilizado deixa-se abater pelas emanações impiedosas que causam verdadeiras tragédias em sua vida, seja de ordem material, mental, física, e que não raro o sofrimento se estende aos que estão próximos, principalmente os familiares. É nesse momento que vem em socorro os Caboclos quebradores de demanda ou Caboclos Mandingueiros, para quebrar (eliminar) a demanda e transformá-la, devolvendo o equilíbrio, fortalecendo e protegendo a pessoa atingida. Os Caboclos que atuam nesse campo são, dentre outros, Caboclo Cobra Coral, Caboclo Ventania, Caboclo Gira Mundo.

<u>Pretos Velhos</u>

QUEM SÃO OS PRETOS VELHOS? Pretos Velhos ou Pais Velhos são espíritos trabalhadores da Umbanda que se apresentam em corpo fluídico de velhos africanos que viveram nas senzalas. São espíritos Guias de elevada sabedoria, que trazem esperança e tranquilidade aos anseios dos que os procuram para amenizar suas dores e aflições. São afetuosos e pacientes, oferecem o amor e a fé aos que lhes pedem ajuda. Tão afáveis e simples que se sentam nos conhecidos "banquinhos de Preto Velho" de modo a ficarem abaixo dos que a eles pedem auxílio ou no máximo no mesmo nível, em uma inequívoca demonstração de humildade.

TODOS OS PRETOS VELHOS FORAM ESCRAVOS E MORRERAM IDOSOS? Não é correto crer que todo Preto Velho e Preta Velha foram negros ou morreram velhos. Muitos servidores do Alto que utilizam essa aparência nunca foram escravos, nem aqui no Brasil nem em qualquer lugar do mundo.

O PRETO VELHO É VELHO MESMO? E PRETO? Não necessariamente. Caboclo, Criança, Preto Velho são roupagens espirituais. O plano espiritual criou uma roupagem que fala a língua da nação brasileira. Ao adentrar no movimento umbandista, no plano espiritual, o espírito faz sua opção: Caboclo, Preto Velho, Marinheiro, ou seja, assume a roupagem perispiritual de um índio, um boiadeiro, um marujo e adota a mensagem espiritual daquela roupagem. O Caboclo nos mostra a simplicidade, a altivez desprovida de orgulho, o amor por si e pela natureza, o poder da natureza. O Preto Velho nos fala da humildade, da sabedoria, quando conversamos com os Pretos Velhos inconscientemente nos postamos aos seus pés em respeito ao seu caminhar. A Criança nos remete a pureza, nos ensina a depositar nossa confiança nas mãos do Pai como faz uma criança, pura e com alegria de viver.

DIZEM QUE PRETO VELHO É FEITICEIRO. MAS FEITICEIRO NÃO É UM SER EGOÍSTA QUE FAZ MALDADE? Não. Feiticeiro é aquele que conhece as forças da natureza e sabe usá-las em benefício da humanidade.

O QUE SIGNIFICA PRETO VELHO QUIMBANDEIRO OU MANDINGUEIRO? São os que trabalham com a Esquerda inclusive nos círculos inferiores, combatendo a demanda. Conhecem a boa magia que nada mais é do que a utilização das plantas, raízes, sementes, ervas preparadas das mais variadas formas para o uso de defumação ou banhos purificadores, para proteção e cura. Fazem mandingas como os amuletos, por exemplo.

AO INCORPORAR UM PRETO VELHO QUE TRABALHA COM FEITIÇARIA, O MÉDIUM TORNA-SE FEITICEIRO TAMBÉM? Em todas as incorporações, independente da Linha de Trabalho, o médium é apenas o veículo de qualquer prática. É preciso que o médium se conscientize que é apenas um instrumento, portanto é injustificável se envaidecer.

QUAL É A DIFERENÇA ENTRE INCORPORAR UM GUIA COMO CABOCLO OU PRETO VELHO, E INCORPORAR UM ORIXÁ? Não se incorpora Orixá porque ninguém suportaria a intensidade de sua energia. Os Orixás possuem trabalhadores espirituais que estão sob suas ordens diretas, chamados Falangeiros, e cuja luz bastante intensa impede que haja, na maioria das vezes, incorporação completa, apenas se aproximam do médium e irradiam sua energia no plano físico através dessa aproximação. O Falangeiro não fala e o médium move-se de forma contida e limitada, alguns inclusive agem de forma cadenciada, parece que estão aplicando um passe. Quando o médium incorpora uma Entidade (Caboclo, Preto Velho, Baiano, Boiadeiro etc.) e estas conversam, dão conselhos, fazem limpeza energética nos assistidos, está incorporando um Capangueiro.

QUAIS SÃO AS MAIORES HABILIDADES DOS PRETOS VELHOS? Têm grande habilidade no manejo das forças da natureza e das ervas medicinais. Estão ligados à vibração de Omulu/Obaluaiê, por isso são feiticeiros poderosos. Fumam cachimbo ou cigarro de palha, benzem com ramo de arruda e com terço católico, conversam e dão conselhos aos que os procuram para desabafar, demandam contra o baixo astral, e suas baforadas nos cachimbos são para limpeza e harmonização das vibrações de seus médiuns e de assistidos. Sugerem remédios e tratamentos caseiros para os males do corpo e da alma. Apresentam-se como tio, tia, pai, mãe, vó ou vovó, vô ou vovô.

O QUE É LINHA DE PRETO VELHO? Quando se fala em Linha de Preto Velho se faz referência a uma grande Linha de Trabalho, ou seja, uma grande faixa vibratória onde espíritos com os mesmos propósitos ingressam para cumprir sua missão.

OS PRETOS VELHOS SÃO ANTIGOS ESCRAVOS ANALFABETOS? TRAZEM OS SINAIS CARACTERÍSTICOS DA ESCRAVIDÃO? O espírito se manifesta com a roupagem fluídica com a qual ele vai poder ser interpretado de forma positiva em um ambiente. De que serviria em um ambiente frequentado por pessoas simples e humildes uma manifestação intelectualizada, fazendo uso de palavras que a maioria não faz ideia do que significa? Os espíritos se adéquam às necessidades humanas formando Linhas de Trabalho dentro da Umbanda e visam, suavemente, agregar as consciências dos que frequentam os Terreiros, permitindo que cada um seja despertado em seu íntimo para uma mudança gradual e benéfica.

POR QUE OS MÉDIUNS INCLINAM O CORPO PARA FRENTE NA GIRA DE PRETO VELHO? Na incorporação dos vovôs e vovós o médium sente vibração que começa com um "peso" nas costas, fazendo com que incline o corpo para frente. Essas Entidades andam apenas para as saudações ao Atabaque, Gongá e Dirigente ou Guia que está comandando a Gira. Ficam sentados durante os atendimentos, e alguns poucos Pretos Velhos se mantêm em pé.

POR QUE OS NOMES DOS PRETOS VELHOS SÃO QUASE SEMPRE IDÊNTICOS? Na época terrível da escravidão, assim que os negros aportavam no Brasil, perdiam o direito de usar o seu nome africano e de praticar as suas antigas tradições. Eram batizados segundo a fé católica e recebiam nomes portugueses, sendo o sobrenome geralmente a identificação da fazenda onde nascera ou para a qual fora vendido. O sobrenome também podia mostrar a procedência da região africana na qual vivia, ou o nome do porto africano por onde tinha sido embarcado para a cruel escravidão em terras brasileiras. Os principais portos eram de Benguela, Cabinda, Costa da Mina e Luanda, e assim os escravos passavam a ser chamados Benguela, Cabinda, Congo, Angola. Por exemplo: Maria Mina, José Cabinda, Joaquim D'Angola, Maria Conga. Na Umbanda, o nome com o qual o Preto Velho ou Preta Velha se apresenta, além de mostrar sua procedência, também lhe distingue sua Linha de *atuação*.

HÁ UMA VOVÓ PRETA CHAMADA MARIA CABINDA E OUTRA CHAMADA MARIA CAMBINDA?
Sim, são duas Pretas Velhas. Embora os nomes sejam quase idênticos, a diferença é que Cambinda (com a letra "m") não é uma região africana e sim a denominação que se dava ao grupo de negros que percorriam as ruas louvando santos católicos, e que hoje conhecemos como Maracatu. Cabinda (sem a letra "m") é uma cidade e também um porto de Angola de onde eram embarcados os negros escravos. Os vovôs e vovós são de Cabinda e não Cambinda, por exemplo, Vovó Cabinda de Angola. O nome da Preta Velha Mãe Cambinda de Guiné pode indicar que era uma negra cambinda e que veio da Costa da Guiné (chamada de Costa dos Escravos), na África.

PRETO VELHO E OMULU É A MESMA ENTIDADE?
Não, Omulu é Orixá. É importante saber que **todos** os Pretos Velhos **"vêm" na Linha das Almas** (Omulu/Obaluaiê), mas cada um recebe a irradiação de um Orixá diferente.

QUANDO É COMEMORADO O DIA DO PRETO VELHO? E O DIA DA SEMANA?
Dia 13 de Maio, quando se

comemora a libertação dos escravos, é comemorado na Umbanda o Dia do Preto Velho. Na semana é segunda feira.

QUAL É A COR DAS VELAS DOS PRETOS VELHOS? A cor das velas, assim como das Guias, são bicolores preta e branca.

COMO É A SAUDAÇÃO DOS PRETOS VELHOS NA UMBANDA? Saúdam-se os queridos pais velhos dizendo *"Adorei as Almas!"*.

Crianças / Erês

AS CRIANÇAS TAMBÉM SÃO CHAMADAS DE ERÊS? Sim, na Umbanda elas são chamadas de Erês, Ibejada ou Beijada, Dois Dois, Cosminhos e Ibêjis. Por influência do sincretismo com os santos católicos são conhecidos também como Crispim e Crispiniano (irmãos e mártires), Cosme, Damião e Doúm (uma característica em relação às representações de São Cosme e São Damião é que junto aos dois santos católicos aparece uma criancinha vestida igual a eles, chamada de Doúm ou Idowu, que personifica as crianças com até sete anos, sendo ele o protetor dos guris nessa faixa de idade). Por influência da cultura indígena também são chamados de Curumins (palavra de origem Tupi-Guarani que designa "criança").

QUAIS SÃO AS CARACTERÍSTICAS DOS ERÊS? Têm características e traços relativos à maneira de agir, de reagir e falar das crianças, além do gosto por brinquedos e doces, por isso simbolizam a pureza e inocência. Incorporados em seus médiuns transmitem grande alegria a todos através de brincadeiras e divertimentos. Quando "chegam" nos Terreiros, os Erês "vêm" sempre brincalhões, travessos, meigos e chorões.

OS ERÊS SÃO APENAS CRIANÇAS? São Entidades de grande atuação e força espiritual, e é voz corrente entre umbandistas que quando uma criança faz uma mandinga só ela tem o poder de tirar.

POR QUE OS ERÊS USAM BRINQUEDOS? Os brinquedos são seus instrumentos de trabalho quando incorporados, por isso é comum ver uma Criança pegar o nome de alguém a quem se quer ajudar e colocar, por exemplo, dentro do carrinho ou boneca, junto com a chupeta, etc.

AS CRIANÇAS VÊM NAS GIRAS APENAS PARA BRINCAR E COMER DOCES? Muitos pensam que durante as Giras elas estão apenas comendo doces ou brincando, mas não é assim que deve ser entendido porque os Erês, quando incorporados, vibram com intensidade e ininterruptamente a energia da natureza (Orixás) a que estão ligados, umas são das cachoeiras vibrando Oxum (Pedrinho da Cachoeira), outras das praias vibrando Yemanjá (Rosinha da Beira da Praia), do mar (Ondinha do Mar), das pedreiras vibrando Xangô (Joãozinho da Pedreira), das matas vibrando Oxóssi (Paulinho das Matas). Basta entrar na sua sintonia infantil, brincando e comendo doce, que acontece toda uma limpeza espiritual. Nas Giras os Erês incorporam nas mais variadas formas, algumas vezes virando cambalhota, outras pulando muito, rolando no chão, etc. Esse tipo de comportamento na incorporação nada mais é do que a forma de descarregarem seus médiuns e as pessoas ali presentes e, ao mesmo tempo, trazer a alegria contagiante para o ambiente.

ERÊ E IBÊJI SÃO AS MESMAS ENTIDADES? Não, Ibêji são Orixás Criança, gêmeos infantis. Os Erês são agrupados na Linha das Crianças, também chamada Linha de Yori ou Linha de Ibêji, e ligados à vibração de Oxum.

QUAL É A DATA COMEMORATIVA DA LINHA DAS CRIANÇAS? É dia 27 de setembro, quando acontece a Festa de Cosme e Damião e têm-se costume de enfeitar os Terreiros com bandeirinhas, muitos doces, brinquedos, bolos e a maioria das Casas de Umbanda abrem suas portas e oferecem fartura de guloseimas e brinquedos para as crianças como forma de agradecimento, e homenagem aos erêzinhos. Da Festa de Cosme e Damião participam pessoas de todas as religiões, é festa linda onde os Erês, com sorrisos e alegria, fazem grandiosos trabalhos. Em atos aparentemente simples como bater palmas e cantar, sem que se perceba, a ajuda que vem do alto já está acontecendo.

POR QUE SE COSTUMA DAR DOCES, REFRIGERANTES, ALÉM DE FRUTAS, AOS ERÊS NOS JARDINS? É onde as oferendas normalmente são feitas.

QUAL É A SAUDAÇÃO AOS ERÊS NA UMBANDA? Saúda-se os Erês dizendo *"Oni Beijada"*, *"Oni Beji"* ou ainda *"Caminha Beijada"*.

QUAIS AS CORES DOS ERÊS E O DIA DA SEMANA?

Suas velas, assim como as Guias, são cor de rosa ou azul claro. O dia da semana de Cosme e Damião é domingo.

É VERDADE QUE OS ERÊS SÃO ESPÍRITOS ADULTOS QUE SE PASSAM POR CRIANÇAS? Não. Se assim fosse seria uma enganação, um teatro. São de fato espíritos de natureza infantil.

POR QUE SE DIZ QUE "O QUE UMA ERÊ FAZ NEM EXU DESFAZ"? A Falange das Crianças é uma das poucas que consegue dominar a magia, por isso são dotadas de imenso poder espiritual.

POR QUE ERÊS SÃO CHAMADOS DE DOIS DOIS? É o nome pelo qual são designadas as pessoas gêmeas.

Baianos

QUEM SÃO OS BAIANOS DA UMBANDA? A Linha dos Baianos é formada por trabalhadores alegres, que ensinam que o ser humano deve viver livre de tudo, sem se preocupar com o alheio. São grandes manipuladores de energia e da magia, e ótimos conselheiros. Trazem sempre palavras de conforto e auxílio para as coisas do dia a dia na vida terrena. Trazem também a esperança de dias melhores e a força para perseguir esses dias porque, ensinam, *"depende de cada um e de mais ninguém mudar os rumos da própria vida"*.

O QUE OS BAIANOS DA UMBANDA ENSINAM? Os Baianos ensinam a importância de se reagir com tranquilidade às dificuldades, contratempos e obstáculos. Mostram que compreender as adversidades, aceitar o que não pode ser mudado, assumir que não se pode ter tudo, e respeitar as opiniões, ideias e pensamentos de outras pessoas faz a diferença entre ser feliz e ser infeliz nessa vida. Ensinam com simplicidade a importância de ter autoconfiança e a armadilha da autossuficiência.

OS BAIANOS GOSTAM DE BRINCAR COM AS PESSOAS? Sim, gostam. Embora espontâneos sempre são muito respeitosos, fazem brincadeiras sadias e jamais provocam ou zombam de ninguém.

COMO SÃO AS GIRAS EM QUE TRABALHAM OS BAIANOS? São descontraídas e bonitas. Essas Entidades movimentam o corpo em passos de danças que se assemelham ao Xaxado e a Capoeira. Muitos falam com o sotaque próprio das regiões do nordeste do Brasil, embora as Entidades que trabalham nessa Linha, como em todas as outras, não foram necessariamente baianos ou baianas.

OS BAIANOS DA UMBANDA TIVERAM FORAM ENCARNADOS NA BAHIA? Como acontece em todas as Linhas de Umbanda, aqui também é apenas a forma como as Entidades se apresentam, um arquétipo. Muitos umbandistas entendem os Baianos como os primeiros sacerdotes da Bahia e do Nordeste, que mantiveram, sustentaram e divulgaram o Culto aos Orixás.

O QUE É ARQUÉTIPO? É um modelo que as Entidades utilizam como referência para o comportamento básico, por exemplo, a Madre Teresa de Calcutá é o arquétipo da bondade. Dessa forma se fazem entender e reconhecer.

POR QUE LINHA DE BAIANOS? POR QUE NÃO EXISTE TAMBÉM A LINHA DE PAULISTAS, GAÚCHOS, CARIOCAS? A Bahia foi a porta de entrada da cultura africana no Brasil. Por lá entraram os Orixás, o axé, os segredos da natureza e sua relação com o ser humano. Assim sendo a espiritualidade, ao permitir a organização de Linha de Trabalho que se manifestaria nos Terreiros trazendo todo o conhecimento da magia dos ancestrais, deu a ela o nome "Linha de Baianos".

A QUAL LINHA DE TRABALHO ESPIRITUAL PERTENCEM OS BAIANOS? Os Baianos pertencem à chamada Linha das Almas, a mesma dos Pretos Velhos. Atuam sob a regência de Iansã e trabalham sob a vibração de todos os Orixás. Melhor explicando, Iansã rege a Linha dos Baianos, mas cada Entidade em particular recebe a vibração de seu Orixá regente. Iansã, sendo Orixá dos ventos, é a grande responsável pelo movimento energético dos planetas, e por serem regidos pela Senhora dos Ventos costuma-se dizer que os Baianos são "movimentadores", não gostam de ver nada nem ninguém parado ou estacionado que logo colocam em atividade, daí se diz que os *"Baianos são ótimos para dar um empurrãozinho"*. Em alguns Terreiros vemos presentes nesta Linha trabalhadores que se apresentam como Cangaceiros (Lampião, Maria Bonita, Corisco). Trabalhador ativo nessa Linha é Zé Pelintra, que trabalha também na Linha de Jurema e Linha de Malandros.

O QUE É VIRADA DE BAIANO? Por serem muito atuantes na quebra de demandas não raro acontece a chamada **"Virada de Baianos"**, quando *"viram"* na Esquerda para lidar com energias negativas porque são Guias que mesclam características da Direita e da Esquerda.

QUANDO A "VIRADA DE BAIANO" PASSA A SER TRABALHO DE ESQUERDA? Caso o padrão vibracional do Terreiro, mesmo com a Virada de Baianos, continue pesado e o ambiente incomodado por perturbações, aí então será chamado o Exu do Terreiro. Neste momento, os trabalhadores que de princípio atuavam na faixa vibracional de Entidades de Direita passarão a atuar na faixa Esquerda, ou seja, os médiuns incorporarão seus respectivos Exus para descarrego de forças negativas e o trabalho passa a ser feito com vibrações muito mais densas.

NA "VIRADA DE BAIANO" ESSA ENTIDADE SE TRANSFORMA EM EXU? Não. Nenhuma Entidade de Umbanda se transforma em outra. Em situações em que o Terreiro, o médium ou mesmo as pessoas que frequentam a Casa estão sob a influência de forças negativas, o Baiano (assim como o Preto Velho) pode mudar sua própria vibração assumindo a roupagem fluídica (ou energética) usada quando em missões de trabalho juntamente com os Exus, trabalhos esses que fazem parte da missão dos Baianos. Quem assiste essa ação acredita que se transformou em Entidade de Esquerda, mas não corresponde a verdade. A Gira, nesse caso, continuará sendo da Linha de Direita.

ONDE SÃO FEITAS AS OFERENDAS AOS BAIANOS DA UMBANDA? O QUE É USADO NAS OFERENDAS? São feitas geralmente na natureza ao lado de um coqueiro. Usa como elementos magísticos batida de coco, água de coco, cigarro de palha, fumo de rolo. Nas festas quase sempre são servidos coco, cocada, farofa com carne seca.

QUAL É A COR DOS BAIANOS? A cor de suas Guias e velas é alaranjada ou qual for definida pela Entidade.

QUAL É O DIA DA SEMANA E COMO É A SAUDAÇÃO AOS BAIANOS? O dia da semana para mentalizar os Baianos é quarta feira. Saúdam-se os Baianos da Umbanda dizendo *"É da Bahia, Meu Pai!"*.

O QUE SE PEDE AOS BAIANOS DA UMBANDA? Pede-se a eles que ajudem a lidar com as adversidades, que tragam esperança e alegria no viver, pede-se auxílio quando é preciso resolver problemas e situações cotidianas e de amparo ao próximo. Pede-se também para o desmanche de trabalhos de magia negra, para a realização de rituais de "abertura de caminhos", para encaminhamento de espíritos sofredores (kiumbas). Dão passes, conhecem orações e rezas fortes e alguns trabalham benzendo com água e dendê.

POR QUE EM ALGUNS TERREIROS OS BAIANOS PARECEM MAIS DUROS, FALAM ALTO E EM OUTROS TERREIROS SÃO MAIS BRANDOS, INCLUSIVE MANIPULAM FLORES E VELAS? O modo como todas as Entidades trabalhadoras se apresentarão depende da forma de trabalho do Chefe da Casa, seus Guias e dos Orixás regentes.

BOIADEIROS, MARINHEIROS, ÍNDIOS, SÃO PERSONAGENS MENOSPREZADAS NA PIRÂMIDE SOCIAL. ISSO SIGNIFICA QUE ESSES ESPÍRITOS QUE ASSUMEM TAIS ROUPAGENS SÃO ATRASADOS OU ESQUECIDOS? De forma nenhuma. Esses "personagens" foram escolhidos pela espiritualidade por serem ricos em significado. Os índios, por exemplo, foram desprezados, massacrados. Os boiadeiros são homens que vivem reclusos no campo, levando o gado, espoliados pelos donos das fazendas. Os marinheiros, marujos, pescadores são quase invisíveis socialmente, quase nunca nos lembramos deles. O baiano antigamente saía de sua terra em busca de vida melhor nas cidades grandes do sudeste, sempre exercendo trabalhos menores, além de que grande número de trabalhadores dessa Linha foram Babalorixás e Yalorixás baianos, sacerdotes africanos do culto de Orixás, arrastados à força para o Brasil. A Umbanda veio resgatar isso com espíritos esclarecidíssimos, que entram na Umbanda e, cheios de amor, vem trabalhar com um povo simples, que sofre e que se identifica com seus iguais.

COMO OS BAIANOS AJUDAM OS SIMPLES, OS QUE SOFREM? Através de boas palavras, bons conselhos, e sempre pela manipulação de energia que realizam. E a pessoa, em algum momento, é tocada.

BOIADEIROS

BOIADEIRO É TAMBÉM CHAMADO DE CABOCLO BOIADEIRO? Sim, e também Caboclo da Jurema ou Baiano Boiadeiro. São aqueles trabalhadores que com energia vigorosa conduzem o grande número de espíritos que vão ser tratados dentro dos Terreiros.

QUAL É A FUNÇÃO MAIOR DESSES TRABALHADORES NA UMBANDA? É acompanhar espíritos decaídos que atormentam os encarnados, encaminhando-os para Guias espirituais de socorro. A missão dos Boiadeiros não é dar consulta como os Pretos Velhos e nem passes como os Baianos, e sim a dispersão de energia pesada do Terreiro, dos médiuns e assistidos. Estão sempre atentos a qualquer alteração de energia do local, assim como estão atentos também à entrada de encarnados e desencarnados, como vigias que controlam tudo o que acontece, sempre prontos a interferir e acudir os necessitados.

COMO OS BOIADEIROS SE APRESENTAM NAS GIRAS DE UMBANDA? Embora notáveis por favorecer a limpeza profunda no campo espiritual, são muito autoritários, de poucas palavras, disciplinados, sérios. O arquétipo do Boiadeiro é a figura do tocador de gado, vaqueiro, posseiro, capataz, enfim, dos homens que conduzem e guardam animais e que aprenderam a lidar com toda sorte de circunstâncias desagradáveis e situações inesperadas, fazendo que algo ruim seja transformado em bom.

BOIADEIRO E OGUN SÃO A MESMA ENTIDADE? Não, Ogun é Orixá. Essa Linha é regida por Ogun, embora cada Boiadeiro trabalhe na vibração do seu Orixá pessoal como acontece nas demais Linhas de Trabalho da Umbanda.

QUAL É A DIFERENÇA ENTRE CABOCLO BOIADEIRO E BAIANO BOIADEIRO? Ambos são trabalhadores da Linha dos Boiadeiros, mas os espíritos que se apresentam como Caboclos Boiadeiros são mais ligados à mata sob a irradiação do Orixá Oxóssi. Os Caboclos da Jurema ou Baianos Boiadeiros são Entidades mais ligadas à Bahia, semelhante aos Baianos, e atuam sob a irradiação de Iansã.

POR QUE MUITOS USAM LAÇO E CHICOTE? O laço e o chicote são os seus instrumentos magísticos de trabalhos espirituais. É traço marcante da manifestação desses trabalhadores o movimento circular com os braços levantados, simulando o manejo de um laço.

POR QUE ALGUNS BRADAM COMO SE ESTIVESSEM TOCANDO GADO, COM VOZ ENÉRGICA DIZEM "*ÊÊÊ BOI*", ALTO E RÁPIDO, COM TOM DE ORDEM? Está mandando espíritos enganadores que entraram no local se retirar. É dessa forma que "*descarregam*" o ambiente. Alguns se apresentam dizendo pertencer a diferentes regiões do Brasil como nordeste, sul, centro-oeste.

CHAPÉU DE COURO OU JOÃO BOIADEIRO SÃO OS NOMES DOS BOIADEIROS? Não. Assim como os demais espíritos da Umbanda, também os Boiadeiros são organizados em falanges, por exemplo, Zé do Laço, Zé Mineiro, João Boiadeiro, Chapéu de Couro, Chico da Porteira, são denominações das Falanges e não da Entidade propriamente.

ONDE SÃO FEITAS AS OFERENDAS? São realizadas nas campinas, nos espaços abertos ou beira de estradas.

QUAL É A COR? E O DIA DA SEMANA? Suas Guias e velas são azuis ou vermelhas como Ogun, ou qual seja definida pela Entidade. O dia da semana para mentalizar os Boiadeiros é terça feira.

COMO É A SAUDAÇÃO AOS BOIADEIROS? Saúdam-se os Boiadeiros dizendo *"Xetro Marrumbaxêtro! Jetruá!"*, palavras que não existem nos dicionários, são chamadas onomatopeia, que significa a formação a partir da reprodução aproximada, com os recursos de que a língua dispõe, de um som natural do estralar do chicote (como "din-don" é o som da campainha, "atchim" o espirro, "tibum" o som de alguém caindo).

É VERDADE QUE BOIADEIRO É UM EXU EVOLUÍDO? Não. Seria a mesma coisa que dizer que Exu é uma Entidade inferior que foi *"promovida"* a Boiadeiro. Não existe Guia de Umbanda que sobe de posição ocupando um cargo mais elevado.

QUANDO OS BOIADEIROS FALAM DO "BOI" ESTÃO SE REFERINDO AO BOVINO? Não. Nos Pontos cantados e nas Giras de Boiadeiro sempre se mencionam palavras que tem significado muito especial. Boi se refere ao ser humano, porque é hábito dos Boiadeiros de Umbanda narrar sua missão espiritual de amparar e encaminhar o encarnado ou desencarnado em desunião com as Leis divinas. Quando diz que o *"boi está desgarrado do rebanho"* narra sua missão de resgatá-lo. Como exemplo é o ponto cantado *"Seu boiadeiro olha que linda boiada / Está faltando um, está faltando um / Pra completar a boiada".*

E A QUE SE REFEREM QUANDO FALAM "BOIADA"? Boiada significa um grande número de bois que, normalmente, estão agrupados num só local. Na linguagem figurada dos Boiadeiros, boiada é a multidão de irmãos desequilibrados que essas Entidades *"recolhem"* para encaminhá-las rumo às veredas da evolução espiritual. *"Boiadeiro, boiadeiro / Sua boiada esparramada / Boiadeiro chama seu guia / E vai ver sua boiada".*

A QUE SE REFERE O PONTO CANTADO QUANDO DIZ QUE O "BOI ESTÁ ATOLADO"? Refere-se a irmãos desencarnados que estão presos em plano intermediário entre o mundo físico e o espiritual, descrito no entendimento dos Boiadeiros como região astral pantanosa.

OS PONTOS CANTADOS QUE DIZEM "BOIS ATOLADOS EM LAMAÇAIS" FAZEM ALUSÃO A QUE? Aos irmãos que se meteram em vícios, presos na areia movediça da dependência física ou psicológica, afundados na lama da degradação.

O QUE SIGNIFICA "BOIS AFOGADOS EM RIOS"? Refere-se aos irmãos que caíram nas águas profundas e turvas das paixões humanas, e quando se está em águas profundas perde-se o controle sobre tudo, inclusive sobre si mesmo.

O QUE QUER DIZER O PONTO CANTADO QUANDO MENCIONA "BOI FOI ATRAVESSAR O RIO E FOI ARRASTADO PELA CORRENTEZA"? Refere-se aos irmãos que tiveram tudo puxado para longe de si, objetos ou pessoas, levado pela correnteza.

VÁRIOS PONTOS CANTADOS FALAM DE "BOIS QUE SE EMBRENHARAM NAS MATAS E SE PERDERAM". REFEREM-SE A QUE? Referem-se aos irmãos que agem de maneira descuidada e sem refletir, e de repente se encontram em complicações desesperadoras, sob ameaça grave e colocando em perigo a própria existência e integridade. Buscam saídas, mas não conseguem sair nem enxergar o outro lado e até mesmo o céu devido à quantidade de árvores e galhos que há nas matas. Ou seja, problema de difícil resolução.

COMO ENTENDER QUANDO FALAM EM "LAÇAR E TRAZER DE VOLTA"? E QUANDO FALAM EM "CHICOTE"? Laçar é recolher os espíritos rebelados que se desgarraram e trazê-los de volta para a grande corrente evolucionista da humanidade. Laço e chicote é uma forma de linguagem figurada para demonstrar que sua missão é resgatar os espíritos rebelados contra a Lei de Deus, mesmo que seja preciso usar de força caso ofereçam resistência. No ponto cantado *"Me chamam Boiadeiro / Boiadeiro eu não sou não / Eu sou laçador* *de gado / Boiadeiro é meu patrão"* demonstra a humildade desta Entidade ao cantar que é simples obreiro de Deus (laçador de gado) e que Boiadeiro é Ogun, o Orixá regente da formidável Linha espiritual de Boiadeiros.

Marinheiros

POR QUE OS MARINHEIROS DA UMBANDA FICAM COM O CORPO BALANÇANDO DE UM LADO E OUTRO? ESTÃO BÊBADOS? Quando os Marinheiros chegam aos Terreiros agem como se estivessem *"desembarcando"* do mar, também chamado Calunga Grande, gingando pra lá e pra cá, gargalhando e abraçando, *"balançando"* e cumprimentando todos com fortes apertos de mão. Os Marinheiros de Umbanda oscilam como quem está se equilibrando no convés de um navio em alto mar. Parecem bêbados, mas que ninguém se engane que embriagados não estão. Na incorporação os médiuns vão com o corpo para frente e para trás porque, como trabalhadores espirituais que se manifestam nas irradiações *"ondulantes"* do mar de Yemanjá, estão em harmonia com as vibrações desse Orixá.

QUAL É A RELAÇÃO DOS MARINHEIROS DA UMBANDA COM IEMANJÁ OU RAINHA DO MAR? A Linha ou falange dos Marinheiros tem sua origem na vibração da Rainha do Mar (Iemanjá).

É VERDADE QUE O CORPO DO MÉDIUM SENTE A FORÇA DA ARREBENTAÇÃO, A FORÇA DAS MARÉS? Sim. É através dos seus *"balanços"* que os Marinheiros fazem a limpeza da carga acumulada nos Terreiros de Umbanda, principalmente após trabalho mais pesado, levando toda a negatividade para as ondas do mar sagrado, por isso dizem *"Já lavei o chão do navio (tombadilho). Agora está tudo bem limpo"*!

COMO É O TRABALHO DOS MARINHEIROS DA UMBANDA? Seu trabalho é realizado em descarrego, passe, no desenvolvimento dos médiuns e em outros trabalhos que possam envolver demandas e descargas pesadas. Não são muito indicados para se conversar ou solicitar consulta.

COMO É A SAUDAÇÃO AOS MARINHEIROS? Saúda-se essa linha dizendo *"Salve a Marujada!"* ou *"Salve o Povo do Mar!"*.

ONDE SÃO FEITAS AS OFERENDAS? E A COR? Fazem-se oferendas aos Marinheiros na orla do mar. Suas Guias são geralmente azul claro e as velas branca, azul ou bicolor branca e azul.

QUAL É O DIA EM QUE SE COMEMORA A LINHA DOS MARINHEIROS E O DIA DA SEMANA? O dia de comemoração aos Marinheiros é 13 de dezembro e na semana, sábado.

É VERDADE QUE OS MARINHEIROS SÃO ESPÍRITOS DE BAIXA EVOLUÇÃO? Muitos afirmam isso porque desconhecem que todas as Entidades que atuam na Umbanda o fazem em estrita obediência a espíritos superiores de extraordinária sabedoria e sublime bondade. Como permitiriam os Mestres Superiores que espíritos de baixa evolução se apresentassem nos Terreiros para ajudar aos necessitados? Quem soltaria um tigre faminto em uma escola para crianças?

OS MARINHEIROS SÃO ESPÍRITOS DE EMBRIAGADOS QUE COMPARECEM AOS TRABALHOS DE UMBANDA SÓ PARA SE EMBEBEDAR? Os Marinheiros, quando se inicia a Gira, dão a impressão que estão alcoolizados porque o balanço que fazem é um ponto de descarrego do ambiente. Criam uma onda de energia no ambiente assim como as ondas do mar, santuário aberto para onde tudo é levado a fim de ser purificado e depois devolvido. Eles não "balançam" porque estão bêbados, **ou alguém já viu algum Marinheiro cair no chão do Terreiro?**

TODO MARINHEIRO "BALANÇA" QUANDO SE INICIAM OS TRABALHOS? Não, muitos andam normalmente. Depende da irradiação que ele atua.

É VERDADE QUE MARINHEIRO PARA TRABALHAR BEM TEM QUE INGERIR BEBIDA ALCOÓLICA? Esta é a interpretação de muitos umbandistas que nem mesmo sabem definir o que é "trabalhar bem". Quando há uma diferença muito grande de ligação energética entre o médium e seu Guia, por exemplo, quando o médium tem problemas pessoais dos quais é difícil desligar o pensamento, é possível realizar maior sintonia entre eles ingerindo pequeníssimos goles de bebida alcoólica, deixando a mente do médium mais permeável de modo a receber às energias irradiadas pelo Guia Marinheiro, facilitando a incorporação.

MAS HÁ MARINHEIROS QUE NÃO CONSOMEM "PEQUENÍSSIMOS" GOLES, E SIM GARRAFAS CHEIAS DE BEBIDA. O Guia é um espírito que se preparou e obteve a permissão da Lei Divina para vir ajudar os encarnados, eles sabem com maestria manipular os elementos usando-os nas quantidades necessárias. Se o médium é alguém que aprecia bebida alcoólica e a ingere sem nenhuma moderação, o faz movido pelo próprio despreparo, e justifica a sua fraqueza dizendo que "quem bebe é o Marinheiro". Desnecessário dizer que a mistificação do médium nesse caso é do tamanho da sua embriaguez.

O QUE DIZER AOS QUE FREQUENTAM TERREIROS EM QUE MARINHEIROS BEBEM LITROS DE UÍSQUE E CACHAÇA DURANTE A GIRA? Caia fora.

A QUE SE REFERE À PALAVRA "MAR" NOS PONTOS E NAS CONVERSAS COM OS MARINHEIROS? Refere-se à vida do ser humano.

O QUE QUEREM DIZER COM "O MAR TÁ BRAVO"? Querem dizer que concordam que a pessoa está passando por grande dificuldade.

QUANDO FALAM A PALAVRA "BARCO" SIGNIFICA UMA CANOA OU ALGO ASSIM? Não. É por "barco" que designam o médium ou os assistidos que pedem conselho.

QUEM É O "CAPITÃO DO NAVIO"? Deus. Também se referem a Ele como Capitão Maior.

QUANDO OS MARINHEIROS DIZEM QUE "LAVARAM O TOMBADILHO" QUASE NINGUÉM COMPREENDE. Tombadilho é o convés do navio, mas na linguagem dessas Entidades significa o Terreiro. Então querem expressar que já limparam a carga negativa do ambiente.

<u>Ciganos</u>

OS CIGANOS PERTENCEM A LINHA DO ORIENTE? No passado a Linha dos Ciganos era uma falange da Linha dos Povos do Oriente, agora constitui Linha própria de trabalho.

QUEM SÃO OS CIGANOS DA UMBANDA? São Entidades conhecedoras do antigo esoterismo e magia baseada no poder da natureza, e poucos os Terreiros trabalham com eles.

EM QUE OS CIGANOS FAVORECEM AS PESSOAS? Alegres, as energias que vibram em suas Giras favorecem a prosperidade, a boa sorte e a união familiar. Observam as fases da Lua para os trabalhos sendo a Lua Cheia a mais favorável. O arquétipo do Cigano é um ser de alma livre, desapegado. É necessário que se esclareça que nessa Linha há trabalhadores que tiveram encarnação como cigano, e há também os que jamais o foram labutando por afinidade com a magia cigana.

COMO SÃO AS FESTAS DOS CIGANOS NOS TERREIROS? Suas festas são das mais lindas da Umbanda, com muita música e alegria, alguns Terreiros levam violinos, pandeiros, viola. As mesas nos dias de festa estão fartas com frutas, flores silvestres, rosas, velas, incenso, arroz cru simbolizando a prosperidade, trigo e pães representando a fartura, moedas para atrair riqueza, o vinho que é a bebida universal do povo cigano. Não são esquecidos os símbolos dos quatro elementos da natureza que são pedras de cristal representando a terra, vela acesa em representação do fogo, cálice cheio de água e o incenso representando o ar. Durante a festa acende-se uma fogueira porque o fogo representa a purificação das pessoas e do ambiente (tudo na Umbanda tem um significado).

POR QUE HÁ SEMPRE MUITA COR NOS TRABALHOS ESPIRITUAIS DOS CIGANOS? De fato os Ciganos usam muitas cores nos trabalhos, mas cada um tem cor de vibração no plano espiritual em concordância com seu Orixá. Aos Ciganos sempre são acesas duas velas, uma geralmente branca e outra da cor estipulada pela Entidade. Alguns Terreiros mantêm altar separado do gongá onde são mantidos incenso, pedra da qualidade e cor apropriada dependendo da vibração do Orixá sob a qual o Cigano trabalha, uma taça com água e uma segunda taça com vinho. Para as Ciganas costuma-se substituir o vinho pelo licor doce.

QUAL ORIXÁ REGE A LINHA DOS CIGANOS? É uma Linha espiritual sob a irradiação de Oyá-Iansã, cuja cor de vibração é salmão ou coral, cor utilizada também nas Guias, embora alguns Terreiros tenham adotado o amarelo e vermelho.

COMO É A SAUDAÇÃO AOS CIGANOS? E ONDE SÃO FEITAS AS OFERENDAS? Saúda-se dizendo *"Arriba Cigano!"* ou *"Salve Santa Sara Kali!"* ou ainda *"Salve todo povo Cigano!"*. As oferendas são feitas junto a árvore na mata ou jardim.

QUAL É O DIA EM QUE SE COMEMORA O CIGANOS DA UMBANDA? E NA SEMANA? O dia de comemoração aos Ciganos é 24 de maio, dia da padroeira Santa Sara Kali, santa católica protetora do povo cigano e provedora de sorte, amor, saúde, fartura e vida longa, e que na Umbanda representa a orientadora dos Ciganos para o bom andamento das missões espirituais. Na semana, quinta feira. Pedem-se aos Ciganos principalmente a cura, amor e prosperidade.

ALGUNS AFIRMAM QUE SE OS GUIAS DE UMBANDA FOSSEM DE FATO ESPÍRITOS DE CIGANOS NÃO FALARIAM ATRAVÉS DE MÉDIUNS NÃO CIGANOS OU, SE O FIZESSEM, FARIAM NO IDIOMA CIGANO. Os ciganos encarnados em nosso plano espiritual falam o idioma Romani que não é língua oficial em nenhum país e não possui escrita, sendo usado apenas como meio de comunicação oral. Outros milhões de ciganos falam diferentes dialetos e línguas dependendo de sua procedência geográfica. Esses são valores culturais de um povo. Os Guias de Umbanda não se pautam pela cultura de um povo e sim pela sua essência. Essa é opinião que se forma induzida pelos que, antes de buscar conhecimento adequado, distribui o fruto da própria arrogância. Acham-se sábios ao ponto de questionar o propósito da espiritualidade. Teoria infundada de presunçosos que transferem para os Guias e Mentores o peso da própria desinformação e preconceito. Os Ciganos da Umbanda falam em linguagem na qual podem ser entendidos. Que proveito teria se não se entendesse nada do que falam?

POR QUE TRABALHAR COM UMA LINHA COMPOSTA POR ESPÍRITOS EXCESSIVAMENTE APEGADOS AO OURO QUANDO ENCARNADOS? Ciganos não possuíam documentos nem endereço fixo, não tinham renda fixa ou comprovada, portanto estavam socialmente desassistidos. Não havia alternativa senão comprarem ouro, transformarem inclusive em dentes de ouro como forma de segurança financeira para si, para sua família e descendentes. Não era apego, era segurança.

POR QUE DIZEM QUE CIGANOS ROUBAM CRIANCINHAS? Antigamente se a mulher engravidava e não era casada, ou sendo casada não desejasse o filho, ela o abandonava ainda recém-nascido perto de acampamento dos ciganos, que nunca rejeitavam cuidar de um desamparado e findavam por criar o enjeitado. E se alguém perguntasse pelo filho desaparecido era sempre mais fácil dizer que os ciganos roubaram. Os ciganos não roubavam crianças, ao contrário, as criavam.

OS CIGANOS TRABALHAM COMO EXUS NA LINHA DE ESQUERDA? Não. Muitos confundem Exu Cigano e Pombogira Cigana com os trabalhadores da Linha de Cigano. Como Linha Auxiliar, eles somente trabalham a Esquerda nos caminhos de Exu. Mas não são Exus.

Linha Do Oriente

É VERDADE QUE A LINHA DO ORIENTE É UMA DAS MAIS ANTIGAS DA UMBANDA? Sim, é verdade. Essa é uma Linha específica de cura, muito antiga na Umbanda e regida pela delicada energia de Oxalá, o Orixá que inspira a fé e a espiritualidade.

O QUE FAZEM OS TRABALHADORES DESSA LINHA? Os trabalhadores que se manifestam nessa Linha fazem cirurgias espirituais, perispirituais, visitam o paciente no lugar onde ele estiver, fazem tratamentos e curas através de reiki, da imposição das mãos, cromoterapia, fluidoterapia, homeopatia, acupuntura, chás, florais. Há mentores de cura, mestres turcos, doutores chineses, médicos alemães, mongóis, egípcios, maias, em alguns Terreiros apresentam-se índios e xamãs.

É VERDADE QUE MUITOS PRETOS VELHOS TRABALHAM NA LINHA DO ORIENTE? É verdade. Por exemplo, Pai Jacó (ou Jacob) que entende a misteriosa Cabala Hebraica, e o Caboclo Pena de Pavão que trabalha utilizando-se das forças e conhecimentos indianos.

COMO É UMA GIRA DA LINHA DO ORIENTE? São organizadas em equipes de cirurgia, de oração, de proteção, de passes espirituais voltados para males do físico, da mente, doenças provenientes de processos cármicos e do espírito. Os trabalhadores da Linha do Oriente interagem com seus médiuns através de incorporação e também através da intuição. Nesse caso o médium psicografa as receitas do tratamento. São entidades espirituais muito calmas, falam pouco, e alguns nem falam, apenas deixam mensagens escritas.

É UM TRABALHO SEMELHANTE AO DAS OUTRAS LINHAS? Não, quando atuam esses trabalhadores nos Terreiros as Giras são bem diferentes. Não há utilização das ferramentas tradicionais como fumo, e os atabaques são batidos lenta e suavemente, haja vista que nada pode perturbar o silêncio necessário nessas Giras.

SÃO ESPÍRITOS QUE TIVERAM ENCARNAÇÃO FÍSICA NO ORIENTE? Novamente aqui não significa que todos os trabalhadores tenham tido encarnação física no Oriente no sentido geográfico, que abrange uma região enorme e com diferenças religiosas e culturais. Trata-se nesta Linha da vibração de cura de trabalhadores que, quando encarnados, professavam crenças não comuns no Ocidente como Hinduísmo, Xintoísmo e trazem seus conhecimentos de cura e conforto para a Umbanda, religião universalista que abraça todos os trabalhadores que queiram praticar a caridade, independente de sua origem.

COMO É A SAUDAÇÃO A ESSA LINHA E ONDE SÃO FEITAS AS OFERENDAS? A saudação para essa linha é *"Salve o Povo do Oriente!"* e também *"Salve o Povo da Cura!"*. As oferendas podem ser feitas em colinas descampadas ou praias desertas, e também podem ser oferendados nos santuários e gongás domésticos.

COMO SÃO AS GUIAS DE TRABALHO DA LINHA DO ORIENTE? As Guias costumam ter 108 contas sendo metade branca e outra metade amarela, mas não é regra.

QUAIS AS CORES E DIA DA SEMANA? As cores das velas são branca, rosa, amarela, alaranjada e azul clara. O dia da semana é quinta feira.

QUE TIPO DE MEDICINA É PRATICADA PELOS TRABALHADORES DA LINHA DO ORIENTE? Pode-se dizer que é praticada a medicina da alma. Entendem que as doenças são resultado do desequilíbrio e abuso com o próprio corpo. Ensinam que há enfermidades do espírito uma vez que há doentes, porém não há doenças. Inclusive a medicina tradicional já começa a compreender isso, atualmente fala-se de doenças psicossomáticas que são moléstias resultantes da mente enferma, como úlceras estomacais ou duodenais, ou ainda pressão alta como consequência de estresse e de conflitos, enfim, estados de tensão muito prolongados que originam lesões graves em vários órgãos.

COMO SE PODEM ENTENDER AS DOENÇAS CÁRMICAS? São doenças que se manifestam devido a débitos contraídos em vidas passadas como consequência de danos físicos cometido contra qualquer ser vivente ou a si mesmo. As enfermidades graves costumam exercer uma função de expiação na vida do espírito.

OS TRABALHADORES DESSA LINHA TRABALHAM EM BENEFÍCIO DE OUTROS ASPECTOS DA VIDA ALÉM DOS MALES FÍSICOS? Não. Trabalham em benefício somente da saúde, sendo o trabalho da Linha do Oriente, em alguns Terreiros, denominados "Gira da Saúde".

ELES CURAM ATRAVÉS DOS REMÉDIOS ALOPÁTICOS? Nenhum Guia de Umbanda prescreve medicamentos da medicina tradicional. Para isso temos os médicos.

MALANDROS

COMO É A UMBANDA DE ZÉ PELINTRA? É formada por uma linda falange de Malandros de Luz voltada para a prática da caridade, cujos trabalhadores ajudam aos que necessitam de auxílio espiritual e material, ensinando incansavelmente sobre o amor e a tolerância entre todos os irmãos do planeta Terra, aconselhando que o respeito ao ser humano é a base fundamental para o progresso individual e social.

LINHA DE MALANDRO É FORMADA POR VAGABUNDOS? É obrigatório que se entenda que não são malandros no sentido de vagabundos e velhacos que lançam mão de artimanhas para enganar. Zé Pelintra não é o malandro que abusa da confiança alheia para levar vantagem sobre alguém ou alguma situação. Ao contrário, rígidos demasiadamente com seus médiuns no que diz respeito ao caráter e honestidade em todos os sentidos, os espíritos de luz que vestem a roupagem fluídica de Zé Pelintra ensinam a importância de ser maleável para adaptar-se em diversas situações, especialmente naquelas em que não se é muito bom, de ter flexibilidade para encarar as coisas e assim sair de dificuldades.

O QUE ENSINAM OS MALANDROS? Ensinam a importância de olhar a vida com bom humor, com pensamento positivo, ensinam a não duvidar de que todos são capazes de transpor os maiores obstáculos e se renovar sempre.

POR QUE ALGUNS MÉDIUNS BEBEM E FUMAM MUITO QUANDO INCORPORADOS EM GUIAS DA LINHA DOS MALANDROS? É impensável que trabalhador da Linha dos Malandros, quando incorporado, use tóxico (cigarros e charutos são usados apenas como defumador astral), sirva-se de bebida alcoólica de forma exagerada, ofenda os assistidos e tente seduzir as mulheres. **O médium que assim procede causa desgosto a Entidade, desconhece a Umbanda e não tem respeito por si mesmo.**

COMO SÃO REPRESENTADOS OS TRABALHADORES DA LINHA DOS MALANDROS? Pode ser representado de três formas a considerar sua missão no astral. A primeira é como um malandro carioca do bairro da Lapa do Rio de Janeiro, quando Zé Pelintra usa a tradicional calça, paletó e sapatos brancos (ou brancos e vermelhos), gravata escarlate e chapéu branco com fita nas cores vermelha ou branca ou preta. A segunda é como Mestre da Jurema, e nesta forma de apresentação usa camisa comprida branca ou quadriculada com mangas dobradas, calça branca dobrada nas pernas, lenço no pescoço nas cores vermelha ou branca ou preta, traz na mão a bengala e o cachimbo e costuma estar com os pés descalços. A terceira forma de representação é na linhagem dos Baianos ou das Almas, onde utiliza roupas de algodão comumente usadas entre os escravos diferenciando-se apenas por lenço vermelho ou cachecol vermelho, e fita vermelha ou branca ou preta em seu chapéu de palha, bem como a bengala típica.

AS ENTIDADES SE VESTEM ASSIM COMO FOI DESCRITO NO MUNDO ESPIRITUAL? Evidentemente que não. São apenas representações e não a forma como se vestem ou se apresentam nos Terreiros. São simbolismos para o entendimento humano.

POR QUE HÁ MANEIRAS DIFERENTES DE APRESENTAÇÃO COMO AS QUE FORAM AQUI DESCRITAS? Porque apesar de trabalharem todos na falange de Zé Pelintra são espíritos de diferentes vibrações e variados conhecimentos. E também porque se adaptam a forma de trabalho do Terreiro.

QUAL A MISSÃO DE ZÉ PELINTRA DOS PORTOS E CABARÉS? É conhecido e respeitado por seus poderes em livrar seus filhos e fiéis de perseguições e traições.

QUAL A MISSÃO DE ZÉ PELINTRA DA BAHIA OU ZÉ PELINTRA DAS ALMAS? São antigos sacerdotes do Candomblé baiano ou das religiões dos escravos africanos, poderosos em desmanchar feitiços e mazelas de seus filhos e protegidos.

QUAL A MISSÃO DE MESTRE ZÉ PELINTRA OU PRETO JOSÉ PELINTRA? É assim conhecido no Catimbó ou Jurema, é erveiro capaz de receitar chás medicinais para a cura de qualquer mal, benzer e quebrar feitiços.

POR QUE ESSA ENTIDADE SE MANIFESTA EM PRATICAMENTE TODAS AS GIRAS? Seu Zé é a única Entidade da Umbanda que tem condições de transitar em todos os níveis vibratórios e em dois rituais diferentes e opostos como a **Linha das Almas**, onde trabalham Caboclos e Pretos Velhos, e a **Linha do Povo de Rua** que se destina a Exus e Pombogiras. Ou seja, Zé Pelintra trabalha em qualquer Gira, desde que seu trabalho seja realmente necessário.

HÁ VÁRIOS OUTROS TRABALHADORES ESPIRITUAIS NA LINHA DOS MALANDROS ALÉM DE ZÉ PELINTRA? Sim, há outros Malandros com nomes distintos, tais como Zé Pretinho, Zé da Navalha e inclusive há Malandras como Maria Navalha e Maria Preta.

COMO É A SAUDAÇÃO AOS MALANDROS? Saúda-se essa linha dizendo *"Salve os Malandros!"* ou *"Salve a Malandragem!"*.

QUAIS SÃO AS CORES E O DIA DE COMEMORAÇÃO? Suas Guias são branco e preto, branco e vermelho, vermelho e preto, e do mesmo modo as velas. O dia de comemoração aos Malandros é 12 de outubro, dia da semana de vibração é terça feira.

O QUE SE PEDE AOS TRABALHADORES DESSA LINHA? Pede-se aos Malandros a limpeza, purificação e abertura de caminhos.

QUAIS SÃO AS FLORES QUE SE PODE OFERECER E OS LOCAIS DE OFERENDA? As flores ofertadas aos Malandros são os Cravos vermelhos e também os brancos, as oferendas são feitas na subida de morros, encruzilhadas ou no local de seu campo de atuação.

QUAL ORIXÁ REGE A LINHA DOS MALANDROS? São regidos por Ogun e podem atuar sob a irradiação de outros Orixás.

POR QUE USAM FITAS NO LAÇO DOS CHAPÉUS DE CORES DIFERENTES? Os Malandros que se apresentam com fita vermelha no chapéu são trabalhadores da Linha das Almas, com fitas pretas são os da Linha das Estradas, e os que atuam na cura usam uma fita branca, que é símbolo do curador regido por Oxalá.

ZÉ PELINTRA SE VESTE DE FATO COM ROUPAS COMO AS DESCRITAS AQUI, COM BENGALA E CHAPÉU? Não. São formas de apresentação simbólica. Apenas elementos representativos da Linha dos Malandros com a finalidade de nos fazer entender e reconhecer suas características e missões espirituais.

ZÉ PELINTRA É EXU? Zé Pelintra não é Exu, mas trabalha junto dele assim como também trabalha junto com Boiadeiro,

Baiano, Preto Velho, Caboclo, enfim, onde precisar dele.

O QUE QUER DIZER ZÉ PELINTRA "VIRADO NA ESQUERDA"? Significa simplesmente que ele está trabalhando junto com Exus, Pombogiras e Exus Mirins.

TODOS OS TRABALHADORES DA LINHA DE MALANDRO FORAM MALANDROS EM VIDAS PASSADAS? Não. Os trabalhadores são agrupados a partir de suas afinidades vibratórias e evolutivas e de suas especialidades, ou seja, são reunidos em campos de atuação. Assim como em todas as demais Linhas, nem sempre o trabalhador espiritual desta Linha foi malandro carioca, Mestre da Jurema ou sacerdote do Candomblé, embora muitos se agrupem a partir de tais afinidades.

Elementais Ou Espíritos Da Natureza

O QUE SÃO ELEMENTAIS? São seres espirituais relacionados com os elementos da natureza e que colaboram na sua harmonização, sempre orientados por espíritos benfeitores.

ELES TÊM UMA FINALIDADE NA ORDENAÇÃO DE NOSSO MUNDO? São essenciais para a vida neste mundo, pois que é pela ação direta deles que chegam às mãos dos homens e mulheres as ervas, flores e frutos, oxigênio, água e tudo o mais que a ciência denomina como sendo forças ou produtos naturais.

POR QUE QUASE NUNCA SÃO VISTOS E MUITOS OS CONSIDERAM PERSONAGENS DE FÁBULAS INFAN-

TIS? De fato sua existência é percebida por alguns poucos, mas a grande maioria os ignora considerando serem apenas personagens de fábulas infantis. O ser quase nunca os vê ou percebe porque vivem nesse mundo como se estivessem em uma dimensão paralela. São invisíveis aos olhos humanos porque os sentidos subdesenvolvidos são incapazes de funcionar para além das limitações dos elementos mais densos. **Aliás, diga-se que são tantos os espíritos que estagiam nas mais variadas dimensões da natureza que o ser humano sequer imagina.**

TODOS OS ELEMENTAIS VIVEM JUNTOS NA NATUREZA? Eles se agrupam segundo suas afinidades e vivem em quatro elementos: as Ninfas no elemento água, os Silfos no elemento ar, os Elfos, Gnomos ou Duendes na terra, e as Salamandras no fogo. Os Gnomos cuidam das florestas, das matas, dos desertos, das regiões geladas, protegem os animais e produzem fenômenos naturais sob a supervisão de seres mais elevados. As Ondinas cuidam dos mares, das águas e fenômenos naturais ligados as águas. Os Silfos cuidam dos ventos e produzem furacões. As Salamandras cuidam de tudo que se relaciona com fenômenos naturais ligados ao fogo. **Cada espécie somente pode habitar e locomover-se no elemento ao qual pertence, e nenhum pode subsistir fora do elemento apropriado, porque o elemento está para o Elemental como o ar para o ser humano ou como a água para os peixes, e nenhum deles sobrevive em elemento pertencente à outra classe.**

OS MAÇONS ACREDITAM NOS ELEMENTAIS? Sim. Os Maçons chamam os Elementais de *"operários silenciosos"*, a Teosofia afirma que Elementais são seres de uma cepa de evolução paralela à humana, mas que atuam próximos em virtude de serem entes que cuidam da terra, água, fogo e ar.

O ESPIRITISMO ENSINA SOBRE OS ELEMENTAIS? Sim. Há vasta menção na literatura Espírita a esses espíritos que exercem ação nos fenômenos da Natureza.

OS ELEMENTAIS TAMBÉM SÃO ORIENTADOS E SUBORDINADOS AOS ORIXÁS? Tudo nas faixas vibratórias dos humanos e dos elementais está subordinado aos Orixás. Sereias são regidas por Yemanjá; as Ondinas, que são sereias mais velhas, são regidas por Nanã; as Ninfas são regidas por Oxum.

TODOS OS TERREIROS TRABALHAM COM ELEMENTAIS? Não. Alguns Terreiros trabalham com Ondinas, Ninfas e Sereias, mas são pouco solicitadas para trabalhos junto à natureza até porque nem todos conseguem compreende-las corretamente. É um mistério que precisa ser mais estudado e o conhecimento compartilhado.

ONDINAS, SEREIAS, GNOMOS E FADAS SÃO PERSONAGENS DE HISTÓRIAS INFANTIS. NÃO SERIAM APENAS FÁBULAS? Os nomes são apenas denominações do vocabulário humano. Em meio ao dia a dia atribulado e a correria diária espalham-se outros seres vivos que tem consciência, conhecimento, que raciocinam e que interpretam. O universo todo está repleto de vida e todos os seres colaboram para o equilíbrio do mundo. **O ser humano não crê que além dele existam outros seres vivendo nesse planeta ou em outra dimensão, porque é profundamente ignorante quanto aos "mistérios" da criação.** A maioria das lendas e estórias consideradas folclore encobre a realidade do mundo astral, com maior ou menor grau de fidelidade. São fatos que ficarão encobertos até que o ser humano esteja preparado para confrontar determinadas questões.

QUAIS AS TAREFAS OS ELEMENTAIS EXECUTAM? Inumeráveis. Protegem os vegetais, os animais, os homens, contribuem para tempestades, chuvas, maremotos, terremotos, interferem nos fenômenos "normais" da Natureza sob o comando dos Orixás que operam em nome do Criador. Deus *"não exerce ação direta sobre a matéria. Ele encontra agentes dedicados em todos os graus da escala dos mundos"* (O Livro dos Espíritos, questão 536).

EXISTE DIFERENÇA ENTRE ELEMENTAIS E ELEMENTARES? Sim, os Elementais são entidades espirituais relacionadas com os elementos da natureza, ou seja, trabalham em contato direto com a natureza através dos quatro elementos primordiais: ar, água, fogo e terra. Os Elementares são criações plasmadas de substâncias astrais pela força do pensamento, também chamada "formas-pensamento".

COMO INTERPRETAR OS NOMES DOS GUIAS

Para conhecer mais sobre a interpretação dos nomes sugerimos a leitura do livro "Descomplicando os Guias de Umbanda - Para Leigos"

OS NOMES DOS GUIAS DE UMBANDA SÃO SIMBÓLICOS OU SÃO NOMES REAIS? Na Umbanda as Linhas de Trabalhos espirituais são formadas por espíritos incorporantes que têm nomes simbólicos. Cada Linha, assim como cada Guia individualmente, está ligada a um ou mais Orixás, e através dos seus nomes simbólicos pode-se identificar sob a vibração de qual Orixá o Guia trabalha (o Guia também é regido por Orixá), sua missão junto ao médium, especialidades de sua Linha etc.

COMO EU POSSO ENTENDER A MISSÃO DE CADA ENTIDADE? Para entender a missão de cada Entidade é preciso conhecer os pontos de força dos Orixás, assim como seus campos de atuação no planeta e na vida de cada ser humano. *Para obter esse conhecimento de forma simples, sugerimos a leitura dos livros "Os Orixás na Umbanda" e "Descomplicando os Guias de Umbanda".*

É POSSÍVEL IDENTIFICAR A QUEM PERTENCE O PRINCÍPIO "ABRIR"? Toda Entidade que leva "Abrir" no nome atua sob a irradiação de Ogun, pois é o Orixá que "abre os caminhos". Assim, sendo Ogun o Orixá dos Caminhos, é também a origem da linhagem de Entidades que levam "Abre" (de abrir ou desatar) no nome.

NOS NOMES SIMBÓLICOS DAS POMBOGIRAS TAMBÉM ESTÃO CONTIDAS A IDENTIFICAÇÃO DE SUA SERVENTIA A UM DETERMINADO ORIXÁ? Sim, e também sua missão junto ao médium e as especialidades de sua Linha. Porém nem todos os nomes falados pelas trabalhadoras dessa indispensável Linha de Esquerda são conhecidos ou verdadeiros, porque é muito comum a Entidade não revelar seu nome por inteiro.

É POSSÍVEL IDENTIFICAR O ORIXÁ QUE REGEM OS CABOCLOS QUE LEVAM "SETE" NO NOME? O número **Sete** representa uma Entidade que trabalha nas sete Linhas de Umbanda, embora seja sempre associado a Oxalá. Por exemplo, **Pombogira Sete Rosas**, onde Rosas são de Oxóssi. Se disser que seu nome é **Sete Rosas Vermelhas ou Sete Rosas Pretas** entende-se que essa Entidade atua também nas vibrações de Ogun (Vermelha) ou de Omulu (Preta).

É PORQUE NEM SEMPRE O NOME COMPLETO É DITO PELA POMBOGIRA QUE SURGE UMA GRANDE QUANTIDADE DE NOMES COM MARIA PADILHA OU MARIA MULAMBO OU SETE SAIAS? Sim. Mas podem ser das Almas, das Matas, das Encruzilhadas, das Porteiras, das Pedreiras, etc. Da mesma forma como há Tranca Rua das Almas, da Encruzilhada, de Embaré, das Matas, e alguns dizem ser apenas **Tranca Rua**.

É TAMBÉM PORQUE OS NOMES DOS EXUS NÃO SÃO REVELADOS INTEIROS QUE EXISTEM TANTOS OS EXUS TRANCA RUA, VELUDO, TIRIRI? Sim, é por isso. **Exu Veludo** que pode ser da Meia Noite, Exu Veludo Cigano, Exu Veludo Sete Encruzilhadas, Exu Veludo Menino (Veludinho), Exu Veludo dos Sete Cruzeiros, Exu Veludo das Almas, Exu Veludo dos Infernos, Exu Veludo da Calunga, Exu Veludo da Praia, Exu Veludo do Oriente, Exu Veludo do Lixo. Porém muitos dão o nome de apenas Exu Veludo. É comum um Exu dizer que seu nome é **Exu Tiriri**, porém existem Tiriri das Encruzilhadas, das Matas, dos Infernos, Menino, da Calunga, das Almas, da Figueira, do Cruzeiro, da Meia Noite, Cigano e cada um desses tem serventia a Orixás distintos.

EXUS, POMBOGIRAS E MIRINS

Para conhecer mais sobre os Guias de Esquerda sugerimos a leitura do livro "Descomplicando os Guias de Umbanda - Para Leigos"

COMO EXPLICAR AS FORÇAS DE EXU E POMBOGIRA DE MANEIRA SIMPLES DE ENTENDER? Pombogira é o desejo, a expectativa de possuir ou alcançar algo. Exu é a vontade e força interior que impulsiona a realizar de modo a atingir os desejos. Colocado de outra forma, imagine uma tarde chuvosa e fria de domingo em que se está quentinho debaixo do cobertor em casa, assistindo um filme na televisão. De repente dá uma vontade enorme de comer maça, mas não tem a fruta em casa. Se não tiver a vontade firme de sair debaixo da aconchegante coberta, trocar de roupa, andar sob a chuva até o -

mercado para comprar a maçã vai ficar o resto do dia desejando a fruta. Essa é a diferença entre desejo e vontade. Pombogira é o desejo de comprar um carro novo, Exu é a vontade que impulsiona a pessoa a trabalhar arduamente para comprá-lo. Um é o complemento do outro. Desejo sem a ação da vontade é inútil. A vontade não acontece se antes não existir o desejo.

SE POMBOGIRA REPRESENTA O DESEJO E EXU REPRESENTA A VONTADE, ENTÃO AMBOS DÃO AO SER HUMANO ESTÍMULOS DIFERENTES? Exatamente. O desejo vem antes da vontade porque ninguém luta pelo que não deseja. Por exemplo, ninguém luta para morar debaixo de uma ponte, mas milhões de pessoas lutam para ter a casa própria, primeiro se deseja nunca mais pagar aluguel e depois coloca a vontade para conseguir. Deste modo **Exu e Pombogira são duas forças que se complementam e impõem o equilíbrio aos seres humanos.**

QUAL É A FUNÇÃO DE EXU E POMBOGIRA? Estimular o ser humano. Estímulo é encorajamento, empurrão, Exu e Pombogira auxiliam as pessoas em suas lutas diárias.

É CORRETO PEDIR A POMBOGIRA E EXU QUE ME GUIE PELOS CAMINHOS CERTOS A FIM DE TER SUCESSOS EM MEUS INTENTOS? É correto. Porém é errado pedir que eles deem o objeto do desejo porque não estão à disposição para satisfazer caprichos e fantasias, e nem são responsáveis pelo sucesso alheio. São trabalhadores da Luz que nos amparam na luta pela vida. Os excessos que se assiste em algumas Casas de Umbanda, infelizmente, devem-se ao desequilíbrio gerado pela falta de estudo dos médiuns. São os que se pautam pela preguiça de aprender ou pela mentira de que o conhecimento atrapalha o Guia. Há também os que por conveniência afirmam que não precisam aprender nada porque o Guia sabe tudo.

NÃO ENTENDO QUANDO DIZEM QUE EXU, POMBOGIRA, EXU E POMBOGIRA MIRINS SÃO TRABALHADORES QUE AUXILIAM O SEU MÉDIUM EXTERIORIZANDO O QUE ESTÁ NO ÍNTIMO DE SUAS ALMAS. Por exemplo, da mesma forma que uma casa é a expressão de quem a habita e a conserva, as palavras e tudo o que vem do interior do ser humano é a exteriorização de sua alma, revelando seus instintos mais escondidos. Exu grosseiro, Pombogira escandalosa, Exu Mirim malcriado apenas demonstram a alma de seus médiuns.

Exu, O Senhor Do Livre Arbítrio

É VERDADE QUE EXU TRABALHA NA ESQUERDA PORQUE É ESPÍRITO SEM LUZ? Exus, Pombogiras e Exus Mirins são espíritos que trabalham na escuridão em benefício da Luz, e cujo trabalho é absolutamente indispensável aos seres. Muitos entendem erroneamente que Direita e Esquerda significam lados e que a Esquerda é a posição não merecedora de confiança ao contrário da Direita, lado considerado bom e correto.

POR QUE O LADO DIREITO É CONSIDERADO O BEM E O LADO ESQUERDO O MAL? Usamos as palavras direita e esquerda como polaridades que os Guias trabalham e não lados. As ações humanas, em sua grande maioria, são absolutamente maléficas e desprovidas de consideração e amor pelo próximo. Sabendo que nossos atos e pensamentos geram energia, e que essa energia é detectável inclusive por aparelhos e devidamente comprovada nos laboratórios, imagina-se a carga negativa agregada em torno do planeta. Esse fardo pesado tem de ser neutralizado, e quem o anula são os Guardiões e Guardiãs que militam no campo denso e negativo que chamamos "Esquerda". Uma de suas missões é "diluir" os fluidos espirituais corrosivos que nós mesmos criamos com pensamentos impróprios e atos nocivos. Daí entende-se que os Guardiões e Guardiãs não são negativos. Os Guias que denominamos de "Direita" são aqueles que nos orientam a uma transformação dando recursos, energias, intuição, mas não estão em nosso lado direito ao contrário do que pensam alguns.

ESQUERDA E DIREITA SE COMPLEMENTAM? Os Guias denominados de Esquerda trabalham com as energias que nós não sabemos administrar. Os da Direita nos incentivam a buscar a iluminação.

POR QUE EXUS E POMBOGIRAS FUMAM E BEBEM? Os trabalhadores da Linha de Esquerda utilizam o cigarro, charuto e cigarrilha como defumadores individuais porque esta é a real finalidade, utilizam a bebida para descarregar energias densas e, quando muito, bebem um **golinho** para limpar o campo energético do médium. Se o médium não teve orientação ou aprendeu por imitação dos irmãos mais velhos que Exus são pinguços, que as Pombogiras além de beber precisam fumar como convém a toda "mulher da vida", e que o Exu Mirim, tendo sido um "menino de rua" quando encarnado precisa ser desbocado, mal educado e "cheirador de cola", então há algo errado com esse médium.

AS PESSOAS TEM MEDO DA LINHA DE ESQUERDA PORQUE JÁ VIRAM MUITO EXU CACHACEIRO, POMBOGIRA LEVIANA E EXU MIRIM DELINQUENTE.

Isso existe tão somente no inconsciente do médium por falta do mínimo de esclarecimento. Ou então incorporação neste padrão baixo de vibração são os obsessores e zombeteiros usando o nome dos Guias da Linha de Esquerda para montar seu circo particular. E o pior é que tem gente que acredita. Em qualquer plano espiritual nos círculos próximos do nosso, assim como na sociedade humana no plano físico, os espíritos sempre se agrupam por afinidade, ou seja, se unem de acordo com seu nível vibracional.

EXUS E POMBOGIRAS DÃO ASSISTÊNCIA AOS ENCARNADOS EM SUAS NECESSIDADES MATERIAIS?

Exatamente. Por se tratar de Entidades que trabalham com energias compactas e carregadas, atuam nos Terreiros na assistência aos encarnados em suas necessidades materiais, nos assuntos urgentes que necessitam de solução imediata, cortam demandas, desfazem os trabalhos de obsessão estabelecidos pelos desencarnados que perseveram no mal, impedem a influência nociva dos que conseguem penetrar no íntimo das criaturas (daí o conselho do Mestre "Orai e Vigiai"), ajudam a limpar os ambientes retirando os "malfeitores" antes que consigam sugar a energia vital levando a pessoa à ruína física e mental.

O QUE É EXU GUARDIÃO? Todo médium da religião de Umbanda tem um Guardião de Esquerda que corresponde à vibração de seu Eledá (Coroa), ou seja, é aquele que tem grande evolução espiritual e recebe instruções diretas dos Orixás. Uma das funções do Exu Guardião é determinar quem irá cumprir ordens recebidas e de que forma serão executadas. Esse Exu guarda a vibração do Orixá, nunca encarnou e nem irá encarnar entre os seres humanos, quase nunca incorpora, é raro quando se manifesta através de um médium e quando o faz geralmente não revela seu nome, não conversa com os assistidos e jamais dá consulta. Apenas médiuns com missões de relevância ímpar tem um Exu Guardião como Guia Pessoal. Esse Exu não é bom e não é mau, é apenas justo e por isso é neutro. Ou é apenas neutro, por isso é justo. Ao Exu Guardião pede-se somente amparo, sustentação e proteção referente às coisas espirituais.

O QUE É EXU DE LEI OU EXU DE TRABALHO? Exus de Trabalho são os Exus que dão aconselhamento nos Terreiros, incorporam nos médiuns e desempenham importante papel junto deles, olhando com atenção os problemas dos assistidos. **São os Exus de Trabalho que se manifestam nos Terreiros porque seu campo vibracional ainda é próximo das vibrações do ser humano.** Eles fazem parte da segurança de um Terreiro. Todo médium pode ter mais de um Exu de Trabalho, e quando há vários, apenas um deles será o Exu de frente, identificado pelo seu médium porque será aquele que dará consultas e se colocará a serviço do Guia Chefe. Aos Exus de Trabalho o médium poderá pedir ajuda na solução de problemas seus e de outras pessoas, referentes a coisas do dia a dia.

O QUE SÃO KIUMBAS OU EXU PAGÃO? Erroneamente denominam os espíritos obsessores e moralmente atrasados de Exu. **Zombeteiros, mistificadores, obsessores ou perturbadores não se chamam Exus, chamam-se Kiumbas e muito frequentemente tentam mistificar, iludindo as pessoas de boa fé usando nomes dos verdadeiros trabalhadores da Linha de Esquerda.** São conhecidos também como "Rabo de Encruza" e muitos os chamam de Exu Pagão, **mas não são Exus**. Estes não fazem distinção entre o bom e o mau, entre o bem e o mal. Atrasados no entendimento espiritual, são eles que, se fazendo passar por Exu de Trabalho, aceitam praticar qualquer tipo de coisa em troca de "despacho" com sangue de animais, galinha preta na encruzilhada ou no cemitério e outras aberrações do tipo. Também são eles que "baixam" nos Terreiros e bebem até deixar o médium desfalecido. Com exagero para impressionar se arrastam no chão, fazem os dedos dos médiuns ficarem em posição de garras, são esses infelizes que falam palavras de baixo calão de modo a envergonhar quem os ouvem, outras vezes usam expressão pomposa e empolada para causar uma impressão psicológica em quem assiste.

O QUE SÃO EXUS DE CEMITÉRIO? São os Exus e Pombogiras que trabalham nos cemitério e são chamados "Povo da Calunga Pequena", que na Umbanda é outro nome que se dá para o campo santo ou cemitério. São trabalhadores de serventia de Omulu/Obaluaiê na Linha das Almas. Trabalham para cura e para manter um padrão vibracional de modo a afastar espíritos de pouca luz, ritual que na Umbanda é chamado de "Descarrego". Como em toda a Criação há ordem, o Povo da Calunga Pequena é comandado pelo Exu Caveira. Nesta Linha, além dos Exus e Pombogiras propriamente ditos, também é valoroso colaborador Zé Pelintra das Almas, originariamente trabalhador da Linha de Malandros.

O QUE SÃO EXUS DE ENCRUZILHADA? Há os Exus e Pombogiras que trabalham nas Encruzilhadas e estão quase sempre sob o comando de Ogun, Orixá quem rege os caminhos através dos quais todos devem passar. Além das encruzilhadas rege também as estradas, trilhas e passagens. É da responsabilidade desses Guias abrir e fechar os caminhos em todos os sentidos (amor, saúde, trabalho). Como exemplo de Exu desta Linha de Trabalho é Tranca Rua. Ao "**trancar**" ele fecha, paralisa, bloqueia a passagem. Por "**rua**" entende-se caminho no sentido de rumo, direção, destino. Tranca para auxiliar no progresso. Por exemplo, alguém que faz uso imoderado de drogas, dorme pouco preferindo se divertir durante toda a noite, Exu Tranca Rua lhe fecha os caminhos. Exu Mirim o conduz a situações em que o desfecho é a prisão em uma cadeia, ou outro tipo de clausura tal como uma doença grave. Ao trancar a rua oferece uma oportunidade de mudar de direção agindo com moderação e disciplina.

POR QUE A UMBANDA ESCOLHEU A ENCRUZILHADA COMO UM PONTO DE FORÇA? Porque encruzilhada é o ponto em que dois caminhos se encontram e o ser humano tem dois rumos a seguir, mas precisa escolher apenas um deles. É o momento de difícil decisão e grande solidão, pois escolha é desafio individual e intransferível. Ao perceber que as defesas materiais e espirituais estão ameaçadas, deve buscar proteção nos Exus da Encruzilhada.

O QUE SÃO EXUS DA ESTRADA OU DA RUA? Exus das Estradas são chamados "Povo da Rua" e trabalham sob a regência de Ogun. Muito perspicazes, não admitem que lhe faltem com a verdade porque conhecem a intenção de uma palavra, mesmo que não seja verbalizada e que exista somente em pensamento. Nesta Linha, além dos Exus e Pombogiras, também auxilia Zé Pelintra das Estradas que é trabalhador da Linha de Malandros.

EXUS DA SERVENTIA DE QUAIS ORIXÁS COSTUMAM DAR PASSES? De nenhum Orixá, porque Exus não dão passes.

SE EU SOUBER QUEM É MEU ORIXÁ POSSO, A PARTIR DAÍ, SABER O NOME DO MEU EXU? Não. É preciso que ele se identifique. Depois então seu nome pode ser interpretado.

É VERDADE QUE QUEM USA EXUS NOS TRABALHOS É A MAGIA NEGRA E O SATANISMO? Exus são Entidades trabalhadoras da religião de Umbanda, portanto não são usados. Magia Negra é ritual voltado para o mau, cuja finalidade é levar sofrimento aos inimigos, e Umbanda é religião cujos trabalhadores estão comprometidos com a Caridade. Satanismo é culto a Satanás que é figura inventada para manipular as pessoas de modo a desumanizá-las e assim impor autoridade através do medo. Perpetuar o terror e a desgraça é o que muitas religiões fizeram com mais empenho no decorrer dos séculos, e lamentavelmente com bastante sucesso. A Umbanda não ensina o medo que paralisa, e nem tem figuras medonhas que aterrorizam os umbandistas. As estátuas de Exu com chifres e pés de bicho e Pombogira com os seios à mostra, só servem aos comerciantes inescrupulosos que ganham a vida fabricando e vendendo aberrações.

POMBOGIRA

DIZEM QUE POMBOGIRA É "UM DIABO DO INFERNO". Pombogira é "vítima" de uma crença da existência do inferno, um lugar onde as almas pecadoras são enclausuradas após a morte, submetidas a penas eternas e governado por entidade imensamente maldosa. Contraditoriamente, Deus que está em todos os lugares por acaso não está nessa região infernal, mesmo sendo Ele onipresente. Nessa cultura religiosa encurralada entre o medo da danação eterna e o medo da opinião alheia, a distorção própria da alma humana torna-se fobia quando, além de diabo, Pombogira também é portadora de "defeito imperdoável" que é ser mulher.

O ESPÍRITO SE TORNA POMBOGIRA COMO RESGATE CÁRMICO POR TER SIDO PROSTITUTA? AFINAL, QUAL É A MISSÃO DE POMBOGIRA? Espécie de "coisa ruim fêmea" acredita-se que sua única missão espiritual é encontrar solução para os fracassos alheios, pensam que sua redenção é arrumar a vida amorosa dos outros e proporcionar ou interromper qualquer tipo de união sexual. É senso comum que Pombogira resgata os erros que cometeu por ter sido "mulher de vida fácil" servindo de para-choque para as frustrações de quem não impõe limite à baixa autoestima. Sem contar que grande parte dos que recorrem a "pombagira de mentirinha" estão longe de um código de ética que lhes impeça de desejar e fazer mal ao outro, bastando que não lhes atendam aos anseios mais infantis. Essa pombagira ordinária teria sido em vida uma mulher de baixos princípios morais, capaz de dominar os homens por suas proezas no coito, movida pelo poder do dinheiro e libertinagem, e depois que morreu virou "diabo prostituta". Assim é Pombogira para quase todos os que não conhecem a Umbanda e, infelizmente, para grande parte dos umbandistas. Se Exu é insultado por adeptos de outras religiões e ultrajado pelos próprios umbandistas que alimentam as distorções, como poderia ser melhor com Pombogira?

DIZEM QUE A PROVA DE QUE É OU FOI PROSTITUTA É QUE *"POMBOGIRA É MULHER DE SETE EXUS"*.

Esse é um grosseiro erro de interpretação. Na verdade Pombogira é única no meio de uma hierarquia de sete Exus chefes de legião. Ela não é mulher **DE** sete Exus, e nem é Pombogira e mais sete Exus chefes de legião, **ELA É UMA ENTRE OS SETE**. São eles: **1.** Exu Sete Encruzilhadas da serventia de Oxalá, **2.** Exu Tranca Ruas da serventia de Ogun, **3.** Exu Marabô da serventia de Oxóssi, **4.** Exu Gira Mundo da serventia de Xangô, **5.** Exu Tiriri da serventia de Yori (Crianças), **6.** Exu Tata Caveira da serventia de Yorimá (Preto Velho), **7. Exu Pombogira da serventia de Yemanjá.**

POMBOGIRA É MULHER E EXU É HOMEM? Pombogira é uma força de vibração feminina, do mesmo modo como Exu vibra o poder masculino, mas não são vibrações de gênero físico. São como o yin e yang, dia e noite, par e ímpar, um não é capaz de criar sem o outro, assim são Exu e Pombogira. Homens, mulheres, tudo no universo tem um componente masculino e um feminino, nada nem ninguém é 100% masculino nem feminino. **Os espíritos que conosco se comunicam nos Terreiros viveram em nosso mundo de seres encarnados**, Pombogiras foram prostitutas, camponesas, amantes, esposas, freiras, mães, avós, exerceram profissões variadas e hoje, por afinidade fluídica, trabalham na Linha de Esquerda que é mais uma corrente de trabalho espiritual na Umbanda.

POR QUE POMBOGIRA BEBE MUITO E SE OFERECE AOS HOMENS DURANTE A GIRA? Não há nada nessas Entidades de Luz que justifiquem as incorporações onde médiuns bebem até "secar" a garrafa de espumante, e se insinuam para os homens da corrente e da assistência, quando não chegam ao ponto extremo de roçar no corpo do outro. Claramente é ação da vontade da médium (e do médium), encoberta sob a desculpa de que está "possuída" pelo espírito de uma prostituta. Ou então são kiumbas levando médiuns a atitudes tão baixas. Já foi dito que Exu trabalha com a vontade enquanto Pombogira atua no desejo do ser humano, inclusive os desejos internos que não se confessa a ninguém, a verdadeira face além das aparências. Pombogira trabalha as paixões humanas e tudo aquilo que arrebata a alma. Paixão é sentimento intenso que possui a capacidade de alterar o comportamento e o pensamento, não importa se é gostar ou detestar, é desejo sentido de maneira extrema por alguém ou por uma coisa, não importa se é prejudicial e se causa desespero.

POR QUE POMBOGIRA É MUITO PROCURADA PARA TRABALHAR OS DESEJOS DE ORDEM AMOROSA E SEXUAL? Por ser uma Entidade que lida as paixões humanas são, dentro dos Terreiros, muito procuradas para trabalhar os desejos de ordem amorosa e sexual, insistentemente perguntadas sobre traição de marido, de esposa, de amante, solicitadas para conseguir namorado, e deixa-se de lado uma ajuda inestimável que só Pombogira pode dar no sentido de auxiliar para não se cair na armadilha das ilusões, de superar as dores sem traumas severos.

A POMBOGIRA É EXU FÊMEA? Não, a Pombogira não é Exu fêmea assim como a mulher não é homem fêmea. Essa é linguagem machista da qual nem as valorosas Guardiãs escapam.

POMBOGIRA É ESPÍRITO DE PROSTITUTA? Há muitas pessoas que associam a Pombogira a prostitutas, às mulheres sedentas de sexo se expõem aos homens. As distorções provenientes da desinformação são próprias dos seres humanos que, mesmo não entendendo sobre o assunto, formam opiniões sem base concreta e distorcem a realidade. Essas nossas irmãs em Oxalá nada mais são do que espíritos desencarnados, do mesmo modo como nossos irmãos Exus, que viveram sobre a terra e hoje, por afinidade fluídica, formam mais uma corrente de trabalho da Umbanda. Foram mães, donas de casa, médicas, lavradoras, prostitutas, enfermeiras, enfim, tiveram profissões das mais diversas, pois que a profissão que um espírito exerceu quando encarnado não determina seu grau de evolução e comprometimento com a caridade. Trabalhar na Linha das Pombogiras exige muito preparo espiritual, discernimento e conhecimento da alta magia.

SE NÃO SÃO PROSTITUTAS POR QUE SE DIZ QUE POMBOGIRAS SÃO MULHERES DA VIDA? Na linguagem humana *"mulher da vida"* significa biscate, devassa, promíscua, meretriz, vadia, piranha, puta e outros adjetivos depreciativos. *"Homem da vida"* significa estadista, político, presidente, governador, chefe de estado, comandante, soberano, ou seja, uma pessoa que governa. Se nossa linguagem é tão injusta com as mulheres que são mães e filhas dos homens, por que seria diferente com uma trabalhadora do astral que carrega a vibração do "desejo". Só se pensa o desejo da forma sexual, mas desejo é muito mais que sexo. Pombogira é o desejo de caminhar para frente rumo às conquistas, de avançar a despeito dos tropeços, de prosseguir apesar das dificuldades. Anseios que não são próprios de um gênero, todos desejam, homens e mulheres, serem pessoas melhores, conhecer e usufruir coisas modernas, desenvolver suas habilidades, crescer espiritual e intelectualmente. Quem não deseja um bom emprego para ter e dar uma vida confortável aos que ama? Quem não deseja uma boa casa onde possa abrigar sua família em segurança? Quem não deseja reconhecimento profissional? São os desejos de Pombogira que nos leva para frente e para o alto. Mas o entendimento miúdo liga Pombogira ao desejo de sexo, e assim ficou como "mulher da vida".

É VERDADE QUE POMBOGIRA É O BRAÇO DIREITO DE EXU? Braço direito significa o principal colaborador e aquele que acata qualquer ordem. Pombogira não é subordinada a Exu para acatar suas ordens. São duas forças complementares, e nem Exu e nem Pombogira é mais importante para ter o outro a seu lado só para auxiliar.

DIZ-SE QUE POMBOGIRA É COMPANHEIRA DE EXU PORQUE SÃO CASADOS? Não há Exu casado nem amasiado, o mesmo para Pombogira. Não existe vínculo matrimonial na espiritualidade. Pombogira é companheira de Exu porque ambos atuam nos mesmos caminhos e trabalham nas mesmas questões, de forma complementar.

POR QUE EXU E POMBOGIRA SÃO REPRESENTADOS POR TRIDENTES? Na Umbanda considera-se que a haste do tridente, estando apoiada na terra, representa a ligação do ser humano com o plano material, e suas pontas voltadas para cima representam a ascensão humana por meio da experiência terrena, através dos três caminhos que todos percorrem, e que recebem as vibrações de Exu e Pombogira: 1) o caminho da esquerda onde a vontade individual é satisfeita, 2) o caminho da direita onde a vontade coletiva é satisfeita, 3) o caminho do meio onde há um equilíbrio entre a satisfação da vontade individual e coletiva.

POR QUE HÁ TRIDENTES REDONDOS E QUADRADOS? Porque Pombogira é representada pelo tridente redondo e Exu pelo tridente quadrado.

POMBOGIRA PODE AJUDAR EM QUESTÕES COMO TRAIÇÃO NO NAMORO OU CASAMENTO? Deslocar a força das Pombogiras para essa finalidade é falta de proveito. A essa Entidade de Luz deve ser solicitada ajuda em questões mais relevantes como saúde, problemas espirituais negativos, auxílio para os que sentem dor, inclusive física.

POR QUE OS MÉDIUNS DIZEM "MEU EXU", "MINHA POMBOGIRA"? SÃO PROPRIEDADES DELES? Quando dizem "meu" não quer dizer "de minha propriedade", mas com quem se tem comunhão, com quem se está envolvido ao ponto de compartilhar experiências. Dizem "meu" no sentido de "ser do meu relacionamento" e com quem se aprende.

Exu Mirim E Pombogira Mirim

EXU MIRIM E POMBOGIRA MIRIM SÃO CRIANÇAS? SÃO PEQUENAS PROSTITUTAS E TROMBADINHAS? Se para muitos leigos e inclusive alguns umbandistas Exu é um marginal e Pombogira prostituta, Exu Mirim não podia ser nada melhor. Dizem que foi, quando encarnado, uma criança delinquente, um trombadinha e por isso ao incorporar seu médium tem o hábito de insultar, fazer gestos indecentes, falar palavras de baixo calão. Mas Exu Mirim não é nada disso, são os médiuns que tendem a repetir o comportamento de seu Dirigente nas incorporações, e se ele acredita que essa Entidade é um "tinhoso infantil", se o Dirigente está convencido que Exu Mirim precisa ser obsceno, então aquele Terreiro terá uma falange inteira de "espírito de porco". Interessante que do mesmo modo como evocam Exu bêbado e Pombogira rameira, há médiuns que trabalham com os Mirins mesmo acreditando serem eles pivetes sem educação. E a pergunta que não encontra resposta é: **como podem incorporar e pedir ajuda a essas Entidades se acreditam que são espíritos tão atrasados?** Felizmente estão longe da verdade.

QUEM SÃO OS GUIAS QUE SE APRESENTAM COMO POMBOGIRA E EXU MIRINS? São trabalhadores que tem acesso a campos e energias que os outros Guias não têm. Todos os Terreiros que trabalham com eles conhecem sua força, respeitam essa Linha de Trabalho poderosa, e os médiuns e assistidos sentem os *"Exuzinhos"* tão queridos como todas as outras Entidades.

EXUS MIRINS SÃO COMO OS ERÊS? Ambos são espíritos que trazem em seu fundamento o mistério dos Orixás. Jamais se deve vê-los como criancinhas divertidas e espirituosas como os Erês.

BEBIDAS E OFERENDAS AOS EXUS E POMBOGIRAS

QUAIS AS BEBIDAS DE EXU? Exus utilizam bebidas com teor de álcool absoluto, ou seja, com álcool puro, sem adição de água, como o conhaque e a aguardente (a qual na Umbanda dá-se o nome de marafo), e as Pombogiras fazem uso de champanhe e anis, mas **não induzem jamais o médium ingerir a bebida porque eles apenas utilizam o conteúdo fluídico do líquido, deste modo a bebida pode ficar num copo e não precisa ser engolida.**

QUAIS AS OFERENDAS PARA EXU E POMBOGIRA E EM QUE LUGAR SÃO DADAS? As oferendas para Exu e Pombogiras são dadas nas encruzilhadas das matas e campos e podem ser frutas, incensos, ervas e bebidas, e esta última apenas para captar a energia dos elementos que as fabricaram. Quem vai à encruzilhada ou cemitério fazer entrega de sangue, carne, ossos, animais, não tem noção do que está fazendo nem da espécie de força maligna com a qual está se associando. E o mais grave é que, unidos pela intenção, a levará consigo para onde for inclusive para a casa onde vive com a família e filhos.

MEDIUNIDADE NA UMBANDA

Para conhecer mais sobre a Mediunidade na Umbanda sugerimos a leitura do livro "Mediunidade na Umbanda – Você é uma Antena"

QUAL É A DEFINIÇÃO DE MEDIUNIDADE? "Mediunidade, na essência, é afinidade, é sintonia, estabelecendo a possibilidade do intercâmbio espiritual entre as criaturas, que se identifiquem na mesma faixa de emoção e de pensamento." (Chico Xavier)

QUEM SÃO OS ESPÍRITOS TRABALHADORES NA UMBANDA? Os espíritos são seres humanos desencarnados e continuam sendo como eram quando encarnados, bons ou maus, sérios ou brincalhões, trabalhadores ou preguiçosos, cultos ou medíocres, verdadeiros ou mentirosos. Eles estão por toda parte e não estão ociosos, pelo contrário, eles têm as suas ocupações.

COMO OS GUIAS DE UMBANDA SE COMUNICAM COM OS SERES QUE ESTÃO LIMITADOS AO CORPO FÍSICO? Comunicam se quiserem ou se puderem através dos denominados médiuns. A comunicação se dá em conformidade com o tipo de mediunidade, sendo as mais conhecidas pela fala (psicofonia), pela escrita (psicografia), pela visão (vidência) e pela intuição, da qual todos guardam experiências pessoais.

É VERDADE QUE QUEM TEM MEDIUNIDADE PRECISA DESENVOLVER SENÃO VAI SER PERTURBADO POR ESPÍRITOS, OU QUE A VIDA NÃO VAI PRA FRENTE? Não é verdade. Do jeito como se coloca a questão parece que a pessoa não tem escolha e soa como ameaça. Outros ainda dizem que a mediunidade é como uma espécie de moeda a se pagar por dívidas contraídas no passado, como um carma ruim que o médium tem que resgatar. Mas a mediunidade não é um carma pesado imposto por um deus vingativo. Todos são livres para escolher se quer ou não desenvolver a mediunidade.

A MEDIUNIDADE É A CAPACIDADE DE COMUNICAR-SE COM O PLANO ESPIRITUAL? Sim, e não há nem mesmo um único ser humano encarnado que não seja capaz dessa interligação. Em todos os momentos da vida toda gente tem auxílio do plano espiritual, pode-se dizer que **é uma faculdade humana** da mesma forma que a memória, inteligência, etc.

TODOS SÃO MÉDIUNS DE UMA FORMA GERAL? Pode-se dizer que dizer que sim na medida em que todos estão em contato com os Espíritos e são por eles influenciados. Alguns consideram a mediunidade como uma espécie de "sexto *sentido*", ou seja, um sentido além dos cinco sentidos físicos.

A MEDIUNIDADE É UM PRIVILÉGIO? Não é um privilégio e sim dom inerente a todos os seres e cada um o manifesta em determinado grau, e cada criatura assimila as forças superiores ou inferiores com as quais sintoniza.

POSSO RECORRER A MEDIUNIDADE NA UMBANDA PARA RESOLVER MEUS PROBLEMAS? A mediunidade na Umbanda não é um balcão de atendimento ou um pronto socorro ao qual se recorre para resolver problemas, curar doenças, conseguir emprego ou trazer "o amor" de volta. Não serve como oráculo para dizer o que a pessoa deve fazer ou decidir, porque nem os Guias de Umbanda tem autorização do Criador para interferir no livre arbítrio do ser humano. Ninguém vai acertar os números da Mega Sena porque frequenta Terreiro, nem os Guias vão dar um jeito de enriquecer alguém não importa quantos "despachos" fizer ou quantas velas acender. Muitos que procuram um Terreiro para afastar "espírito" que não deixa a vida "ir pra frente", faria melhor se mudasse de atitude e começasse a pensar onde está errando e como corrigir. Desempregado terá mais êxito se, ao invés de ir ao Terreiro pedir para o Guia lhe arrumar emprego, matricular-se em curso de atualização ou aprender nova profissão.

A MEDIUNIDADE É CASTIGO? A mediunidade não é castigo, não é punição, não faz milagre. Os médiuns e seus Guias não são entidades com poderes especiais e com conhecimentos acima da maioria, porque tanto um como outro só conhece o que suas experiências e vivências lhes proporcionaram, e ambos só vão crescer mediante esforço pessoal, igual a todo mundo.

É CORRETO AFIRMAR QUE A MEDIUNIDADE NA UMBANDA É SINTONIA E TROCA DE EXPERIÊNCIA

ENTRE O MÉDIUM E SEUS GUIAS? Corretíssimo. A mediunidade na Umbanda é um aprender constante porque raramente há perda de consciência, sendo assim o médium sempre aprenderá e somará às suas as experiências envolvidas por todas as partes. A mediunidade na Umbanda é aperfeiçoamento diário dos valores e sentimentos, e é trabalho incessante porque não estando pronta e acabada necessita de estudo, aperfeiçoamento pelo tempo, pela honestidade e compromisso.

POR QUE SE DIZ QUE SOMOS ANTENAS? ISSO SÓ ACONTECE COM OS UMBANDISTAS? Todos são iguais à antena e não importa se é umbandista, católico, evangélico, mulçumano, judeu, se não tem nenhuma religião ou se simplesmente não acredita em nada. Somos antena destinada a receber e transmitir sinais que se irradiam pelo éter. Tudo ao redor está tomado por "ondas mentais" formadas a partir dos próprios pensamentos e do pensar de todos os seres encarnados e desencarnados. É igual aos sinais de rádio e televisão em que alguém transmite e alguém recebe.

TODAS AS PESSOAS SÃO COMO ANTENAS? Sim, não há exceção. **Todas** as pessoas são como antenas abertas que captam sinais vindos de **todas** as direções para o centro da antena onde está o "captador" que na Umbanda é chamado Orí, e é onde são concentrados todos os sinais, mesmo os mais fracos. O Orí, também chamado de Coroa, fica no topo da cabeça que é o ponto onde se recebe todas as irradiações provenientes dos mundos visíveis e invisíveis (espiritual) para o bem e para o mal. Algumas religiões denominam o Orí de "Sahasrara", que é o 7º Chakra chamado de Chakra da Coroa ou Coronário.

É VERDADE QUE CADA PESSOA É UM APARELHO DE TELEVISÃO E POSSUI MEIOS PRÓPRIOS PARA "PEGAR" UM CANAL EM PARTICULAR, FILTRANDO OU EXCLUINDO OS DEMAIS? É verdade. Se a pessoa sintonizar seu receptor numa faixa de frequência que quem está transmitindo é cheio de ódio, inveja, rancor, *é esse programa que vai passar em sua vida*. A pessoa começa a ficar com raiva de tudo, incomodada, não encontra sossego e como consequência as coisas em sua vida começam a dar errado. Ela vai ao Terreiro para *"abrir seus caminhos que estão fechados"*, mas não adianta.

O QUE É SINTONIA ENTRE AS MENTES? Vamos dar um exemplo: imagine um sujeito que bebe álcool ao ponto de cair pelas esquinas. Convide-o para ir a uma festa onde só será servido guaraná. Mesmo que ele aceite, vai se sentir deslocado. Agora o convide para ir jogar conversa fora no botequim. Na hora ele aceita porque estará junto daqueles que tem interesses semelhantes, encarnados e desencarnados. Comumente os espíritos que eram viciados no alcoolismo enquanto estavam encarnados, não conseguindo se livrar da dependência, ao desencarnarem transmitem sugestões mentais da bebida, e aquele cuja antena captar essa faixa de frequência vai ceder aos apelos para o viciado usufruir das emanações do álcool que ele, embriagando-se, libera.

COMO FUGIR DA ARMADILHA DE ESTAR SINTONIZADO COM MENTES QUE ME ABSORVAM AS FORÇAS E ME INDUZAM RUMO AO FUNDO DO POÇO? Escolhendo qual canal sua televisão vai sintonizar. A antena está aberta, mas isso não significa que a TV tem que sintonizar todos os canais. A prática da caridade rompe os sentimentos inferiores e o misericordioso será um transmissor de fraternidade, consequentemente entrará numa faixa de frequência do bem. Sentindo que sua televisão está recebendo sinais de inveja, ódio, vingança, imediatamente mude de canal, só você pode.

O QUE QUER DIZER COM "TODO MUNDO PODE ESCOLHER A SINTONIA DE SUA ANTENA E FILTRAR O PROGRAMA QUE VAI ASSISTIR"? Cada ser humano que vive, seja no corpo físico ou fora dele, recebe sinais que combinam com seu modo de ser, ou seja, assiste aos programas que sua antena interna captou. E retransmite inclusive programas gerados pelos seus pensamentos e vontade de acordo com o próprio modo de pensar e agir. Se cultivar maus pensamentos, más palavras e atitudes ruins certamente entrará em sintonia com frequência semelhante. Muitos reclamam que a vida está uma droga, que tem *"trabalho de macumba feito para as coisas não andarem"* e é bom que se esclareça que na imensa maioria das vezes não tem nada feito, é a própria pessoa causando a sua ruína com palavras irresponsáveis, pensamentos descuidados e atos inconsequentes.

O QUE SÃO OS SUGADORES DE ENERGIA? Cada um tem seus pensamentos, crenças e outras particularidades. Porém há um ponto em comum entre todos os seres que é seu componente energético e sua influência na natureza e em outros organismos da criação. Pensamentos emitem energias, a mente sintoniza e o espírito absorve energias do ambiente. Estamos imersos em um incalculável e profundíssimo oceano de vibrações e energias e nele transitamos, influenciamos e somos influenciados por ondas energéticas e vibratórias, das quais absorvemos "forças vivas" das mais diversas, e de forma automática. Quando as criaturas se aproximam são estabelecidas as mais diversas combinações energéticas, uns influenciando os outros. Sempre que há aproximação entre as pessoas ocorre uma mistura ou associação de "forças vivas". Isso quer dizer que as pessoas estão permanentemente trocando energia entre elas. Por exemplo, quase todos já tiveram a terrível experiência de, depois de ter se encontrado com determinada pessoa, sentir-se fraco, com mal estar, inexplicavelmente desanimado, tornando-se vítima da ação de sugador de energia, indivíduo que tem a lastimável capacidade de tornar o ambiente desagradável e subtrair as forças alheias. É preciso constante vigilância sobre os próprios pensamentos para evitar a sintonia mental e espiritual com seres desequilibrados.

COMO DESCOBRIR QUAL É A MINHA MISSÃO ESPIRITUAL NESSA VIDA? Preste atenção aos convites da espiritualidade e estude-se como ser humano, pergunte a si mesmo o que faz aqui nesse plano de existência. Todos somos espíritos encarnados com um carma a resgatar, com novos aprendizados a compreender diariamente. *"A maior missão na vida de todos os que aqui encarnam é aprender a usar o seu livre arbítrio" (Zé Pelintra).*

O Médium da Umbanda

QUAL A DEFINIÇÃO DE MÉDIUM? "Médium é toda pessoa que sente num grau qualquer a influência dos Espíritos. Essa faculdade é inerente ao ser humano e, por conseguinte, não constitui um privilégio exclusivo." (Allan Kardec, O Livro dos Médiuns, capítulo XIV).

O ESPÍRITO CONTINUA A EXISTIR APÓS A MORTE DO CORPO FÍSICO? Muitas religiões e filosofias espíritas e espiritualistas, dentre as quais a religião de Umbanda, afirmam que o espírito continua a existir mesmo depois da morte física, apenas os encarnados não podem mais vê-los com os olhos da matéria. Os que negam a existência de vida após a morte dizem que o que os olhos não veem não existe.

COMO O MÉDIUM PODE IMPEDIR QUE ESPÍRITO MENOS ESCLARECIDO FALE O QUE BEM QUISER? Entidades perversas e grosseiras raramente chegam a entrar no Terreiro porque há sustentação dos Exus no entorno, e é por isso também que não se aconselha o médium incorporar em outro local, considerando que kiumbas não são atraídos onde há um padrão vibratório digno. Guias de Umbanda jamais são inconsequentes seja no agir ou no falar, os médiuns são responsáveis por todas as comunicações porque tudo o que ele atrai é resultado de seu hábito mental, assim se o médium não distingue os seus pensamentos dos pensamentos de quem se comunica, além de faltar-lhe bom senso também precisa repensar sua conduta intelecto-moral.

QUE RESPONSABILIDADE TEM O MÉDIUM SE PRATICAR UM ATO SOB A INFLUÊNCIA DE ESPÍRITO?

Responsabilidade total. Quando ouvimos dizer que alguém cometeu determinado ato porque estava sofrendo a atuação de espírito inferior, mesmo que seja verdade, não se isenta de forma alguma da responsabilidade integral por qualquer ato que venha a praticar, porque o espírito encontrou ali respaldo para suas atuações maléficas, encontrou sintonia.

E SE A PESSOA NEM MESMO PERCEBER QUE ESTÁ AGINDO SOB A INFLUÊNCIA DE ESPÍRITO INFERIOR?

Aí a situação torna-se ainda mais dolorosa porque a sintonia é tão perfeita que ambos trocam mutuamente os sentimentos e energias, e suas intenções são tão iguais que a pessoa que está agindo sob a atuação de espírito inferior nem tenta se defender, ela não quer ser afastada do obsessor, um emaranhou-se no outro como o parasita e seu hospedeiro.

EU TENHO RECEIO DE SOFRER ATAQUES DE MAUS ESPÍRITOS SE FREQUENTAR A UMBANDA.

Para que as influências, tanto negativa quanto positiva, atuem na vida é fundamental haver sintonia. Lembre-se que o corpo é seu, a mente é sua, portanto nenhuma força tomará conta de você se você não permitir ou sintonizar com ela.

QUAIS OS PERIGOS QUE SE SUJEITAM OS MÉDIUNS NO QUE DIZ RESPEITO A SUA MEDIUNIDADE? PRINCIPALMENTE OS QUE JÁ TRABALHAM NA UMBANDA HÁ MUITO TEMPO? O primeiro e mais penoso é a vaidade. Grande parte dos médiuns se acredita privilegiada porque possui mediunidade como se fosse mérito pessoal. Ser preguiçoso é outro, recusando-se aos convites de estudo e achando que o Guia sabe tudo e dele é toda a responsabilidade. Trabalhar mediunicamente em qualquer local e a qualquer hora, na sala da casa da vizinha, por exemplo, porque ela "está com um problemão e precisa falar com o Guia". Fazer trabalhos mediúnicos na própria residência ou na casa de quem se dispuser a emprestar um espaço é outro perigo, além de ser um abuso com a espiritualidade. Exceção nos casos em que o médium, não encontrando um Terreiro com o qual se identifique, sinta necessidade de pedir força aos seus Guias espirituais, o que deverá ser feito em dia e hora determinados. Cobrar dinheiro ou favores é um passo em direção a obsessores.

POR QUE OS GUIAS SE AFASTAM DOS MÉDIUNS? Por advertência quando o médium se esquece de que ele é um simples instrumento, e que sozinho, sem a cooperação de todas as Entidades, nada faria. Se o médium não corresponde moralmente ou se esquece dos ensinamentos fundamentais da religião, os Guias se afastam. Outra razão pode ser por bondade, quando o médium está debilitado por doença física, assim que recupera a saúde os Guias retornam e neste caso a interrupção não significa punição, pelo contrário, demonstra afeição e zelo do Guia para com o médium. Outra razão é a provação cujo objetivo não é punir, mas sim desenvolver a paciência, de modo a forçar o médium a meditar sobre as lições muitas vezes ensinadas através dele mesmo, quando o Guia utilizou seu corpo físico como veículo mas ele sequer ouviu. Todas as palavras, lições, instruções dos Guias tem a finalidade de instruir os filhos de fé, e se o médium é o meio pelo qual os Guias falam suas mensagens, dele é que se esperam maiores progressos.

É CORRETO O MÉDIUM TRABALHAR SOZINHO PORQUE CONSIDERA QUE NÃO PRECISA DE NINGUÉM?

Os médiuns não devem jamais se esquecer do espírito de fraternidade que norteia a Umbanda. Fraternidade é um termo oriundo do latim que significa "irmão", mas não Apenas consanguíneo como também irmão na Luz. A união de seres que possuem o mesmo objetivo e que juntos trabalham para o bem geral é um dos fundamentos da Umbanda.

OS MÉDIUNS SE RECORDAM DE TUDO O QUE OCORREU DURANTE A INCORPORAÇÃO?

Na mediunidade semiconsciente e inconsciente, ao findar a incorporação, geralmente o médium nada ou bem pouco se lembra do ocorrido ou da mensagem transmitida, porém não é regra e pode ser que se lembre de tudo. Geralmente fica uma sensação vaga, semelhante ao despertar de um sonho em que permanece uma impressão, mas que não se sabe afirmar com certeza do que se tratou. Na mediunidade consciente lembra-se de tudo.

O GUIA TOMA O CORPO DO MÉDIUM? Não. É como se o médium fosse o "café", o Guia fosse o "leite" e ambos misturados formam o "café com leite", uma terceira consciência.

É CERTO AFIRMAR QUE NENHUM GUIA OU ESPÍRITO SE APOSSA OU "ENTRA" NO CORPO DE UM ENCARNADO, MÉDIUM OU NÃO? Sim, é certo. A incorporação acontece mais em nível mental. Nos processos obsessivos causados por espíritos inferiores podem ocorrer transtornos psíquicos, e os que têm pouco conhecimento acham que um Espírito mau se apoderou do corpo do enfermo. Foi esse fenômeno que deu origem às práticas de exorcismo.

POR QUE É IMPORTANTE QUE O MÉDIUM ESTUDE PARA SER MAIS ÚTIL AO GUIA? SE O GUIA SABE TUDO POR QUE O MÉDIUM TAMBÉM PRECISA SABER? O médium consciente e semiconsciente é um intérprete do pensamento do Guia, e o que ele fala é uma ideia que lhe foi sugerida. Cabe ao médium exprimi-la conforme sua capacidade própria de entendimento. A mediunidade será tanto mais proveitosa quanto maior forem os conhecimentos e cultura do médium, vocabulário, gestos, etc. Importantíssimo também são as qualidades morais do médium na medida em que seus atos, pensamentos e palavras aproximam Guias bons e sábios, considerando que o oposto também é realidade, aproximando espíritos trevosos. Estudo constante e bom senso fazem a diferença para os que têm como finalidade servir a religião de Umbanda com equilíbrio e sem fantasia.

COMO É PARA O GUIA QUE SE SERVE DE MÉDIUM SEM CONHECIMENTO? Quando o Guia se serve de médiuns pouco esclarecidos é mais longo e penoso o seu trabalho, porque suas mensagens são incompletas e suas manifestações ineficientes. Imagine um médico obstetra (Guia) que vai fazer uma cirurgia e tem como auxiliar um enfermeiro (médium) que não conhece os instrumentos cirúrgicos. O médico pede um bisturi e ele não sabe qual é, pede uma pinça e ele não faz ideia de qual seja, o enfermeiro simplesmente não procurou aprender porque o médico sabe tudo. De que serve esse auxiliar?

O QUE É PRECISO PARA QUE O MÉDIUM TENHA UMA PERFEITA INCORPORAÇÃO? O principal é que tenha confiança em sua própria mediunidade, nos Guias que o assistem e no Terreiro que frequenta.

O MÉDIUM SABE DE ANTEMÃO A OPINIÃO DO GUIA SOBRE OS ASSUNTOS? Não. Só vai tendo consciência do que ele transmite à medida que os pensamentos do Guia vão passando pelo seu cérebro.

QUANDO O GUIA AUXILIA O MÉDIUM NO PROCESSO DE INCORPORAÇÃO? Quando a união entre médium e Guia está bastante fortalecida inclusive pela confiança. Frequentemente o Guia auxilia o médium imprimindo mais vigor à ação telepática através da imposição das mãos no cérebro material do médium, dando-lhe um sentimento maior de segurança.

Desenvolvimento

O QUE DEVE SABER UM MÉDIUM ANTES DE SE INICIAR NA UMBANDA? Antes de iniciar o desenvolvimento mediúnico na Umbanda é preciso que o filho de fé entenda que ele será mais um "prestador de serviço", planejado e orientado pelos Guias Espirituais, e acima de tudo deve estar disponível como **mais um** instrumento da Espiritualidade Maior, dedicando-se com humildade ao quinhão que lhe compete. Não há regra para o desenvolvimento mediúnico na Umbanda, cada Dirigente possui sua própria maneira de proceder, porém há três quesitos básicos que todos devem ter em mente.

QUAL É O PRIMEIRO QUESITO QUE TODA PESSOA QUE VAI SE INICIAR NA UMBANDA DEVE SABER? O primeiro e que vale para todos, é o iniciante conhecer o Terreiro e constatar a seriedade do seu Dirigente e o comprometimento do corpo mediúnico.

QUAL É O SEGUNDO QUESITO QUE TODA PESSOA QUE VAI SE INICIAR NA UMBANDA DEVE SABER? O segundo é ter afinidade com a Linha do Terreiro. Alguns mesclam princípios do catolicismo, outros do espiritismo, Candomblé, outros ainda preservam o culto iniciado pelos indígenas. Mas é importante entender que a Umbanda **apenas mistura certos conceitos das diversas religiões, porém não é nenhuma delas.**

QUAL É O TERCEIRO QUESITO QUE TODA PESSOA QUE VAI SE INICIAR NA UMBANDA DEVE SABER? para o desenvolvimento mediúnico são as Giras chamadas de Desenvolvimento, feitas em dias separados das Giras de Atendimento, aonde os médiuns vão, gradativamente, percebendo a proximidade de seus Guias, conhecendo as sensações no corpo e na mente. Após um tempo a ligação mediúnica vai se fortalecendo até tornar-se natural e fácil, quando então o médium estará pronto para o trabalho na Umbanda.

PODE-SE SER UMBANDISTA E SER CATÓLICO AO MESMO TEMPO? Provavelmente causaria certa confusão porque são religiões totalmente diferentes, a crença dos católicos não é a mesma dos umbandistas, a religião de Umbanda é bela, livre, adora a natureza, não angustia ninguém com ameaça de danação eterna, fala de amor sem culpa, portanto são religiões tão diferentes quanto o dia e a noite. Pensando nas religiões Católica e Protestante, ambas cristãs, mas que não tem nem a mesma Bíblia em comum imagina a confusão de se professar duas religiões.

HÁ UMBANDISTAS QUE SÃO INCLINADOS AOS RITUAIS DO CANDOMBLÉ PRINCIPALMENTE DEVIDO A SUA BELEZA. PODE-SE SER UMBANDISTA E CANDOMBLECISTA AO MESMO TEMPO? O Candomblé é, inegavelmente, a religião que mais valoriza a beleza dos elementos visuais e da estética no encanto das danças, na lindeza dos trajes, na imponência do "sagrado". Mas Candomblé e Umbanda são duas religiões profundamente diferentes em seus fundamentos. Na Umbanda quem dá consultas, passes e aconselhamentos são Entidades espirituais através de incorporação nos médiuns, e no Candomblé a consulta acontece apenas por meio do jogo de búzios através dos Babalorixás e Yalorixás (Pais e Mães do Santo, respectivamente). No Candomblé incorporam-se somente os Orixás e na Umbanda jamais se incorporam Orixás. No Candomblé os espíritos dos mortos, chamados Eguns, são prontamente repelidos e afastados, e na Umbanda são chamados Guias e são os Mentores Espirituais que representam a base da fé umbandista. No Candomblé há "obrigações" que são cerimônias internas e fundamentos completamente desconhecidos pelos umbandistas. São duas religiões distintas, e é inimaginável que em uma Casa de Candomblé se adote práticas da Umbanda. Infelizmente, o oposto não é verdadeiro.

PODE-SE SER UMBANDISTA E ESPÍRITA AO MESMO TEMPO? O mesmo raciocínio de que causaria profunda confusão vale para o espiritismo, que é uma ciência de observação e uma doutrina filosófica nascida na França, em Paris, quando em 18 de Abril de 1857 Allan Kardec publicou o "Livro dos Espíritos". A Umbanda nasceu em 16 de Novembro de 1908, quando o primeiro culto foi realizado na casa do médium Zélio de Moraes, em São Gonçalo, no Rio. Mais de 50 anos marcam o advento do Espiritismo do surgimento da Umbanda. Embora sejam duas religiões diferentes é aconselhável que os umbandistas estudem a doutrina espírita e as obras de Allan Kardec para entender as questões relacionadas às atividades de comunicação com o Mundo Espiritual, o desenvolvimento da mediunidade etc. Porém ambas são fundamentadas em crenças distintas.

O QUE O MÉDIUM PODE ESPERAR DURANTE AS GIRAS DE DESENVOLVIMENTO? No início, durante as Giras de Desenvolvimento, é comum o médium sentir a energia do Guia em seu corpo astral e ter uma espécie de "choque" que lhe sacode o corpo. **Saiba que é normal**, não significa que o *"Caboclo é forte demais"* (esse é argumento dos que se deixam levar pela vaidade).

Há quem, durante o desenvolvimento, sente arrepios devido à troca de energia entre ele (médium) e o Guia.

Há quem tem movimentos involuntários ou tremores que acontecem quando o Guia age nos centros de energia do médium, denominados chakras, com a finalidade de incorporar ou simplesmente habituá-lo às sensações para incorporações futuras.

Há médium que sente vontade de cantar, rir e chorar devido às descargas energéticas que são emanadas para reequilíbrio de seu emocional.

Há quem sente as pontas dos dedos formigarem, e essa ocorrência é simplesmente porque os médiuns concentram energia nas mãos, com o amadurecimento ele aprenderá, através da imposição das mãos, utilizar essa energia para realizar limpezas espirituais e doar para cura.

Os bocejos também são normais, significam que o médium está sendo preparado para entrar em condição de relaxamento, estado que antecede a incorporação.

Quando o médium está em processo de desenvolvimento é comum e normal sentir falta de ar, às vezes parece que está caindo num "poço". Tudo isso é frequente e tem explicação.

QUAL O PRAZO PARA UM MÉDIUM INICIANTE SE TORNAR UM MÉDIUM EM CONDIÇÕES DE PARTICIPAR ATIVAMENTE DAS GIRAS? Não há um prazo para terminar o desenvolvimento, é variável e na verdade nem importa porque o que vale não é a duração, mas a qualidade.

O MÉDIUM QUE AINDA ESTÁ EM DESENVOLVIMENTO PODE ATENDER AOS ASSISTIDOS? Não pode, mas infelizmente atendem. É muito arriscado para ambos que assim ocorra porque pode o assistido sair da Gira muito mais perturbado do que chegou. Deve-se ter em mente de que se trata de médium "em desenvolvimento", por isso com grande chance de interferências na comunicação do Guia, o que é perfeitamente normal nesta fase. Sabemos que as mensagens dos Guias quase sempre são tomadas como verdade principalmente pelos assistidos, e há risco especial quando os envolvidos são parentes ou conhecidos próximos, pois a interferência do médium é ainda maior devido às questões armazenadas em sua mente. O mais prudente, e que deveria ser norma em todos os Terreiros, é que o médium só trabalhasse incorporado nos dias de Gira aberta após o término de seu desenvolvimento.

É VERDADE QUE MÉDIUNS EM DESENVOLVIMENTO PODEM INCORPORAR O ESPÍRITO ERRADO?

Na verdade o médium não incorpora o espírito errado, o que ocorre é que devido à pressa e um sentimento de urgência que "tem que incorporar", o médium produz uma incorporação sem que ele esteja de fato sendo um instrumento mediúnico da ação espiritual. Nesse caso acontece o que se chama "animismo". Animismo não é mistificação, essa última é quando um médium aparenta estar incorporado induzindo os outros a crer em uma mentira, criando uma fraude consciente. Denomina-se animismo o fenômeno em que o médium revive suas próprias recordações de vidas passadas, e as expressa durante as consultas nas Giras. Por não haver ali um Guia que se comunique é um fenômeno injustamente mal visto.

PODE UM MÉDIUM INCORPORAR UM OBSESSOR SE FAZENDO PASSAR POR UM GUIA DE LUZ?

Se estiver despreparado, sim. O médium de Umbanda é fortemente pressionado em muitos Terreiros onde precisa incorporar um Guia que é obrigado a dar o nome, depois precisa riscar o Ponto, e muitas vezes sem ter tido nenhum tipo de orientação ou estudo. Com isso o médium abandona sua condição de passividade e passa a conduzir a incorporação ao invés de permitir que o Guia faça isso. Ele acredita estar incorporado com uma Entidade quando, na verdade, quem está presente é outra. O melhor que o médium iniciante tem a fazer é, durante o desenvolvimento, empenhar-se em apenas afinar sua percepção sobre seus Guias, procurar conhecê-los e nunca se colocar à frente deles. O médium de Umbanda deve se oferecer como instrumento da espiritualidade e não pretender que a espiritualidade se prontifique ao seu serviço.

COMO EXPLICA GUIAS QUE TRABALHAM COM UM MÉDIUM INCORPORAREM EM OUTROS? OS GUIAS PODEM ESTAR EM VÁRIOS LUGARES E VÁRIOS MÉDIUNS DIFERENTES AO MESMO TEMPO? É POSSÍVEL INCORPORAR EM VÁRIOS MÉDIUNS SIMULTANEAMENTE? É possível a Entidades que alcançaram alto grau de elevação se manifestar em pensamento em vários médiuns ao mesmo tempo, mas não é este o caso nos Terreiros de Umbanda. O nome que o Guia revela, sendo igual a outros que trabalham com outros médiuns, é na verdade o nome da falange de trabalho. Todos os trabalhadores pertencentes àquele grupo se manifestam com o mesmo nome quando estão em trabalhos nos Terreiros. Mas são Guias de individualidades distintas. Assim, Vó Maria Conga são vários espíritos da mesma falange, em vários lugares, utilizando o mesmo nome.

POR QUE UM GUIA IMITA OUTRO QUANDO INCORPORADO? Não são os Guias que imitam, mesmo porque cada espírito tem sua própria particularidade e personalidade. Igual ao ser humano encarnado eles também têm características que os tornam seres únicos. É o médium que devido a sua ansiedade e má preparação busca referência em outros médiuns mais antigos, e passam a imitá-los. O médium tem o dever de se preparar de modo a oferecer condições ideais para que seus Guias se manifestem segundo suas próprias naturezas.

COMO O MÉDIUM INICIANTE FAZ PARA SABER O NOME DAS ENTIDADES QUE VÃO TRABALHAR COM ELE? Na hora certa as Entidades se apresentam. Ou podem dar intuição ao médium sobre seu nome. O certo é que o médium saberá no momento em que os Guias acharem apropriado. Os iniciantes não devem se preocupar com essa questão.

A MAIOR ANGÚSTIA DO MÉDIUM INICIANTE É SABER SE É ELE OU O GUIA QUEM ESTÁ FALANDO. O QUE FAZER? Essa preocupação mostra que o médium é honesto consigo e com os outros, caso contrário não se perturbaria com essa dúvida. Na verdade é a principal questão que castiga nove em cada dez médiuns iniciantes e é causa de abandono da Umbanda. A interferência do médium quando ainda está conhecendo e se familiarizando com o processo de incorporação é grande. E é absolutamente normal que o médium interfira. Temos um indicativo da interferência quando o médium fica imóvel, não permitindo que o Guia se movimente nem saia do lugar. Também é influência do médium quando a Entidade incorporada não pronuncia nem mesmo uma palavra, porque o médium se cala. Por insegurança o médium interrompe a incorporação ou cai com frequência. Do mesmo modo se pode entender que é parte da imaginação do médium quando o "Guia" fala alto quase gritando, se move com exagero, usa linguagem ou sotaque que ninguém. Os tiques também são próprios do médium e não do Guia, assim como opiniões despropositadas e brincadeiras ácidas ou preconceituosas. Considere sempre que o discurso de um Guia de Luz tem sabedoria que normalmente difere da opinião dos encarnados, porque nunca tomam partido em nenhuma questão ou conflito de modo a não exacerbar os ânimos. Mesmo que seus médiuns estejam envolvidos em divergências eles nunca escolhem um lado, porque reconhecem que todos estão no caminho em busca do entendimento e necessitam de esclarecimento e ajuda.

ALCANÇAR UM DOMÍNIO ESPIRITUAL SIGNIFICA QUE O MÉDIUM ESTARÁ INCONSCIENTE DURANTE AS INCORPORAÇÕES? Não. Ser consciente ou inconsciente não é determinante para um médium desenvolver um bom trabalho espiritual. Não se pode jamais esquecer que em toda incorporação mediúnica há participação também do espírito encarnado. Domínio espiritual se alcança com esforço.

INCORPORAÇÃO NA UMBANDA

O ESPÍRITO ENTRA NUM CORPO COMO ENTRAMOS EM UMA CASA? Muito pelo contrário. Identifica-se com um Espírito encarnado, cujos defeitos e qualidades sejam os mesmos que os seus, a fim de obrar conjuntamente com ele. Mas, o encarnado é sempre quem atua, conforme quer, sobre a matéria de que se acha revestido. "Um Espírito não pode substituir-se ao que está encarnado, por isso que este terá que permanecer ligado ao seu corpo até ao termo fixado para sua existência material." (Kardec)

QUAIS OS TIPOS DE MEDIUNIDADE? Conforme o tipo de faculdade que possui o médium permanece com as percepções normais, e neste caso é denominado de **"médium consciente"**. Se seu estado de percepção for muito mais sensível, é chamado **"médium semiconsciente"**. Se adquirir uma forma semelhante ao sonambulismo, este será o **"médium inconsciente"**. Seja qual for a mediunidade é importante todo médium de Umbanda perceber a colossal responsabilidade que tem por tudo o que se fala e faz através dele. É de necessidade fundamental entender que o corpo mediúnico de **um Terreiro de Umbanda pode ser comparado a uma orquestra, onde todos os sons sempre são dos instrumentos: os médiuns são os instrumentos, os Guias são os sons.**

Incorporação Consciente

O QUE ACONTECE NA INCORPORAÇÃO CONSCIENTE? Na mediunidade consciente o médium recebe o pensamento do Guia e em seguida transmite a mensagem de seu modo particular, com suas palavras e capacidade de expressão. Por isso há tanta diferença de postura entre as Entidades, sendo algumas mais eruditas, outras menos instruídas, e a tendência é atribuir a simplicidade da manifestação ao Guia quando na verdade, quase sempre se trata da limitação cultural do médium. Porém, que fique claro, que isto em nada diminui o valor dos ensinamentos nem do trabalho espiritual do médium e do Guia. Com o tempo e principalmente com estudo, vai ficando cada vez mais fácil para o médium captar e entender as ideias recebidas através de sugestões mentais que recebe das Entidades, mas sempre será o médium que as interpreta e comunica com suas próprias palavras, adquirindo com o passar da fase de desenvolvimento inclusive a capacidade de expressar também os sentimentos da Entidade, com o mínimo de interferência pessoal. Através do estudo e da confiança para com o Guia chega-se a tal entendimento que poderá nem haver mais interferência.

UMA DÚVIDA QUE ANGUSTIA OS MÉDIUNS, PRINCIPALMENTE OS INICIANTES, É QUE PARECE QUE É ELE QUEM AGE E FALA E NÃO UMA ENTIDADE ALHEIA. Esse sentimento é normal porque o médium está começando a conhecer a transmissão do pensamento de modo ostensivo, tudo é novidade para ele. Como prova de que tal comunicação não é "pura imaginação", vemos médiuns dando mensagens que ultrapassam o seu entendimento ou concepção comum que tem da vida, ou falando sobre coisas pessoais com quem jamais viu e sobre fatos que não eram do seu conhecimento.

NA INCORPORAÇÃO CONSCIENTE O MÉDIUM SE AFASTA DO CORPO? Na incorporação consciente não se afasta, apenas sintoniza-se mentalmente com o Guia para receber telepaticamente a influência e transmiti-la, porém às sugestões mentais não são acrescidos sentimentos e sensações. Tem plena consciência do que está acontecendo, e se sabe que o médium está recebendo uma influência fora do comum quando o assunto tratado está fora das cogitações do médium ou mesmo contrária a seus pontos de vista. Ao finalizar a incorporação o médium lembra-se de tudo o que ocorreu, pois permaneceu com suas percepções normais.

INCORPORAÇÃO SEMICONSCIENTE

O QUE ACONTECE NA INCORPORAÇÃO SEMICONSCIENTE? Com o passar do tempo, e já familiarizado com a sintonia mental e a vibração energética dos seus Guias, o médium continua a receber telepaticamente as ideias e a transmiti-las, porém suas mentes estarão tão perfeitamente sintonizadas e ocasionando plena harmonia vibratória, que ambos estarão magnetizados como um imã. A força mental e vibratória do Guia atuando sobre o sistema nervoso do médium faz com que tenha pensamentos e sentimentos que ele entende inequivocamente não serem seus, tem ideias que vem de fora, sugestões mentais carregadas de sensações. O médium recebe as mensagens, interpreta-as e expressa com suas palavras. Terminada a Gira, muitas vezes o médium só lembra vagamente do que foi tratado.

NA INCORPORAÇÃO SEMICONSCIENTE O MÉDIUM SE AFASTA DO CORPO? Na incorporação semiconsciente o médium não se afasta do corpo, mas sintoniza mente-a-mente e se harmoniza com a vibração energética do Guia para receber telepaticamente a influência estranha, e posteriormente transmiti-la.

INCORPORAÇÃO INCONSCIENTE

O QUE ACONTECE NA INCORPORAÇÃO INCONSCIENTE? Na incorporação inconsciente efetua-se o "ajuste perispiritual" entre o médium e o Guia que transmite diretamente a mensagem, e o médium fala como em estado de sonambulismo. É importante entender que nenhum Guia "toma" o corpo do médium assumindo o lugar da sua alma, o que ocorre é que ambos se comunicam de perispírito a perispírito, ou seja, mente-a-mente, e esse estado na Umbanda chama "incorporação". Não raro os Guias incorporados expõem assuntos que transcendem os limites do conhecimento do médium.

NA INCORPORAÇÃO INCONSCIENTE O MÉDIUM SE AFASTA DO CORPO? Sim, o médium afasta-se do corpo ao qual, segundo os clarividentes, fica unido por um cordão fluídico e ele entra em estado de sonolência ou transe. Quando a mensagem é transmitida por essa forma de mediunidade de incorporação o médium estará totalmente ausente, porém esse tipo de mediunidade exige afinidade total do médium com o Guia, ambos devem vibrar na mesma sintonia. Embora inconsciente da mensagem, o médium muitas vezes permanece junto do Guia, auxiliando-o. Ou quando tem plena confiança no Espírito que se comunica, poderá afastar-se em outras atividades. Importante esclarecer que a incorporação é de responsabilidade do médium, e por isso se algo lhe acontecer ele poderá despertar automaticamente. O mesmo não acontecerá se, ao invés do Guia, estiver sob a influência de obsessor. Os trabalhadores espirituais de diversos Terreiros distintos têm explicado que, nas últimas décadas, não encarna médium totalmente inconsciente porque não é mais finalidade na Umbanda que assim seja.

NA MEDIUNIDADE INCONSCIENTE O MÉDIUM ESTÁ A MERCÊ DA VONTADE DO GUIA? PODE O GUIA FA-

ZER O QUE QUISER? Não, mesmo na incorporação inconsciente o médium é o responsável pela boa disciplina do desempenho mediúnico, porque somente com o seu consentimento o Guia poderá realizar algo. Mesmo estando em condições de passividade total, se o Guia comunicante quiser realizar algo que venha contra seus princípios, ele imediatamente tomará o controle do seu organismo, despertando.

INCORPORAÇÃO INCONSCIENTE É MELHOR QUE CONSCIENTE? OU AINDA, O MÉDIUM INCONSCIENTE É MAIS EVOLUÍDO QUE O CONSCIENTE? De forma nenhuma. Não existe incorporação melhor que outra. E o tipo de mediunidade não está relacionado com grau de evolução do médium nem é comprovação de força espiritual do Guia. Também pode ocorrer que, de acordo com o interesse dos Guias, apenas certas manifestações sejam conscientes no médium e outras não.

A MEDIUNIDADE INCONSCIENTE TRAZ SUPERIORIDADE MEDIÚNICA AO MÉDIUM? É GARANTIA DE QUALIDADE? Não. O que dá superioridade e garantia em qualquer tipo de mediunidade é a qualidade moral do médium, a responsabilidade e seriedade com que encara sua missão.

O QUE É PERISPÍRITO? Quando o Espírito está encarnado, o perispírito é o que serve como elo entre o Espírito e o corpo. Desencarnado, o perispírito faz o papel de corpo com o qual o Espírito se manifesta, é através do perispírito que o Espírito recebe as sensações do ambiente ou nele atua. Tem a mesma forma do corpo físico e é conhecido como "**arquivo da alma**", porque tudo que fazemos ao nosso corpo material também se manifesta no perispírito. Por exemplo, um fumante de longa data nesta encarnação sofrerá as consequências do fumo após a morte do corpo físico uma vez que não só os pulmões são lesados, mas também o perispírito. E essa lesão repercutirá em nova existência, por meio da reencarnação, uma vez que o perispírito serve de molde para a formação do corpo em vida futura, onde será possível que, reencarnado, o novo corpo desenvolva alguma doença pulmonar. Outro exemplo, um fumante inveterado sentirá falta da nicotina após o desligamento do corpo físico. Da mesma forma o alcoólatra.

POR QUE A MEDIUNIDADE INCONSCIENTE ERA MUITO MAIS COMUM NO INÍCIO DA UMBANDA HÁ CEM ANOS? Porque os primeiros trabalhadores espirituais da religião que nascia precisavam fazer coisas incomuns para serem acreditados. Eram constantemente incitados a andar sobre as brasas para provar que não se tratava de uma fraude, ou beber litros de cachaça sem deixar o médium bêbado. Mas esse tempo passou e hoje não é preciso provar nada porque há os que acreditam e para esses não há porque provar coisa alguma. E há os que não acreditam e para esses do mesmo modo não há porque provar coisa alguma, porque simplesmente não acreditam. Assim hoje em dia são raros os médiuns completamente inconscientes, porque seriam largamente prejudicados na medida em que não aproveitariam dos conselhos, lições e boas palavras dos Guias que com ele trabalham no campo fértil da caridade, que é o pilar da religião de Umbanda.

O MÉDIUM RECEBE AS PALAVRAS DOS GUIAS? Não, todo médium, inclusive o umbandista, não recebe palavras dos Guias, recebe pensamentos. Portanto não transmite palavras, transmite pensamentos.

POR QUE POR QUE É TÃO DISSEMINADO EM TERREIROS DE UMBANDA MÉDIUNS QUE RECEBEM GUIAS ESPIRITUAIS QUE FALAM EM LÍNGUAS INDECIFRÁVEIS OU EM DIALETOS OBSCUROS? Difícil explicar como o Guia transmite para os médiuns, em sua imensa maioria consciente, palavras que o próprio médium desconhece. Mais difícil ainda explicar como, desconhecendo, pode transmitir-lhes os pensamentos. Exemplar a prática já adotada em 1930 na União Espírita Trabalhadores de Jesus, quando médium começava a engrolar imediatamente se dizia ao espírito julgado presente *"Meu irmão, vós estais faltando com a caridade para conosco; ide ao espaço e aprendei a língua que falamos e depois podeis voltar"*.

ANIMISMO E MISTIFICAÇÃO

O QUE É ANIMISMO? A palavra "Animismo" vem do latim "Anima", que significa Alma. Animismo é a intervenção da própria personalidade do médium nas comunicações espíritas, é a própria alma do médium comportando-se como se fosse outra Entidade espiritual. O médium não está querendo enganar ninguém, acontece inconscientemente. Em vez de transmitir mensagens e ideias dos Guias transmite algo que estava adormecido em seu inconsciente. Considerando que todos reencarnaram inúmeras vezes e tiveram várias existências, e em cada uma dessas existências desenvolveram personalidades distintas e acumularam conhecimentos diferentes, cada ser humano é a soma de todas as suas vidas. Todas as pessoas neste plano evolutivo possuem informações que vão muito além de seu saber na vida atual, porque é soma da vivência e do aprendizado de cada uma das vidas passadas. Na manifestação anímica o médium pode expressar sabedoria que ele, na vida atual, não possui a nível consciente. Daí decorre, muitas vezes, que não há como saber se a comunicação é erudição do Guia, ou é a manifestação dos próprios conhecimentos do médium que se encontravam latentes no inconsciente.

ANIMISMO OCORRE COM MÉDIUNS EXPERIENTES?
Com médiuns experientes, na grande maioria das vezes, o que ocorre é um estado intermediário com maior ou menor participação da alma do médium em relação ao Guia que por ele se expressa. Assim sendo sempre haverá participação do médium. O animismo não é, portanto, defeito mediúnico e nem deve ser tratado como distúrbio ou desequilíbrio da mediunidade ou do médium. Na verdade, retirando o preconceito e o medo que esse tema causa nos umbandistas, o animismo deve ser considerado também parte do fenômeno mediúnico, já que *"O médium não é um telefone. Ele capta o fluxo mental da entidade e o*

transmite, utilizando-se de seus próprios recursos" (Richard Simonetti, "Mediunidade - Tudo o que você precisa saber").

A ATUAÇÃO ANÍMICA DO MÉDIUM ACONTECE DE FORMA CONSCIENTE OU INCONSCIENTE? Quase sempre inconsciente, de modo que o próprio médium dificilmente consegue perceber a sua própria interferência ou participação no fenômeno que manifesta, não consegue separar o que é seu do que é criação mental do comunicante, mesmo quando o fenômeno, em si, é consciente.

ANIMISMO É MISTIFICAÇÃO? Não. O termo "animismo" passou a ser usado de forma negativa e pejorativa, significando tudo aquilo que é produzido por um médium sem a contribuição ou participação de nenhuma Entidade ou Guia. É o pesadelo de grande parte médiuns, especialmente os iniciantes, porque costuma ser confundido com mistificação e fraude. Animismo não é mistificação e essa desorientação apenas causa angústia em quem está começando na religião de Umbanda.

O ANIMISMO É UM PROBLEMA PARA OS MÉDIUNS INICIANTES? O animismo faz parte de todo o processo de incorporação, e não há nenhum problema se na fase de desenvolvimento a comunicação for obra da alma do próprio médium, pois um dos objetivos do desenvolvimento é quebrar a timidez e o constrangimento. Aquele que está iniciando não deve se inquietar por medo de "falhar" nas incorporações ou de mistificar, o animismo costuma apresentar-se intenso em quase todos os principiantes e é absolutamente normal. Depois, com o passar do tempo, sua influência nas comunicações cai para níveis aceitáveis. **Por essa razão é que não julgamos apropriado médium em processo de desenvolvimento trabalhar nas Giras de Caridade (atendimento).**

EXISTEM CASOS EM QUE A INFLUÊNCIA DA ALMA DO MÉDIUM É TÃO ELEVADA QUE O TORNA IMPRODUTIVO? Sim, existe. E os Guias da Casa, juntamente com o Dirigente, fazem extensivo trabalho para equilibrá-lo. Com o tempo o médium aprende a transmitir com toda a fidelidade possível o pensamento do Guia, interferindo o mínimo no que ele tem a dizer. Por não haver incorporação sem participação anímica não é justo nem responsável, ao perceber o fenômeno do animismo, estigmatizar o médium como se ele fosse uma fraude. É necessário ajudá-lo a traduzir com palavras adequadas o pensamento que lhe está sendo transmitido pelas Entidades trabalhadoras na Umbanda.

COMO SE PODE DEFINIR UM BOM MÉDIUM? Essa resposta encontra-se muito objetivamente nos ensinamentos de Kardec: "Assim como o espírito manifestante precisa utilizar-se de certa parcela de energia que vai colher no médium para movimentar um objeto, também para uma comunicação inteligente ele precisa de um intermediário inteligente, ou seja, do espírito do próprio médium. (...) O bom médium, portanto, é aquele que transmite, tão fielmente quanto possível, o pensamento do comunicante, interferindo o mínimo que possa no que este tem a dizer. Reiteramos, portanto, que não há fenômeno mediúnico sem participação anímica. O cuidado que se torna necessário ter na dinâmica do fenômeno não é colocar o médium sob a suspeita de animismo, como se fosse um estigma, e sim, ajudá-lo a ser um instrumento fiel, traduzindo, em palavras adequadas, o pensamento que lhe está sendo transmitido sem palavras pelos espíritos comunicantes."

O QUE SIGNIFICA ENTRAR EM SINTONIA COM OS ESPÍRITOS? Sintonia significa entendimento, acordo mútuo, harmonia. Portanto duas almas sintonizadas estarão com as mentes perfeitamente entrosadas, havendo entre elas uma ponte magnética unindo-as profundamente. Estão "respirando" na mesma faixa, pensando e desejando na mesma frequência. Espiritualmente os iguais se atraem. Se o ser humano vai alimentando sentimentos inferiores, se concede licença para fazer certas maldades porque ninguém está vendo, como por exemplo, maltratar um animal, está alimentado sintonia com energia que lhe é compatível. Se não conseguir interromper essa sintonia atrairá para si categoria de espíritos que se sintonizam com tais sentimentos, e é quase certo que por eles será dominado. O oposto também é verdadeiro, ou seja, há sintonia com Espíritos de Luz, entidades benfazejas que enchem de bênçãos a vida da pessoa.

SE NA MEDIUNIDADE HÁ SEMPRE MAIOR OU MENOR PARTICIPAÇÃO DA ALMA DO MÉDIUM EM RELAÇÃO AO GUIA, COMO EXPLICAR A ENTIDADE

QUE NÃO FALA O IDIOMA PÁTRIO DO MÉDIUM? ACASO ESSE NÃO TEM ACESSO ÀS INFORMAÇÕES DE QUE DISPÕE O MÉDIUM? Essa é uma questão delicada, e pela lógica é improvável a veracidade de alguns que se expressam em línguas estranhas devido ao desconhecimento do idioma pátrio do médium, como é o caso de alguns Ciganos que só conhecem seu dialeto nativo, ou de Caboclos que apenas entendem língua indígena. Interessante é que, em todos os casos presenciados por esta autora os Guias entendiam, mas não falavam o português, explicando seus pensamentos por meio de gestos, expressões corporais e fisionômicas. Tal comportamento talvez ultrapasse a sensível fronteira do animismo, ou há motivo desconhecido da Entidade para agir assim.

O QUE É MISTIFICAÇÃO? Mistificar é fazer alguém crer em uma mentira ou em algo falso, abusando de sua boa fé. Mistificação na incorporação é a fraude consciente do médium que simula premeditadamente a falsa incorporação com intenção de enganar os outros. Médium mistificador, portanto, é aquele que **FINGE** estar em transe mediúnico ou recebendo comunicação de um Guia, quando na verdade está apenas inventando a mensagem para impressionar e tirar proveito das pessoas que estão à sua volta. Há também os espíritos mistificadores que são mentirosos, hipócritas e obsessores. Em Terreiro onde impera a verdadeira caridade e onde não há espaço para a vaidade eles não se manifestam, pois **não há mistificadores sem mistificados**.

COMO SABER QUANDO SE TRATA DE UMA MISTIFICAÇÃO? São várias situações em que o mistificador se incrimina, basta ficar atento. Inicia com a certeza de que os Guias de Umbanda jamais se ofendem ao ponto de humilhar ou ameaçar, e seria um contra senso se o fizessem porque eles mesmos aconselham os filhos de fé a serem mansos de espírito, porém nunca usam linguagem doce e suave para seduzir com o intuito de ludibriar. Infelizmente na maioria dos casos é o médium falando escondido atrás do nome do Guia, como a criança que fala escondida detrás da parede acreditando não ser reconhecida.

QUAIS AS PRECAUÇÕES QUE SE DEVE TER AO VISITAR UMA CASA DE UMBANDA PELA PRIMEIRA VEZ?
A maioria das pessoas que procura os Terreiros está predisposta a aceitar tudo o que vem do mundo invisível sem questionamento. Quem já conhece o Terreiro e já comprovou a seriedade e o compromisso com a caridade dos que ali trabalham, não precisa ficar preocupado. *Mas ao visitar uma Casa de Umbanda pela primeira vez, assim como os demais templos e igrejas de qualquer vertente religiosa, convém receber todas as informações com prudência e discernimento, passar tudo o que foi visto e ouvido pelo crivo da razão e da lógica, perceber se as palavras são de bom senso.* E não se esquecer de que onde a Luz se propaga há que ter moral elevada. Essa é a receita para se evitar os médiuns e os espíritos trapaceiros e mistificadores.

O QUE É MÉDIUM MISTIFICADOR? É o médium que finge estar incorporado, e conscientemente simula sempre com intenção de enganar os outros. Não havendo incorporação de Guias, o médium apenas inventa a mensagem para impressionar ou agradar as pessoas que estão à sua volta. Ou às vezes para dizer coisas que não teria coragem de falar em seu nome, e usa desse subterfúgio para dar seus recados. Infelizmente a mistificação não é feita somente por médiuns, mas também por Dirigentes e nesse caso torna-se mentira ainda mais cafajeste.

O QUE ACONTECE NOS TERREIROS ONDE OS MÉDIUNS E ATÉ DIRIGENTES COMETEM ATOS DOS MAIS BAIXOS FAZENDO - OU PENSANDO QUE FAZEM - O MAL A OUTROS, PROCURANDO ATENDER SEUS DESEJOS DESQUALIFICADOS MORALMENTE? Nestes lugares, por afinidade vibratória, se ligam às criaturas do astral inferior que são quem praticamente dão as ordens a todos e a tudo o que lá se faz. Não raro é lugar onde reina o mexerico e a discórdia entre seus membros, onde a violência e vingança são o sinal dominante.

POR QUE AS ENTIDADES DE LUZ DEIXAM ESSAS COISAS ACONTECEREM EM TAIS TERREIROS? Os Guias de Luz empreendem grandes esforços a fim de mostrar o valor da verdadeira caridade, mas o livre arbítrio, que é o poder que cada ser humano tem de escolher suas ações e o caminho que quer seguir, sempre é respeitado. Persistindo no erro são deixados à própria sorte. Com o tempo, atolados no lodo astral ao qual se meteram por livre vontade, procuram os Terreiros que são conduzidos pelo amor a Deus e começarão dura caminhada rumo à cura de seus males espirituais e físicos. Não raro também procuram outras religiões e apontam a Umbanda como causa de seus desvios morais e deficiência de caráter.

CULPAR A RELIGIÃO E SEUS ABNEGADOS TRABALHADORES PELOS PRÓPRIOS ATOS DESPREZÍVEIS NÃO DEMONSTRA MESQUINHEZ? Cada um entende com a compreensão que lhe é própria moral, intelectual e espiritualmente.

OBSESSÃO, POSSESSÃO E VAMPIRISMO

O QUE É OBSESSÃO? É sentimento incontrolável que ultrapassa todos os limites, como um desejo excessivo e uma ideia fixa. Obsessão é a fixação em uma ideia que domina doentiamente a mente e o espírito de uma pessoa. A obsessão acontece dependendo de com quem ela se envolve, e de acordo com a sintonia mental. As imperfeições atraem espíritos com os idênticos vícios e falhas morais, ou como se costuma dizer, os iguais se atraem. As brechas psíquicas para as obsessões são abertas por cada um na medida em que o que prende um obsessor junto ao encarnado não são as afinidades fluídicas e sim morais.

O QUE É A OBSESSÃO SIMPLES? É quando um ou vários espíritos influenciam a mente da pessoa com suas ideias.

O QUE É A FASCINAÇÃO? É quando há uma ação constante e direta sobre o pensamento da pessoa por espíritos ardilosos que se dedicam a ganhar-lhe a confiança, ao mesmo tempo em que paralisam seu raciocínio até chegar ao ponto em que aceita tudo o que lhe é sugerido como se fossem verdades incontestáveis, mesmo sendo os mais completos absurdos. A subjugação é influência tão forte sobre a mente do obsidiado que este não mais raciocina nem age por si mesmo, tornando-se um fantoche do espírito ou dos espíritos que o influenciam.

HÁ QUANTOS TIPOS DE OBSESSÃO? Há 6 tipos: de desencarnado para encarnado, de encarnado para desencarnado, de encarnado para encarnado, de desencarnado para desencarnado, obsessões recíprocas e auto-obsessão.

O QUE É OBSESSÃO DE DESENCARNADO PARA ENCARNADO? É o domínio que alguns espíritos têm sobre uma pessoa encarnada e nunca é praticado senão por inferiores que procuram dominar o obsediado.

O QUE É OBSESSÃO DE ENCARNADO PARA DESENCARNADO? Dá-se, por exemplo, através da ligação anormal e obstinada à pessoa querida que já desencarnou, seja através de sentimento de revolta ou de perda, até se tornar obsessão. Consciência culpada, inveja, ódio, vingança também são as causas da terrível compulsão. *Note que há obsessão de encarnado para desencarnado.*

O QUE É OBSESSÃO DE ENCARNADO PARA ENCARNADO? Acontece domínio não só mental, mas muitas vezes físico por causa de ciúmes, paixão, e até do que o atormentador chama "amor", embora seja amor por si mesmo e nada mais. Ódio, orgulho ferido, inveja e outros sentimentos inferiores também são causa da obsessão entre encarnados.

O QUE É OBSESSÃO DE DESENCARNADO PARA DESENCARNADO? Há espírito que obsedia espírito numa prova incontestável de que os sentimentos não mudam com a morte do corpo físico. Amor ou ódio, simpatia ou aversão permanecem em qualquer dimensão em que se esteja.

O QUE SÃO OBSESSÕES RECÍPROCAS? Acontece quando uma individualidade dependente da outra, estejam na dimensão do espírito ou da matéria. Isso ocorre quando há ligação tão estreita que não se sabe "onde um termina e outro começa". Obsessor e obsidiado se nutrem das emanações um do outro de tal forma que é muitíssimo perigoso desligá-los rapidamente. Como exemplo de triste obsessão é o caso de um marido possessivo que vampiriza o corpo físico da esposa, ou o pensamento de uma namorada abandonada que vampiriza a ambos, ela própria e o infeliz ex-namorado. Ainda se pode citar como exemplo o alcoólatra incorrigível e seu "colega de copo", espírito também alcoólatra quando encarnado, ambos perturbados e com a preocupação constante de satisfazerem o seu vício. O desencarnado se "cola" ao perispírito do usuário (ou "copo vivo") para inalar, aspirar, sentir os efeitos da droga, e assim convivem em regime de escravidão mútua.

O QUE É AUTO-OBSESSÃO? Auto-obsessão é a mais difícil de ser admitida. Reconhecível quando a pessoa vive em função de si mesma, ou descuida totalmente da saúde ou se preocupa em excesso. Aquele que se imagina portador de doenças incuráveis percorrendo médico após médico, sem encontrar a cura para a doença que não tem é um auto-obsessor, do mesmo modo o infeliz que, não encontrando as respostas em si mesmo, busca nas religiões e não se adapta a nenhuma. A vítima de si própria padece de ciúme exagerado ou orgulho excessivo, sofre antecipadamente por situações que provavelmente jamais acontecerão. O opressor que se comporta de maneira tirânica para obter o poder completo também sofre de auto-obsessão.

O QUE É POSSESSÃO ESPIRITUAL? É quando acontece influência mental, invasão nos pensamentos, controle e até subjugação sobre uma pessoa.

O QUE É POSSESSÃO MENTAL? É quando se dá a posse dos pensamentos. Por exemplo, "José" nutre-se de ódio tão violento por "João" ao ponto de ficar transtornado, e diante do odiado "João" nem é mais "José" que age, ele está possuído, atraiu para si um espírito perverso que vibra no mesmo diapasão. Há tantas situações em que uma pessoa age com palavras agressivas e depois diz "nem sei como pude ter falado aquilo", ou em situações piores em que age com violência, agride, mata e nem se lembra do que fez e diz "parecia que não era eu".

COMO OS ESPÍRITOS TREVOSOS CONSEGUEM DOMINAR ASSIM? Pela cegueira que o ciúme, a revolta, o ódio e toda gama de sentimentos inferiores causa. Se uma pessoa tem o campo mental favorável e outra consciência toma posse, ela fica "cega de ódio". Entra em faixa negativa que funciona como "imã" para que outras inteligências sejam atraídas e a comande.

O QUE É POSSESSÃO FÍSICA? É quando "o indivíduo tem muitas vezes consciência de que o que faz é ridículo, mas é forçado a fazê-lo, tal como se um homem mais vigoroso do que ele o obrigasse a mover, contra a vontade, os braços, as pernas e a língua". *(Kardec)*

O QUE É VAMPIRISMO? É o ato de desencarnados prisioneiros dos desejos e caprichos humanos, dos recursos materiais e de seus pensamentos inferiores, dos quais extraem a essência vital.

O QUE É VAMPIRO OU SUGADOR DE ENERGIA? O vampiro é aquele que suga a energia de alguém ou alguma coisa. Por exemplo, um fumante quase sempre tem a companhia de um espírito viciado que recolhe o fluido emitido pelo cigarro, e o mesmo se dá com o álcool, com sexo lascivo e até com a alimentação. Muitos já vivenciaram a sensação de não sentir fome, mas necessidade de comer, que muitas vezes pode ser descrita como uma fome emocional originada de ansiedade, estresse e depressão, mas há também a fome espiritual, impulso que se dá às vezes em razão da ação dos tais vampiros que vêm se alimentar dos fluidos do alimento. Todo tipo de vício que o ser humano adquire tem um viciado correspondente na espiritualidade que pode ser nominado, para efeito de entendimento, de *"vampiro"*. No livro espírita "Sexo e Destino" André Luiz relata um caso em que a pessoa não está bebendo, mas ela tem o campo mental favorável, ela vibra na mesma sintonia e não demora está sendo influenciada para beber.

COMO EVITAR SER VAMPIRIZADO POR TAIS CRIATURAS? Entendendo que tudo em excesso faz mal, tudo o que é demais, sobra. Fumo, drogas, bebidas alcoólicas, comida com exagero, tudo isso atrai para perto os desencarnados que ainda estão ligados a tais coisas, e tudo farão para desfrutar através dos encarnados os vícios que ainda não superaram.

TAMBÉM HÁ OS QUE VAMPIRIZAM AS ENERGIAS ALHEIAS E ESTÃO ENCARNADOS? Sim, e com os quais se convive diariamente nas casas, fábricas, escritórios, lojas. Podem ser irmãos, maridos e esposas, amigos, chefes, colegas de trabalhos, vizinhos, enfim, qualquer um do convívio.

O QUE É ENERGIA VITAL? É a energia que circula pelo corpo humano e está em tudo: na natureza, nos alimentos, nos líquidos que bebemos, é absorvida através do ar que respiramos. Como o nome diz, a energia vital é mais importante e que é necessária para a manutenção da vida porque a afeta de maneira essencial.

ONDE SE ENCONTRA A ENERGIA VITAL E COMO SE PODE RESTABELECER? A energia vital é abundante no universo, pode-se recompô-la através da respiração, alimentação adequada, absorção do fluido cósmico universal ou vital através dos chackras.

POR QUE ALGUMAS PESSOAS VAMPIRIZAM AS ENERGIAS ALHEIAS? Porque não conseguem receber nem recompor. Atuam sem consciência do que fazem, e por serem incapazes de absorver as energias das fontes naturais estão constantemente desequilibrados energeticamente. Como são indispensáveis para nutrir o corpo físico e, principalmente, o corpo espiritual, buscam as fontes mais próximas que normalmente são as pessoas de convívio diário.

É VERDADE QUE TODOS OS SERES QUE DISPÕE DE INDIVIDUALIDADE EM ALGUM MOMENTO DA VIDA VAMPIRIZAM A ENERGIA ALHEIA? Sim, por exemplo, nas situações em que os pensamentos ficam desordenados ou os sentimentos inadequados, e as coisas se desorganizam. *A maioria não dá importância ou nem desconfia que o modo de vida, a qualidade dos pensamentos, sentimentos e sensações são de inteira importância para repor naturalmente a carga energética vital em quantidade suficiente para manter a vida.* E deve-se estar ciente de que o sugador sempre se aproxima de pessoas que têm boa carga de energia vital.

O QUE É SIMBIOSE ENERGÉTICA? Independente da intenção ou do que se esteja pensando, querendo, desejando, sempre que uma pessoa se aproxima de outra ocorre à troca de energia, chamada simbiose energética. A proximidade com parentes, amigos, amantes, desafetos, transeuntes desconhecidos, cada um emanando sentimentos nem sempre positivos de paz, gratidão, bondade, sendo o mais comum, devido à baixa evolução dos que habitam essa dimensão espiritual, pensamentos e sentimentos negativos como ódio, mágoa, egoísmo, inveja, vaidade, orgulho, ganância e cobiça, assim como os desvios sexuais que se expressam em exageros, agressividade e desamor causam enormes desequilíbrios. Todas as emanações energéticas se misturam e se combinam e há troca permanente de vibração. Nesse emaranhado sempre haverá os mais voltados para si mesmo (a principal característica do sugador é o egocentrismo) e, não tendo nenhuma energia para trocar, **ao vampiro só resta sugar.**

É VERDADE QUE A MAIORIA DOS SUGADORES O FAZ COM PESSOAS AS QUAIS TEM ALGUM LAÇO AFETIVO? Sim, porque através da amizade, do romance ou de um simples coleguismo profissional doa-se mais energia do que para um completo desconhecido, e o vampiro se aproveita disso. Mas só existe sugador porque existem os que se dispõem a serem sugado ou por pena ou por não terem ainda compreendido. O melhor conselho para quem encontrar com um sugador de energias é livrar-se dele o mais rápido possível.

COMO IDENTIFICAR UM SUGADOR DE ENERGIA? O que se derrete em elogios para lustrar o ego alheio, bajula excessivamente, procura seduzir com palavras escolhidas que claramente não saíram do coração, está com certeza sugando a energia. É preciso não deixar o orgulho cegar e cair fora. Aquele que conta suas mazelas, narra as infelicidades e tragédias com detalhes, tudo faz de modo a despertar no ouvinte a compaixão, fala esperando que o outro se apiede de suas desgraças está na verdade esvaziando a energia vital do interlocutor. É preciso dizer a esse "desfavorecido" que se queixar de nada resolve, e que melhor faria se procurasse achar solução para seus problemas. Falando assim causará no "pobre coitado" um abalo inesperado de modo a interromper a subtração das energias. E caia fora. Se ao encontrar com um conhecido este logo começa a cobrar a visita que não fez, o telefonema que não recebeu, é certo que antes de se despedirem o que está sendo intimado estará com as reservas de energia bem baixas. A melhor atitude é argumentar que se não visitou também não foi visitado, se não telefonou, tampouco ele. E cair fora. O colega de trabalho que critica tudo e todos, nada nunca é bom o suficiente, maldiz a vida e calunia os colegas é um sumidouro de reserva energética. Não se pode jamais concordar com ele, e o melhor a fazer é cair fora. O sujeito que reclama do sol e da chuva, do dia e da noite, a tudo se coloca de modo a formar obstáculo, reclama supostos direitos e a qualquer coisa expressa oposição, deve ser deixado falando consigo mesmo. Aquele que fala durante horas, que conta histórias intermináveis, cheias de detalhes e minúcias de modo a cansar pela insistência está na verdade levando aquele com quem interage à perda da estabilidade e da firmeza. Não se deve demorar em sua companhia. Quem acha que nada se resolve com diálogo, que *"dá um boi pra não entrar em uma briga, mas uma boiada pra não sair"*, de fala áspera e agressiva, sempre raivoso, provocativo, dono total da razão até em assuntos dos quais nunca ouviu falar, busca fazer a pessoa com quem fala se descontrolar e cair na armadilha de discutir com ele. Esse é um vampiro sugador de energia e o melhor a fazer é manter a calma e ficar o menor tempo possível em sua presença. O eternamente preocupado acerca de seu próprio estado de saúde - embora não haja razão genuína para isso - portador de todas as doenças já diagnosticadas e novas, age assim para chamar atenção. Contando minuciosamente os pormenores do padecimento desperta cuidado e deixa inquietos os que com ele conversa. Enquanto o ingênuo estremece com os detalhes da moléstia o sugador lhe esgota as energias. É preciso interromper educadamente a lamentação interminável e cair fora.

É VERDADE QUE AS COMPANHIAS ESPIRITUAIS QUE NOS CERCAM SERÃO DE ACORDO COM AS NOSSAS AÇÕES E PENSAMENTOS? Sim. Os perversos só estão onde podem satisfazer sua crueldade, independente de estarem ou não encarnados. Não é suficiente ir ao Terreiro e achar que os Guias de Luz vão levar um atormentador para longe e tudo estará resolvido, porque será uma solução temporária na medida em que um vai e outro logo vem. É preciso eliminar em si aquilo que os aproxima.

COMO SÃO ATRAÍDOS OS ESPÍRITOS ATRASADOS? Como moscas atraídas pelo mau cheiro que exala das feridas os espíritos impiedosos são seduzidos pelas chagas da alma.

O QUE É PROVA E EXPIAÇÃO DE UM ESPÍRITO? O planeta Terra é mundo de prova e expiação, cuja diferença é que prova é o resgate escolhido por cada um quando está consciente de seus débitos e necessidades, mas a coisa se complica com aqueles que vivem em expiação, que é o resgate imposto pela Justiça Divina a espíritos que insistem teimosamente no erro.

MUITOS NÃO CONCORDAM QUE ESTE SEJA UM MUNDO DE PROVA E EXPIAÇÃO, DIZEM QUE PENSAR ASSIM É PESSIMISMO. Aos que discordam que vivemos em mundo-escola convido a pensar nos horrores próprios da esfera em que moramos sem opção de escolha, tais como o terrorismo, holocausto, genocídio, estupro. Reflita sobre os horrores das guerras, a extinção forçada dos pobres animais, racismo, homofobia, humilhação, tortura. Avalie a sede e a fome que devastam vidas em mundo onde metade está faminta e a outra metade obesa. Medite sobre a inclemência da natureza e os trabalhos penosos, quando não literalmente escravos. Neste mundo há os que incendeiam vivos índios, moradores de rua, cães e gatos. Considere a perversidade dos homens demonstrada na inquisição da Igreja Católica, nos campos de concentração de Hitler, nos massacres de Osama Bin Laden, Mao Tsétung, Saddam Hussein, George Bush, Lênin, Stálin, nos terroristas do Estado Islâmico. São provas incontestáveis de que nem todos os seres humanos são dotados de humanidade.

COMO DEVE PROCEDER AQUELE QUE DESEJA MODIFICAR SUAS COMPANHIAS ESPIRITUAIS? Deve primeiro modificar-se. É preciso entender que pensamentos emitidos é convite claro para os que pensam de maneira semelhante se aproximar. **A chave do bem viver é cuidar da frequência vibratória que sintoniza.** Cada gesto indigno, cada ação desonrosa, cada pensamento degradante, cada palavra mentirosa vai ligando a pessoa aos espíritos infelizes.

COMO IDENTIFICAR OS QUE ESTÃO EM EXPIAÇÃO?
Os que estão em expiação geralmente aceitam mal as situações difíceis que se apresentam, mostrando a todo o momento sua revolta. Atravessam a existência a reclamar do peso de sua cruz.

MISÉRIA MATERIAL É UMA EXPIAÇÃO? A miséria não é necessariamente uma expiação, podendo ser uma opção do espírito que julga importante a pobreza material para uma provação, entendendo que será útil ao seu progresso. Por outro lado é necessário observar que pessoas com alto padrão de vida podem estar amargando pesada expiação, porque ao contrário do senso comum, posição social não determina a natureza das experiências vividas pelo espírito. A pessoa rica financeiramente pode estar em processo de desolada purgação como consequência, e o desfavorecido de posses pode ser feliz com o que tem e é. Porém, o livre arbítrio é fator preponderante na vida de todo ser humano, e aquele que faz planos de quitar as dívidas nessa esfera espiritual pode viver com tolerância as provações se conseguir despertar do sono profundo que vive, lembrando-se de si mesmo e desapegando das coisas materiais que o fascina.

COMO IDENTIFICAR OS QUE ESTÃO EM PROVAÇÃO?
Os que estão em provação aceitam melhor as adversidades porque as dificuldades foram idealizadas por eles, desta forma tendem a aceitar com mais equilíbrio e sem revolta. Como um aluno que se submete a exame, tenta fazer o melhor, habilitando-se a estágio superior.

O QUE SIGNIFICA DESCARGA OU DESCARREGO NA UMBANDA? Significa que se vai afastar perturbações espirituais ou obsessores que estão atormentando uma pessoa, uma casa de comércio ou residência, ou os médiuns de um Terreiro de Umbanda.

O QUE SÃO AS GUIAS E PARA QUE SERVEM

Para conhecer mais sobre as Guias sugerimos a leitura do livro
"O Ritual de Umbanda - Para Leigos"

O QUE SÃO AS GUIAS? Também conhecidas como "Cordão de Santo", "Colar de Santo" ou "Fio de Contas", as Guias são uma espécie de colar colorido usado por todos os filhos de fé durante as Giras e faz parte do Fundamento da Umbanda. Após ser confeccionadas e imantadas pelo Guia do Dirigente do Terreiro ou pelo Guia do médium a qual pertence, torna-se uma espécie de para raios de descargas pesadas em defesa de quem as usa. Também se torna mais uma ferramenta de ligação entre o médium e seu Guia.

COM QUAL MATERIAL DEVEM SER CONFECCIONADAS? São confeccionadas com sementes, pedras, porcelanas, conchas, cristais, enfim, sempre com produtos naturais por serem condutores de energia. Os produtos feitos de plástico, por exemplo, as miçangas ou materiais que se equivalem, não podem ser usados de nenhuma forma porque o plástico é isolante e, sabendo-se que através dele não passa corrente elétrica, tampouco o fluido dos Guias. Devem-se, portanto, utilizar miçangas de porcelana, cristal ou louça, e com a cor correspondente ao Guia ou ao Orixá. A medida deve ir até a altura do umbigo. Em alguns Terreiros é costume utilizar certo número de miçangas enfiadas uma a uma em fio de aço, de náilon ou fibra vegetal, mas normalmente são confeccionadas seguindo o padrão do Terreiro.

AS GUIAS PRECISAM SER CONSAGRADAS? Usar uma Guia no pescoço sem ter sido consagrada e imantada é apenas um colar. Sendo as Guias ferramentas pessoais são também intransferíveis. Embora vendidas em lojas de artigos religiosos, o ideal é que o próprio médium as confeccione, manipule e utilize. Em alguns Terreiros as Guias podem ser feitas por outros filhos de fé desde que escolhidos pelo Dirigente ou Guia Chefe para essa finalidade.

QUANTOS TIPOS DE GUIAS EXISTEM? Existem pelo menos quatro tipos de Guias que são usadas pelos médiuns: Guia de Proteção, Guia de Tratamento, Guia do Orixá e Guia das Entidades.

O QUE É GUIA DE PROTEÇÃO? É aquela que quando um médium entra para a Gira de Desenvolvimento deve providenciar, chamada **Guia de Oxalá,** de cor branca, ou **Guia das Sete Linhas,** contendo as sete cores dos Orixás de Umbanda. Quem decide qual das duas Guias é a tradição do Terreiro.

O QUE É GUIA DE TRATAMENTO? É frequentemente de cor branca e que se dá para o assistido usar durante o tempo que durar o tratamento, devidamente cruzada e imantada, representando a força e vibração de Jesus/Oxalá.

O QUE É GUIA DO ORIXÁ? É a Guia que está ligada à faixa vibratória do Orixá do médium, confeccionada na cor relacionada ao Orixá, geralmente de uma só cor, embora existam Terreiros que trabalham com Orixás cruzados e aí a Guia terá duas ou mais cores.

O QUE É GUIA DAS ENTIDADES? É aquela que não tem um padrão ou cor predefinida porque cada Entidade pede a Guia de acordo com a sua necessidade. Pode ser feita de materiais diversos como coquinho, olho de cabra, dentes e é de grande importância que se siga exatamente a recomendação da Entidade quanto ao modelo e confecção porque tem um fundamento igual ao ponto riscado.

COMO SÃO AS GUIAS DAS ENTIDADES? As cores variam de acordo com o Terreiro, normalmente confeccionadas seguindo um "padrão da Casa". **Lembrando sempre que qualquer elemento especial que se acrescente ao Fio**

de Contas simples deve ser a pedido da Entidade ou de acordo com a doutrina do Terreiro, porque Colar de Santo não é adorno para enfeitar médium.

COMO SÃO FEITAS AS GUIAS DE PRETO VELHO? São feitas com contas nas cores preta e branca. É usual acrescentar semente da planta Lágrimas de Nossa Senhora, também conhecida como Conta de Lágrimas ou ainda Capim Rosário, usada na confecção do terço. Essas Guias são herança dos antigos africanos na época em que os negros eram cativos, essa semente era o material que se encontrava mais à mão porque estava plantada em todos os lugares. É semente cinza com uma palha dentro. Usam-se também favas, cruzes, figas feitas de arruda ou guiné.

COMO SÃO FEITAS AS GUIAS DE CABOCLO? São feitas com contas de cor verde, porém podem ter outra cor dependendo do Orixá regente do médium. Alguns Caboclos podem pedir nas Guias sementes de Açaí, de Coronha (também chamada de Olho de Boi), dentes, bambus, penas, conchas ou outro elemento do mar, sempre de acordo com a origem vibratória da Entidade.

COMO SÃO FEITAS AS GUIAS DE BAIANOS? São feitas na cor alaranjada e podem conter coquinho, semente ou fava conhecida popularmente como Olho de Boi, ou outra semente denominada Olho de Cabra, pedaços de couro e búzios.

COMO SÃO FEITAS AS GUIAS DE BOIADEIRO? São confeccionadas na cor azul ou vermelhas e podem conter além das miçangas, Olho de Boi, Olho de Cabra, pedaços de couro.

COMO SÃO FEITAS AS GUIAS DE CIGANOS? São feitas de cores diversas, muito coloridas, e podem conter fitas, pedras diversificadas e em especial Ágata de Fogo.

COMO SÃO FEITAS AS GUIAS DE MARINHEIRO? São confeccionadas na cor azul clara e podem conter conchas e âncoras.

COMO SÃO FEITAS AS GUIAS DE MALANDROS? São contas nas cores branca, vermelha e preta intercaladas, e podem conter adereços de ferro e aço.

COMO SÃO FEITAS AS GUIAS DE EXU? São feitas nas cores preta e podem conter sementes de Olho de Cabra, tridente, búzios pretos, pedras Ônix, Obsidiana ou Hematita, além de instrumentos de ferro, aço, etc.

COMO SÃO FEITAS AS GUIAS DE POMBOGIRA? São confeccionadas com miçangas da cor vermelha e pode conter tridente, além de instrumentos de ferro, aço.

COMO SÃO FEITAS AS GUIAS DE SEREIAS? Podem ser feitas com conchinhas recolhidas à beira-mar.

O QUE SIGNIFICA FIOS DE UMA SÓ "PERNA"? É o nome que se dá ao colar simples de uma só fiada de miçangas, cuja medida deve ir até a altura do umbigo.

OFERENDAS

O QUE É OFERENDA? Oferenda é aquilo que se oferece. O dízimo, que é a décima parte de algo doado voluntariamente para ajudar organizações religiosas, é uma oferenda.

COMO É A OFERENDA DOS CATÓLICOS? Chama-se a Liturgia Eucarística e inicia-se com a preparação das oferendas que são o pão e o vinho, e ao serem consagrados entendem que se tornam o corpo e o sangue de Jesus. O ofertório é parte do ritual católico em que são consagrados e ofertados o pão e o vinho com água, oferendas de dinheiro e outros objetos que podem ser levados com caráter simbólico.

COMO É A OFERENDA NO BUDISMO? Os Budistas oferendam flores, arroz, velas, lamparinas, incensos, mandalas, água, chás, frutas, pó de sândalo. As oferendas de lamparinas, por exemplo, é simbolicamente a oferta de luz para dispersar obstáculos de todos os seres. O propósito de fazer oferendas no Budismo é desenvolver e aumentar a mente de generosidade e reduzir a avareza.

COMO É A OFERENDA NO CANDOMBLÉ? No Candomblé as oferendas são de origem animal, abatido pelo chamado Axogun ou Ogã de Faca ou ainda Mão de Faca, que é quem sabe as técnicas complexas para o sacrifício. O animal vai para as mãos da cozinheira chamada Iyagbasé, que é a única responsável por fiscalizar e executar tudo o que se refere à alimentação da Casa de Candomblé, tanto para o Orixá como para todos os presentes. Normalmente a Iyagbasé (pronuncia Iabassê) é maior de 60 anos porque nessa idade não menstrua mais.

COMO É A OFERENDA NA UMBANDA? A regra mais importante deixada pelo Caboclo das Sete Encruzilhadas quando da fundação da religião, é que jamais de faça oferendas que contenha sacrifício animal. Utiliza-se o chamado "sangue verde", de origem vegetal obtido nas cascas das árvores, folhas, frutos, sementes e flores. Usa-se também o "sangue" de origem mineral que são água, sal e carvão. Deste modo **as oferendas são feitas basicamente com flores, frutas, velas e bebidas.**

OFERENDAS E DESPACHOS SÃO AS MESMAS COISAS? As oferendas da Umbanda são, por infelicidade, constantemente confundidas com os despachos de encruzilhada, com as macumbas que alimentam o astral inferior e cujos ofertantes (tanto os que fizeram quanto os que mandaram fazer) só conseguem de verdade a companhia de vampiros que, após se alimentarem da carne putrefata do pobre animal, vão em busca dos desajuizados que com eles fizeram "negócio". **Engana-se quem acha que será atendido em seus sinistros propósitos mutilando, matando, enterrando vivos os pobres animais.** Os espíritos de baixa vibração estão interessados apenas em sorver o fluido vital do sangue enquanto os animais são mortos, e depois da carne em decomposição. **Como os que assim agem podem acreditar que O Criador permitiria a uma pessoa de má índole, com o auxílio de um Espírito perverso que necessita do sangue de um animal**

inocente, fazer mal ao seu próximo?

ONDE SÃO FEITAS AS OFERENDAS E QUAL A FINALIDADE? Na verdadeira religião de Umbanda as oferendas são feitas junto à Natureza e sempre com a finalidade de absorver, nos campos de força dos Orixás presentes no mundo natural, as energias dali irradiadas tal qual o sedento junto à fonte de água cristalina. Nos pontos de força os filhos de fé estabelecem sintonia com os Orixás e suas emanações, descarregando as energias negativas e recebendo eflúvios benéficos e positivos que reequilibram os corpos inferiores. Em resumo, **oferenda é um meio para se colocar em sintonia vibratória e mental com os Orixás.**

HÁ UMA FORMA CERTA DE SE FAZER OFERENDA?
Não há uma receita nem fórmula nem maneira certa ou errada de se fazer uma oferenda, o que importa é a intenção e o pensamento durante o ato. Não é preciso fórmula mirabolante, apenas que seja feita como o coração mandar. *Se colocar uma melancia aberta debaixo de árvore frondosa, regada de caldo de cana, e pedir com fé* para que haja harmonia em seu local de trabalho, ESTARÁ REALIZANDO UMA OFERENDA. *Se colocar uma melancia aberta debaixo de árvore frondosa, regada de caldo de cana, e pedir com fé* para que um colega de trabalho que está lhe prejudicando seja demitido, ESTARÁ REALIZANDO UMA DEMANDA. Para a espiritualidade o que vale é a intenção, muito além do ato e dos elementos com os quais é realizado.

É PRECISO ENTREGAR AMALÁ (COMIDA RITUAL) NAS OFERENDAS? Alguns Dirigentes acreditam que é preciso entregar no amalá (comida ritual) os elementos correspondentes ao Orixá ao qual se está oferendando. Outros acreditam que deve haver uma ritualística que incluam movimentos e procedimentos específicos, desenhos para criar poderes mágicos, invocação. Porém nada disso será útil se não houver nas palavras e pensamentos o verdadeiro querer do ofertante, seja desejando o amor seja endereçando a dor.

OS GUIAS DE UMBANDA E OS ORIXÁS PRECISAM DE OFERENDAS MATERIAIS? *Que fique bem claro que nenhum Guia de Luz, trabalhador de Umbanda assim como nenhum Orixá precisa de oferendas materiais. Elas são úteis à concentração de quem oferece, e que uma simples oração feita com a mais profunda fé no silêncio do coração é mais eficaz que todas as oferendas que se possa fazer se o ofertante não estiver imbuído de boas intenções.*

É VERDADE QUE A OFERENDA É ESSENCIAL PARA SE CONSEGUIR AJUDA DAS ENTIDADES? Não basta oferenda para conseguir qualquer coisa que se precise ou se queira. **É preciso esforço.** Os Guias de Luz e os Orixás não vão tornar as obrigações mais aprazíveis nem as responsabilidades menos implacáveis em troca de oferenda, não há barganha com a espiritualidade. Nenhum Preto Velho jamais vai pedir parte das posses financeiras de alguém em troca de chance de progresso espiritual ou financeiro. Os pedidos que são feitos nas oferendas só acontecem se for do merecimento de quem ofertou, e sendo assim nem precisava de oferenda.

TODOS OS MÉDIUNS SÃO OBRIGADOS A FAZER OFERENDAS? O QUE SÃO? PARA QUE SERVEM? Não são todos os Terreiros que adotam essa prática. Oferendas são oferecidas para as Entidades ou Orixás com o objetivo de conseguir força espiritual. Quando feita com fé e respeito eleva a força fluídica que se encontra ao redor do perispírito da pessoa que ofertou, e que a Entidade oferendada manipula e direciona para ajudar na realização de um pedido. A Entidade apenas manipula a energia fluídica que envolve a oferenda, é importante deixar bem claro que, ao contrário da crença comum, as oferendas na Umbanda não são para as Entidades ou Orixás comerem, até porque estão em planos mais elevados de onde extraem outros tipos de energia de acordo com as suas condições, mas servem para que absorvam teores energéticos da natureza e os revertam para o próprio ser humano, de acordo com a sua necessidade. Outra razão da oferenda é que quando feitas na natureza estão ligadas às forças sutis do mundo natural tais como da mata limpa, praia limpa, montanha, cachoeira, e deste modo tem-se auxílio dos espíritos elementais que os habitam. Assim as oferendas servem para restituir as energias a fim de equilibrar física, mental e espiritualmente. As oferendas não são obrigações, Orixás e Guias de Umbanda não obrigam ninguém a oferecer coisa nenhuma, muito menos pedem ou exigem que se adquiram objetos e elementos caros, cujo dinheiro pago vai fazer falta no orçamento. Quem quiser oferendar basta algo simples como uma flor.

Nunca é demais lembrar que a Umbanda respeita a natureza, e o verdadeiro umbandista recolhe os elementos que usa em seus cultos e oferendas quando feitos ao ar livre, seja na mata, seja na praia, cachoeira ou em qualquer lugar. Alguidás, velas, palitos de fósforo, nada deve ficar emporcalhando o ambiente, nem mesmo a parafina da vela em uma pedra é admissível deixar.

MAGIA E SEUS ELEMENTOS

O QUE É MAGIA NA UMBANDA? Importante esclarecer que Magia na Umbanda não é superstição, crença ou prática irracional resultante da ignorância e do medo do desconhecido. Magia na Umbanda é conhecimento "oculto" acerca da natureza e suas forças misteriosas. E esse conhecimento se obtém através do estudo registrado em textos escritos e também transmitidos oralmente pelos Guias. A Umbanda é permeada constantemente por atos de magia, e aqui são pontuados alguns deles.

Ponto Riscado

O QUE É PONTO RISCADO? Também chamado de **GRAFIA DOS ORIXÁS**, é o conjunto de sinais referentes aos Guias de Umbanda. Assim como cada homem e mulher um tem sua assinatura que os identifica e é única, não existindo duas iguais, assim são os pontos riscados das Entidades que trabalham na Umbanda.

JÁ VI OS SÍMBOLOS DOS PONTOS RISCADOS EM OUTRAS RELIGIÕES. TODOS TÊM O MESMO SIGNIFICADO? Não, esses símbolos na Umbanda tem significado próprio. Por exemplo, a estrela de seis pontas para o Judaísmo simboliza o selo de realeza representativo do reinado de David (daí o nome Estrela de David), mas na Umbanda a estrela de seis pontas representa a justiça, portanto é símbolo de Xangô.

O QUE DIZER DOS TERREIROS QUE OBRIGAM A ENTIDADE RISCAR O PONTO? A Entidade vai riscar o Ponto quando ela achar que é o momento, ninguém além dela pode decidir isso. Somente vai riscar o Ponto quando estiver em total sintonia com o médium e quando entender que o médium está preparado. Obrigar o Guia riscar o Ponto só vai causar ansiedade e aflição no médium que vai buscar na internet alguns "desenhos" só para satisfazer a expectativa do Dirigente. Não tem nenhum valor espiritual.

DUAS ENTIDADES COM O MESMO NOME TERÁ O MESMO PONTO RISCADO? Não. Embora sejam trabalhadores da mesma falange possuem suas individualidades e missões espirituais próprias. Pode haver alguma semelhança, mas nunca será igual.

COMO SABER SE O PONTO RISCADO PELA ENTIDADE ESTÁ CORRETO? Isso quem saberá é o Guia Chefe do

Terreiro, pois cabe a ele confirmar. Se não está correto o médium será orientado para firmar a incorporação, sempre com o carinho e respeito que o médium merece.

POR QUE EM ALGUNS TERREIROS OS DIRIGENTES PEDEM QUE AS ENTIDADES RISQUEM OU CANTEM SEUS PONTOS? Porque alguns Dirigentes fazem a confirmação da Entidade, dos Orixás e das falanges desta forma. Mas somente os Guias com incorporação completa junto aos seus médiuns conseguem isso, e o que se vê são Dirigentes que pressionam os médiuns iniciantes para riscar ou cantar o Ponto, o que gera ansiedade injustificável, sendo inclusive motivo do abandono da religião por alguns irmãos que passaram a duvidar de sua mediunidade por causa de exigência descabida.

Pemba

O QUE É PEMBA? É uma espécie de giz colorido com que se riscam os Pontos e são de cores variadas como branco, vermelho, amarelo, rosa, roxo, azul, marrom, verde e preto. Por si a Pemba não tem valor, apenas nos sinais grafados através dela é que lhe é atribuída grande importância. Quando se fala "**Lei da Pemba**" refere-se à Umbanda propriamente dita, e quando se fala "**Filhos de Pemba**" é referencia aos filhos de Umbanda.

O QUE SIGNIFICA A FRASE NA MÚSICA "EU ABRO A NOSSA GIRA COM DEUS E NOSSA SENHORA, EU ABRO A NOSSA GIRA SAMBORÊ, PEMBA DE ANGOLA"? Samborê vem do Cabula e do Omolokô, que são duas religiões surgidas dos povos vindos da África, para quem a palavra *"samba"* significa *"pular com alegria"*, assim esse trecho do ponto cantado declara a alegria por estar iniciando a Gira. A Pemba é originária dos rituais Bantu (Congo e Angola) onde é reverenciada e sempre há uma reza para ela. Note que também nos pontos cantados constata-se a herança dos povos do Candomblé.

POR QUE SE USA A PEMBA PARA RISCAR AS MÃOS, PÉS E CABEÇA DOS MÉDIUNS? Geralmente para dar-lhes proteção.

QUAL É A DIFERENÇA ENTRE AS CHAMADAS PEMBA DE ANGOLA, DO CONGO, DA COSTA E DE MOÇAMBIQUE? Não tem nenhuma diferença além do preço. A força não está na pemba e sim nos sinais que o Guia firmou.

POR QUE AS PEMBAS SÃO COLORIDAS? Porque representam as Linhas de Trabalho das diversas Entidades espirituais da Umbanda. Um Caboclo de Ogun irá riscar seu ponto de vermelho que é a cor do Orixá Ogun, os Caboclos de Oxóssi usam a cor verde, de Xangô é marrom etc.

PÓLVORA

PARA QUAL FINALIDADE SE UTILIZA A PÓLVORA NA UMBANDA? Pólvora, também chamada FUNDANGA ou TUIA, é utilizada na Umbanda para descarrego, ou seja, para afastar perturbações espirituais. Assim como o fogo no campo físico serve para esterilizar, no campo energético a pólvora tem a propriedade de purificar consumindo por inteiro as formas-pensamentos que são as chamadas larvas mentais ou miasmas, larvas astrais e outros parasitismos.

O QUE É RODA DE FOGO OU CAMINHO DE FOGO?
Chama-se Roda de Fogo ou ainda Caminho de Fogo o ritual de purificação considerado a força máxima da limpeza espiritual. Geralmente desenha-se um Ponto Riscado com pólvora ou com a pemba, em seguida acende e deixa queimar. Esse ritual varia de acordo com o Terreiro na forma como é feito, mas não na intenção que é igual em todos os Terreiros de Umbanda.

A QUEIMA DE PÓLVORA É PARA "QUEIMAR" OS ESPÍRITOS? Não. Quando se realiza a queima da pólvora, ao contrário do que alguns pensam não se queima nenhum espírito, o ponto de fogo ou queima de fundanga (pólvora) é para descarga ou desintegração de placas no perispírito sobrecarregado de fluidos nocivos.

O QUE SÃO LARVAS MENTAIS E LARVAS ASTRAIS?
As larvas mentais não são seres, nem espíritos e nem alma, são aglomerado de energia negativa e roubam a vitalidade do hospedeiro, podendo comparar as larvas mentais a parasitas. As larvas astrais são criações mentais geradas a partir de pensamentos e sentimentos desequilibrados que se alimentam dos atos, pensamentos e desejos negativos e destrutivos e que se apropriam da saúde, bem-estar, prosperidade e equilíbrio mental/emocional. Todo tipo de vício atrai larvas astrais, cada uma

de acordo com suas necessidades. Há larvas astrais que encontram prazer no álcool, e por isso se grudam na aura de alcoólatras e os incentivam a beber cada vez mais.

É FATO QUE LARVAS ASTRAIS SÃO ATRAÍDAS POR SANGUE? Sim, seja qual for o tipo, astral ou mental, invariavelmente são atraídas por sangue fresco como há nos matadouros, porque os vapores do sangue dão a sensação de vida. Os que fazem oferendas com sangue dos pobres animais sequer imaginam que estão satisfazendo o instinto pernicioso de larvas e não de Entidades trabalhadoras de Umbanda. **É só pensar: por que e para que um Espírito de Luz iria pedir sangue?**

COMO ESSAS LARVAS DO MENTAL E DO ASTRAL SÃO ATRAÍDAS? Por empatia ou por afinidade. Elas se alimentam dos pensamentos e desejos negativos e destrutivos. Pessoas de má índole, que vivem ambicionando o que é dos outros e constantemente desejando o mal alheio, estão sempre cercadas por larvas astrais. São parasitas e é preciso que se livre deles.

FOLHAS E ERVAS

POR QUE SE USAM FOLHAS E ERVAS NA UMBANDA? As folhas e ervas são curandeiras desde a remota antiguidade. É do conhecimento geral suas propriedades aromáticas, alimentares e medicinais, e em muitos casos são tão ou mais eficazes que os medicamentos industrializados. No Brasil o conhecimento das propriedades das plantas medicinais é uma das maiores riquezas da cultura indígena. O índio, com conhecimento milenar, retira das plantas diversos remédios para a cura e prevenção de doenças em rituais repletos de elementos desconhecidos pelos homens brancos. Considerando que a Umbanda é formada também pela religiosidade indígena, herdou a crença e o conhecimento segundo o qual das plantas e ervas emanam fluídos benéficos que os umbandistas usam para diversos fins. Das cascas, folhas e flores extraem emulsões para o preparo de banhos, amacís, imantações. Acreditam os umbandistas que nas ervas e folhas ritualísticas estão contidas grande concentração de energia dos elementos naturais da terra que as sustentam, como a energia da luz do sol, a intensidade do ar, o vigor da água das chuvas que as alimentam, dando às folhas e ervas a força da Criação. Quando utilizadas para defumação entra em comunhão com o simbolismo da terra e água através do vegetal que queima (ervas), com a potência do fogo no carvão em brasa e com o ar que alimenta a combustão. Enfim, seu uso é indispensável, *pois "sem folha não tem sonho, sem folha não tem vida, sem folha não tem nada".*

AS VELAS

HÁ UMA FORMA CORRETA DE ACENDER VELA NA UMBANDA? Se acender a vela de forma automática, nada mais será do que tacar fogo no pavio de cera misturada com parafina, e estará gastando dinheiro inutilmente. Quando se acende uma vela não pode ter pressa, deve-se concentrar na chama que é calor e luz, ir de encontro ao próprio íntimo buscando respostas, entrando devagar em sintonia com os seres com os quais tem afinidade, anjos, Orixás, elementais, encantados, santos, Guias, não importa o nome que se dê. É preciso saber da grandeza e importância do momento, pois a energia emitida pela mente daquele que acende a vela irá se misturar à energia ígnea (do fogo), buscando alcançar a essência (ou a mente) da entidade. A energia emanada pelo pensamento juntamente com a intensidade do fogo viajarão no espaço pedindo auxílio àquele que vai atender a razão da queima da vela, de acordo com o merecimento do pedinte. Quem usa das próprias forças mentais com o auxílio das velas para ajudar alguém recebe em troca energia muito positiva. O oposto também acontece se inverter o fluxo de energia, ou seja, se o pensamento estiver negativo, carregado de ódio, de vingança e a finalidade for prejudicar o outro às vezes é alcançado, mas o retorno é infalível.

É VERDADE QUE A ENERGIA DO RETORNO SEMPRE É MAIOR? Sim, é verdade. Para o bem e para o mal. Porque ela volta com a energia de suas intenções somada a energia daquele que a recebeu.

PODE-SE DIZER QUE AS VELAS SÃO MÁGICAS? Sim, se considerarmos que mágica é a movimentação de energias.

POSSO ACENDER VELA DENTRO E FORA DE CASA? Não há problema. Os lares em que há harmonia e equilíbrio possuem proteção natural advinda da Espiritualidade que impedem o acesso de espírito ainda em perturbação em qualquer nível.

SE EU ACENDER UMA QUANTIDADE GRANDE DE VELAS TENHO MAIS CHANCE DE ENTRAR EM SINTONIA COM AS ENTIDADES? A intenção de acender uma vela gera energia mental no cérebro, e é essa energia que a Entidade irá captar em seu campo vibratório. Deste modo não é a quantidade de velas que se acende que é determinante, mas a qualidade, que é a fé e a mentalização daquele que acende a vela. Assim sendo é inútil acreditar que se pode "comprar favores" ou "ter mais proteção" de um Guia ou Entidade negociando ou acendendo um número grande de velas. Os espíritos captam em primeiríssimo lugar as vibrações de nossos sentimentos, quer acendamos velas ou não.

COMO DEVO INTERPRETAR AS CHAMAS E A QUEIMA DA VELA? QUANDO ELA NÃO ACENDE IMEDIATAMENTE, POR EXEMPLO, SIGNIFICA QUE ESTOU "CARREGADO"? OU SE A CERA SE ESPARRAMA É SINAL QUE HÁ FORÇAS NEGATIVAS ATRAPALHANDO A VIDA? As velas são simplesmente a extensão da vontade e dos pensamentos daquele que a acende. Quem acende uma vela sem concentração, sem intenção, de forma mecânica, está apenas acendendo um pavio inserido em parafina. A função do pavio é ser queimado para produzir fogo, e quando a vela não acende ou esparrama significa somente que o pavio foi mal colocado durante a fabricação.

AS VELAS TAMBÉM SÃO USADAS PARA PREJUDICAR O PRÓXIMO? Infelizmente há os que usam as velas para causar mal aos outros. Há práticas condenáveis que produzem suas próprias velas a partir de gordura de animais determinados para aquela intenção, e cujo pavio é feito com os cabelos de quem se deseja mal. Nada de positivo pode vir daí.

BEBIDA E FUMO

OS GUIAS DE UMBANDA SÃO ALCOÓLATRAS E VICIADOS EM NICOTINA E TABACO? Os trabalhadores espirituais da Umbanda não são alcoólatras e nem fumantes viciados em nicotina. O álcool e o fumo são ferramentas de trabalho úteis e necessárias, e tem que haver um compromisso sério de orientação aos médiuns para que sejam esclarecidos sobre o uso desses elementos, pois a falta de entendimento tem levado muitos irmãos umbandistas a cometer excessos absurdos que difamam a verdadeira missão de caridade prestada pelas Entidades e Guias espirituais, arcando a religião com o doloroso ônus dos exageros cometidos por médiuns desorientados e o julgamento ultrajante dos que criticam injustamente a Umbanda.

POR QUE ALGUMAS ENTIDADES TRABALHADORAS NA UMBANDA UTILIZAM O CHARUTO E O CACHIMBO? São utilizados tão somente como **defumadores individuais**. Nada além. Lançando a fumaça sobre a aura, os chacras e o corpo físico vão os trabalhadores atuando em benefício dos que tem fé, ao modo dos passes espirituais. As cigarrilhas são muito utilizadas pelas Pombogiras e Caboclas, os cigarros, inclusive de palha, são utilizados por quase todos os trabalhadores espirituais, mas **o Guia jamais traga a fumaça**. Quando dão preferência ao cigarro de palha impregnam o tabaco com sua energia espiritual e pensamentos que lhes são próprios, e transformam o "pito" em um desagregador de energias pesadas. Algumas entidades, inclusive, cospem em "caixinha" para evitar ao máximo a ingestão da nicotina pelo médium.

POR QUE ALGUMAS ENTIDADES TRABALHADORAS NA UMBANDA UTILIZAM A BEBIDA? A bebida, assim como o fumo, é utilizada na Umbanda para descarregar as energias densas, queimar larvas e miasmas astrais. Pelo fato de o álcool poder ser ingerido, é usado para limpar tanto o externo (quando o Guia pede que se passe a bebida nas mãos, por exemplo) como o interno (quando o Guia pede que a pessoa tome um **golinho** da bebida).

O QUE É CURIADOR? Manipuladas, as bebidas recebem o nome de "**curiador**", que são as utilizadas por cada Linha de Trabalhos. Caboclos "bebem" cerveja ou água de coco; Pretos Velhos "bebem" café e em alguns utilizam vinho; Crianças "bebem" guaraná ou outros tipos de refrigerantes e sucos de frutas; Baianos "bebem" água de coco ou batida de coco; Boiadeiros "bebem" cerveja escura; Marinheiros "bebem" rum e alguns "bebem" cerveja clara; Exu "bebe marafo" (pinga) e alguns "bebem" uísque ou vinho, e embora não seja comum, cerveja; Pombogira "bebe" champagne ou sidra.

OS GUIAS FUMAM E BEBEM PORQUE SÃO VICIADOS? Entender o fumo e o álcool como apego dos espíritos incorporantes à matéria é desconhecimento infantil acerca dos trabalhos magísticos caritativos realizados dentro do ritual de Umbanda. Eles não precisam desses elementos para si, utilizam-nos para a criação de um ritual. O álcool e o fumo são ferramentas de trabalho úteis e necessárias oferecidas pela natureza, e algumas vezes utilizadas por ter fácil combustão. Sempre que há excessos de beberagem é por conta do médium despreparado e mal orientado, e que sabe bem o que está fazendo.

MUITOS CLASSIFICAM A UMBANDA COMO "BAIXO ESPIRITISMO" POR CAUSA DA BEBIDA E DO FUMO DOS QUAIS FAZEM USO AS ENTIDADES. O uso do fumo e do álcool pelas Entidades que se manifestam na Umbanda leva os críticos da religião a classifica-la como "baixo espiritismo", assim como seus trabalhadores espirituais classificados em grau evolutivo inferior, e quem assim o faz compra o livro apenas pela capa sem se importar com o conteúdo. Criticam sem procurar conhecer sua essência e natureza, como o vaidoso que não tem interesse por nada que não seja o espelho.

COMO SE ARRANJA O MÉDIUM QUE NÃO É FUMANTE QUANDO INCORPORA UM GUIA QUE GOSTA DE FUMAR? Não há Guia que gosta de fumar. O cachimbo, charuto, cigarro de palha, cigarro com filtro, são defumadores individuais e utilizados apenas como instrumentos na ação dos trabalhos umbandistas. São usados com cuidado pelas Entidades que nunca tragam a fumaça, pois não são tabagistas.

TEM GUIA QUE TOMA QUANTIDADE CAVALAR DE BEBIDA. Nunca é o Guia. O próprio médium é que consome a bebida em quantidade despropositada. Neste caso pode ser que o Guia se afaste e deixe o médium com os efeitos da bebida que consumiu sem necessidade. Quando utilizada de fato pelo Guia, fica resquício mínimo da bebida no organismo do médium e não provoca nenhum prejuízo ao mesmo.

E O QUE SE PODE DIZER DOS GUIAS QUE INCORPORAM E JÁ PEDEM BEBIDA SENDO O DIRIGENTE DO TERREIRO OBRIGADO A NEGAR? Os exageros provêm de duas fontes: ou de médium despreparado e que presta um grande desserviço à religião de Umbanda, pois tais excessos são atribuídos pelos desavisados às Entidades trabalhadoras, e por isso taxadas injustamente de atrasadas e primitivas; ou provêm de espíritos mistificadores e aí o problema é o Dirigente incompetente, cujo comando é deficiente.

OS MARINHEIROS PARECEM SEMPRE EMBRIAGADOS. É a irradiação em que eles atuam que os fazem parecer bêbados. Aquele balanço é um ponto de descarrego no ambiente, esses trabalhadores trazem a energia e a vibração do mar. Muitos atuam normais, sem esse balanço. Marinheiro que se encharca de rum e cachaça, não existe. Existe médium despreparado.

HÁ DIRIGENTES QUE BEBEM BASTANTE QUANDO INCORPORADOS, PRINCIPALMENTE EM GIRA DE ESQUERDA. O Dirigente foi preparado por seus mentores e

Guias para a missão sacerdotal, tem o amparo direto da espiritualidade durante as Giras, pois a responsabilidade dele (ou dela) é total e é o para-raios das descargas do Terreiro, dos filhos da casa, dos visitantes encarnados e desencarnados, das irradiações pesadas e doentias dos que por ali passam. Portanto nunca se questiona a forma como ele ou ela dirige o trabalho. Os Exus e Pombogiras são os que fazem uso com mais frequência da bebida por serem trabalhadores com missões mais próximas às faixas vibratórias densas da Terra, e consequentemente necessitam das energias etéreas extraídas de matérias como alimentos e álcool para poderem realizar seus trabalhos que por falta de entendimento e palavra adequada chamamos "magia". O marafo (bebida alcoólica) sempre em pequenas quantidades, assim como a pólvora, são usados para limpar e descarregar os que procuram ajuda nos Terreiros.

LITURGIA, RITOS E SACRAMENTOS

Para conhecer mais sobre as Liturgias, Ritos e Sacramentos da Umbanda sugerimos a leitura do livro "Os Rituais de Umbanda"

SÓ A UMBANDA TEM RITUAL? O QUE É ISSO? Cada religião segue seus próprios rituais para comunicar-se com Deus através de atos, posturas e gestuais que demonstram devoção, e que podem ser entendidos como representação de humildade e agradecimento.

ASSENTAMENTO

O QUE É ASSENTAMENTO? A definição de assentamento é "força ou poder assentado". Mas o que é força e o que é poder? Quando na Umbanda se fala "**força**" faz referência às Entidades, ou seja, os Caboclos, Pretos Velhos, Crianças, Marinheiros, Boiadeiros, Baianos, Ciganos; e quando fala "**poder**" faz menção aos Orixás. O Assentamento traz a força (Linha de trabalho ou Guia espiritual) e o poder (Orixá) para dentro do Terreiro.

DE QUE MODO SE FAZ ASSENTAMENTO PARA GUIA OU ORIXÁ? Normalmente para assentar uma Força (Linha de Trabalho ou Guia espiritual) ou um Poder (Orixá), escolhe-se um ponto e ali se depositam certos elementos como pedras, ervas, símbolos, de modo a ter uma força maior dos Orixás ou das Entidades.

QUAL A FINALIDADE DO ASSENTAMENTO? A energia emanada do Assentamento passa a dar sustentação aos trabalhos espirituais e conceder proteção a Casa. **Sustentar** é dar apoio, segurança, amparo. Alguns chamam esse ponto apenas de Assentamento, outros de **Assentamento de Orixá**. O local escolhido é permanente, não deve ser mudado a não ser que o Terreiro mude de endereço físico.

QUANTOS ASSENTAMENTOS TÊM EM UM TERREIRO? Costuma-se ter no mínimo dois assentamentos: o "**Assentamento do Altar**" que é onde se assenta os elementos dos Orixás ou das Entidades, e o "**Assentamento da Tron-

queira" que visa à defesa energética do local e é onde se deposita os elementos ou ferramentas da Esquerda (Exu e Pombogira).

O ASSENTAMENTO FICA ESCONDIDO? O assentamento não fica às vistas dos frequentadores, mas não tem nada de misterioso ou perigoso que se deve esconder, é apenas usual que fique em local de pouco acesso.

O FUNDAMENTO SÓ PODE SER VISTO PELO DIRIGENTE? O fundamento de Assentamento não é ferramentas para uso somente de Dirigente nem se constitui em segredo, nada impede que o filho de fé peça ao Dirigente que mostre e ensine sobre os Assentamentos de sua Casa.

USA-SE SANGUE ANIMAL NO ASSENTAMENTO? Jamais. A Umbanda é uma religião que vivencia absolutamente a natureza, e deste modo nos cultos não se mata nem machuca nenhum ser vivo, **em nenhuma hipótese e sob nenhum pretexto**. Como a ideia dos assentamentos é influência do Candomblé, na Umbanda substituímos o sangue pelas ervas ou água.

O ASSENTAMENTO É FEITO DE IGUAL FORMA PARA TODOS OS ORIXÁS? Não. São feitos de acordo com o Orixá regente do Terreiro porque cada um tem suas ferramentas, seus elementos, cores, pedras, punhais, pontos riscados, terra, ervas, bebidas, fumo, pemba, enfim, são vários os elementos consagrados ao Orixá.

FIRMEZAS

O QUE SÃO FIRMEZAS? As Firmezas são diferentes do Assentamento porque são feitas para fins específicos. Por exemplo, quando se acende uma vela para o anjo de guarda de um ente querido pedindo proteção, se está direcionando e intensificando a energia mental de modo às súplicas chegarem até aquele que pode auxiliar. Ao acender a vela eleva-se o pensamento ao protetor espiritual ao qual o apelo é feito, e a energia emitida pela fé é vinculada a chama da vela. Ao terminar a prece a vela é deixada sobre um altar ou um móvel, e a vibração de amor, assim como a essência dos sentimentos emanados durante a prece, fica firmada na vela acesa. **Enquanto estiver acesa dela será irradiado constantemente o pedido de auxílio. Quando ela se acabar, a firmeza perderá a força.** A vela está firmada e não assentada, porque a irradiação só dura enquanto estiver acesa.

PARA QUAL FINALIDADE SÃO FEITAS AS FIRMEZAS? Podem ser feitas em casa para limpar o campo energético, para descarregar o ambiente, para ajudar o filho, esposa, marido, amigos. Podem ser firmadas para as Linhas de Trabalho, Orixás, santos, anjo de guarda, enfim, canalizada para onde estiver a devoção.

O QUE É FIRMEZA DE ESQUERDA? A Firmeza de Esquerda é igual ao explicado acima só que direcionada para Exu, Pombogira e Exu Mirim.

FIRMEZA PODE SER FEITA DENTRO DE CASA? Sim, apenas as Firmezas da Esquerda se recomenda fazer fora de casa.

E QUEM MORA EM APARTAMENTO E NÃO TEM QUINTAL? Nesse caso pode fazer atrás da porta da entrada, mas se não puder deixar vela acesa porque mora com outras pessoas que não compartilham da mesma crença pode também deixar na lavanderia. E se também na lavanderia não for possível pode deixar atrás da porta do próprio quarto.

DISSERAM-ME QUE NÃO PODE ACENDER VELA DENTRO DE CASA NEM MESMO PARA O ANJO DE GUARDA. Essa é opinião de alguns Espíritas para quem acender vela dentro de casa atraí espíritos perdidos, maneira de pensar que não é compartilhada pelos umbandistas. Toda vela que se acende tem um destinatário, ou acende para um Preto Velho ou para um Caboclo etc. Não há motivo para temer porque toda vela acesa com propósito nobre é uma Firmeza.

FIRMEZA E ASSENTAMENTO SÃO IGUAIS? Não. Firmeza é uma simplificação do Assentamento, mas tem as mesmas funções. Um ponto de sustentação é uma Firmeza. Um ponto de força é um Assentamento. A Firmeza pode ser iluminada de vez em quando ou somente quando se fizer algum pedido à Entidade firmada. O Assentamento deve ser realimentado constantemente e geralmente em dia da semana definido. Tanto o Assentamento quanto a Firmeza tem a função de amparar e proteger.

TRONQUEIRA

O QUE É TRONQUEIRA? Tronqueira, também chamada Canjira, é uma casinha que fica assentada do lado esquerdo da entrada de todo Terreiro. É nessa "casinha" onde está o Assentamento do Exu Guardião e da Pombogira Guardiã do médium Dirigente, cuja função, entre tantas outras, é tomar conta da entrada. Tronqueira um portal que impede as forças hostis se servirem do ambiente religioso de forma deturpada. É para a Tronqueira que os fluidos negativos são atraídos e dali dispersados para as profundezas da terra (como se fosse um fio terra).

BATER CABEÇA

O QUE É BATER CABEÇA? "Bater cabeça" é o ato em que o médium se prostra no chão ou simplesmente se encurva frente ao Gongá.

EM QUAIS LUGARES SE BATE CABEÇA NO TERREIRO DE UMBANDA? Na Umbanda se "bate cabeça" defronte ao Gongá (altar) e os Atabaques, e aos pés ou diante do Dirigente dependendo do costume da Casa. É preciso entender que quando se ajoelha em frente ao Dirigente ninguém está prostrado diante do homem ou da mulher que dirige o Terreiro (e que é um ser humano cheio de defeitos como os médiuns), mas em reverência aos Orixás, ao Guia chefe do Terreiro e a toda corrente espiritual **representada naquele momento pelo Dirigente**.

O MÉDIUM PRECISA BATER CABEÇA NO GONGÁ? Não precisa, mas bate em sinal de humildade e reverência. É um gesto simbólico que representa o oferecimento de seu Orí (Coroa) para o Orixá e seus enviados. É também um pedido de benção.

CRUZAR

O QUE É CRUZAR? Cruzar significa formar cruz. A cruz é o símbolo de Omulu/Obaluaiê, o Orixá das passagens, dos entrecruzamentos. Quando se chega ao Terreiro saúdam-se as forças do Alto e do Embaixo, da Esquerda e da Direita que tomam conta da Casa, desenhando com os dedos, no chão, o símbolo da cruz. **Com esse rito o médium atravessa o portal dos mundos, e o sinal da cruz é a chave que abre a porta da passagem.** Objetos também podem ser entregues aos Guias para que sejam cruzados, de modo a empregar neles a força da Entidade que lhe é própria e ligar ao poder que rege o Terreiro.

AO ENTRAR NO TERREIRO SÓ CRUZAR COM OS DEDOS O SOLO BASTA? Sim, mas muitas pessoas fazem uma oração que ajuda a se concentrar no propósito, dizendo *"Eu saúdo o seu alto, o seu embaixo, a sua direita e a sua esquerda e peço em nome de Omulu/Obaluaiê que se abra o portal do sagrado para mim"*.

CONSAGRAR

O QUE É CONSAGRAR? Consagrar é tornar sagrado. Ele deixa de ser profano e passa a ser sagrado, ou seja, deixa de pertencer ao mundo material e passa a pertencer ao plano espiritual. Por exemplo, as Guias são simples colares, mas quando consagradas adquirem poder de resguardar o médium contra ataques de ordem mental ou espiritual.

IMANTAR

O QUE É IMANTAR? A palavra imantar vem de "imã" e quer dizer "magnetizar". Magnetizar significa "exercer poderosa atração sobre algo". Dessa forma entende-se por imantar o ato de transportar uma força ou poder de uma pessoa ou objeto para outro, por exemplo, pode-se dar uma Guia para um Preto Velho imantar e assim será agregada a força dele ao objeto.

QUAL É A DIFERENÇA ENTRE CRUZAR, CONSAGRAR E IMANTAR? Cruzar está associado a cruz, então quando se diz que um objeto foi cruzado significa que ele foi vinculado às forças que regem o Terreiro ou que regem o médium. **Consagrar** significa tornar sagrado, então quando se diz que um objeto foi consagrado significa que ele se tornou sagrado para o médium e para a Umbanda. **Imantar** vem da palavra imã, então quando se diz que um objeto foi imantado significa que ele foi carregado de um poder ou de uma força.

SACUDIMENTO

O QUE É RITUAL DE BATE FOLHA OU SACUDIMENTO? O Bate Folha, também chamado de **SACUDIMENTO**, é um ritual cuja finalidade é descarregar o ambiente ou pessoas, fazendo uma limpeza ou reorganização energética, geralmente utilizando um amarrado de ervas da escolha da Entidade que está dirigindo o ritual, geralmente feito durante as Giras com ervas apropriadas para cada situação. O termo Sacudimento é mais comum no Candomblé, mas também é utilizado na Umbanda.

Passe

O QUE É PASSE UMBANDISTA? O passe é a sintonia da mente do Guia com a mente de quem o recebe, formando entre ambos uma corrente mental através da qual o Guia emite energia para a pessoa. É certo dizer que o Guia faz uma transfusão de energia (igual a uma transfusão de sangue) com a finalidade de rearmonizar seu corpo, mente e alma. O Guia pode retirar a energia doada de seu próprio corpo astral ou da Natureza, e emanar para os centros vitais de quem recebe o passe. Na Umbanda aprendemos que em uma simples troca de olhar, num mero aperto de mão, na relação sexual ou num inocente abraço a troca energética acontece. Portanto, orai e vigiai.

Roupa Branca

POR QUE USA ROUPA BRANCA? Usa-se o branco por duas razões. A primeira é que o branco é a soma de todas as cores, por isso é a cor que representa Oxalá que é considerado o Orixá Maior na Umbanda. A segunda razão nos remete ao dia 16 de novembro de 1908, dia da fundação da Umbanda pelo Caboclo das Sete Encruzilhadas quando foi determinado que os filhos de fé sempre vestissem branco durante os cultos, muito provavelmente porque assim há igualdade entre todos, não havendo nada que diferencie os umbandistas. Todos vestidos igualmente não há distinção social nem se evidenciam disparidade financeira, são somente humildes servidores da Fraternidade e Caridade em nome do Amor.

O QUE É DEFUMAÇÃO? A defumação, também chamada **incenso**, é um elemento importantíssimo em qualquer Terreiro de Umbanda porque, junto com os Pontos Cantados, harmoniza o ambiente e modifica de modo a equilibrar o estado de consciência dos médiuns e assistidos a fim de receber os Guias que vão ali praticar a caridade. A queima de ervas e resina é depurador que desmancha a couraça de energias negativas que envolvem muitos dos assistidos, e permite que a Gira comece a receber as vibrações dos Orixás e da corrente espiritual da Casa. Na Umbanda cada erva tem um significado e poder, e **a principal função da defumação é perfumar, limpar e harmonizar o ambiente e dissipar as energias negativas**. A maioria usa benjoim, alecrim, alfazema, arruda, guiné, manjericão e palha de alho.

BANHOS

O QUE É BANHO RITUALÍSTICO? Banho Ritualístico é literalmente um banho que se toma com ervas, folhas ou flores misturadas à água, a fim de promover a troca energética entre a pessoa e a natureza, cuja finalidade é normalizar as forças espiritual, física, emocional e mental daquele que se banha. Há quatro tipos de Banhos Ritualísticos na Umbanda, denominados Banho de Descarrego, Banho de Defesa, Banho de Energização e Banho de Fixação, todos fundamentais para os médiuns porque com ele há troca ou reposição das energias.

PARA QUE SERVEM OS BANHOS COM ERVAS? Servem para harmonizar o corpo astral do médium e sintonizá-lo com seus Guias.

QUAL A FINALIDADE DO BANHO DE DESCARREGO OU BANHO DE DESCARGA? São feitos com a finalidade de livrar a pessoa de cargas energéticas negativas. No presente plano evolutivo todos estão interligados através dos pensamentos, são reféns de suas palavras, atos e intenções de modo que vai criando uma "casca" que se gruda no corpo astral. Dois tipos comuns de Banhos de Descarrego são os que usam sal grosso e os que utilizam as ervas.

QUAL A FINALIDADE DO BANHO DE DEFESA OU BANHO DE PROTEÇÃO? Tem como finalidade empregar as propriedades energéticas e fitoterápicas de plantas e raízes com o objetivo de reequilibrar os corpos físico, emocional, mental e espiritual.

PARA QUE SERVEM OS BANHOS DE ENERGIZAÇÃO? São para fortalecer principalmente o mental de modo a facilitar a incorporação e conseguir melhor sintonia com os Guias. Também são feitos por quem deseja ou precisa se harmonizar com seu Orixá e Guia de Frente, **portanto quando o médium vai trabalhar em Gira de Umbanda o Banho de Energização é indispensável**. Também é aconselhado quando a pessoa precisa mais força de si própria ou encorajamento.

O QUE SÃO BANHOS DE FIXAÇÃO? São banhos preparados que "abrem" todos os chacras e deixa aguçada a percepção mediúnica, por isso são **feitos apenas por médiuns e somente quando vão participar de Giras fechadas aos assistidos**.

O QUE SÃO BANHOS NATURAIS? Além dos banhos preparados há os Banhos Naturais, que são aqueles realizados em locais de vibração da natureza e considerados excelentes para equilíbrio dos corpos físico, mental emocional e espiritual. **ÁGUA DE MAR:** é ótima para descarrego e para energização, faz vibrar a energia de Yemanjá. **ÁGUA DE CACHOEIRA:** a água que bate nas pedras é um poderoso "desinfetante" de impurezas, sob a vibração de Oxum. A queda d'água em contato com o corpo descarrega e restitui energias. **ÁGUA DE RIOS E LAGOAS:** é amplamente conhecida por ter emanações de cura. Se o rio tiver **pouco movimento**, com as águas quase paradas como a lagoa ou mangue, tem energia purificadora e curadora. Se o **rio tiver corredeira** e a lagoa movimento, a energia da água é energética e equilibradora. **ÁGUA DE MINERAL/MINA:** equilibra os chacras com a harmonização de Oxalá e Nanã. **ÁGUA DE POÇO:** é recomendada para os males no físico, mas também desajustes no corpo espiritual porque tem a força transformadora e curadora de Omulu. **ÁGUA DE CHUVA:** energiza e purifica. Depois de cair no chão é muito indicada para descarrego de ambientes internos com a vibração de Iansã.

COMO SÃO ESCOLHIDAS AS ERVAS USADAS NOS BANHOS E DEFUMAÇÕES? As ervas são escolhidas para serem queimadas na defumação ou usadas nos banhos de acordo com o objetivo que se quer obter, por essa razão utilizam-se mais de um tipo de erva ao mesmo tempo.

Gongá

O QUE É GONGÁ? Gongá é ponto principal de Axé no Terreiro também chamado de Congá, Altar, Peji e Jacutá. É um ponto de grande força e poder de onde irradiam as vibrações que favorecem a realização das Giras. O Gongá, para efeito de entendimento, age durante a Gira como um reservatório de distribuição onde a energia espiritual e mental de todas as orações, cânticos de louvor, pontos cantados, força de cada pensamento, emanações mentais dos encarnados e desencarnados e as súplicas são concentradas e depois de tratadas são distribuídas aos médiuns e assistidos.

QUAL É A DIFERENÇA ENTRE GONGÁ E TRONQUEIRA? O Gongá e a Tronqueira são campos de força do Terreiro, sendo que o primeiro irradia energias positivas a todos e o segundo absorve as energias negativas de todos, de modo que a força no Terreiro, mesmo que ninguém veja, está atuante e em grande movimento, ajudando a todos.

COMO DEVE SER MONTADO UM GONGÁ? Não há uma forma predeterminada de como montar um gongá. **O gongá deve ser feito como manda o coração, seguindo como regra a simplicidade.** Gongá não é para ostentar riqueza, não é para alimentar orgulho, não é para chamar atenção nem exaltar vaidade.

O QUE É PONTO DE AXÉ DE UM TERREIRO? Dos Orixás são emanados o poder, a energia e a força presentes em cada ser humano e em cada entidade e matéria existentes no Universo. A essa emanação que ampara homens e mulheres se dá o nome de Axé. Pode ser representado por um objeto imantado e consagrado, e que por isso está carregado com a energia dos Orixás ou Guias espirituais. O Gongá é um ponto de Axé.

Gira

O QUE É GIRA? Gira refere-se à Sessão umbandista com cânticos e danças para cultuar as Entidades e Orixás, e também designa a "corrente espiritual". Embora seja variada nos diversos Terreiros quanto ao ritmo e costumes, é consenso que há três tipos básicos: Gira Festiva, Gira de Desenvolvimento e Gira de caridade.

O QUE É GIRA FESTIVA? É aquela em que se comemoram datas específicas do calendário umbandista, como a Festa das Crianças (Erês) com farta distribuição de doces.

O QUE É GIRA DE DESENVOLVIMENTO? É reservada apenas para os "filhos da Casa", não tendo a participação de assistidos, ocasião em que se dedica exclusivamente ao "desenvolvimento" mediúnico dos médiuns iniciantes, bem como das práticas ritualísticas do Terreiro.

O QUE É GIRA DE CARIDADE? É a que se dedica ao atendimento das pessoas em geral feito pelas Entidades trabalhadoras em auxílio dos que procuram amparo, sempre fiel ao compromisso com a Caridade. Nela, os assistidos conversam com Entidades como Preto Velho, Caboclo, etc., com o propósito de obter ajuda e conselho para suas vidas, cura de males físicos e problemas espirituais diversos.

QUAL É A FORMA CORRETA DE FAZER UMA GIRA DE UMBANDA? A forma correta é como é feita em cada um dos Terreiros e ninguém deve julgar porque seria uma intromissão injustificável. A maneira como é conduzida a Gira em cada Terreiro só diz respeito ao Dirigente e aos trabalhadores no nível terreno e espiritual.

POR QUE HÁ TANTAS DIFERENÇAS DE CULTO DE UM TERREIRO PARA O OUTRO? A Umbanda é uma religião genuinamente brasileira que nasceu sob a influência das religiões africana, católica, espírita, e devido a essas diferenças há Terreiros que tenderão a exaltar mais uma ou outra influência. Quando um umbandista sente o chamado e funda um novo Terreiro, traz consigo a raiz da casa de onde veio, o modo como os trabalhos eram conduzidos lá e, não raro, todo o rito. Com o tempo vai percebendo qual é necessidade missionária de sua própria missão e vai adequando o culto aos objetivos da corrente espiritual do seu próprio Terreiro.

HÁ QUANTAS CORRENTES DE CULTO DE UMBANDA? Muitas, porém algumas usam o nome de Umbanda e fazem sacrifício de animais, trabalhos de amarração e cobram pelos atendimentos, e estas **NÃO SÃO** Umbanda sob nenhum argumento nem justificativa. Apropriaram-se indevidamente do nome de linda religião que só faz o bem e a caridade.

POR QUE HÁ GIRAS ESPECÍFICAS DE EXU UMA VEZ AO MÊS? É importante que haja para descarregar, expurgar, encaminhar e limpar o Terreiro e os médiuns dos trabalhos feitos durante o mês. Exus e Pombogiras são os que dão o primeiro combate às forças sombrias, são eles também que trazem as ordens dos Orixás para os níveis mais baixos em que estão os seres humanos, lembrando que são os executores do carma e atuam para o desmanche de trabalhos trevosos. Naturalmente é necessário Gira específica e frequente para limpeza e descarrego.

POR QUE O MÉDIUM TRABALHA DESCALÇO NAS GIRAS? Nem todos trabalham descalços, mas o ideal é que não se use nenhum tipo de calçado, primeiro por uma questão de humildade, segundo porque facilita a incorporação, e por último porque além de descarregar mais facilmente as energias pesadas no solo também capta a vibração positiva que vem do chão.

POR QUE HÁ CERTAS GIRAS EM QUE OS MÉDIUNS SAEM ESGOTADÍSSIMOS? São vários os motivos. Os médiuns iniciantes gastam muita energia no processo de captar e entender as ideias recebidas dos Guias. Outra causa pode ser a falta de preparação adequada do médium, como por exemplo, não tomar o banho de ervas antes dos trabalhos, pois muitos não entendem a importância da energia das ervas no perispírito e não se preparam adequadamente. Entidades mal intencionadas também "sugam" a energia do médium. Em um determinado momento do trabalho em Gira aberta o Guia chefe da cabeça do médium toma a frente do trabalho, capta sua energia espiritual e a distribui entre todos os trabalhadores da corrente mediúnica, de modo a formar um escudo de proteção com a finalidade de proteger o campo astral dos médiuns da corrente da ação de espíritos desordeiros e sofredores. Em trabalhos muito "pesados" a energia recolhida é grande, o que também desgasta o médium.

Amací

O QUE É AMACÍ? É um banho ritual de lavagem de cabeça, para limpar o campo energético do médium afim de melhor aproximação de energias dos Espíritos mais elevados da Umbanda. Os que não são médiuns e nem participam como trabalhadores da corrente espiritual também podem fazer o Amací, e é uma boa oportunidade para limpar o campo energético do corpo e trazer fluídos melhores (devem estar vestidos com roupa branca). Acontece anualmente com a finalidade de preparar os médiuns para receber as energias do Terreiro de forma mais intensa, e também entrar em contato direto com o poder de seu Orixá de frente. É feito com folhas maceradas que se deixa repousar após colheita, pedindo a proteção de Ossaîn, Orixá responsável pelas ervas e folhas. Escolhidas as plantas conforme a orientação do Dirigente ou do Guia Chefe do médium, são maceradas na água de cachoeiras, nascentes ou rios e que tem por finalidade a lavagem de cabeça do médium, pois é onde vibra o Orixá. Pode-se dizer que este é o primeiro sacramento da Umbanda.

SE EU FIZER O AMACÍ ESTAREI COMPROMETIDO E NUNCA PODEREI SAIR DA UMBANDA? É importante salientar que o Amací não é um compromisso perpétuo com a religião e nem tampouco com o Terreiro, e que nada na Umbanda prende o filho de fé, portanto nada que se faça é uma responsabilidade pétrea da qual não será possível desistir quando quiser.

DEITADA

O QUE É DEITADA? Não são todos os Terreiros que adotam o ritual chamado **D**EITADA PARA O **O**RIXÁ ou **D**EITADA PARA O **S**ANTO. Consiste em rito onde o médium fica recolhido durante algumas horas sobre uma esteira, podendo ser no espaço das Giras próximo ao altar ou em outro local determinado pelo Dirigente porque varia de acordo com o Terreiro. A finalidade da Deitada é proporcionar ao médium caminho para reflexão através de poderosa conexão com seus Orixás, Guias e seu próprio Orí (cabeça). Nesse ritual o médium fica recolhido durante algumas horas, e nessa comunhão com os Mentores o médium eleva seus padrões mentais e espirituais, adquirindo condições de receber orientação do alto.

COROAÇÃO

O QUE É COROAÇÃO? Coroação é um tipo de "Primeira Comunhão" na Umbanda, um ritual fundamental e muito emocionante porque simboliza o desenvolvimento do médium, um rito de passagem que ele alcançou mediante esforço e dedicação. Representa o ponto em que médium e Guias juntos já possuem domínio suficiente para desenvolverem bom trabalho de caridade desinteressada. Em algumas Casas é no dia da Coroação que o Guia Chefe incorpora e se apresenta por inteiro, ocasião em que reafirma seu nome (porque já o terá feito antes), risca o ponto, apresenta a Falange na qual trabalha. Então, simbolicamente, ao som de cânticos entoados por todos os presentes, o Guia Chefe da Direita do Terreiro coloca no Orí (cabeça) do médium incorporado uma Coroa quase sempre confeccionada com folhas e ervas trançadas, que **simboliza a ligação afetiva e moral do médium com seus Guias espirituais,** assim como a união e respeito de todos, médiuns e Entidades, aos Orixás e a corrente mediúnica do Terreiro. Ao coroar o Guia Chefe do médium e o próprio médium ao mesmo tempo, tem a beleza da virtude que se conquista através do trabalho desinteressado em benefício de todos os irmãos, filhos de Oxalá.

O MÉDIUM QUE FAZ A COROAÇÃO TORNA-SE SACERDOTE DE UMBANDA? Não tem nenhuma relação com a formação sacerdotal. A Coroação é o subir de mais um degrau na imensa escadaria do crescimento espiritual.

Batizado, Casamento e Funeral

O QUE É O BATIZADO NA UMBANDA? Nas religiões de origem africana **a finalidade do batizado é criar um laço entre o ser humano e seu Orixá, tornando o corpo um verdadeiro altar.** Na Umbanda o batismo é ritual sagrado e simbólico que significa submissão da criatura humana a Olorum (Deus). É a invocação das bênçãos divinas de Oxalá, um ato de amor aos Orixás e aos Guias de Luz, reafirmando na cerimônia o compromisso por toda a existência carnal com a Caridade. Ao receber o batismo o batizado aceita de boa vontade o trabalho e dedicação para com a religião de Umbanda. O batismo acontece na Umbanda, além de opção pessoal do médium ou assistido que queira adotar a Umbanda como religião, também por opção dos pais quando do nascimento da criança. *"O batismo é, portanto, uma apresentação às divindades da Umbanda, para que enviem as suas vibrações ao espírito encarnado e assim ele passe a receber a proteção dos Orixás. O espírito e o mental do que foi batizado passam a ser amoldados sutilmente na nova vida, na nova religião, revestidos com uma aura protetora divina."*

PODEM SER REALIZADOS OS CASAMENTO NA UMBANDA? Sim, pode e deve. O Brasil é um estado laico, que significa não pertencente a uma religião e nem tampouco ser sujeito a ela, onde por lei há liberdade para os cidadãos manifestarem a sua fé religiosa qualquer que seja ela, sem haver controle ou imposição de uma religião específica. Muitos umbandistas, talvez por desconhecimento de que a Umbanda tem seus ritos e sacramentos próprios, ainda se casam na igreja católica, lá batizam suas crianças, porém as religiões de matriz africana tem todo o respaldo legal para realizar tais atos tanto quanto cerimônias realizadas em catedrais, mesquitas, sinagogas e templos. **Os umbandistas tem que casar em seus Terreiros, batizar os filhos e a sí mesmos reafirmado no ato do batismo e do casamento a entrega e amor aos Orixás por escolha pessoal,** porque casamento na Umbanda não é considerado um dever religioso. As formalidades do registro civil precisam ser observadas para que a cerimônia seja reconhecida, e então, no lugar de um juiz de paz a união é realizada por um Sacerdote de Umbanda. **Não é preciso nem é correto o umbandista recorrer a outras religiões para realizar seus rituais e cerimônias.**

O QUE É FUNERAL NA UMBANDA? Funeral é um ritual religioso de despedida que se realiza logo após a morte de um ser humano. A morte para os umbandistas é apenas a passagem da dimensão terrena para a dimensão espiritual, onde os que desprendem do corpo serão sustentados pela vibração de Omulu/Obaluaiê, que é quem rege o instante da passagem do corpo material para o espiritual. Guardião dos Mortos e das Almas, são seus falangeiros e capangueiros que amparam os seres no momento do desenlace, afim de que o espírito possa cortar os laços de apego com esse mundo e com seu corpo físico. A grande maioria precisa de ajuda e amparo, pois o processo de desligamento é difícil, principalmente porque as pessoas estão ligadas vibratoriamente ao planeta. Oyá Iansã, a Senhora dos espíritos dos mortos, é quem vibra sobre os desencarnados emanando os fluidos necessários de modo a encaminhá-los aos seus planos espirituais correspondentes. É Iansã quem servirá de guia, ao lado de Omulu/Obaluaiê, e indicará o caminho a ser percorrido pelas almas de acordo com o merecimento. O afastamento dos obsessores sempre é feito com o indispensável auxílio desta Ayabá, pois atormentadores não obsediam somente os que estão sob a proteção do corpo físico, simplesmente o fazem com sentimentos, pensamentos fixos, atraindo para perto também os já desencarnados.

ORGANIZAÇÃO, CARGOS E PRÁTICA

Para conhecer mais sobre a organização, os cargos e as práticas da Umbanda sugerimos a leitura do livro "Os Rituais de Umbanda"

DIRIGENTE

O QUE É DIRIGENTE? Dirigente também é chamado de Sacerdote, Pai ou Mãe de Terreiro, Pai ou Mãe do Santo, Padrinho ou Madrinha de Umbanda, Chefe de Terreiro, Zelador(a) de Santo e Cacique de Umbanda. São termos usados para designar a pessoa responsável ou que possui autoridade máxima na Casa, e deve dirigir e comandar os trabalhos espirituais. O ideal é que o Terreiro tenha um líder e não um chefe, devido ao espírito de liberdade que predomina na Umbanda.

TODO MÉDIUM TEM A POSSIBILIDADE DE SER SACERDOTE? Sim. Basta querer. Os fundamentos necessários para abrir uma Casa de Umbanda são ensinados pelos Pais ou Mães do Santo aos seus filhos e filhas de fé que manifestem vontade de ter seu próprio Terreiro, mas infelizmente alguns se sentem ameaçados e tendem a isolar o médium com o pensamento de que este quer tomar seu lugar, pensamento mesquinho e despropositado que se torna uma das causas de número reduzido de Terreiros da religião de Umbanda.

QUAL É A MAIOR E MAIS PENOSA FUNÇÃO DO DIRIGENTE? Ajudar o filho de fé desenvolver raciocínio coerente para que não caia nos excessos da superstição. Ao Chefe da

Casa cabe exercer a capacidade de julgamento sem considerar simpatia ou antipatia pessoal. Os ensinamentos que os verdadeiros Dirigentes passam aos médiuns é a necessidade de desvincular a fé da paixão que gera o fanatismo, fé fundamentada na reflexão e no pensamento analítico, longe de cegas crenças, de lorota sem base na razão ou no conhecimento que levam a criar falsas obrigações e a temer coisas inócuas. Difícil missão haja à vista que muitos também creem em coisas equivocadas. Eles têm a função de cuidar e zelar da vida espiritual dos médiuns, orientar e dirigir os trabalhos abertos e fechados ao público. São os responsáveis por fazer cumprir as diretrizes estabelecidas pelo Astral.

É PRECISO ESTUDAR PARA SER DIRIGENTE? Na religião de Umbanda muitos Dirigentes não têm nenhum tipo de graduação porque quase não há cursos destinados a tal atividade (e os poucos disponíveis são pagos), sendo seus conhecimentos adquiridos na prática.

POR QUE ALGUNS DIRIGENTES NÃO ADMITEM QUE OS FILHOS DA CASA VISITEM OUTROS TERREIROS? É PREJUDICIAL O UMBANDISTA IR À CASA DE UMBANDA QUE NÃO SEJA A SUA? O Católico não é proibido de frequentar igreja além de sua paróquia, o Protestante pode tranquilamente participar de outros cultos, judeus são bem vindos em qualquer sinagoga, os rituais budistas estão abertos a todos os visitantes e o mesmo nas mesquitas dos muçulmanos. Alguns Dirigentes de Umbanda realmente fazem restrição que seus seguidores frequentem outros Terreiros, quase sempre alegando que a "energia" do outro "atrapalha". Porém, sendo a Umbanda *"a manifestação do Espírito para a caridade"*, trata-se de argumento insustentável, é igual dizer que só em seu Terreiro há "a verdadeira Umbanda", sendo que nos outros lugares há emanações ruins. Geralmente o que de fato atrapalha é o temor que alguns têm de "perder" seus seguidores para outros Terreiros. Aí prejudicial não é o lugar e sim a insegurança.

Mãe Pequena e Pai Pequeno

O QUE É MÃE PEQUENA E PAI PEQUENO? Há uma hierarquia dentro dos Terreiros de Umbanda, visando a organização e disciplina, sem as quais não seria viável seu pleno funcionamento. O Dirigente, ou Pai e Mãe do Santo, é a autoridade máxima e responsável por tudo o que ocorre nas Giras. O Pai Pequeno ou Mãe Pequena são as segundas pessoas no comando, cuja função é substituir o Dirigente em sua ausência, e com a obrigação indiscutível de fazer com que tudo ocorra rigorosamente dentro da linha determinada pelo líder principal. Em algumas Casas o Pai Pequeno, *Bàbá Kékere*, e a Mãe Pequena, *Ìyá Kékere*, são escolhidos pelo Dirigente.

Cambone

O QUE É CAMBONE? Cambones ou Cambonos(as) são médiuns de sustentação que não incorporam. Auxiliam o chefe de Terreiro e o Guia Chefe garantindo segurança, firmeza e proteção para os médiuns de atendimento, para os assistidos e para o trabalho de um modo geral. É o(a) Cambone quem atende os

Guias Espirituais incorporados em suas necessidades materiais. Também cabe ao Cambone fiscalizar o comportamento de todos dentro do Terreiro, incluindo aí as Entidades trabalhadoras para certificar que nada saia da normalidade, e caso aconteça é sua obrigação acionar a direção do Terreiro. Importante salientar que Cambone é médium de sustentação e auxiliar dos trabalhadores, e não empregado ou serviçal de ninguém. Como é responsável por zelar pelos Axés dentro do Terreiro é preciso que seja de absoluta confiança do Dirigente da Casa.

OGÃS OU CURIMBEIROS

O QUE É CURIMBEIRO OU OGÃ? Ogãs, Curimbeiros ou Tabaqueiros são os médiuns que não incorporam. Responsáveis pelo canto e pelo toque (ritmo) nos Atabaques, a maioria é intuitiva e sacerdote nato, cuja missão espiritual é "falar" pelo Orixá porque suas mãos são instrumentos de comunicação entre o mundo visível e invisível. Em muitos Terreiros é Coroado como Ogã para exercer a função.

CURIMBEIROS TAMBÉM TÊM OS SEUS GUIAS E ORIXÁS? Sim, apenas não se apresentam de modo a serem reconhecidos através da incorporação. São Entidades espirituais que auxiliam nos ritmos dos atabaques e considerados Guardiões dos mistérios que envolvem os Pontos Cantados. Forma corrente espiritual de mestres da música que conhecem o som sagrado dos tambores.

POR QUE AS PESSOAS CANTAM E BATEM PALMAS JUNTO COM OS ATABAQUES? O ritmo das curimbas (atabaques), unido ao movimento da dança e da música juntamente com as palmas que as acompanham, induz a um estado de percepção aumentada. A Umbanda utiliza amplamente as danças e tambores rítmicos para provocar o estado de consciência no qual os médiuns entram em contato com seus Guias, facilitando a incorporação. Os tambores estimulam a sensibilidade e permitem que energias individuais e coletivas se unam nos rituais de Umbanda, tornando os Ogãs os "cavalos" que levam os médiuns em viagens a outros círculos de consciência.

QUAL É A FUNÇÃO DOS OGÃS? Durante a Gira os Ogãs marcam cada parte do ritual, por exemplo, a defumação, abertura, chamada, sustentação e subida das Entidades, e fechamento do ritual. São polos captadores e distribuidores de energia de formidável ajuda aos médiuns, porque estão em compasso com todos os trabalhadores da corrente mediúnica do Terreiro, físicos e espirituais. Pelas mãos dos Ogãs os Pontos Cantados transmutam-se de meras músicas em poderosas preces cantadas.

OGÃS DEVEM SER SEMPRE DO SEXO MASCULINO? No Candomblé sim, porém não na Umbanda, onde não há distinção de gênero. Homens e mulheres podem igualmente ocupar todos os cargos no Terreiro.

OGÃS MULHERES TOCAM BEM A CURIMBA? Tão bem quanto os homens.

DIZEM QUE AS MULHERES NÃO TÊM FORÇA FÍSICA PARA BATER NO COURO DO TAMBOR COM AS MÃOS. Não se tocam os atabaques com força como se estivesse ali desabafando mágoas e frustrações. Não se descarrega força física nos tambores. Os atabaques devem ser tocados com amor e fé, é preciso dialogar com eles. Os tambores são segredos que só os Ogãs que nasceram com a missão sabem desvendar, independente do gênero ao qual pertença.

Atabaques ou Curimbas

O QUE É CURIMBA OU ATABAQUE? Os atabaques vieram com os africanos que falavam a língua yorubá, de onde vem o culto dos Orixás, e se chama "Rum", que significa tambor grande, "Rumpi" que designa o tambor médio, "Runlé ou Lé", nome dado ao menor tambor dos três. **A denominação "atabaque" foi dada em nosso país. Outras culturas africanas diferentes que vieram para o Brasil utilizam outros tambores com formas diferentes, geralmente chamados "Engomas".**

POR QUE FOI ESCOLHIDO O ATABAQUE SE EXISTEM INÚMEROS INSTRUMENTOS? Na África o toque dos atabaques comunicava todos os acontecimentos sociais, nascimento, casamento, morte, plantio, colheita e para cada acontecimento existia um som diferente. Herdeira dos ritos e tradições religiosas africanas, a Umbanda utiliza os atabaques muito além do simples instrumentos de percussão. Os atabaques são tão importantes na liturgia da religião de Umbanda que os próprios Guias quando chegam cumprimentam o Gongá e depois os Atabaques, e ao se despedir, fazem o mesmo ritual. Durante as Giras são tocados para manter a vibração harmônica e equilibrada, e auxilia o corpo mediúnico a permanecer em concentração mental.

ALGUNS CRÍTICOS DA UMBANDA, EM ESPECIAL OS ADEPTOS DO ESPIRITISMO, GOSTAM DE AFIRMAR QUE TEMPO VIRÁ EM QUE SERÃO ABOLIDOS OS "BARULHENTOS ATABAQUES" E OS GUIAS TRABALHADORES ESTARÃO "EM SILÊNCIO SENTADOS AO REDOR DE UMA MESA", A EXEMPLO DO QUE OCORRE EM SEUS CENTROS. Entendendo como sendo a sua a "mais perfeita filosofia/religião que Deus ofereceu ao homem para lhe servir de guia e modelo", quais os donos de escravos que proibiam expressamente a dança e música dos negros com a alegação de que produzia som demoníaco e horroroso, os assustados "senhores de engenho modernos" jamais criticaram o instrumento musical chamado Órgão, por muito tempo indispensável nas igrejas católicas, nem os sinos e mais recentemente o violão. Nem se ouve murmúrio sobre os conjuntos instrumentais que alegram os cultos neopentecostais. Pois bem, da mesma forma que os sinos dobram nas igrejas chamando os fiéis para as missas, os atabaques chamam os Guias e a força dos Orixás, e pelas mãos dos Ogãs os filhos de fé podem vislumbrar uma ínfima parte do mistério espiritual conhecido somente pelos Orixás, que são manifestações da consciência divina.

SE ALGUNS ADEPTOS DO ESPIRITISMO SÃO TÃO CRUÉIS COM A UMBANDA EM SEUS JULGAMENTOS, POR QUE SOMOS ACONSELHADOS A ESTUDAR OS SEUS LIVROS? A reposta foi dada pelo próprio Codificador quando disse que Espiritismo não é a ideia de uma única pessoa (e muito menos a dele), mas a essência das instruções ditadas pelos Espíritos superiores. Assim, a obra Espírita não lhes pertence. Acrescenta Allan Kardec que qualquer pessoa pode estudar seus ensinamentos, pois os conhecimentos ali expostos encontram-se no livro da natureza. Os que pretendem ser exclusivos não devem ser levados a sério, estão engatinhando espiritualmente.

POR QUE EXISTE TANTO PRECONCEITO EM RELAÇÃO À MÚSICA NA UMBANDA SE MUITAS OUTRAS RELIGIÕES TAMBÉM FAZEM USO? O atabaque já era usado pelo Candomblé de antigamente e pelos escravos, portanto discriminado pela hierarquia branca da igreja católica. Consequentemente, a "boa sociedade" passou a pensar nele como instrumento de negro, coisa do demônio, objeto de macumba, claro que carregado de todo preconceito e discriminação tão profundamente enraizado quanto a cara de pau dos que, mentindo, negam que tem preconceito racial. No Antigo Testamento existem várias menções não só ao tambor, mas vários outros instrumentos utilizados em louvores a Deus. No Novo Testamento foram suprimidos em benefício da voz humana, inclusive o Órgão foi abolido dos cultos porque os padres consideravam profanos devido a serem utilizados nos cabarés, e com o passar dos anos foram readmitidos. A música que agradava a Deus no Antigo Testamento envolvia o uso de vários instrumentos de música, inclusive os desprestigiados tambores.

POR QUE TODOS NOS TERREIROS DE UMBANDA SÃO CONVIDADOS A ACOMPANHAR OS PONTOS CANTADOS COM PALMAS? Quando se inicia a Gira as palmas não são compassadas, alguns batem mais rápido que outros, cantam em tom mais alto ou fora do momento. Passados poucos minutos o ritmo e o tempo vão se afinando entre todos. É nesse momento que os problemas vividos durante o dia e a correria do cotidiano vão se assentando. A frequência cardíaca, ou seja, a quantidade de vezes que o coração bate por minuto, desacelera acompanhando a cadência das palmas, começa a haver mudança de atividade no cérebro, o médium aos poucos ingressa em estado diferenciado de consciência que propiciará a sintonia com seu Guia de trabalho, e logo toda a corrente de trabalho do Terreiro está em sintonia. Os assistidos, harmonizados com os cantos, o soar dos atabaques e as palmas, permanecem equilibrados devido ao padrão vibratório do ambiente.

Pontos Cantados

O QUE SÃO PONTOS CANTADOS? A música é uma das mais antigas e valiosas formas de expressão da humanidade e na Umbanda se faz do canto instrumento de comunicação com Deus, com Orixás, Guias e com o mundo espiritual. Sendo um dos Fundamentos da Umbanda, **os Pontos Cantados são formas de**

oração, são como mantras que, juntamente com as palmas cadenciadas, servem para causar um estado de tranquilidade e paz interior, acalmar a mente e os sentidos, e ligam os médiuns e assistidos às forças superiores. A música é a comunicação direta com a alma e com Deus.

DE ONDE SE ORIGINAM OS PONTOS? Os Pontos tradicionais são cantados desde o nascimento da Umbanda a mais de um século, e foram trazidos à luz pelas Entidades da corrente espiritual, chamados **Pontos de Raiz.** Não são modinhas pueris com rima fácil como afirmam alguns, ao contrário, as letras são simples para facilitar a memorização, e identificam a Entidade trabalhadora, sua falange, sua "mironga" (segredo, mistério, magia) e os ritmos variam de acordo com a vibração espiritual e Linha que identifica cada Entidade. Há os chamados Pontos Terrenos que são criados pelos fiéis para homenagear um Orixá ou um Guia ou falange. Quando compostos com bom senso e sabedoria são aceitos enternecidamente pelos Guias. Porém alguns são absolutamente ridículos, sem fundamento, sem lógica, sem noção, chegando a envergonhar.

NO PONTO DE OGUM IARA, POR EXEMPLO, SAÚDAM-SE OS CAMPOS DE BATALHA PARA ENALTECER A VIOLÊNCIA? *"Se meu Pai é Ogun / Ogun vencedor de demanda / Ele vem de Aruanda / Pra salvar filhos de Umbanda / Ogun, Ogun, Ogun / Ogun Iara, salve os campos de batalha / Salve a Sereia do Mar".* A violência não é defendida e jamais é estimulada na Umbanda. Deve-se entender por "campos de batalha" a própria vida do ser humano e a luta incessante para vencer sua inclinação para as coisas que o afasta da Luz, suas próprias inferioridades. Uma guerra de muitas batalhas contra a própria inveja, ciúme, apego, violência e mesquinhez. De sua luta nesse campo de batalha depende o crescimento espiritual, o sossego interior e a paz familiar.

TEMAS GERAIS

TELEPATIA

TELEPATIA EXISTE? Sim, existe. Pensamentos, emoções ou atitudes podem ser transmitidos de uma mente para outra apesar da distância corporal que as separa. Comum a todos os seres, cada criatura pode transmitir suas ideias ao seu semelhante e na maior parte das vezes nem está consciente disso.

COMO FUNCIONA A TELEPATIA ENTRE ENCARNADOS? Um cérebro ativo envia ondas que são captadas por outro cérebro receptor passivo, por que ambos sintonizam-se na mesma faixa vibratória de transmissão mental.

SE OS ENCARNADOS PODEM SE COMUNICAR ENTRE SI PELOS FIOS DO PENSAMENTO, IGUALMENTE PODEM OS DESENCARNADOS? Sim, e podem muito mais facilmente, porque eles se encontram livres dos embaraços da matéria. Quando um Espírito (encarnado ou desencarnado) pensa, imediatamente envia ondas de fluidos que vibram na direção desejada. Os desencarnados, mesmo os que estão nos estágios inferiores da evolução, em geral possuem facilidade de captar essas ondas e imagens.

AS EVOCAÇÕES E ORAÇÕES SÃO UMA ESPÉCIE DE TELEPATIA? As Evocações são, na verdade, um chamamento direcionado mais intensamente do pensamento para um Espírito alvo. Deste modo, se os encarnados enviam seus pensamentos aos desencarnados, o oposto também se dá, os desencarnados também transmitem seus pensamentos aos encarnados. Eis aí a mediunidade.

ARUANDA

O QUE É ARUANDA? Originalmente Aruanda era o porto principal de Angola, situado no continente africano, de onde partiam os negros sequestrados e trazidos ao Brasil na condição de escravos, e essa região ficou na memória coletiva dos cativos como o lugar onde encontrariam novamente a liberdade. Considerando que Aruanda era um local de reencontro e felicidade pela volta ao lar, convencionou-se denominar "o espaço" onde, teoricamente, habitam espíritos trabalhadores do bem e da caridade como Luanda ou Aluanda ou Aruanda. O livro "*Tambores de Angola*", psicografado pelo médium Robson Pinheiro através do espírito de Ângelo Inácio, explica que *Aruanda é uma colônia específica no plano espiritual, onde residem espíritos de muita luz, constituídos em sua maioria de Pretos Velhos e Caboclos, e que são os responsáveis espirituais pela Umbanda.* Vimos no filme "Nosso Lar" as chamadas "Cidades Astrais", que nada mais são do que comunidades agrupadas em grandes egrégoras com até dezenas de milhares de almas.

EGRÉGORA

O QUE É EGRÉGORA? Egrégora é a denominação da força espiritual criada a partir da soma de energias coletivas, sejam elas mental, emocional ou espiritual, fruto da congregação de duas ou mais pessoas.

O QUE É NOSSO LAR? Nosso Lar é a mais famosa (embora não a única) cidade astral ou colônia astral relatada em livros espíritas.

POR QUE OS MUNDOS ESPIRITUAIS SÃO DESCRITOS DE MANEIRA MUITO VAGA E ÀS VEZES PUERIL? As ideias de Deus, em todo o mundo, são descritas de forma relativa ao grau de intelectualidade e capacidade de entendimento dos povos. Tem níveis muito sutis no universo que nossa mente não entende e nem temos palavras para expressar. Na hora de comunicar a ideia se recorre ao que é mais familiar

CATIMBÓ, JUREMA SAGRADA E JUREMÁ

O QUE É CATIMBÓ E JUREMA SAGRADA? Catimbó é uma religião originária da região norte e nordeste do Brasil, resultante da fusão entre os rituais africano, indígena e católico. Eram praticadas pelos sertanejos embaixo de árvores frondosas nos terrenos da caatinga, onde mesas eram repletas com imagens de santos, crucifixos e velas agregadas às crenças de origem africana, trazidas pelos negros escravos. O Catimbó foi perseguido e proibido por lei, tendo inclusive muitos adeptos sido mortos, e como forma de resistência houve uma junção com rezas católicas para poderem disfarçar suas práticas, e assim se explica a influência católica sofrida por mais essa religião. Quando os africanos fugiam dos engenhos onde eram escravizados encontravam abrigo nas aldeias indígenas, e negros e vermelhos trocavam o que tinham de conhecimento, inclusive religioso. Os africanos contribuíram com o seu saber sobre o culto dos mortos (chamados eguns) e dos Orixás, e os índios com a cultura das invocações dos espíritos de antigos pajés. Aos conhecimentos de índios e negros somou-se o saber dos portugueses, banidos no Brasil por serem considerados hereges pela Inquisição, e que traziam na bagagem a compreensão da natureza, das propriedades curativas de ervas e plantas e de sua força viva. Dessa mistura surgiu o culto a **Jurema Sagrada ou Catimbó**. Os negros, de origem banto, incorporaram os Caboclos a esse culto e passaram a chamá-lo de "Candomblé de Caboclo" ou "Samba de Caboclo".

O QUE É JUREMA? Jurema, chamada em algumas regiões do Brasil de Catimbó, vem do tupi-guarani e designa uma frondosa árvore que depois de crescida vive mais de 200 anos, onde índios enterravam os mortos junto de sua raiz e passavam a cultuá-los para que evoluíssem espiritualmente e habitassem o tronco, ajudando a todos da tribo em suas necessidades. A planta Jurema, nativa do agreste e sertão nordestino, é matéria prima para um dos maiores fundamentos do culto da Jurema

Sagrada que é uma bebida psicoativa (alguns afirmam que não é alucinógeno, mas sim erva de poder e força), à base de infusão das folhas com casca do tronco e da raiz misturado com mel de abelha, garapa de cana-de-açúcar e cachaça ou vinho que, acredita-se, alimenta e dá forças aos "encantados". A ingestão da Jurema, em conjunto com os toques e as cantigas rituais do Catimbó, provoca um estado de transe profundo, interpretado pelos catimbozeiros como a incorporação dos Mestres da Jurema. Estas entidades espirituais, que habitariam o Mundo Encantado ou Juremá, teriam sido adeptos do Catimbó que, ao morrerem, se "encantaram", ou seja, foram transportados a esta sublimação espiritual, de onde poderiam atender os vivos pela realização de curas e aconselhamento, desde que para tal fossem requeridos através da incorporação. Parecido com o Santo Daime, o **"Vinho da Jurema"** é servido a iniciados e clientes e a receita exata não é conhecida nem mesmo pelos praticantes, somente os Mestres conhecem o segredo.

QUANDO NA UMBANDA SE CANTA O PONTO "DEFUMA COM AS ERVAS DA JUREMA, DEFUMA COM ARRUDA E GUINÉ, BENJOIM, ALECRIM E ALFAZEMA, VAMOS DEFUMAR FILHOS DE FÉ", A QUE SE REFERE? Estão sendo chamadas as forças desse mundo encantado e mágico, porque cada erva tem uma finalidade, e é preciso conhecê-las. Na Umbanda a Jurema representa o universo vegetal, tem uma ligação profunda com Ossaîn que é o Orixá que manipula as ervas.

COMO SÃO CHAMADOS OS MÉDIUNS DO CATIMBÓ? ELES INCORPORAM OS MESMOS GUIAS DA UMBANDA? Os médiuns do Catimbó, chamados Catimbozeiros, incorporam seus mestres que são Caboclos, Pretos Velhos, Baianos, Boiadeiros ou Mestres que tiveram encarnação como catimbozeiros. Um grande Mestre da Jurema que foi juremeiro (também chamado catimbozeiro) José Pelintra de Aguiar, o Zé Pelintra. Diz a lenda que José Pelintra de Aguiar nasceu em Pernambuco, migrou para o Rio de Janeiro onde se estabeleceu no morro, vivendo pela Lapa como um malandro, e no final da vida voltou a Pernambuco, tornando-se Mestre da Jurema. **Jurema ou Catimbó não é Umbanda, são religiões distintas.**

O QUE É JUREMÁ? Importante não confundir Juremá com Jurema (sem acento). Se na Umbanda os Caboclos vêm de Aruanda, no Catimbó eles vêm do Juremá. É o mundo espiritual do Catimbó onde moram os Encantados, Mestres e Caboclos. Imagina-se que o Juremá seja composto de aldeias, cidades, estados ou reinados. A Grande Cidade do Juremá ou Cidade da Jurema ou Aldeia do Juremá é um centro de poder de onde emergem as falanges dos mensageiros de luz, Guias, conselheiros astrais, espíritos de luz, Caboclos, Caboclas, Capangueiros e etc. Diz a lenda que o número dos que lá habitam é maior do que os grãos de areia de todas as praias de nosso planeta.

QUEM HABITA O JUREMÁ? Habitam o Juremá os Caboclos e os Mestres. São inclusive essas duas categorias de entidades espirituais que tem seus assentamentos nas mesas de Jurema. Os Caboclos da Jurema são identificados como entidades indígenas que trabalham principalmente com a cura através do conhecimento das ervas, dão passes e realizam benzeduras com folhagens. São associados às correntes espirituais mais elevadas. Alguns Caboclos cultuados na Jurema-Catimbó são conhecidos na Umbanda, como Tupinambá, Rompe Mato, Arariboia, Urubatão, e no Catimbó entende-se que trabalham para o bem, mas que também podem ser entidades perigosas quando usados contra alguém, por isso são muito temidos e respeitados.

COMO SÃO EXPLICADOS OS MESTRES DA JUREMA?
Os Mestres Juremeiros são descritos como espíritos curadores de descendência escrava ou mestiça, e quando em vida possuíam conhecimento de ervas e plantas curativas. Morreram em decorrência de alguma tragédia e tornaram-se "*encantados*", podendo assim voltar para "*acudir*" os que ficaram "*neste vale de lágrimas*". Alguns deles se iniciaram nos mistérios e "ciência" da Jurema antes de morrer, outros adquiriram esse conhecimento no momento da morte. Também são denominados Caboclos da Jurema.

CABOCLO DA JUREMA COM CABOCLA JUREMA SÃO AS MESMAS ENTIDADES? Não. Cabocla Jurema, na Umbanda, é uma Entidade Guia Chefe da Linha de Oxóssi, embora também evocada no Catimbó. O nome Jurema é citado em muitos pontos cantados justamente por estar ligados a todos os maiores poderes espirituais responsáveis pela guarda e manutenção da vida que alimenta o planeta Terra, principalmente o poder das mães da natureza.

HUMAITÁ

O QUE É HUMAITÁ? Trata-se de uma fortificação defensiva militar paraguaia situada na confluência dos rios Paraguai e Paraná. Lá aconteceu a batalha do Humaitá (1868), durante a Guerra do Brasil com o Paraguai, devido àquele país ter invadido o Mato Grosso. Carente de soldados, iniciou-se o recrutamento para a formação dos Corpos de Voluntários da Pátria, tendo a palavra *"voluntários"* se tornado piada, pois a população era forçada a se alistar. Os donos de escravos negociavam com os recrutadores e mandavam os negros lutar em seu lugar e de seus filhos. Duque de Caxias, a fim de aumentar o número de soldados, prometera a liberdade aos escravos que lutassem. Nas senzalas os negros firmavam ponto ao Pai Ogun para que protegesse seus filhos, maridos, netos e irmãos. As tropas pediam a proteção de Ogun, seja diretamente ao Orixá, seja na forma de São Jorge. Assim a palavra "Humaitá" entrou para as cantigas de Umbanda e assumiu outro sentido, passando a ser um lugar sagrado onde mora Ogun, porque aquela foi uma terra de pranto e de dor, e ao mesmo tempo onde se provou a fé dos negros. Humaitá passou a ser visto como símbolo de vitória, lugar de vencer demandas e desafios. Os escravos lutaram uma guerra que não era deles e ainda assim não esmoreceram, pois estavam sob a proteção de Ogun. Ao término da Batalha de Humaitá as tropas de Caxias saíram vencedoras. Há vários lindos Pontos cantados de Ogun que fazem referência a este lugar, que começou a ser transmitido até se tornar conhecido como a MORADA DE OGUN.

DEMANDA

O QUE É DEMANDA? Muito utilizado nos Terreiros, significa desentendimentos, conflitos, obstáculos colocados intencionalmente no caminho do indivíduo e agressões de toda espécie (inclusive as de natureza psicológica ou energética).

CATIÇO

O QUE É CATIÇO? Os chamados Catiços são espíritos que já tiveram encarnação na Terra. São espíritos incorporantes que dão consulta, trabalham sob as irradiações dos Orixás e denominados Caboclos, Erês, Pretos Velhos e todas as demais Linhas que compõem a egrégora umbandista. Também são chamados Guias.

CANJIRA

O QUE É CANJIRA? Alguns entendem que é um lugar no Terreiro destinado à realização de algumas danças religiosas. Outros entendem que é outro nome que se dá à Tronqueira.

YORUBÁ, IORUBÁ E NAGÔ

O QUE É YORUBÁ, IORUBÁ E NAGÔ? Nagô ou Anagô era a designação dada aos negros comprados na antiga Costa dos Escravos, um dos mais importantes centros de exportação do comércio de escravos no continente africano. Eles falavam o idioma **yorubá** que hoje é usado em ritos religiosos afro-brasileiros. A palavra **iorubá** designava uma das maiores etnias do continente africano em termos populacionais.

GESTUAIS E SAUDAÇÕES

O QUE SIGNIFICA AS SAUDAÇÕES NA UMBANDA? Saudar é cumprimentar, honrar e respeitar alguém ou alguma coisa, e na Umbanda saudação é o momento em que também se louva e reverencia.

O QUE SIGNIFICAM OS GESTUAIS QUE OS UMBANDISTAS FAZEM? Necessário entender que quando o umbandista entra no Terreiro está penetrando em ambiente sagrado, e deve pedir licença para adentrar naquele local. **Os gestuais são os sinais de respeito e ao mesmo tempo um pedido de permissão. A porta do Terreiro é a passagem ao sagrado,** ninguém pode simplesmente entrar nesse universo venerável como se estivesse entrando pela porta dos fundos da própria casa. A Tronqueira, que é onde está à firmeza de Esquerda, é mais um portal indispensável a quem pretende transpor o limiar dos mundos profano e sagrado.

POR QUE QUANDO SE CHEGA AO TERREIRO DEVE-SE IMEDIATAMENTE SAUDAR A TRONQUEIRA? Porque ela representa o limite entre a rua e a Casa espiritual, é o espaço destinado às Firmezas e Assentamentos de Exus e Pombogiras da Casa.

O QUE É BATER PAÓ? (pronuncia-se Paô) É uma palavra em iorubá que são palmas em cadência sincopada, empregadas como saudação a Exu, normalmente feita na Tronqueira.

POR QUE OS UMBANDISTAS TOCAM O CHÃO DO TERREIRO A PONTA DOS DEDOS? Este ato representa uma saudação ao chão onde está firmada a Força dos Orixás regentes do Terreiro, e também de onde, simbolicamente, vem a Força desses Orixás. Ao sair do Terreiro nunca se dá as costas para o Gongá, também como forma de respeito.

É CERTO DENOMINAR O CONGÁ COM OS NOMES ALTAR, PEJI OU JACUTÁ? Sim.

COMO SE REVERENCIA O CONGÁ? Em alguns Terreiros é costume o médium prostrar-se ao chão (deitar no chão de barriga para baixo) em postura de humildade. Em alguns Terreiros é costume o médium reverenciar o Gongá em pé. Há Terreiros em que o médium apenas deita-se de barriga para baixo em frente ao Gongá, e toca o solo com a testa em ato de louvor aos Orixás.

POR QUE SE SAÚDA O DIRIGENTE NA ABERTURA DAS GIRAS? Tem uma conotação especial. É preciso ter em mente que o Dirigente do Terreiro naquele momento é o representante dos Orixás aos quais os médiuns irão se unir, e também o representante dos Guias e Mentores da corrente mediúnica que se manifestarão através dos médiuns.

POR QUE NORMALMENTE O MÉDIUM BEIJA O DORSO DA MÃO DO DIRIGENTE (GUIA E MENTORES) E EM SEGUIDA LEVA O DORSO DA MÃO DO DIRIGENTE A PRÓPRIA TESTA (OJU ORÍ)? Isso significa que sendo a cabeça (Orí) que comanda e rege simbolicamente o médium, com esse gesto, coloca-se o médium subordinado ao poder dos Orixás e dos Guias que comandam o trabalho, representados pelo Dirigente. Por ser mais higiênico o médium pode substituir o beijo no dorso da mão por um toque em seu próprio queixo, em seguida leva o dorso da mão do Dirigente à sua própria testa.

POR QUE OS MÉDIUNS INCLINAM-SE EM REVERÊNCIA DEFRONTE AOS ATABAQUES? Porque durante a Gira sempre está presente toda uma corrente de espíritos que auxiliam nos toques e cantos das Curimbas ou Atabaques, e é essa Corrente Espiritual que se está cumprimentando.

POR QUE QUANDO SE SAÚDA A ESQUERDA E A TRONQUEIRA DO TERREIRO OS MÉDIUNS ENTRELAÇAM OS DEDOS COM AS PALMAS VOLTADAS PARA BAIXO FAZENDO MOVIMENTOS CIRCULARES? É uma forma ritualística de cumprimentar a Linha da Esquerda. Na Umbanda diz também *"saravar"* como sinônimo de cumprimentar. Está assim demonstrando respeito pela força espiritual dos trabalhadores da Linha de Esquerda e, ao mesmo tempo, dando-lhes boas vindas. As palmas voltadas para o chão é uma forma de captar as vibrações dos Exus e Pombogiras que vem do solo.

POR QUE ALGUNS GUIAS CUMPRIMENTAM AS PESSOAS BATENDO OMBRO NO OMBRO? Esta forma de cumprimento é sinal de fraternidade e amizade.

O QUE SIGNIFICA BATER CABEÇA PARA O SANTO?

Sendo a cabeça que comanda e rege o médium, o bater cabeça significa que esse médium respeita, obedece e se subordina de livre vontade aos Guias e Orixás. Na Umbanda a expressão usual é "Bater Cabeça" somente.

AJOELHAR-SE PERANTE O GONGÁ OU AO DIRIGENTE NÃO SERIA POSIÇÃO DE SUBSERVIÊNCIA E INFERIORIDADE?

Os orgulhosos e vaidosos pensam assim, os humildes e caridosos entendem o quanto são pequenos diante de Deus e ajoelham-se em demonstração de respeito e amor pelos bons espíritos que nos assistem. Nenhum Guia jamais pediu que um filho de Umbanda se ajoelhasse.

POR QUE SE TOCA O SOLO QUASE SEMPRE TRÊS VEZES?

É uma herança africana que a Umbanda incorporou em seu ritual. O número três significava o "assim seja". Deste modo quando, por exemplo, o nome de Ogun era pronunciado, os africanos tocavam três vezes o solo em um gestual que representava *"Que Ogun venha até nós, que assim seja"*.

POR QUE SE TOCA O SOLO?

Também por tradição da cultura africana. Vindos sequestrados para o Brasil na terrível condição de escravos, os africanos enterravam secretamente objetos sagrados em solo brasileiro para não perderem totalmente o contato com suas raízes, e o transformava em "chão" dos seus Orixás. Hoje, em todos os Terreiros, a força dos Orixás regentes da Casa está firmada debaixo do chão em respeito à tradição. Ao tocar o solo, o filho de Umbanda pede permissão para entrar na Gira e força para realizar sua missão.

POR QUE NA MAIORIA DAS CASAS DE UMBANDA OS MÉDIUNS, AO INICIAR A GIRA E CUMPRIMENTAR O DIRIGENTE OU GONGÁ, GIRAM EM TORNO DE SI MESMOS? É forma de expressão para indicar uma ideia, chamada Simbolismo. Em alguns Terreiros o giro é feito à esquerda (sentido anti-horário) porque representa a volta ao passado, aos ancestrais, a união do médium com seus antepassados e seus Orixás. O médium está, nesse ritual, simbolicamente, unindo o passado ao presente para promover a unidade entre os mundos sagrado e profano. Em outros Terreiros o médium gira à direita (no sentido horário) que é o sentido da vida.

POR QUE A UMBANDA É CONSIDERADA A RELIGIÃO DOS PÉS DESCALÇOS? Os umbandistas tiram os sapatos em respeito ao solo do Terreiro, e também para reafirmar em cada Gira a simplicidade e humildade de seus ritos. Também há de se considerar que uma descarga energética mais pesada se dissipa no solo.

POR QUE NOS GESTUAIS QUASE SEMPRE HÁ TOQUE NA CABEÇA? Por herança africana. A cabeça, para os africanos, era a parte mais importante do corpo, considerada sagrada, pois é a cabeça quem comanda tudo. O mito por trás do ato de tocar a cabeça é o seguinte: a cabeça, sendo a parte mais sagrada do corpo, é composta pela cabeça física, pela cabeça interior (que chamamos de mente ou personalidade) e pela consciência (ou espírito). Durante o planejamento reencarnatório, a cada espírito é dada uma personalidade para vivenciar seu destino e acontecimentos determinados de antemão. Esse espírito também recebe a força dos ancestrais ou legado ancestral, que é aquilo que herdará dos antepassados e que não se limita somente às características físicas, tendo inclusive um profundo efeito sobre sua personalidade porque, mesmo sem o saber, será influenciado por acontecimentos que ocorreram aos seus pais, avós, bisavós e antepassados mais remotos, cujas emoções e memórias podem estar presentes em sua composição emocional e espiritual. Nesse planejamento reencarnatório o espírito recebe também seus Orixás. Considerando esse mito entendemos a representação ritual na Umbanda da seguinte forma: A testa representa o destino (odú), a parte da frente da cabeça (oju orí) significa o futuro, a nascente. A nuca ou a parte da trás da cabeça (ìpakó orí) representa o passado, os ancestrais e suas heranças, o poente. A têmpora direita, ou seja, o lado direito da cabeça (opá òtúm) representa o Orixá masculino. A têmpora esquerda ou o lado esquerdo da cabeça (opa osí) representa o Orixá feminino.

QUANDO SE DIZ QUE O ESPÍRITO HERDARÁ O LEGADO DOS SEUS ANTEPASSADOS E QUE NÃO SE LIMITA ÀS CARACTERÍSTICAS FÍSICAS, SIGNIFICA QUE HERDA TAMBÉM O QUE? Além da aparência física também estão latentes os dons, os sofrimentos, doenças, talentos, dívidas cármicas que ficam em inatividade parcial na memória de suas células, até sair do estado dormente e readquirir a mesma força e atividade como quando viva no antepassado. Atualmente há um método psicoterapêutico chamado Constelação Familiar que olha para as diversas consciências das quais somos tomados, com o mesmo princípio dos antigos africanos.

A UMBANDA ADOTOU OS RITUAIS E PRECEITOS AFRICANOS? Não todos, mas alguns que explicam os gestos e saudações, considerando que a religião de Umbanda foi formada basicamente da fusão espiritual de três etnias: o branco (colonizador), o índio (nativo da terra) e o negro (trazido como escravo). Na Umbanda nada é feito ao acaso, tudo tem fundamento, por exemplo, o ritual do Amací que é um ritual onde éfeita a lavagem com ervas da coroa ou orí (o centro da cabeça) do médium, cujo objetivo é reconhecer e conjurar as forças nela contida.

***

ZÉ PELINTRA

Advogado dos pobres, Mestre da Jurema, Malandro, Catimbozeiro, Dono da Noite, Rei da Magia, são muitos nomes para Zé Pelintra e sobre o qual não há meio termo: ou é amado ou é temido. Temido pelos que presenciaram médiuns despreparados dando voz a espíritos trevosos com os quais se unem pelo nível vibracional, e que se passam por Entidades de Luz para se divertirem e zombarem. Aqueles que presenciaram médiuns obsessores de si mesmos, desequilibrados, "recebendo" um Zé Pelintra vulgar, beberrão, vingativo, debochado, bocudo, tem razão de ficarem amedrontados. Outros amam verdadeiramente porque tiveram a oportunidade de conhecer de fato um trabalhador da religião de Umbanda que luta para ver os filhos em pé, que encanta pela gentileza sincera, que brinca com todos sem jamais perder o respeito por ninguém, seja homem ou mulher, e que a todos dá amor e que recebe igualmente muito amor.

PARA PENSAR

Tanto desconhecimento e preconceito acerca de Exus e Pombogiras chegam a bloquear a incorporação dos Guardiões e Guardiãs, sendo que em alguns Terreiros nem mesmo admitem trabalhar com a Linha de Esquerda por considerá-los espíritos rasteiros, sem evolução. Alegam que eles riem alto, gargalham, bebem cachaça, fumam charuto, e que assim procedendo demonstram que estão presos aos vícios carnais. Muitos umbandistas acreditam que basta prometer a Exu uma garrafa de cachaça para ele fazer tudo o que se pede inclusive "amarrar a vida" do desafeto. A Pombogira é vista como uma prostituta desclassificada que acaba com casamentos a troco de cigarrilha, bijuteria, batom e outras miudezas. Há ainda mulheres desequilibradas que dizem incorporar a Pombogira para "amarrar homem na cama" e quanto a isso, francamente, é tão grotesco que é melhor nem comentar. Para coroar a desinformação dizem que Exu Mirim é filho de Exu com Pombogira e é especialista em levar o desespero à vida alheia, desde que como pagamento receba cigarro sem filtro, farofa com pimenta e uma dose de cachaça. Nesta visão pouco esclarecida as Entidades de Esquerda se tornaram seres espirituais de dois gêneros, ao mesmo tempo em que são involuídos também são imbecis que trabalham a troco de migalhas. Levados pela desinformação que dá munição à infâmia, para piorar esse quadro já bastante tenebroso, há filhos de fé que tem expostas imagens de Exus retratados como o capeta dos católicos, corpo vermelho, rabo pontiagudo, pés de bode e provando que tudo o que é ruim ainda pode piorar, algumas estátuas de Exus tem chifres, o "coitado" é retratado com cornos. Há um enorme esforço em rebaixar esses valorosos trabalhadores de Umbanda, e com eles os umbandistas conscientes sentem-se também inferiorizados por constatar que em tão linda religião ainda há espaço para excesso de desinformação e grosseria.

VOCÊ SABIA QUE tudo na vida são afinidade e comunhão, que almas ignorantes atraem criaturas ignorantes, que doentes afinam-se com doentes, e que enquanto não mudar o padrão mental não adianta procurar ajuda em Terreiro?

"Mo nì omobìnrin ti Aféfe. Èmi ní Aloyá."

Eliana Pacco

Oyá - Iansã (Cláudia Amaral Argoud)

Livro 1 – Descomplicando os Guias de Umbanda

Livro 2 – Mediunidade na Umbanda

Livro 3 – Os Orixás na Umbanda

Livro 4 – O Ritual de Umbanda

Livro 5 – As Perguntas e Respostas da Umbanda

Umbanda, Muito Prazer!

Para saber mais sobre nossos títulos e autora, ou enviar seus comentários sobre este livro, mande email para elianapacco@gmail.com